The Good Liars

Anita Frank

D1364197

ONE PLACE. MANY STORIES

HQ
An imprint of HarperCollins*Publishers* Ltd
1 London Bridge Street
London SE1 9GF

www.harpercollins.co.uk

HarperCollins*Publishers*
Macken House, 39/40 Mayor Street Upper,
Dublin 1, D01 C9W8, Ireland

This edition 2023

First published in Great Britain by
HQ, an imprint of HarperCollins*Publishers* Ltd 2023

ISBN: 9780008455224

This book is produced from independently certified FSC™ paper
to ensure responsible forest management.

For more information visit: www.harpercollins.co.uk/green

This book is set in 10.7/15.5 pt. Sabon by Type-it AS, Norway

Printed and Bound in the UK using 100% Renewable Electricity at
CPI Group (UK) Ltd, Croydon, CR0 4YY

For David

A Mother's Shame

Spring 1920

Her chest was tight as she walked to the village hall, though whether from a lingering effect of the influenza she had somehow survived or due to her current unease, she was unable to say. A good many had already gathered outside by the time she arrived – neighbours, many once considered friends – all of whom now fell silent at her approach, though they leant together to whisper as soon as she had passed.

She kept her focus on the door before her, refusing to falter in her task, even if her reception justified the anxiety that had nearly kept her at home. But she could not have stayed away. Her purpose was too great. She could not let him down.

Clutching her handbag, her stomach knotted, she mounted the steps and pushed open the door.

The murmurous chatter inside stilled immediately. Heat rose in her cheeks as eyes turned upon her. Mouths pinched with displeasure; eyebrows hitched with surprise; foreheads furrowed. On seeing more than one head shake with disgust, she almost turned tail and ran.

But then she thought of her boy, her beautiful boy, and

a wave of anger enveloped her. Her son was as good as theirs, better even – better than most, certainly. Buoyed with defiance, she walked through them all to take her place in the queue.

Heart hammering, she inched forward, waiting her turn. She tried to ignore the whispered comments and pointed stares, but each broke through her fragile defences to land a brutal blow. At last, she found herself facing the Reverend, a ledger spread wide before him, a cashbox to his side.

Before she could lose her nerve, she opened her bag and placed her hard-earnt money upon the table.

'That's my donation.'

The Reverend had the good grace to look uncomfortable.

'I'm afraid we cannot accept it.'

'Why not?' she demanded, a quiver in her voice. 'My money's as good as the next man's.'

'What seems to be the problem?' Counsellor Jones asked, breaking free from a cluster of onlookers.

Her mouth dry, she turned to face him. 'I've come to pay my money. My son served his country. His name deserves to be on the memorial, along with the other boys from the village who fought and gave their lives.'

Reaching down, he swept the money back towards her.

'This memorial is to record the names of the glorious dead, those honourably fallen, men the community wishes to remember and is proud to do so. I lost two sons on the Somme, and quite frankly it would be an insult to their memory, and to the memory of all the other brave boys who died so courageously, to have the likes of your son listed alongside them. Now, unless you wish to make a donation as an act of remorse, I suggest you show some common decency and leave.'

'My son has a right—'

'Your son is a disgrace, madam!'

The words knocked the wind from her lungs. Her throat ached as tears blurred her vision, but she would not let them fall. She would not give him – give any of them – the satisfaction. Instead, she fostered her rage, fanning its flames with indignation and resentment as she scooped the spurned notes and coins back into her bag.

Later, she would be unable to recall the words she shouted as she left the hall, though she would be able to remember every insult thrown after her, every derogatory comment made about her boy. She would not remember how she made it home, but she would remember her knees buckling as she closed the door behind her. She would be unable to say how long she sat there crying, her heart breaking, but she would recall that the room was dark by the time she found the strength to stand.

What she would have no trouble remembering was her sense of shame. Not for her boy. She was ashamed of *herself*. For not fighting harder. For not arguing better. For allowing them to win. She would forever be ashamed of letting him down.

And whenever she had reason to reflect on that day, she would ask herself:

What kind of mother fails her child the way I failed my son?

And her heart would break once more.

Prologue

It is Ida Stilwell who opens the door. Her surprise, which she makes no attempt to mask, clearly indicates she has been expecting someone else. Her budlike mouth forms a perfect 'Oh', a delicate breath giving voice to the exclamation.

As it is, a man occupies her doorstep – a tall, broad man, sporting a brown bowler hat and dressed in a mackintosh with a worn suit lurking underneath, a spot of breakfast surreptitiously lingering just below the knot of his tie. He dips his head, then removes his hat, exposing a generous sweep of silver hair, wiry, but neatly clipped at the sides. He holds the bowler before him, in meaty fingers tinged with nicotine, and whilst those hands might have looked more at home on a manual labourer, there is nothing about this man to suggest he toils for his living. He smiles, exposing comfortingly crooked teeth, greying where they disappear into his gums.

'Mrs Stilwell?' His voice is low and oddly melodic with a gravelly undertone, but there is another note, hidden deep within the ensemble, that appears to put Ida on her guard.

'Yes?' She draws herself up an extra inch or two, lifting her

4

chin with intent, like an animal attempting to look imposing in the face of danger.

'I am so sorry to call unannounced like this—' he reaches into the gulley of the mackintosh and delves into the inside pocket of his suit jacket '—but I was wondering . . .' he pauses, issuing a flash of a smile as he pulls out a small leather case which he flicks open for her perusal '. . . whether I might just take a few minutes of your time?'

The policeman – an inspector no less – seems to fill the small lobby. The joyless gloom of the beamed vestibule ensures his expression is wreathed in shadows, though the bulk of him remains plain to see, solid and straight in his buff coat. Ida's bemused smile falters as he expresses his need to speak to the entire household, but she quickly resumes the role of gracious chatelaine.

'Won't you come through?'

She leads him across the red and black quarry-tiled floor. He is forced to duck under the low lintel that takes them into the reception hall. He notices how she appears emboldened once they have crossed the threshold, as if somehow the grandeur of their new surroundings inspires her to confidence. He pauses to admire the seventeenth-century hall, lined with panelling that gleams like chestnuts fresh from their casings. The morning sunshine beams through the crisscrossed leading of its large windows to cast a thousand diamonds across the ancient chequerboard flags of slate grey and pale dove. But the most impressive attribute of the room is the fireplace, a floor-to-ceiling rockface of carved stone, emblazoned with a family shield guarded by two heraldic figures standing either side. The sizeable grate occupying the yawning cavern at its base contains the charred remnants of what he takes to be the previous night's fire, the thick bed of ash underneath still waiting to be cleared away. The sight momentarily draws Ida's attention, and though she makes no comment, the fleeting dip in her neatly plucked brows suggests she is disappointed he has not been met by a hearty blaze. The room is undeniably imposing. But it is also cold and uncomfortable, and the smell of soot hangs stale in the air.

'Do take a seat while I round up the others.'

She gestures him onto the brown leather sofas that flank the fireplace. They strike him as jarringly modern set, as they are, against the Tudor and Jacobean pieces that otherwise furnish the hall – though, to his mind, those sturdy antiques, so dark and heavy in nature, are rather oppressive.

'Most kind, thank you.'

The sofa gasps as he collapses upon it, as if winded by his assault. He folds himself forward, his forearms propped on his knees, the bowler turning in his restless fingers. His eyes continue to skim the room even as Ida disappears back beneath the doorway through which they came. A small curve plays at the edge of his mouth.

She returns a few minutes later, looking even bolder now that she brings with her reinforcements. The Inspector struggles to his feet, leaving his bowler to occupy the space beside him. He smiles affably at the new arrivals.

The first young man bounds towards him like an energetic Setter, his hand out in greeting.

'Inspector Hume? How do you do, I'm Maurice Stilwell.'

The husband, the Inspector thinks, as he shakes the

proffered hand, assessing as he does so the master of Darkacre Hall. He is tall and willowy – gangly even. A flop of brown hair grazes his dark eyebrows, and he is forced to sweep it back with irksome regularity. He offers the Inspector an easy smile of boyish charm, the confidence of a public-school training, coupled, no doubt, with the instinctive euphoria of having survived four years in the trenches – for the Inspector has done his homework. He had thought the experience might have left the young man with a harder edge, but there is still something intrinsically soft and delicate about him – indeed, the only evidence of what he has endured are the fine strands of silver that thread his hair and the periodic twitch at the edge of his right eye.

'Mr Stilwell, my apologies for imposing on you like this.'

'Not at all, not at all.' Maurice steps back to reveal the two fellows behind him. 'Allow me to introduce my brother, Leonard.'

The Inspector's eyes drop to the pitiable remnants of the man occupying the wheelchair before him. The familial resemblance is immediately clear, but this man shows his suffering – it is carved upon his face and starkly evident in the missing parts of his body. A tartan blanket hangs limp over the seat of the chair, while his left shirt sleeve has been folded back on itself at the elbow and pinned into place. To his mortification, the Inspector experiences a moment of hesitation, but the young man holds out his right hand, and, rallying, the Inspector takes it. The handshake is firm. Defiantly so.

'How do you do, Mr Stilwell?'

Leonard Stilwell responds with a brief nod, his eyes sliding away as he withdraws his hand.

The Inspector is rather relieved to be able to turn his attention to the third man. 'Strapping', is the first thought that enters his head. The contrast between the two men could not be more pronounced. The man who had pushed the wheelchair into the room is tall, taller than the Inspector, who, at five feet eleven inches, doesn't consider himself a small man by any means. Dark-blond hair lies in furrows, thick and dense, and the Inspector suspects his penetrating blue eyes could render a man uneasy, if caught in their icy depths too long.

'Victor Monroe,' he introduces himself. 'How do you do?'

The voice is rich and debonair, his manner assured and privileged, and yet, from what the Inspector has gleaned from his local enquiries, the man is a permanent houseguest at Darkacre and has been since boyhood. He wonders briefly why he has never struck out, put down roots elsewhere, gathered his own court about him – for such a prime example of a man could easily govern his own principality, indeed, should revel in doing so. And yet, he lingers here amongst friends, like a cuckoo in the nest.

'A pleasure, Mr Monroe,' the Inspector says, taking his hand. He is a little surprised by the unnecessary pressure the man applies to his grip – a warning perhaps? He flexes his fingers once they have been released, suppressing an urge to chuckle.

'Would you like some tea?' Ida asks.

The Inspector turns to face her. There is no sign of a maid, which again, would marry with what he has learnt so far. There has been difficulty in securing staff locally – it seems no love is lost on the once esteemed family. He detects an underlying anxiety that he might answer in the affirmative, so, instead, he allows a slow smile to warm his eyes.

'You are most kind, Mrs Stilwell, but I've not long had one.'

'Oh,' the answer comes with a satisfied mew that betrays her relief. 'Oh well, do sit down,' she says again, and he does so, moving his hat to the arm of the sofa to make space – but it seems no one wishes to sit near him. Mrs Stilwell tucks herself into the far edge of the sofa opposite, crossing her legs, her hands folded across her upper knee. Her fingers look a little weathered, and her nail polish is chipped. As Maurice Stilwell collapses down next to her, she makes an almost imperceptible movement, drawing herself in, like a jar top being screwed tighter into place. It amuses the Inspector that her husband appears oblivious to the subtle recoil. Maurice's long legs stretch forward in a most relaxed manner, though he remains unable, the Inspector notices, to control that periodic tic about his eye. It flickers three times in quick succession before vanishing once again.

Victor positions Leonard's wheelchair beside the sofa, before perching on its broad leather arm. The Inspector is forced to tilt his head back to observe him, and he wonders whether the apparently casual seating arrangement isn't perhaps a deliberate ploy. He smothers a private smile.

'So—' it is Maurice who speaks, stepping up to his duties as man of the house, though with Victor present, the Inspector thinks the mantle seems oddly out of place upon his shoulders '—how can we help you, Inspector?'

There is a brief pause while the Inspector collects his thoughts. He offers them a self-deprecating smile, hoping his mattress of grey hair will explain the length of his deliberation.

'I'm looking into an old matter actually. A case that occurred before the war.' He treats them all to his amiable smile as he scans their politely inquisitive faces. 'A missing boy. Bobby Higgins.'

It might be the shifting light within the room, but Ida Stilwell appears to pale, though the fixed spread of her lips fails to waver. The silence is punctuated by the rhythmic tick of a wall clock located somewhere behind him.

'Gosh, Bobby Higgins,' Maurice says at last, 'that was some time ago.'

'Yes, yes, it was.' The Inspector apologises as he digs into the inside pocket of his jacket once more, this time extracting a small leather-bound notebook, a stub of pencil tucked under the elastic band that holds it shut. The band pings as he removes it. He lifts the cover and leafs through a few pages, conscious of their intense scrutiny as he does so. He taps the pencil against the sought-after entry. 'He was reported missing on the thirty-first of August, 1914.' He looks up. 'And was never found.'

'Yes, terribly sad.' Maurice speaks now with a degree of gravity, his pleasant features carefully arranged into a perplexed look of sorrow. 'His poor mother.'

'Yes, indeed . . . her only child, I understand.'

'That's right. She had been widowed young, I believe, and never remarried. Well, I suppose with Bobby being the way he was . . .' Maurice trails off. The Inspector raises his eyebrows. 'Well, he was . . . you know . . .'

'Simple. The boy was never right,' Victor drawls, making no effort to conceal his evident boredom. 'He probably wandered off or got himself into some mischief. I thought it was decided he'd fallen into the river and drowned.'

The Inspector nods slowly, looking again at his neatly written notes.

'Looking through the paperwork, I understand that was the preferred theory.'

'Is there any reason to doubt it?' Maurice asks, pitching forward, a deep crease marring his brow.

'Well . . .' the Inspector sighs and slowly shakes his head. 'Rivers have a way of surrendering their victims over time. A body is washed downstream, or floats to the surface . . .'

'It could have been carried for miles,' Victor interjects, 'there's a strong current around here.'

'And yet I don't think it would have got further than the weir without someone noticing,' the Inspector counters, 'and it was summer, the river levels were low – such a hot summer, 1914,' he tuts and shakes his head again. 'Curious.'

'But couldn't it – I mean the body – have got caught up on something, snagged out of sight, a fallen tree trunk or some other debris?' Maurice proposes with the eagerness of a keen student.

'Indeed, it could have.' The Inspector closes the notebook, and Maurice looks chuffed with himself, as if he has supplied the right answer and solved the mystery single-handedly. 'But there was an effort to dredge the river,' the Inspector counters again. 'Not conclusive of course, these things seldom can be, but . . .' he shrugs, his dissatisfaction clear. 'It seems a lot of effort was made by the local community to find the boy.'

'He was hardly a boy,' Ida pipes up sharply. The sudden weight of the Inspector's attention causes her to flush. She smooths her skirt over her knee. 'He must have been in his late teens.'

'Seventeen,' the Inspector supplies. He switches his focus to Victor, tipping back his head to meet the man's cool eyes. 'But as you say, somewhat retarded.'

'I think we can all agree it's a tragic case, a mystery indeed,'

Victor says, 'but why are you here asking us about it after all this time?'

The Inspector places his broad hands over the narrow notebook. 'Some new information has come to light.'

'New information?' Leonard echoes, his voice rusty. The Inspector shifts in his seat to better address him.

'Yes, hence why I'm here. A new . . . *witness* . . . has come forward, suggesting the boy was perhaps here on the day he disappeared.'

'Here?' Ida exclaims.

'Well, not at the house. On the grounds, in the estate.'

The Inspector flicks through the notepad once again, giving Ida, Maurice, and Victor the opportunity to exchange a darted glance. He is satisfied they are oblivious to the fact that he has clocked the hurried exchange. Leonard alone has kept his eyes fixed firmly forward.

'Well . . . we uh . . .' Maurice clears his throat. He splays his hands in apparent bemusement, his long fingers stretching as he does so. The Inspector idly wonders whether he plays the piano, because such fingers could easily straddle the ivories. 'We have extensive grounds here, Inspector, and Home Farm, of course. It's not beyond the realms of possibility the boy may have wandered onto our land. We don't patrol it with shotguns after all.' He laughs.

The sound is a little girlish, but the Inspector's eyes brighten with appreciation at the attempted levity. 'Do you remember where you were that day?'

The laughter dies as he submits the four of them to the beam of his broad smile.

'We were all here.' It is Victor who responds. Confident.

Challenging almost. 'It was a rather special occasion.' Leonard snorts, his eyes trained on his lap. A muscle flexes in Victor's jaw. He meets the Inspector's gaze. 'You see, we had all enlisted by that time. We were joining our regiment the following day.'

'So, it was your last day of freedom,' the Inspector deduces quietly.

'And life was never to be the same,' Leonard murmurs, more to himself than to anyone else, it seems to the Inspector, who can't help feeling a pang of pity on hearing the young man's leaden tone.

'So, I'm afraid, Inspector, the boy could well have been hereabouts, but we were all rather preoccupied and unlikely to have noticed.'

'And you played no part in the search for him?'

'How could we? Our train left at seven o'clock the following morning.'

'We were all rather the worse for wear, I'm afraid,' Maurice admits, shamefaced. 'We nearly didn't make the bloody thing.'

'We didn't even know the boy was missing, not until later.'

'And how did you find out?'

'I think,' Victor looks across at Ida, 'Ida wrote to Maurice, didn't you?'

'Yes . . . yes, that's right.' Her shoulders hitch in brittle motion. 'You know how it is, you mention bits of local news.'

'I don't suppose you'd know when that was?' the Inspector asks.

She laughs. 'No, goodness, I wouldn't have a clue. But I'm sure that's it, I'm sure I wrote of it.'

'And, of course, we were a local regiment, Inspector,' Maurice chips in. 'Other men from the area were with us, and more joined later. News carries. I can't remember the specifics of how we heard every detail, but, well, the story reached us in its entirety over time.'

'I see.' The Inspector taps the pencil against the notebook cover. 'To the best of your knowledge, were the woods ever searched?'

'The woods?' Maurice asks, eyes wide.

'The woods by the river. The river is close, isn't it, to the front of the house? Just across the lawns. A very attractive setting, if you don't mind me saying.'

'The river threads through the valley,' Maurice answers, apparently bemused by the Inspector's unexpected observation, 'and the woods run along it in part.'

'Do you swim ever?' the Inspector asks with the affability of a genial uncle, his large hands resting lightly in his lap.

'Swim?'

'In the river? Refreshing on a hot summer's day . . . and fourteen, as I say, was such a scorcher.'

Maurice fumbles for an answer. It is Victor who comes to his rescue. 'We sometimes swam in the river, but only on occasion. I think we're all too old for that type of thing now, of course.'

The Inspector laughs, swiping the air with his hand as he sits forward once again. 'Oh, don't say that! I'm fond of a dip myself on a warm summer's day and I'm sure I have many, many years on all of you.' His chuckles subside. 'So, the woods were never searched.'

There is a pregnant pause. Once again, it is left to Victor to fill it. 'As I said, Inspector, we weren't here to know the details of what was done.'

'Mrs Stilwell? Do you happen to recall?'

Startled at being put on the spot, Ida appeals to the others, but when no lifeline is forthcoming, she shakes her head, a dainty, quivering movement. 'I'm sorry, I don't remember. I might not have been told. You see, my father-in-law was, unfortunately, not in the best of health then, so, with the boys away, it's highly likely the matter would have been dealt with by our farm manager at the time, a Mr Durham. Perhaps you should ask him?'

'Of course, a very valid suggestion.' The Inspector lays the pencil against the notepad cover. Having secured it in place with the elastic band, he tucks the bundle into his inside pocket. 'Well, I'm sorry to have imposed on your time, but I'm sure you understand.' He grunts as he struggles free of the sofa's embrace. The others rise out of manners. Leonard, naturally, remains where he is, staring into the far distance, only rallying himself at the last minute to acknowledge the Inspector's imminent departure, abruptly shaking his proffered hand as he makes his farewells.

Maurice, Ida, and Victor escort the Inspector to the front door. He steps out, then pauses to absorb the scene beyond the gravel forecourt: the expanse of lawn that gently slopes to the river's edge and the strand of meadow on the far side that gives way to the woodland bordering the horizon. He turns back to them.

'I may need to trouble you again in the future, I'm afraid.'

'Of course, if there's any way in which you think we can help,' Maurice says, thrusting his hands deep into his trouser pockets, hunching his shoulders against the unwelcome breeze pushing in through the open doorway.

'Well, the mother is still alive, and it would bring great comfort to her, I'm sure, to have some conclusion to the matter, one way or another.' The Inspector dons his bowler hat.

'This witness, Inspector . . .' Victor steps out onto the worn flagstone beyond the doorway. 'Why have they come forward now? After so long?'

The Inspector pulls a face. 'Well, Mr Monroe, people sometimes don't appreciate the significance of something they have witnessed until long after the fact – they might, for example, look upon a recollection with fresh eyes. In other cases, it might be something that has been troubling them for years, and their conscience can no longer bear it.'

'So, what exactly does this new witness say they've seen?'

'Well, please understand, Mr Monroe, I'm not really at liberty to divulge the contents—'

'The contents?'

'Of the letter, Mr Monroe. We have received a letter.'

I promise you that what I have written here is a true and honest account of what took place that day.

The Inspector looks up at the pewter-coloured clouds above and sniffs the air like a bloodhound detecting scent. 'Rain, if I'm not mistaken.' He smiles, his eyes crinkling at their edges.

I implore you – let justice be done.

'You'd better batten down the hatches – I hear there's a storm coming.'

Chapter One

She slams the car's door, then watches as it pulls away, its exhaust fumes cutting into the back of her throat as it disappears down the road, leaving her with only her large case and the trepidation churning in her stomach. For a moment she considers running after it, waving it to a stop, so she can climb back into the relative safety of its confines. But it is too late for that now. So instead, she watches the purple vapour gradually dissipate until, like the car, it is no longer visible, and the whole episode might have been little more than a figment of her imagination.

She lets out the breath she has been holding and bends to pick up the suitcase at her feet. Its weight drags her down, as if it too is intent on anchoring her to the spot. This will not do. She lets out another breath, short and sharp this time, and thrusts out her chin with more determination than she feels, firmly telling herself this is the beginning of an adventure. She will see it through, come what may. There is no going back.

A shoulder-high flint wall borders the road, containing the dense woodland that stretches behind it. It is broken by two frost-cracked brick pillars that hail the start of a driveway, one of which bears a wooden sign announcing 'Darkacre Hall'. No doubt it had once been pristine, a gleaming white background with ornately scrolled letters in glistening black paint, but now the wooden panel shows signs of rot, and what remains of the lettering has faded to shades of grey, so that it takes an educated guess to confirm she is in the right place. A pair of wrought-iron gates, bleeding rust from beneath their scraped epidermis, sag open either side, and as she approaches, she notes the tangled weeds entwined around their bottom edge, suggesting they have stood undisturbed for some time. She feels a stir of foreboding as she passes through them.

The bleak light of the day dims further under the wood's bristling canopy. Looking up, she catches glimpses of the wan sky through the branches' verdant shawls, now drab after the long summer and no longer blessed with the vibrancy they had displayed in the spring, when they were fresh with the splendour of the new season. A stiff breeze lifts the boughs and the leaves shiver, whispering their unease, as if realising their days are numbered.

The trees' sighs are soon drowned out by another sound: a low rumble that grows increasingly distinct. She has not gone far into the woods before the driveway rises over a hump-backed bridge straddling the broad river before her. White crests form across its surface as it thunders over the boulder-strewn riverbed. Fed by recent downpours, it displays unusual velocity and strength, its angry roar smothering the sound of bird calls above.

On reaching the peak of the bridge, she takes pause. Wandering over to the crumbling stone parapet, she drops her bag and plants her palms, the roughness of the lichen-spattered stone penetrating her cotton gloves. She leans over and peers into the gushing brown torrent that is, to her surprise, not far off the curve of the supporting arch beneath her. She can almost feel the river's fury and frustration as it surges against the edges that confine it, yearning to break free. It would not take much, she thinks, for it to burst its banks and spread itself wide.

A gust of wind sweeps across her face. She looks up at the darkening clouds overhead. A rook suddenly takes flight from a nearby beech tree, cawing loudly, its black wings beating. She shivers, struck by the ominous portent. Subduing her fears, she picks up her case and walks on.

The arbour drive seems to channel the wind, and soon it is cutting through her light wool coat and grazing her cheeks like a stubbled lover. A chill nestles between her shoulder blades. The unseasonably warm start to September has long misled her, but it is the end of the month now and the day's intermittent sunshine little more than a cool sham, a warning that summer is indeed over, and autumn hails.

The drive drags on, its loose chippings jabbing through the thin soles of her shoes. Her suitcase grows heavy; it bangs relentlessly against her calf, leaving her quite bruised. She switches hands to relieve the agony, but soon her arm muscles feel wrenched, and the fresh fingers ache. She stops to set it down, groaning with relief to be free of its burden. She wonders how on earth she will manage the rest of the way – there is not yet the merest hint of a house.

Stripping off her gloves, she massages the bleached welts cut by the case's handle. She is tired now, and fraught tears sting her eyes, but she chastises herself for being silly as she thrusts her fingers back into their cotton corsets. Picking up her case, she walks on.

The wood finally breaks, and she is rewarded with a broad vista of parkland, a bucolic scene dotted with great oaks and grazing sheep, their plaintive calls carrying on a softening breeze. She discovers she is in the bottom of a wide valley, the horizons edged with swells of woodland, while the river runs its length.

Her chest tightens. There, still some distance away, is Darkacre Hall – a white sail cloth neatly threaded with broad tar stiches, its diamond-paned windows glinting in the sunshine that momentarily pierces the shrouded sky.

With the end in sight, her pace quickens. The nagging sense of trepidation now serves as a distraction from the painful strain of carrying her case. In her haste, she stumbles, but catches herself in time. She feels foolish for tripping over her own feet, for setting her heart racing so unnecessarily. The thickening clouds smother the sun once more and the day dulls again. As the breeze teases the stray strands of hair that have escaped her neat hat, she finds herself questioning, not for the first time, whether she is doing the right thing coming here.

Poplar trees flank the end of the drive, towering over her like sentinels as the magnificent, beamed structure of Darkacre Hall looms large. Fifty yards beyond the last pair, the drive fans out into a gravelled forecourt. The chippings crunch under her feet, creating another note in the rich symphony carried on the wind, already chorded with bird song, bleating sheep and the distant rush of the river.

She realises she is holding her breath as she reaches the front door, an arch of ancient, age-blackened timber, studded with square nail heads, each the breadth of a knuckle. In a flight of fancy, she imagines herself in a fairy tale: an innocent lost, seeking shelter at a strange castle, uncertain as to what dangers might lurk behind its daunting façade. Her pulse quickens as she reaches for the twisted metal loop of the bell pull. She yanks it down and hears a faint clanging just beyond the door. Quite inexplicably, she experiences the strange sensation that she is no longer alone, and though her flesh prickles, she takes comfort from the thought.

After a minute or two she hears the clatter of footsteps and the screeched protest of a bolt hauled from its bed. The door yawns open.

'I'm Miss Sarah Hove,' she says. 'I believe I am expected.'

Chapter Two

Ida feels a bite of irritation that the girl has mistaken her for the maid. But then, what can she expect when she is forced to answer the door wearing a pinafore, with hair limp from the steam of the iron and fingers ingrained with dirt from scrubbing potatoes?

She has been reduced to the role of skivvy ever since her housekeeper, Mrs Gibbons, handed in her notice – without warning – leaving on the unlikely excuse she had, *quite out of the blue*, received *a most generous* offer of employment from a young couple newly moved to Brighton where her sister resided.

Ida has done her best to find a replacement locally, but her efforts have been in vain. The war might be over, but it seems people like to bear a grudge. Her attempts to enlist the services of an agency were met with humiliation – she received a curt response that the wages she had suggested were insufficient, given the outlined role, and Maurice stubbornly insisted it was all they could afford to offer. The double death duties they have been forced to pay are now taking their toll, compounded, of course, by the cost of Leonard's inescapable needs.

She, understandably, has refused point blank to assist him in any way. She has no intention of becoming his nursemaid – the very thought makes her shudder. She can't help feeling it would have been better for them all if he had just died in France, instead of returning home, a successful mistake of modern medicine – better to be a dead hero than a burdensome cripple. She has suggested that he be moved to a specialist home, or hospital, somewhere better equipped to care for his needs, but Maurice won't hear of it. His refusal rankles her. But then, lots of things about Maurice rankle her these days. He is no longer the man she married, and not for the first time, she wonders what her life might have been, if she had followed her heart rather than her mercenary streak. Practicalities, her parents had called it, but sometimes, even after all these years, she still feels the calling of her heart. She wonders if she will ever be free of it, and, increasingly, whether she should even try. But she knows, deep down, she is a coward, with far too much to lose.

Rallying, she offers the young woman before her a flustered smile, thanking her lucky stars once again for the unsolicited enquiry that has resulted in her arrival.

'I wasn't sure what time to expect you, hence you caught me out. I do wish you'd telephoned from the station.'

The girl's stuttered apologies fail to register; Ida is too busy removing the sauce-stained pinafore, which she discards upon the settle behind her. She taps her butter-blonde hair into place and then, in her haste to explain herself, trips over her complaints about deserting staff and the difficulties of finding servants since the war. Her grievances are met by a smile that attempts to be sympathetic, though it strikes her as detached, condescending even, leading to a stab of discomfort.

She doesn't like being wrong-footed, and there is something about this girl that makes her feel . . . *inferior*. She fights off her instinctive reaction to be haughty, and instead flings up her hands in a humorous show of mock exhaustion as she slips back into her comfortable guise of charming lady of the manor. She urges Sarah to put down her case, then helps her with her hat and coat, nestling them companionably beside her own on the stand behind them.

'Has it been a horribly arduous journey to get here?'

'Not at all, everything ran smoothly.'

'How did you get from the station? Surely you didn't walk the whole way?'

'I only walked from the main road, and really, it was no trouble. After being cramped up it was quite nice to stretch my legs, to be perfectly honest.'

'But carrying that heavy suitcase!' Ida pouts her disapproval. 'You really should have telephoned.'

'It was no bother.'

'Well, you're here now and that's the main thing. Would you like a cup of tea?'

The offer contains a deliberate hint of discouragement, and Ida is therefore pleased when Sarah politely declines.

'Oh well, if you're sure.' She smiles brightly. 'I'll introduce you to the boys first – they've been dying to meet you – and then I'll show you to your room and give you a little time to settle in. How does that sound?'

Leaving the beamed lobby by the right, they enter a long corridor. A grandfather clock stands tucked against the wall, its pendulum echoing with the solemn resonance of a drum beating the condemned to the scaffold. The corridor's floor is a work of ancient artistry – tessellated stone hexagons, patterned in clusters of four set around a small square flag, like petals around a stigma.

'How old is the Hall?' Sarah asks, her steps faltering as she admires the beauty beneath her feet.

'Most of it dates from the early 1600s. It didn't belong to Maurice's family then, of course. His grandfather bought the estate in the 1820s.' Ida glances sideways at Sarah and smiles. 'It is a very beautiful house, in its own way, but there are times when I wish we lived in a slightly more up-to-date abode. I think some of the plumbing might be original.' She is pleased when her wry humour is rewarded with a soft chuckle, but the accompanying smile proves fleeting.

Though the day outside has unexpectedly brightened, the corridor remains dull and gloomy, its air thick and still. Ida is suddenly conscious of the cobwebs strung across the corners of the ceiling, and that several of the diamond windowpanes, already smeared with grime, sport cracks like battle scars, while the cumbersome Jacobean furniture that sparingly populates the walkway bears a silver lamina of dust. Seeing Sarah's straying observation, she speaks up.

'The wretched housekeeper was an idle, po-faced thing, but she did her best to keep on top of it all. Since she left, I'm afraid I've been struggling somewhat.'

'I'm sorry, I didn't mean . . . it's such a house to maintain.'

'Things have been so difficult since the war.' Ida hesitates, but the prospect of unburdening herself is irresistibly attractive, and in a rapid revision of her initial impression, she now finds there is something about Sarah's quiet demeanour that encourages confidence. She has been deprived of female companionship for so long, and now she detects a glimmer of light in her lonely existence. 'Maurice's father died five years ago and Hugo – Maurice's elder brother – inherited, but he was then killed at Neuve Chapelle. Well, the double death duties, as you can imagine – crippling! And poor Maurice, left to bear the brunt of it while serving at the front. It's hardly any wonder . . .' she trails off. 'Well, it didn't help, I can tell you. It didn't help at all.'

'It sounds terrible.'

'It was. It has been terrible. And to lose Mrs Gibbons after all the other servants . . . I can't tell you the trial I've been through, Sarah.' In an uncharacteristic show of intimacy, Ida's fingers rest with butterfly brevity on Sarah's arm. 'I am so pleased that you have come. We run a quiet house here, informal – we don't stand on ceremony any longer, Maurice won't hear of it. He believes if the war has taught us anything it's that all men should be treated as equal in life as they are in death.'

She pauses, taking the opportunity to study the new arrival, caught in faded light. She is a little disappointed Sarah isn't prettier, but she is pleasant enough to look at it, though her heavy bone structure betrays her working-stock origins. Her hair – a dull, nondescript brown – is rather severely styled in a bun, and her plain navy dress has clearly been designed for practicality rather than elegance, but, nonetheless, Ida is pleased that Sarah is neat and well-kept, her clipped fingernails clean as a whistle, while her skin is bright and clear enough to withstand her lack of make-up. Her voice, though not exactly cultured, is blessedly free of any local accent that might have induced a shudder and she conveys a pleasing degree of intellect. Taken as a whole, Ida can't help feeling relieved and rather hopeful. With burgeoning optimism, she grasps Sarah's fingers.

'I am so glad you are here. I hope we will be friends. I would so like us to be friends.'

'I would like that.'

Pleased, Ida's hand falls back to her side. 'Now come, meet the boys.' She hastens towards the closed door before them, and with an encouraging backward glance, thrusts it open, ducking beneath the low-beamed lintel.

'Hello, my dears, look who I have brought you!'

*

Sarah's heart is pounding as she follows Ida inside. From the laden bookcases that line the walls, she presumes herself to be in the library. The exposed floorboards are a mishmash of widths, lengths and colours even, some honey oak, others as dark as molasses, but most are concealed by a Turkish rug, richly patterned in hues of brick, royal blue, duck egg and cream, its tassel edge matted with age.

The fire smouldering in the grate consists of little more than glowing embers; no effort has been made to replenish it, though a full basket of logs stands to the side of the hearth.

Three men lazily occupy the room. Two of them sit in the pair of wing-backed armchairs flanking the hearth, the floor around them strewn with discarded newspapers, including the salmon-pink pages of the *Financial Times*, and carefully marked sheets of *Sporting Life*. Both are smoking behind their spread broadsheets, the newspapers acting as chimneys, drawing the exhaled cigarette smoke upwards until it hangs below the plasterwork ceiling. The third man is confined to a wheelchair positioned by one of the recessed window seats. A thick plaid blanket lies draped over what should have been his lap, but Sarah sees instantly his thighs have been reduced to little more than stumps. He is the first to acknowledge their entrance, and she is struck by the sadness emanating from his young but weary features. He attempts a smile, but it proves rather insubstantial and quickly wilts on his lips, failing to flower in his eyes. He returns his attention to the garden beyond the panes.

'Hello, hello . . . Who have we here, Ida?' The man on the right of the fireplace rises first, fluttering shut the pages of his newspaper, before tossing it down upon his vacated seat. He stoops to rest his cigarette on the saucer cradling a half-filled cup of tea that sports a cataract-like skim on its surface. He is casually dressed in a V-necked Fair Isle jumper with a shirt and neatly knotted tie underneath, and dark-green twill trousers. He steps forward, holding out his hand.

'How do you do? I'm Victor, Victor Monroe.'

Steeling herself, Sarah takes his hand, meeting his steady gaze with as much confidence as she can muster.

'This is Miss Sarah Hove,' Ida announces brightly.

Victor continues to hold Sarah's hand. Growing uncomfortable, she attempts to extract it without fuss, but his grip tightens.

'I do hope you're not going to make us call you "Miss Hove". I'm sure Ida's told you, we run an informal house here, so I trust you won't be scandalised by us calling you Sarah.'

'Not at all,' she responds, a rigor smile on her lips. She is awash with relief as he finally relinquishes his hold, though she is irritated by the smirk that dashes across his face, as if some point scoring has been achieved at her expense.

'It's a pleasure to meet you, Sarah.' The second young man, already risen from his chair, now advances to shake her hand in a far more cordial manner, serving as a salve on her discomfort. 'I am so glad you have come. I have no doubt you will be a godsend to poor Ida. She has been coping valiantly these last few weeks, but it can't be much fun for her, having only male company.'

'This is my husband, Sarah,' Ida says, moving to stand beside him, her arm snaking through his.

'Oh gosh, I'm such a dolt!' the young man exclaims, patting the hand now gripping his bicep. 'I completely forgot to introduce myself. I'm Maurice Stilwell.'

It strikes Sarah that there is something overly apologetic about him, as if this omission is just one of many commonplace failures and he is pre-empting a reprimand. The flesh by his right eye flickers uncontrollably for a moment, causing his expression to darken with vexation, his easy smile faltering. Ida distracts him by suggesting he brings his brother around, and Maurice bounds off to do her bidding, taking the handles of the wheelchair and manoeuvring it into the gathering at the centre of the room.

'And last but not least!' Ida declares with strained gaiety.

'I'm Leonard. Leonard Stilwell. How do you do?'

He speaks quietly, almost diffidently, and makes no attempt to offer his hand, nor does he make a great effort to meet Sarah's eye. Instead, his gaze flits only briefly her way, absconding at the first opportunity.

'How do you do?' she says, keeping her hands firmly clasped before her.

'Has Ida run through everything with you yet?' Maurice asks, brushing back the heavy fringe that has a habit of slumping across his forehead. 'I'm sure she has; she's frightfully good at that type of thing.'

Victor snorts at this. Disinterested now, he disengages from the group and returns to his chair, retrieving his cigarette and paper before collapsing back down to read.

'I'm going to show her round now, darling,' Ida says, patting Maurice's arm in a somewhat condescending manner. 'I did so want her to meet you and her troublesome charge first.'

Her attempt at jest falls frighteningly flat, assisted on its way by the caustic undertone she hasn't quite managed to conceal. Leonard's chin drops to his chest, his mouth hardening with pained resentment, though Ida appears oblivious to his hurt. She pays him scant regard as he struggles to move himself away, using his only remaining hand in aggressive, jabbing thrusts to the arc of a wheel. Instead, she begins to lightly berate Victor for the state of his overflowing ashtray. As she speaks, Leonard succeeds in rotating his chair into the sought direction but remains unable to push himself back to his spot by the window. Finding his dogged persistence agonising to watch, Sarah is on the brink of offering her assistance when Maurice, finally registering his brother's growing distress, steps forward.

'Here, old chap, let me.'

Sarah is unable to decipher Maurice's backward glance at Ida as he returns his brother to the pool of light before the mullioned window. Leonard says nothing, but stares morosely out upon the garden.

'Well, come Sarah, let me show you around, help you get

your bearings. You can properly acquaint yourself with this rabble later.' Ida gestures her towards the door.

Victor removes his cigarette and leans beyond the wing of his chair to catch Sarah's eye as she turns to leave.

'I shall look forward to us meeting again, *Miss Hove*.'

He holds her gaze for an impertinent length of time. Only when her plain cheeks begin to burn does he return to the pages of his broadsheet, concealing his scornful smirk with the smouldering cigarette.

Chapter Three

'Don't mind Victor, I'm afraid he's always had a bit of an eye for the ladies.'

Though her words are dismissive, Sarah senses Ida's earlier warmth cooling unexpectedly, like a chilly breeze stealing the sun's respite on a winter's day to reveal the true nature of the season.

'I'll show you around quickly,' she says, setting off at a brisk pace down the corridor, retracing their earlier steps, 'just the rooms you'll be in day to day. We don't use all of the house. We so rarely entertain these days; the boys are never keen to, sadly.'

'Do you ever find it lonely here?' Sarah says, careful to keep the tone of her enquiry sympathetic but respectful, cautious of the blurred boundary between employer and employee that Ida has sought to establish, and which now, for some reason, appears in jeopardy.

Ida starts, as if taken aback by Sarah's perception. She comes to a standstill, her attention caught by the rain shower now spotting the window. A sigh escapes her, her sudden ill-humour fading. When she turns back to Sarah, her smile is tinged with sadness, and Sarah suspects it is the first honest display she has witnessed since her arrival.

'Yes . . . yes I do sometimes. The boys, you see, they have a tendency to club together, keep themselves to themselves. I'm always on the periphery somehow. Sometimes I wonder whether I'm not surplus to requirements, whether they wouldn't prefer it if I wasn't here at all.' Something passes behind her eyes before she catches herself. Her steely brightness shines once more as her fingers alight on Sarah's arm. 'Which is why I'm so pleased to have you here. I know already you will make the world of difference. I do so miss female company.'

'I'm sure your friends must be a comfort though.'

'Not so much, these days.' Forcing a smile, Ida carries on down the corridor. 'I mean I do have friends, of course I do,' she says, as Sarah falls in step beside her, 'I seem to spend all my time on correspondence – but there is no one nearby to drop in for a cup of tea and a chin-wag.' She grows wistful. 'Before the war, the house was alive with laughter and jollity. We had weekend parties galore – oh the fun we used to have, I can't tell you! Maurice's parents loved to entertain, and they were forever indulging our whims and turning a blind eye to our high-jinx. We were children playing at being grown-ups, really. But then the war came and . . . well, we lost so many friends, our circle of acquaintance . . .' Sarah watches melancholy overcloud Ida's sunny memories. 'Well, let's just say it was never the same after the war. The missing faces would crowd the house more than the living ones could possibly hope to fill it. Few people visit now.'

Casting off her sadness, Ida leads Sarah past the front door and through to the reception hall. Even here, the day's wan light has failed to penetrate. Instead, it seems to hover outside the vast windows, uncertain of its welcome.

In the near corner of the room, concealed by a projection of panelling, is the beginning of a staircase. Ida starts up the initial short flight of steps but pauses at the first half-landing to point out the portrait of a young man in uniform hanging above them. Its subject has a handsome face with strong features, his blond hair precisely parted. He is wearing a scarlet dress jacket, silver buttons gleaming down its front, its white upright collar brushing his cleanly shaven jaw. His right hand is nestled within the ornate basket hilt of the sabre housed in the scabbard hanging from his waist, while his left rests upon a navy cloth helmet topped by a gilt spike and emblazoned with an officer's star, positioned upon the table beside him. It is, Sarah readily concedes, an impressive image.

'That's Hugo, Maurice and Leonard's older brother, shot by a sniper. Such a dreadful waste. All that promise and then you're gone,' Ida snaps her fingers, 'just like that. So pointless, all of it.' She shivers, chilled by the futility of war. 'It hit them all so hard, his death. Shook Maurice to the core especially. He'd always looked up to Hugo, you see, hero-worshipped him almost.'

Sarah continues to peer into the startling blue eyes of the fallen soldier above her. From the beamed backdrop, she deduces the portrait has been done in the house, probably just before his departure. He emanates the innate hubris of the privileged few, assured of his own immortality. Such blind naivety renders the painting all the more poignant.

Ida begins climbing the second flight of stairs. She calls back over her shoulder, 'Hugo was always the golden child. His father adored him; such the right sort to be heir and take on all the responsibilities of the estate. Poor Maurice has never quite felt up to the job. He was never the strongest character . . .' She stops herself as she reaches the top landing and offers Sarah a weak smile as she hastens to catch up. 'Anyway, enough of all that. Let me show you to your room.'

Coarse beams stripe the walls, bleeding up into the plaster ceiling and disappearing beneath the uneven floorboards that run the length of the corridor. The red runner laid upon them is threadbare in places, and the exposed wood either side of it is thick with dust. There is a morose taint in the air, a vaguely repellent perfume of neglect and mothballs with an undernote of damp.

'I've put you in the Yellow Room,' Ida says as she descends seven steps that see the corridor give way to a broad landing as they reach the far end of the house. Three low doors are arranged around it, each set within beamed frames and constructed from roughly hewn wooden planks the texture of withered skin and as dark as char, with spear-headed wrought-iron hinges that stretch almost their full width. 'You can be on hand for Leonard then. Maurice, Vic and I are at the other end of the house, but if you scream loudly, we'll hear you.' She laughs, then gestures loosely to the door facing them. 'That's a bathroom. We have our own at the other end, so it's just for you and Len really, and on down there is the door to the attic and the back staircase that leads down to the kitchen.' She reaches for the latch on the door nearest them. 'So, this is your room.'

The room is not large by any means. The walls are again encased in wood, but the window is smaller than those down-stairs and fails to permit sufficient light, rendering the room dark and, to Sarah's mind, dreary. A simple stone fireplace stands flush against the panelling – the strong smell of soot in the air suggests it has recently been swept, perhaps in preparation for her arrival. The space is dominated by an ornately carved four-poster bed, its measly proportions reflecting the stature of its original Tudor occupants rather than their twentieth-century antecedents. Covering the bed is a faded yellow silk coverlet, and the curtains flowing from the thin brass curtain pole above the window are of a matching material. A patterned rug in shades of mustard and green mostly covers the floorboards, but it is immediately apparent to Sarah that moths have been at work upon it. The eaten-away clumps impair the image, like missing pieces in an otherwise complete jigsaw. The antique bedstead is oddly juxtaposed with a rather modern mirrored wardrobe. The only other furnishings are a plain chest of drawers and a high-backed wooden chair with a yellow velvet seat that has seen better days.

'It's quite a pleasant room, I do hope you like it.' Ida drifts towards the window. 'There are lovely views over the gardens.'

Sarah makes no attempt to join her in their appreciation. 'Thank you, I'm sure I'll be most comfortable here.'

The comment appears to please Ida. 'Let me show you Leonard's room.'

Back on the landing, she reaches for the latch of the neighbouring door. Sarah stops short, somewhat perplexed.

'Forgive me for saying, but would it not be easier to convert one of the downstairs rooms into a bedroom for him? Surely, getting up and down here must be a tremendous struggle.'

Ida throws up her hands and sighs dramatically. 'You are absolutely right, of course. It would make much more sense and prove easier for everyone but . . .' she huffs and looks away, clearly marshalling her thoughts. 'This has been Leonard's room since he left the nursery. He takes great comfort from being in it – even though it inconveniences everyone else.'

'How on earth does he manage the stairs?'

'One of the boys carries him – every morning, every evening. One of them carries him, and one of them carries his chair. Without a murmur of complaint. I swear they are too saintly.' Ida's lightning smile suggests she would not have such patience or selflessness. 'It's completely impractical, of course – an absurd arrangement – but they won't hear of changing it. At least Len will rest on the chaise downstairs now if he gets tired during the day. It took quite a lot of agitation on my part to persuade him to do that, I can tell you.' She offers a bitter smile and Sarah is once again taken aback by how quickly her sweet demeanour can sour. The latch clicks up.

'Won't he mind?' Sarah asks, already feeling the guilt of intrusion.

'Of course not.' Ida laughs as she pushes open the door.

Sarah experiences an immediate pang as she surveys the room, which she suspects has remained largely unchanged since Leonard was little more than a schoolboy, marching off to war in the wake of the elder brothers he likely adored.

It is a sizeable room, larger, certainly, than the one she has been given. The curtains have only been partially opened, and the room feels dingy, the air fetid, thick with sweat, alcohol, stale smoke, and something unsavoury which Sarah struggles to identify until she catches sight of the unemptied chamber pot shoved under the bed. She quickly looks away.

Muttering, Ida crosses to the window. The curtain rings grate on the brass pole as she thrusts the velvet panels further apart. Fumbling with the latches, she throws the casement wide open. The invasive breeze helps to dispel the unhealthy miasma.

The room is a complete mess. The bed itself is unmade, the top sheet and blankets carelessly tossed back over its bottom edge, and items of clothing have been discarded everywhere – on the chaise positioned at the end of the bed, on a chair, they are even strewn across the floor – while the drawers of the tallboy sag open, their contents casually rifled. Sarah delicately steps over a jumper and an empty whiskey bottle lying on its side as she advances further in.

'I'm so sorry, I haven't been in here for weeks. I had no idea it had got into this state.'

'It's all right. Nothing shocks me,' Sarah says distractedly, for her attention has been caught by the stone fireplace or, more specifically, by the small silver cups and school awards that crowd the mantel above it. Curious, she peers at the inscriptions – *Most promising batsman 1913, Captain first XI 1912, 1st Prize Long Jump 1912, Cross Country Champion 1911.* There are medals too – gold, silver, bronze, their coloured ribbons threaded amongst the bases of the cups.

On the walls, layered upon the panelling, are black and white photographs of sports teams – staggered rows of self-assured young men, brazen smiles for the camera. She finds Leonard in all of them, brandishing rugby balls, tennis racquets, cricket bats and golf clubs. She gasps.

'He was left-handed,' she murmurs, wincing as she thinks of the pinned-up shirt sleeve on his left arm.

'Yes, yes, he was . . . is, well, not now, I suppose,' Ida says. 'They tried to discourage it at school, of course, but his parents were always rather lax about things like that and so he never really mastered using his right hand. Think of the difference it might have made if he had.'

Sarah chooses to ignore Ida's insensitive comment and continues her study of the photographs. He features on horses now, an entire stable's worth, wearing hunting jackets, polo shirts – there is even one of him in racing silks, his knees tucked high against the saddle, dwarfed by the magnificent thoroughbred on which he is mounted, as he grins at the camera without a care in the world. An irrepressible, active, able boy, an energetic man-child. It makes the thought of the legless young man downstairs, a mere fraction of his former self, achingly poignant – and life seem unforgivably cruel. To her surprise, Sarah's eyes are pricked by tears as she turns away.

'Sad, isn't it? Poor Leonard,' Ida sighs, leaning against the windowsill, the infiltrating breeze playing loose strands of hair against her cheek. 'He was always the most active of the boys, wouldn't sit still, not for five minutes – one could get quite exhausted just watching him. Such a shame.' She steps away from the window. 'If there's any way you can help stay on top of this mess, it'd be most appreciated.'

'Is he on medication?'

Ida exhales her answer on a held breath. 'Yes, you're to see to all of that. Three pills a day; they're kept in here.' She crosses swiftly to an oak medicine cabinet mounted on the wall above the washstand – sufficiently high, Sarah notes, to make it unreachable by anyone confined to a wheelchair. Ida removes three brown medicine bottles, typed labels wrapped around their middles. She hands them to Sarah for inspection. The names of two of the medications are immediately familiar but she doesn't recognise the third. Ida comes to her side and reads the labels over her shoulder. A chipped nail taps two of the bottles in Sarah's spread palm. 'Those two are one tablet each, to be taken in the morning, that one . . .' the nail rasps the third bottle '. . . just one at night.' She takes them all back and replaces them in the cupboard. 'They must never be left lying around. You must supervise him taking them and then lock them away in here, every time. Do you understand? That really is terribly important.'

Keen to leave the insalubrious room, Ida ushers Sarah out. She announces she will send Maurice up with Sarah's case, and suggests Sarah takes some time to unpack and settle in, before joining them for dinner.

'Now, Maurice insists you are to be treated as one of the family rather than an employee. Very modern of him, but there we are, he's developed such peculiar convictions of late. Anyway. We don't stand on ceremony these days,' Ida assures her, 'so no dressing for dinner or anything like that – even I have no intention of cooking in my best evening gown. Just stay in what you're wearing. As I keep saying, we run such a quiet house now, most informal.'

Sarah begins to thank her, but the words die suddenly. A frown mars her brow, as her focus strays beyond her new employer.

'What on earth's the matter?' Ida laughs, twisting to follow Sarah's perplexed gaze.

Snapping back to her senses, Sarah releases a jagged breath. Her eyes drop to the floor.

'I'm sorry, I . . . I thought I saw . . .'

'Saw what?' Ida's voice quivers with amusement as she looks again at the empty corridor behind her.

'I . . . I don't know . . .' Sarah shakes her head and forces a smile. 'It must have been a trick of the light. Forgive me, I am clearly more worn out from the journey than I thought.'

'Well, take your time settling in – perhaps have a lie-down. I'll call you for dinner, you don't need to join us until then.'

'Thank you,' Sarah murmurs, faintly apologising again as she backs into her room.

Her eyes stray over Ida's shoulder for a final time before she softly closes the door.

Chapter Four

'So where were you before you came here, Sarah? I'm sorry, Ida's probably told me at some point, but I'm afraid I can't recall.'

They have gathered in the dining room for dinner, a room of modest proportions with treacle-coloured panelling and a half-hearted blaze in the limestone fireplace. Here again, the furniture is bulky and blackened with age, attuned to the period of the house. Sarah is beginning to find the dark wood that dominates the Hall horribly oppressive. The incessant panelling and ancient furniture greedily absorb all glimmers of light. Everything around her appears drab and morose. Even the silverware on the table – the candlesticks, the cruet set, the cutlery – is tarnished, and though the electric lights of the low-hanging brass candelabra above them are lit, two of the bulbs have blown, meaning that, beyond the immediate table, the features of the room are concealed in dense shadow, in which anyone – or anything – might lurk without fear of detection. She finds it a most unsettling thought.

Smoothing her napkin on her lap, she looks across the table to where Maurice is eagerly awaiting her answer. 'I had a position in Hurley, looking after an elderly lady.' She smiles. 'I very much enjoyed taking care of her, and the house, of course. I was quite at a loss when she died, but then an old nursing colleague mentioned having seen Mrs Stilwell's advertisement in the paper. I was afraid the position might have been filled, so I was delighted when she replied to my enquiry.'

'And how are you finding things with us, *Sarah*? Now you've had a chance to unpack and make yourself at home.'

There is a dryness to Victor's tone that borders on sarcasm, and Sarah's shy smile grows cautious.

'Everything is most satisfactory, thank you, Mr Monroe.'

'No, no, no . . .' Maurice sets down his wine glass with more agitation than is warranted. 'I thought we'd already said, no formality. First names for all of us.'

Sarah lowers her eyes. 'Of course, my apologies.'

'I mean, what has been the point of it all, all that waste, all that sacrifice, if nothing changes? Sent to war by an out-of-touch hierarchy to protect a society and lifestyle where they alone benefit—'

'I think there was a little more to it than that,' Vic interjects, with a sardonic hitch of an eyebrow.

'I don't blame the Russian workers for rising up,' Maurice continues over him, forming a fist upon the tablecloth, 'sent to the slaughter while their "betters" stay in the safety of their plush palaces. Regardless of who we fought for, we foot soldiers had one thing in common: we were all dispensable pawns. Little more than cannon fodder.'

'I might remind you, old chap, our class has sacrificed a great deal. Officers' odds were worse than those of the general soldier, first over the top and all that. Further, I would point out we are part of the very bourgeoisie that you'd bring down in an instant.' Victor adopts a teasing tone that doesn't quite mask the mockery lurking beneath it. 'Are you going to slit my throat in an act of proletariat solidarity while I sleep? Should I take to locking my door?'

The building confrontation is temporarily interrupted by Ida's arrival, as she rattles a rather rickety trolley laden with plates and covered dishes into the room. Sarah's offer to help in the kitchen that evening had been reluctantly rebuffed, but Ida has made it clear she expects her to be in full action by the morning. Sarah rises now to help unload the hot dishes, while the men return to their debate. Maurice's rising voice has Ida curdling with disapproval.

'You know what I'm trying to say, Vic. There should be a levelling of society. One man shouldn't be born above another, it's just not right, it's not fair.'

'It's a charming sentiment, Maurice, but hardly realistic or practical, and it's easy enough for you to idealise while sitting here feasting—'

'That's enough both of you! You must forgive my husband, Sarah, he's becoming quite the revolutionary.' Ida pushes away a slip of hair with the back of her hand, her forehead moist from the heat of the range. 'Enough talk of war and politics. Can't we just eat while it's hot?'

Lids clatter as the contents of the various serving dishes are exposed. Maurice and Victor wait for the ladies to help themselves first. Once she and Ida are done, Sarah, who has deliberately taken the empty seat next to Leonard, draws the dishes closer so that he can help himself as best he can. His right hand is clumsy with the serving spoons, but she resists offering her assistance for fear of causing offence, even though she finds his struggle painful to watch. At last, he has a full portion – a thick, leathery chop, roast potatoes, and a variety of soggy vegetables.

Picking up his knife in his right hand, he stares down at his plate.

Leaning towards him, Sarah murmurs, 'May I help?'

'No.'

The single word shoots from him like a bullet and she recoils from the force of its impact.

'Here, let me do it for you, old man.' Maurice hurriedly pushes back his chair, but is pinned in place by Ida's hand, heavy on his forearm.

'No, Maurice, let Sarah do it. That's why she's here after all – to help.' Ida turns her cool gaze on her brother-in-law. 'Don't be silly, Leonard.'

Leonard's knife clatters against his plate, bouncing off its edge to land on the table, soiling the white linen cloth with a smear of gravy. He regards his sister-in-law with steady contempt. A muscle in Ida's clenched jaw twitches tellingly, but she meets his challenging glare without a flicker of concern. The lump of Maurice's Adam's apple leaps and falls behind its curtain of closely shaven skin, but he says nothing, choosing instead to focus on his plate.

With a derisive snort, Victor saws through his hunk of pork, his knife catching on the china plate. He skewers the morsel on the tines of his fork and looks straight at Sarah as he pops it into his mouth, the honeyed light of the candelabra catching his amused expression. His jaw circles slowly.

Sarah eases out a breath. Her hand is trembling as she reaches for Leonard's plate. She draws it towards her as Ida watches on with satisfaction, though Leonard, sparking with anger and burning with unspoken words, has turned his face away. She makes short work of cutting up his food. The only break in the frosty silence is the pin prick tick of the ormolu clock on the mantel. Feeling an overwhelming sense of relief when she is done, Sarah eases the plate back into place, resting the fork against its right-hand rim. Straightening, she gathers up her own cutlery.

With a nod of approval, Ida reaches for her wine glass. 'Perfect.'

Leonard makes no attempt to pick up his fork and instead continues to stare into the pooling darkness beyond the table. Maurice tries to catch his brother's eye, but when he meets with failure, he studies his plate, bearing a look of abject misery.

'Welcome to our happy home, *Miss* Hove,' Victor says blithely. 'Aren't you glad you came?'

'Oh, do shut up, Victor,' Ida snaps.

They eat the remainder of the meal in silence.

*

Victor is glad to see the back of the women when they withdraw at the end of the meal, and he suspects Maurice and Leonard share his sentiment. After-dinner brandy and cigars is the one pre-war tradition they have clung to.

'I don't want a nursemaid,' Leonard protests, raising his crystal snifter to his stubborn-set mouth.

'We've been over this already, Len.' Maurice sprawls in his chair. 'Ida thought—'

'I don't bloody care what Ida thinks, Maurice. I don't want a nursemaid.'

'Ida simply felt it was for the best.'

'Practically, Len, you need help,' Vic says, swilling the brandy in his glass before tossing it back.

'But you help me, both of you. I know I'm a burden—'

'You're not a burden—'

'Except I am, damn it, and I know it! I wish to God—'

'Don't, Len.' Maurice's eye begins to spasm. 'Don't start that nonsense again. You're my brother, the only one I've got left. I'll always look after you, you know that.' There is a hint of desperation in his voice.

Victor pours himself another glass, comparing as he does so the amusing, robust young man Maurice once was, with the fragile fool he has become. The fear and imbalance that had once completely debilitated him still lingers behind the thin veneer of recovery, always threatening, never far away. He is like a finely blown glass – all it would take is a modicum of pressure, one indelicate touch, and he would irreparably shatter into a million pieces.

'I don't want anyone to "look after me,"' Len sulks. 'Isn't it humiliation enough to be like this without having to rely on a stranger for the most intimate of assistance? You cannot imagine, either of you.'

Victor replaces the stopper in the decanter. He cannot imagine what life is like for Leonard, and, more to the point, he has no wish to. He would have put a bullet through his brain by now if he had emerged from the war in a similar state. He washes the thought down with a gulp of brandy, savouring its burn. Poor Leonard, he had tried to end it all, of course. Even now, Vic wonders if it wouldn't have been better for everyone if Maurice had just agreed to stand by that night and let nature take its course. As it was, it turned out to be a missed opportunity for Leonard. All it had done was forewarn Maurice of his brother's intent. Anything that might be used as a tool of self-destruction is kept well out of Leonard's reach now, but Victor knows Ida is of the same opinion as himself. If Leonard wants to end it all, he should have the right to do so. But Victor also knows that should anything happen to Leonard it would break Maurice beyond repair. Isn't that why he is still here when he could have, arguably *should have*, moved on? For an impatient man, some things he considers worth waiting for.

He clears his throat. 'Anyway, your registered objections on the principle aside, what do you think of Sarah?'

'She seems pleasant enough, I suppose,' Leonard admits. 'I have no objection to her on a personal level at all, I never meant that. I just meant that I would have preferred things to stay the way they are. Why, what do you think of her?'

'Ida says she provided the most wonderful references,' Maurice chimes in. 'It was a stroke of good fortune that she wrote in when she did. Poor Ida had had no luck elsewhere, and, as it turns out, she has the perfect experience and no qualms about helping you, Len, or seeing to the household chores. You know, we really are very lucky to have her. I think she'll prove a marvellous asset, Len, I really do.'

'She nursed during the war, didn't she?' Victor asks on the way back to his seat.

'Yes, with the Queen Alexandra's – a professional, not one of those volunteer girls. That's why Ida was so thrilled to

48

receive her enquiry about the housekeeper's position. It makes her uniquely qualified.' He steals a look of apology at Leonard and seems relieved he has not reacted.

'She must have been very young,' Vic muses. 'What do we know about her generally – her family, where she comes from?'

'Oh, you'll have to ask Ida about all that. I think she comes from down south somewhere.'

'Why are you so interested?' Leonard takes a pull on his cigar before leaving it to smoulder on the edge of his pudding bowl, now smeared with Ida's tasteless custard. He reaches again for his brandy.

'I don't know. There's something about her.'

'How do you mean?'

'Don't you think her a little aloof?'

'She was a nurse; she must have seen terrible things. No doubt she's adopted an air of professional detachment after all that,' Leonard argues.

'No, it's not that. There's just something about her.'

'She seemed perfectly pleasant to me,' Maurice insists.

'She doesn't just look at you. It's as if she peers right inside you, right into your soul, searching . . .'

'Searching for what?'

'Your secrets,' Victor concludes quietly, swilling his brandy, mesmerised by the way it refracts the light. 'And yet something tells me, she has no intention of surrendering her own.'

Chapter Five

Ida leads Sarah into the drawing room after dinner, possibly the most inviting room in the house. A fire burns in the grate, spitting and hissing, as logs slip and crumble amongst the crackling flames. Opposite the door stands a grand piano, its lid closed, a handful of books abandoned on its dust-streaked top, while an array of sheet music has been left, forsaken, on its stand.

'They can have their brandy, and we shall have some sherry,' Ida declares, the clatter of her shoe heels vanishing as floorboards give way to a richly decorated rug. She crosses to the drinks table, tucked away against the far wall, its top crowded with decanters and an array of glasses. She fills two with sherry, then hands one to Sarah.

'Chin-chin,' she says, holding the glass aloft before taking a hearty gulp. Her lipstick leaves its stain on the etched rim. 'Do sit down.'

There is the choice of a floral-covered two-seater sofa or one of the assorted armchairs clustered before the hearth. A void has been left in the arrangement – Sarah presumes the space is for Leonard. Ida collapses upon the sofa, throwing one leg casually over the other. She props her elbow on the back of the seat, her fingers playing idly with the wave of her hair.

'Do you find us a queer lot?' she asks, as Sarah takes one of the armchairs.

'Not at all.'

'You'll get used to us, I'm sure. Sometimes I think we've been too much in each other's company. There's never a chance to breathe. But *you*—' she brightens perceptibly, dazzling Sarah with a smile '—you will be like a breath of fresh air. I can feel it already. You'll bring a bit of life to this staid old house.'

Unsure how to react, Sarah covers her feeble smile by taking a sip of sherry, though she has never had much of a taste for it. The wine at dinner has left her head feeling fuzzy, and she is conscious of taking care with her words. Ida shows no such restraint or concern. The alcohol has provided her with an attractive flush of colour, a natural pink spreading beyond the artificial smear of rouge she applied to her cheeks just before dinner. Blessed with a dainty nose, baby-blue eyes, and angled cheekbones, she is a truly beautiful woman. Sarah can't help but feel a stir of jealousy.

Letting out a sudden cry, Ida sets down her glass on the side table and scurries across to a peculiar shawl-covered stand in the corner beyond the piano.

'Mr Tibbs! Why are you still covered up, you poor dear!'

Chattering childishly, she whips away the fringed shawl to reveal a domed bird cage on a brass stand, with a shallow shelf just beneath. Sarah issues a cry of surprise and she shifts in her chair to better see the striking silver parrot perched on the swing inside.

'Hello, Mr Tibbs,' Ida coos.

'*Hello.*'

Ida whirls around, a broad smile cutting into her cheeks, her eyes sparkling with delight.

'There! What do you think of that? Isn't he an absolute marvel?'

Curious, Sarah, still clutching her sherry glass, joins Ida at the bird cage. Ida begins feeding monkey nuts through the bars, taken from a brown paper bag stored on the shelf below.

'What sort of bird is it?' Sarah asks, unnerved by the way the creature has skewered her with its beady eye.

'An African Grey Parrot. Maurice got him for me. Isn't he lovely? I'm going to teach him to say all sorts of things. He's awfully clever, you know. Say "hello", Mr Tibbs.'

'*Hello.*' The bird promptly snatches a nut from Ida's fingers, gripping the shell in its claws as it cracks it apart with its hooked beak.

'How do you do?' Ida speaks in a deliberate manner as the bird devours the nut. 'How do you do?' she repeats with a sing-song lilt, her nose almost touching the bars of the cage. The bird ignores her. 'How do you do?' She frowns with mild irritation, then straightens up and smiles. 'It's how you teach them, you see, repetition. You say a phrase over and over until they say it back to you.'

'How long have you had him?'

'Only a month, and he learnt "hello" so quickly.' She turns back to the cage. 'How-do-you-do?'

Sarah retakes her seat while Ida dallies at the cage side, persisting with the bird's tuition. It isn't long before the repeated mantra begins to grate on Sarah's nerves, but she grits her teeth and says nothing. She is greatly relieved when the men finally put in an appearance, Maurice pushing Leonard through the doorway first, Victor sauntering in after. He makes his way directly to the drinks table.

Sarah had thought Ida might tire of her tutorial once the men joined them, but she finds she is mistaken – indeed Ida does not even acknowledge their arrival. Maurice, however, soon loses patience with her infuriating chanting and demands she stop.

Ida, now peevish, flounces back down onto the sofa. 'How am I supposed to teach him to speak if you won't let me?'

'Teach him when I'm not in the bloody room.'

'Hello, Mr Tibbs,' Ida calls out with an air of defiance.

'*Hello.*'

'Isn't that extraordinary?' She swivels in her seat, seeking out Sarah's agreement.

'Yes . . . quite.'

'He's such a clever little chap,' Ida says, leaning over the side of the sofa to renew her cooing while pointedly ignoring Maurice's muffled expletive. The bird bobs, its neck feathers ruffling, as it proceeds to offer up a chorus of whistles and clicks, much to Ida's delight, though she soon tires of its display. She settles back in her seat, but she seems incapable of sitting still. She takes to jabbing the fire rather ineffectively with the poker, complaining of its lack of vibrancy. Cack-handed with the tongs, she adds more logs until it roars so alarmingly Victor breaks off from his study of *Sporting Life* to advise her she is at risk of setting the chimney on fire.

'Well, this is terribly dull – shall we play some cards?' she suggests at last.

Victor draws on the cigarette clamped between his fingers. 'Oh, go on, why not, I'll play a couple of hands with you,' he says, speaking through the exhaled smoke.

'Oh marvellous! Maurice, be a dear and get the cards, would you?'

Maurice, who has been engaged in muted conversation with his brother since their arrival, pats Leonard's arm in a manner Sarah interprets as apologetic, before rising to do his wife's bidding, leaving Leonard looking lost, the fingers of his right hand playing with the fringe of the tartan blanket covering his lap.

'Actually, I'm not one for cards. I'm more of a chequers or chess player myself,' Sarah blurts out. She catches Leonard's eye. 'I don't suppose you play either of those?'

'Chess, yes,' he stutters with surprise. 'I like chess.'

'But we won't be able to play bridge with only three,' Ida protests.

'Well, there are plenty of other games we can play,' Maurice says, passing her the worn pack of cards. 'The chess set is over here, Sarah, let me show you.'

She accompanies him to the dresser at the far end of the room and crouches down beside him as he opens one of the bottom cupboards. There, amongst an assortment of boxed board games, is a beautiful pearl-inlaid chess set.

'Thank you—' his low voice is full of genuine warmth as he hands it to her '—that was very kind of you. Len struggles with cards – something Ida seems to forget.'

His smile is overshadowed by a furrowed brow as Ida summons him to join her. Under Ida's instruction, Victor, his cigarette dangling precariously from his bottom lip, lifts a games table into position between their seats.

Sarah is relieved to have escaped the card game. The tense knots in her shoulders, which have been plaguing her since

54

dinner, ease a little as she joins Leonard at the small table before the window. As she takes her place, they both agree, it is the perfect size for a chessboard.

It is nearly midnight when Ida decides it is time for them to retire. Maurice, having broken up the charred remains of the fire with the poker, takes the handles of Leonard's wheelchair and manoeuvres him through the doorway into the reception hall. Vic indulges himself with a final drag on his cigarette before grinding it into the ashtray.

'Well, goodnight, *Miss Hove*, I hope you sleep well. Goodnight, Ida,' he says, his fingers brushing the top of Ida's shoulder as he follows Maurice out.

'Right.' Ida gets to her feet with surprising bounce, and, not for the first time, Sarah wonders where she gets her energy from. 'I'm going to make some cocoa – do you want a cup?'

'No, not for me, thank you. I'd better go and see to Leonard.'

'I do hope you didn't find today too awful,' Ida says, delaying Sarah's departure with a gentle hand. 'They can take a bit of getting used to, but they're not a bad lot really. I so hope you'll stay. I think you can make a wonderful difference here.'

'I'm not going anywhere, just yet,' Sarah assures her, adding a smile. 'Goodnight.'

'*Bye-bye*,' squawks Mr Tibbs from the corner, much to Ida's amusement.

The reception hall is in darkness. No lights have been turned on, and the curtains have long been drawn against the moonlight which might have offered some relief. But there is a bulb burning somewhere upon the stairs, and the bottom steps within the panelled protrusion are caught in the periphery of its glow, providing a beacon for Sarah.

She gropes her way towards it as best she can, but being unfamiliar with the positioning of the furniture, she collides with the edge of the sofa, masked by the gloom. She curses under her breath at the burst of pain in her thigh, which she attempts to rub away as she gives the sofa a wide berth and carries on towards the staircase. She draws up short at the poignant sight of Leonard's empty wheelchair, abandoned by the bottom step.

'I hope you know what you've let yourself in for.'

Her heart explodes from her chest as Victor looms out of the darkness, a fresh cigarette smouldering between his fingers, its tip crimson against the pitch black. His lips curl with amusement at her evident shock. As her rapid pulse steadies, she stiffens with resentment.

'It's not a pretty sight that awaits you.'

'I have seen far worse, I'm sure,' she retorts. 'There is nothing quite as gruesome as a wound fresh from the field, before it has been sanitised, stitched and healed.'

He snorts, bringing the cigarette to his lips. His cheeks sink as he draws on it. 'Of course . . .' smoke drifts from his mouth '. . . you were a proper little nursey, weren't you? Not one of those well-intentioned young ladies looking for a bit of excitement and an excuse to cut loose from Mama's silk apron strings.'

'You are very unjust to belittle the efforts of the Voluntary Aid Detachment, Mr Monroe. Their contribution was invaluable, as you would know if you'd ever been injured.'

'How do you know I wasn't?'

'I don't think any casualty who had encountered members of the VAD first-hand would speak of them in such a derogatory manner.'

He responds with a sardonic chuckle. 'You're right, of course. I had a few flesh wounds, a few near misses, but nothing that had me sent down the line beyond the nearest regimental aid post.'

'You were very lucky then.'

'Lucky or just a bloody good soldier.'

'I don't think ability has anything to do with it.'

He leans towards her, so close she can smell the pungent tobacco on his warm breath. 'I wouldn't be so sure of that.'

He continues to study her as he slots his cigarette back between his lips. Lifting the wheelchair, he starts up the stairs.

Sarah, her mouth dry, waits a moment, then follows behind.

The upstairs landing is meanly lit by sparse wall lamps so ineffectual as to be pointless. Sarah chooses to keep her distance as she follows Victor, the chair's wheels squeaking as they roll and jump across the uneven floorboards. He glances back at her as he reaches the top of the downward flight leading to the bottom landing. Hoisting up the chair again he makes a leisurely descent. A golden rectangle of light spills out from Leonard's open door, along with murmurous voices.

Vic leaves the chair just outside. Hanging onto the door post he swings through the doorway, snapping off a mock salute.

'Goodnight chaps.'

He turns to leave. Sarah catches her breath as he faces her. He studies her for a moment, as if attempting to penetrate the layers of her carefully constructed veneer to discover what lurks beneath.

'Goodnight again . . . *Sarah*,' he says at last.

'Goodnight.' She cannot bring herself to use his name.

'Sleep well,' he adds, and though Sarah smarts from the mockery in his tone, she continues to watch him as he retreats up the steps.

She does not look away until he has disappeared into the gloom.

Chapter Six

Sarah finds Leonard positioned on the edge of his bed. In an attempt at coy modesty, his dressing gown lies draped across his lap.

'Shall I stay?' Maurice asks.

'I don't think that's necessary,' she replies.

'Right, well . . .' He rubs his hands together for want of something to do. 'Holler if you need anything. Goodnight, Len. Goodnight, Sarah. See you both in the morning.'

Sarah closes the door behind him, silently lowering the latch into place before turning to face the young man on the bed. She forces a bright smile.

'Now then—'

'In case you're wondering, I hate this. And what's more,' Len blurts out, 'just so we're clear, I never wanted you here. I'm sorry, it's nothing against you personally, but I think you should know.'

'Then why am I here?'

'Ida.' He brutalises his sister-in-law's name, shredding it with contempt.

Sarah clasps her hands together so he can't see them shaking. 'She thought you needed some help?'

'She resents me. She resents that I take up so much of Maurice's time.'

'He's your brother. I'm sure he doesn't mind looking after you.'

He winces. 'I don't want anyone to have to "look after" me.'

'Well, I'm afraid, given your situation, that's a rather unrealistic desire.'

'I hate being so f . . .' he catches the expletive just in time. She can see the struggle it is for him to suppress his temper, like recorking a shaken bottle of champagne, but, in the end, he manages to stopper the explosion, and when he starts to speak again, his voice is steady, though chilling. 'I hate being so utterly dependent. It's pathetic.'

'It's not pathetic. It's just the way things are. Best not to dwell on it too much. It'll drive you mad.'

A harsh bark escapes him. 'Who says it hasn't already?'

She smiles at that. Her nerves begin to dissipate as she finds herself returning to solid ground. This is familiar territory – nursing, caring. She realises that she is more at ease now than she has been sitting in their company all evening, attempting polite conversation. Her confidence blooms as she advances, efficient and business-like, closing the gap between them. 'So, how do you like things done? I'll fit around your preferences – do you want to dress first and wash later or vice versa? What's your routine?'

'Usually, Maurice sits and drinks several generous measures of whiskey with me then stays until I fall asleep. And since the whiskey is used to wash down my medication, that doesn't tend to take too long.'

'Well, that doesn't sound very sensible at all.' She smiles at the young man, and after a brief hesitation, he smiles back.

'No, I suppose it's not really,' he admits, his hostility dissolving into sheepishness, which she finds rather endearing.

'So, let's get you dressed first and cleaned up after and then you can have your medicine. But I'm afraid there'll be no whiskey on my watch.'

She reaches for the dressing gown, but his hand lands on hers before she can pull it away. She takes a deep breath. Her voice softens.

'You've nothing under there that will shock me, Leonard. Let me help you.'

He reluctantly withdraws his hand, angling his face away from her as he does so. She takes up the dressing gown. His amputations are high – there is little more than six inches of his left thigh remaining, while the right is slightly longer, perhaps eight.

'Not a pretty sight, is it?' There is a catch in his voice.

'A good deal prettier than when you arrived at the clearing station, I'm sure,' Sarah retorts briskly, blinking away the images of torn flesh and protruding bone that flash into her mind's eye. She silences the tortured screams that for a moment seem to fill the room. 'Now, what can you do for yourself? You're not a baby, I'm sure you don't need me for everything.'

He laboriously removes his pullover and fumbles free the buttons on his shirt, though he requires her help to fully remove it. Next, he unbuckles his belt. With growing embarrassment, he unbuttons his trousers. He tries – and largely succeeds – in shuffling himself out of them. Sarah helps where necessary and discreetly drapes a towel across his lap while she holds the urine bottle for him. She leaves the towel over the filled container when she sets it down on the washstand, ready for later removal. They work together to get him dressed in his pyjamas, the legs of which have been cut into shorts and neatly hemmed. Sarah wonders who might have done the stitching; she can't imagine Ida being responsible.

'Have you never considered prosthetics?' she asks as he eases himself back against his banked pillows.

'No,' he says, pulling the blankets over his chest.

'Any particular reason?' Sarah shakes a single pill from the appropriate bottle removed from the cabinet. 'They're quite good, you know,' she says, as he takes it from her open palm. 'They might help you feel a bit more . . . like normal life.'

'I don't think I deserve a chance of normal life.' He washes the pill down with the water she passes him, draining the glass before handing it back.

'Why on earth not?'

He removes one of the pillows from behind him, then lies flat, staring at the ceiling above.

'I've done terrible things in my life. I think this is perhaps my just punishment.'

Sarah secures the lid on the pill bottle and sets it down on the bedside table. 'You were a soldier. You did what you had to do.'

She fills the ensuing silence by tidying his room, straightening the drawers in his tallboy and making a start on sorting his discarded clothing.

'When did you become a nurse?'

She is startled by the sudden question. 'Eight years ago. I was posted to France at the outbreak of the war.'

'Did you . . . lose anyone?'

She falters in the folding of a jumper she has deemed clean enough to be put away. 'Didn't everyone?' She places it into a drawer of the tallboy. Only when she has shunted the drawer shut does she answer. 'A brother. Two cousins. Countless friends.'

'I'm so sorry to hear that.' The quiet sincerity in his voice brings unexpected tears to her eyes. She turns away to conceal them. 'It must have made your service all the more meaningful.'

'They were beyond saving. Others were not.' She begins to organise his bedside table, ensuring the handbell is within reach, should he need her in the night. 'But I will never forget them. I will never forget what they must have endured.'

'Nor should you.'

'No,' she says quietly. 'I should not.' She looks down at the bottle of pills. Picking it up, she returns it to the cupboard. 'Now, is there anything else I can do before I leave you?'

'I don't think so.'

'Right. Well, ring if you need anything. I'm just next door.' She bends down to retrieve the chamber pot from under the bed, its unsavoury contents sloshing up the sides as she does so. She empties the urine bottle into it.

'I'm sorry. I'm sorry you have to . . . no one should have to do that.'

'It's nothing.' She shrugs. 'It's just part of the job.'

He turns away from her as she switches off the lamp on the bedside table, but not before she has seen the tear trailing down his cheek. It is not nothing, she realises then. For him it is something very significant indeed, and she wishes she could take back her nonchalance.

'Goodnight, Leonard.'

He does not return the farewell. The light cast from the small fire Maurice must have lit in the grate lifts the darkness enough for her to make her way to the door. She had not even noticed it before – the flickering flames have done little to make their presence known. A cold edge remains in the air. As she reaches for the latch, she inhales sharply.

Behind her, the bed sheets rustle. 'What is it?'

'The strangest thing . . . Like someone just walked over my grave.' Her laugh, though self-deprecatory, contains a definite tremor.

'Are you all right?'

'Yes . . . yes . . . of course,' she assures him at last.

She wishes him goodnight again, as she closes the door behind her.

Chapter Seven

Sarah wakes early the next morning despite her restless night. She tiptoes across the landing to use the bathroom, not wishing to disturb the still slumbering household. Only after she has dressed in the half-light does she throw back the yellow drapes, the rake of curtain rings slicing through the dormant silence with the ruthlessness of a butcher's blade.

The sun has broken the horizon to paint a grey wash over the garden stretching before her, muting the autumnal fall upon the dew-dampened lawns. She can trace the winding path of the river by the thick ribbon of mist suspended above it. The air beside the window feels cold and dank, and she soon retreats.

Once she has dressed her hair, made her bed and tidied away her things, it is time to wake Leonard. Stepping out onto the landing, she is surprised to find his door already open, familiar voices coming from within. She seeks to overcome her nerves by first visiting the bathroom to fill her ewer with water, before carrying it back across the landing. Her steps slow as she reaches Leonard's door.

Maurice is lying across the end of Leonard's bed, propped up by his elbow, his shaven cheek resting in the palm of his hand, while Victor leans with characteristic apathy against the stone casing of the window, smoking.

'Ah, here comes Florence Nightingale herself,' Vic drawls, noticing her first. 'Good morning, Sarah, I trust you slept well?'

Sarah sets the ewer down on the washstand, feeling every inch a matron who has invaded a schoolboys' dorm. 'Good morning.'

Maurice sits up, pushing back his errant hair. 'Good morning, Sarah. How are you? I'm sorry, I hope you don't mind us congregating like this – old habits and all that.' He offers her a rueful smile.

'I'm sure she doesn't mind, Maurice,' Victor pushes himself up and extinguishes his cigarette on the stone sill. 'She hardly strikes me as a battle-axe. You'll find it in your heart to forgive us our little ways, won't you, Sarah?'

'I'd rather you used an ashtray than the windowsill.'

Maurice clears his throat. 'Look here, Len, we'll clear out and let you get sorted. See you in a bit, old chap.'

Out of habit, Maurice pats the end of the bed, betraying a time when he might once have caught his brother's legs. His gauche gait as he leaves the room is at a sharp contrast to Victor's suave confidence. She is relieved to shut the door on them both.

'Sorry about that . . .' Leonard hitches himself up against the pillows. 'They've always been the ones to look after me, you see.'

'Well, I'm here now.'

She assists him with his ablutions and helps him dress, before dispensing his medication. When he is ready, she brings the wheelchair to the bedside. He places his arm around her neck, clearly uncomfortable with the level of intimacy required, as she half-drags, half-lifts him into its seat. She manages to cover her shock at how little he weighs and focuses instead oh arranging the tartan blanket over his lap. She finds it curious that he bothers with it at all, given that everyone in the house must be used to his appearance, but it is clearly an acquired habit, and she presumes that, like a child with a comfort blanket, he is reluctant to relinquish the security it gives him.

'All set?'

She wheels him to the door, pausing as she considers the challenge of reaching the upper bedroom corridor, but the tickle of cigarette smoke in her nostrils gives her the confidence to push on. Victor and Maurice are sitting on the steps, smoking while they wait. Sarah stands aside as, with speed gained from years of practice, they disassemble Leonard and his wheelchair, Maurice whipping his brother up into his arms, while Vic hauls the chair up the short flight of stairs, before they reunite them at the top. Maurice then takes charge, wheeling his brother along the corridor, with Victor ambling alongside, leaving Sarah to trail, redundant, in their wake. They repeat the procedure when they reach the downward flight leading to the reception hall.

'I say, Ida's in the kitchen getting breakfast – would you mind giving her a hand and I'll take Leonard through to the dining room?' Maurice asks, somewhat apologetically.

'Of course.'

The kitchen is at the rear of the house, down a dark service corridor that runs beyond the library. The greater the distance from the main reception rooms, the greater the air of general neglect, and by the time Sarah can hear the clatter of saucepan lids, the painted plaster walls are speckled with grey-green mould, and spiderwebs, as intricate as doilies, cling to the ceiling beams. She even spots what she suspects to be mouse droppings.

In the kitchen, Ida is giving vent to her ill-temper. She looks round when Sarah enters, her face flushed and glistening with sweat.

'Oh, thank God! Be an angel and give me a hand, would you?'

The kitchen is not a particularly large one, and their combined presence, along with the long pine table standing in its midst, seems to fill it. They are forced to dance around each other as Ida manhandles pans from the range onto the warped tabletop, while Sarah searches through cupboards for plates, serving dishes and cutlery.

'I'm so glad you're here to help now. I am not cut out for this,' Ida moans. 'I couldn't believe it when Mrs Gibbons walked out like that. Wretched woman. She left me completely in the lurch.'

'I'm surprised there wasn't someone in the village willing to come in.'

'No . . . no . . . unfortunately not.'

'Not even a young girl?'

'I'm afraid local people don't look to work here these days,' Ida says, loading the serving dishes.

'Why ever not?'

Ida's attention remains rigidly fixed on the congealed porridge she is ladling into a tureen. 'Oh, you know . . . people can be funny like that . . .'

'But surely this house must always have been an important employer around here?'

'People just don't want to work here since the war!' Ida appears to regret her snappishness almost immediately. She rubs her hand across her forehead. 'Sorry, I didn't mean to bite your head off. A lot of things have changed since the war, that's all.'

They bustle around each other, depositing the bacon and scrambled eggs that Ida has haphazardly produced into the remaining serving dishes. Sarah passes no comment on the quality of the food, though the bacon fat is charred, and the egg has caught in the pan. Ida's relief when they are done is marked. She is as out of place in the kitchen as a thoroughbred at a gymkhana.

'We'll have to work out a morning schedule for you,' Ida says. 'I appreciate you can't be seeing to Leonard at the same time as cooking breakfast, but it's quite clear I was not raised to this. The boys might just have to accept some alterations to their precious routine.'

'I'm happy with that, as long as Leonard won't mind being left to manage.' Sarah lifts one of the laden trays from the table.

'Leonard will be fine,' Ida says, taking the other tray, the harshness in her voice speaking volumes. 'The boys are quite capable of looking after him. He certainly doesn't need your ministrations every minute of the day, there's far more important things for you to be getting on with than looking after him. He takes up quite enough of everyone's time as it is.'

Sarah sets her tray back down upon the table. 'You've something on your shoulder . . .'

'Have I?' Ida twists to see as Sarah reaches out to pluck away the offending item.

'It must be from your pillow,' Sarah says, holding up a small white feather.

The colour drains from Ida's cheeks.

'Are you all right?'

'Yes,' Ida replies, tearing her gaze away from the delicate white furl. 'Yes, I'm quite well. You're right, it must have escaped my pillow and got caught in my cardigan. Funny I never noticed it before. Come on,' she says with an uncertain smile, 'we'd best get this up to the dining room while it's all still vaguely warm.'

The men seem unfazed by their unappetising start to the day, drowning the porridge in syrup before digging into the burnt bacon and dry egg with gusto. Sarah, in contrast, picks delicately at the food and instead sates her appetite by drinking several cups of tea. Ida herself seems distracted and on occasion brushes her shoulder, as if she suspects something else might yet be loitering there. She looks round at the sound of disturbed gravel outside. Throwing down her napkin, she pushes back her chair and crosses to the window.

'The postman! Oh, I wonder if there's anything for me!' There is girlish excitement in her voice as she excuses herself, optimism carrying her from the room. When she returns a few minutes later, a single missive in her hand, her shoulders are slumped, and her zest has soured.

'Just one for you, Maurice.' She drops it before him, and retakes her seat with a heavy sigh, though no one comments on her apparent disappointment.

Maurice thanks her, setting down his teacup. He glances at the front of the envelope and frowns, before slipping his finger under the back fold, tearing it apart. 'We were just deciding what to do with the day,' he says as he extracts the single sheet of folded notepaper, 'is there anything you would like to do, Ida?'

'What is it, Maurice?' It is Leonard who speaks, noticing

the darkening of his brother's expression as he scans the letter in his hand.

'It's uh . . . from the Vicar.'

'Ugh, such a boring man.' Ida leans sideways to better confide in Sarah. 'Delivers the most interminable sermons.' She rolls her eyes before turning her attention back to her husband. 'What does he want now?'

'It's . . . uh . . . just about the war memorial. They'll be unveiling it a week on Sunday at a special service.' Maurice makes a fuss of returning the letter to its envelope. His eyes shift about the room as he draws his chair closer to the table. They markedly avoid his wife. He takes a sip of tea.

'Well, I won't be going,' Leonard declares, his mouth forming a stubborn line.

'You ought to, Len, it'll be expected of you.' Victor finishes the last of his breakfast and neatly places his cutlery upon the empty plate.

'I'm not going to be stared at like some exhibit in a zoo. And I have no desire to be the object of people's pity. Nor do I want to see people thanking their lucky stars that their sons are dead and didn't come back looking like me.'

'Oh, Leonard, that's a terrible thing to say,' Maurice cries. Ida is rendered conspicuous by her silence. 'We can't leave you behind all alone.'

'I'll be here,' Sarah points out quietly. 'After all, there's no reason for me to attend.'

At this, Maurice brightens. In fact, Sarah thinks he looks oddly relieved. 'Yes . . . actually . . . why now, if you don't want to go, old man, don't. Vic and I can hold the fort, can't we, Vic? And Ida, darling, there's no need for you to come, you'll only be bored. Why don't you stay here with Len and Sarah?'

'I will not,' Ida rebuffs his suggestion at once. 'You were a commanding officer for a lot of those men, Maurice. As your wife, I have a duty to attend. I'll get your uniforms out. Sarah and I can ensure they're up to scratch, and I'll wear my black; that would be most appropriate, I think.'

'I really don't think there's any need—'

'Maurice, I am going to that memorial. I'm your wife, it would look distinctly odd if I didn't go.'

'No, really, I—'

'Maurice! I am going and that's that.'

'But they don't want you to!'

Maurice's blurted revelation stills the room. He squirms uncomfortably under the collective weight of their shock.

'What?'

The word shoots from Ida like venom. Maurice's eye begins to twitch with such rapidity that he presses the heel of his hand against it, in a vain attempt to calm the spasm. Sarah notices that the hand clutching the letter is now trembling violently.

'You can't go, Ida,' he says at last, his voice uneven. He lowers his hand, but the spasming continues, to his evident frustration. 'I'm afraid they don't want you there.'

'Who doesn't want me there?' Ida plants both palms on the tablecloth as if preparing to spring into attack. 'What are you talking about, Maurice?'

Victor rises from his chair and navigates his way around the table to Maurice's side. He relieves him of the crumpled envelope and extracts the now creased letter from inside. Maurice does not try to stop him. Instead, he seems to shrink, his shoulders curving, and though his hand no longer contains the offending missive, the tremor plaguing it continues.

Vic's eyes narrow as he absorbs the letter's contents. 'The Vicar has written to ask whether you might not attend on the grounds that some bereaved family members have applied to him requesting you don't.'

'That is ridiculous.' Ida throws herself back in her chair. She crosses her arms like a churlish schoolgirl.

'You can't go, Ida,' Victor says, placing the letter on the table before Maurice.

'I will not be told what I can and cannot do—'

'For God's sake, Ida. Can't you just accept that some of the names carved on that stone are there as a direct result of your actions? There are men there who had every right to stay behind, safe with their families. They only ended up in the war because of your maliciousness.'

'Don't, Len,' Maurice whispers, turning to his brother with a look of pleading.

'It's about time some of us around here faced up to the consequences of our actions.' Leonard balls his napkin within his fist and slams it down upon the tablecloth. 'Sarah, take me to the library, would you?' As she pulls his chair clear from the table, he twists round to address the others. 'The rest of you can do what you want, but I won't be attending the ceremony. And if you do have the audacity to go, Ida . . . well, I hope to God you get exactly what's coming to you.'

Chapter Eight

Ida's anger seethes into the following day and the day after. She refuses to eat with them, barely speaks to them, until her building resentment bursts like a boil. She subjects Maurice to her fury, haranguing him at such a volume that the closed door of his study offers no privacy for the humiliating verbal assault. His muffled attempts to console her, to sympathise with her, are met by a screamed rebuke of '*If you were a proper husband* . . .' that penetrates the oaken door with the ease of a hot knife through butter.

Listening from the adjacent library, Leonard grows increasingly indignant on his brother's behalf. Unable to stand it a minute longer, he orders Sarah to take him to them, but Vic intercedes and advises him to leave well alone.

'You know she'll calm down and they'll make up. They always do,' he concludes in a flat voice.

In the end, Maurice and Ida resurface in time to join them for the evening meal that Sarah has rustled up from the meagre supplies found in the kitchen. Ida's anger appears finally spent, though Maurice continues to tiptoe around her as if she were a sleeping tiger, in danger of rousing. He keeps her placid with wine, topping up her glass throughout the meal, until Sarah is convinced Ida has more liquid inside her than food. The near constant flickering of Maurice's eye betrays his worn nerves and the physical cost of walking on eggshells. He looks exhausted.

Perhaps out of sympathy for his brother's suffering, Leonard refrains from making further comment, maintaining instead a sullen silence. It is, to Sarah's surprise, Victor who works to create an easy flow of conversation throughout the meal, the careful captain of a beleaguered ship, steering it past threatening rocks into calmer waters.

As part of his effort to secure safe passage, he suggests they all retire to the drawing room together, insistent the men should forego their brandy and cigars for one night. He seems keen to ensure Ida is kept amused and pleasantly inebriated, so her disgruntled mind will not have the opportunity – the sobriety – to revisit the unpleasant business of the war memorial.

They rise from the dining table, tossing down their napkins. Sarah begins to clear, but Leonard tells her to leave it. She hesitates, uncertain, trying once again to fathom the parameters of her position, but Ida half turns and with a careless waft of her hand slurs, 'Oh yes, do it later, come and keep me company. Save me from all these men,' leaving Sarah with little option but to set down the gathered plates and follow.

'Good God, it's freezing!' Ida exclaims as she steps out into the reception hall.

'There's a nice fire waiting for us in the drawing room,' Maurice promises.

'It's so cold, unusually cold,' she complains, hugging his arm, relishing his warmth, their quarrel apparently forgotten.

The others mumble their agreement. Leonard tucks his tartan blanket firmly about his waist as Sarah pushes the wheelchair towards the drawing room door.

'It's bloody cold,' Vic growls. 'Cold as a damn grave in here. The fire should have been lit.' He throws a pointed look Sarah's way, before striding out to reach the relative comfort of the other room, where she had troubled to light a fire earlier.

Sarah hangs back, waiting for the others to cross the threshold before following with Leonard. She fights back a wave of misery.

Maurice settles Ida down on the sofa while Victor stokes the neglected fire into a hearty blaze. Kicking off her shoes, Ida stretches her stockinged toes towards the towering flames, luxuriating in their heat. She sighs with contentment as Maurice plies her with a measure of sherry so generous it threatens the rim of her glass. Having carefully delivered it, he begins to root through the records stacked beneath the gramophone, until at last he sets one spinning.

The rasp of the needle against shellac fills the air, then an orchestra wheezes into play and a ballroom favourite blasts forth from the brass horn. Ida, her cheeks rosy from alcohol, howls with delight, slapping her hand down on the arm of the sofa. 'Oh Maurice! Do you remember this one? Tell me you remember, or I'll hate you forever!'

'Of course, I remember.' He perches on the sofa arm beside her, propped in position by his outstretched legs, casually crossed at the ankle. 'This, Sarah, was the tune the band was playing when I asked Ida to dance for the very first time. She looked me up and down and said . . . tell Sarah what you said, darling—'

'I said: "You're going to have to give me a very good reason why I should!"'

'So I said—'

'How about a Tudor mansion and eight hundred acres in Gloucestershire,' Leonard finishes drily, his eyes meeting Sarah's.

'How could I resist? So, I danced with him!' Ida throws back her head and laughs, her hand on Maurice's.

'And she bagged him three months later,' Victor adds with an asperity that matches Leonard's. Hearing the record reaching its conclusion, he leaps up to change the disc. 'Can't stand that bloody song,' he mutters, his cigarette jiggling on his lips. He lifts the gramophone's arm, cutting short the final chord.

'How long have you been married?' Sarah asks, as she fulfils Leonard's request to be moved to the table by the window, where the chessboard awaits them.

'Gosh, so that was 1913 . . . seven years,' Ida says, the laughter dying from her voice.

'Separated for nearly five of them.'

'Six,' Ida corrects Maurice swiftly. Their eyes lock. She looks away first. Flustered, Maurice rises to join Victor at the gramophone, loudly suggesting what should be played next, but Vic has already set a disc spinning. Finding himself redundant, Maurice crosses instead to the drinks table where he sloshes whiskey into a glass. He eagerly downs the first gulp.

'You two are looking very glum and serious in the corner there.' Victor sidles across to join Sarah and Leonard as they set out the chess pieces, interrupting their quiet discussion on Leonard's ongoing treatment options. Leonard glares at him.

'Sometimes people choose to discuss serious matters, Victor, rather than idle away their time contemplating the mundane,' he says, with a little more bite than necessary.

'Sounds perfectly dull. Shall I help you escape, Mistress Hove? We could move some furniture aside and dance if you like. I'm sure we can find a suitable tune.'

'Thank you, but I'd rather not.'

'And so, you are rejected again, Vic.'

Something passes between the two men, a coded exchange that Sarah is unable to decipher, though the tension that accompanies it is easy to interpret. Victor issues a soft snort and moves away, but only as far as the sofa where Ida is still lolling, humming along to the music. He steals a glance across to the gramophone where Maurice is deliberating over the next record. Taking advantage of his distraction, Victor leans down and whispers something into Ida's ear, his lips so close that Sarah is certain they must have brushed her skin. Ida turns away, the corner of her mouth rising slyly into her cheek. Straightening up, Vic takes another drag on his cigarette.

'They tossed a coin for her,' Leonard says, his voice low. Sarah realises he has been watching her watching them, and the guilty heat of a peeping Tom floods her cheeks, but he passes no judgement. 'That first night. She caught their attention as soon as she walked into the party. They tossed a coin to see who would ask her to dance first. Maurice called it, and once he'd set out his store for Ida . . . well, poor old Victor, with no fortune and only pleasant middle-class parents to boast of, didn't have a chance.'

Over by the gramophone, Maurice has finally made his choice. Knocking back his whiskey, he sets down his glass and calls for Ida.

'I wish to God Vic had won the toss that night and held onto her,' Leonard says, his eyes upon them as Maurice, laughing, hauls Ida to her feet and begins turning her about the room.

'You don't like her much, do you?' Sarah murmurs, emboldened by his confidence.

'Ida's beauty is only skin deep, Sarah. Never forget that – however much she may try to charm you into believing otherwise.'

Giddy and drunk, Ida loses her balance and falls back onto the sofa. Maurice doubles up, hooting with laughter, his hands planted on unsteady knees.

'My God but you're a bit tipsy, darling!'

'Oh, do shut up, Maurice,' Ida moans, hanging her head in her hands, looking suddenly green around the gills.

'Sarah, would you be an absolute dear and make my drunken wife a mug of cocoa? I fear she needs sobering up,' Maurice calls over, before begging a cigarette off Victor.

'You don't have to.' Leonard plants his hand on her arm, but Sarah is already on her feet.

'It's all right. I wouldn't mind a cup myself, to be honest, and it is my job.' She offers him a smile, before addressing the room. 'Would anyone else like one?'

With no further takers, she plunges into the cold of the reception hall before crossing the draughty lobby into the corridor that leads past the library to the kitchen far beyond. Here too the air is frigid, and her skin ripples in complaint as she moves in and out of the insipid pools of light cast by the wall sconces.

When she reaches the library, her steps stutter. The door

stands ajar. Throwing a cautious glance over her shoulder, she makes a tentative advance, reaching out to press her palm against the roughly hewn wood. Her heart hammering, she steps inside. In the fireplace, embers glow against ash-silvered logs, while the Turkish rug is strewn with moonlight, the curtains having not yet been drawn. She fills her lungs, then lets out a shuddering breath. Turning on her heel, she begins to run.

'Goodness, that was quick,' Maurice calls out as she bursts into the drawing room, but his expression quickly changes when he sees the tension in her body and the fear in her eyes. 'Sarah? What on earth's wrong?'

'Would you . . . would you be able to come for a minute?'

'Sarah, what is it?' Alarmed by her uneven voice, Leonard jabs at the wheel of his chair so he can better face her.

'It's just . . . Are we the only ones here? Or is there someone else in this house?'

Chapter Nine

'What on earth are you talking about?' Sarah's question, coupled with her palpable alarm, douses Ida's merry inebriation like a bucket of cold water, sobering her up with impressive speed. 'Of course there's no one else here, it's just us. Why would you even ask?'

'I was on my way to the kitchen, and I passed the library door – it was *open*.' Sarah takes an urgent step forward. 'I know it was shut when I brought up the dinner, and we've all been together ever since.'

'You're probably just mistaken.' Unconcerned, Victor returns his attention to the decanter of whiskey in his hand and the empty glass in the other.

'I'm not! And there's something else . . . I smelt tobacco . . . pipe tobacco.'

'So you think someone has come in here to smoke a pipe?' Victor laughs.

'I'm not making it up.' Desperate for support, Sarah directs her appeal to Leonard. 'I know that door was shut. I know it.'

Leonard holds her anxious gaze for one beat, then two. He turns to his brother. 'Look, Maurice, there's no harm in just checking, surely. I'd go myself, but . . .'

'Oh, for God's sake, I'll go.' Vic replaces the decanter's stopper with ill-tempered force.

'I'm not sure you should go alone.' Ida leaps to her feet. 'Maurice, go with him.'

'Take me with you,' Leonard urges.

'Oh, for goodness sake, what use would you be?' Ida's eyes narrow with vicious contempt.

'Perhaps we should all stay together?' Sarah positions herself behind the wheelchair.

'Yes,' Ida declares, clawing at Maurice's arm. 'I certainly don't want to be left alone.'

'Oh, for God's sake . . . come on then.' Victor throws back his whiskey, resigned.

Muttering about the absurdity of the escapade, he leads the way across the two halls and down the corridor to the library. The party moves with a hushed excitement that overwhelms any real feelings of fear, progressing towards their destination with the giddy anticipation of thrill-seekers readying to brave a fairground's haunted house.

They cluster together just short of the library door. Maurice unhitches Ida from his arm, so she promptly attaches herself to Sarah instead. The levity that has carried them thus far vanishes as he and Victor move towards the gaping doorway. The door creaks as under Vic's light touch it lists further into the darkened room. He feels for the light switch. With a click, the cloth-shaded wall lights battle the gloom with their muted glow.

Ducking under the lintel, Maurice and Victor boldly advance into the middle of the room. Sarah edges Leonard's chair into the doorway. Ida clings to her so tightly, their hips butt.

Faint yet discernible are the distinctive mellow notes of pipe tobacco.

'Do you smell it?' Sarah whispers.

The three men look to each other, grave now, and for the first time, Sarah catches a glimpse of the soldiers they once were, the warriors who braved the muddy expanses of No Man's Land, who blew their whistles and went over the top without a backward glance. Those battle-hardened cores remain, she realises, even though they choose to pretend a seamless return to the insouciance of their youth. It is Victor though that takes command.

'Sarah, take Ida and Leonard back to the drawing room and wait for us there. Were any of the outside doors left unlocked as far as you're aware?'

She shakes her head. 'No. I checked the kitchen door when I was cooking, it was locked, and I locked the back door when you and Maurice came in from your walk earlier.' Seeing his surprise at this she adds, 'Locking up in the evening is a force of habit. My previous employer was most particular. The other doors haven't been unlocked all day.'

Vic nods. 'Go now. Maurice and I will check the house from top to bottom.'

'Shouldn't you escort us first to the drawing room?' Ida increases her hold on Sarah's arm. 'If someone is in here and they accost us on our way back . . .'

'You won't be alone, Ida,' Maurice points out.

'Well, Leonard's hardly able to fight anyone off, is he?' she snaps, anxiety giving rise to petulance. 'I'm afraid!'

After some persuasion, Ida finally relents and returns to the drawing room with Sarah and Leonard. Unnerved, she paces the room, hugging herself.

'I hate this house.' She pauses to rest her fingers against the bars of Mr Tibbs' cage but snatches them away as the bird lunges for her.

'A Tudor mansion . . . I thought it was your dream come true.' Leonard's tone is scathing. 'It's certainly a step up from your parents' modest townhouse.'

She whirls round, her temper flaring. 'At least my parents were able to afford the upkeep of their *modest* home. This place is going to the dogs and dragging me with it.' A splinter of laughter escapes her. 'More the fool if anyone has broken in here. God knows there's nothing of any value left to steal.'

Leonard's retort is interrupted by Maurice and Victor's return.

'Well?' Ida clutches her knotted hands to her stomach.

'Nothing.'

'Nothing?'

'We've checked every room, upstairs and down,' Victor says. 'All the outside doors are locked, and all the windows are shut. There's no sign of a forced entry anywhere. I don't see how anyone could have possibly got in.'

'What if they got in earlier in the day and hid somewhere?' Ida says. 'They might easily have snuck in through an open door.'

'We've searched the house, Ida – we've even been up into the attics. There's no sign of anyone.'

'What about the cellar?' Sarah chirps up.

'The cellar door is locked, and the key is on the outside,' Vic informs her. 'I hardly see how anyone could manage that.'

'But it doesn't make any sense . . .'

'I suspect the library door was always open, Sarah.' Sarah finds herself caught in the cold depths of Victor's disparaging gaze. 'You just didn't realise. You've managed to work yourself up into quite a panic.'

'But the pipe smoke—'

'Is gone. Perhaps . . .'

'Perhaps what?'

'Perhaps it was never really there.'

'But even you smelt it,' Sarah says, objection ringing in her voice.

'A residual smell.'

'How could it be a residual smell?'

'Well, that's the funny thing, you see.' It is Leonard who speaks. There is something about his quiet interruption that commands attention. 'The pipe tobacco. I recognised it immediately.' He looks to Maurice and Victor. 'Didn't you?'

Under his scrutiny, the two men shift uneasily, exchanging glances that convey a very different message to the one housed in their reassuring words.

'What? What is it?' Sarah demands, her eyes darting between them.

'That particular tobacco scent is very familiar to us,' Leonard admits.

'How so?'

Maurice clears his throat. 'Well, the fact is . . . it was our brother Hugo's favourite blend.'

Chapter Ten

The next morning, Sarah finds herself alone in the kitchen with Ida, washing up the breakfast things. There has been no talk of the previous night's events, Victor having dismissed Ida's speculation as to a supernatural cause as little more than fanciful nonsense, while Maurice and Leonard chose to reserve judgement. Leonard, though, had seemed distracted as Sarah assisted him into bed, leaving her to wonder if Ida's suggestion had touched a nerve.

'I hardly slept a wink last night,' Ida complains, the tea towel she had picked up with a generous offer of help remaining idle in her hand, as she watches Sarah dry the last of the dishes. 'You look washed-out too.'

'Yes . . . it was difficult to sleep after that.'

Ida considers her. 'You have a tendency to be a bit pale,' she muses. 'You should wear rouge, to make a bit more of yourself. There are less men around these days, and you want to improve your chances, surely? You don't want to end up an old spinster, after all.' She dumps the tea towel on the table as Sarah returns the final plate to the dresser, her cheeks already a little pinker. 'Come on, let's take tea in the drawing room.

The boys are still at the table with the morning papers. They won't miss us for a little longer.'

The house seems less ominous with the faint strains of autumnal sun lifting its corridors and halls. Sarah sets down the tray of tea things on a table by the sofa, while Ida whips the shawl from Mr Tibbs' cage. She proceeds to coo in the sickly sweet tone she reserves just for him, as she retrieves the paper bag from the shelf on his stand.

'Goodness! I didn't realise I was getting through these monkey nuts at such a rate. Mr Tibbs, you need to be a better student, or we will have run out before you've learnt a new phrase.'

'Don't you have any more?' Sarah asks, pouring the tea.

'Oh, there's a big bag of them in the pantry yet. Maurice picked up a good supply last time he went into town. Now Mr Tibbs, pay attention, say "pretty lady". There you are, you greedy guzzle. "Pretty lady".'

Sarah carries over a cup of tea which Ida receives with a smile. She indulges Mr Tibbs with one more nut, before sitting down with a sigh.

'Ida, can I ask you . . .' Sarah perches on the edge of the chair across from her, her tentative manner immediately securing Ida's attention. 'Has anything like last night happened in the house before? Have you ever been aware of any . . . presence?' Lacking the courage to hold Ida's inquisitive gaze, she focuses instead on the cup of tea she is nursing in her lap, her fingers tightening their grip on the saucer. Her eyes flick upwards, just the once.

'Goodness me, no! Why on earth do you ask that?'

'It's just . . . I wonder sometimes, that's all.'

'Wonder what?'

Sarah takes a deep breath. She forces herself to look Ida square in the face. 'After my brother died, a friend of my mother's suggested she go to one of those spiritualist meetings.'

'A séance, do you mean?' Ida asks. She wriggles forward in her seat, taut with anticipation.

'Not a séance, no. We did end up going to a séance, but initially we just went to a meeting. It was held in a hall in our local town. There were quite a few bereaved people in the audience, as you can imagine. Men and women alike. I hadn't wanted to go.'

'Why not?'

'I was afraid, I think.' Sarah braves a smile. 'But Mother was desperate . . . and insistent. Have you never thought of going to one? After Hugo, I mean?'

Ida grimaces before thinking better of it. 'No. I certainly never felt the need, and Maurice when he came back, well, let's just say, given the state he was in, I don't think it would have been wise. But I've read about them, in the papers,' she says eagerly, 'and if I had lost somebody, you know, somebody I cared about, I think I would be inclined to go.'

Beyond the window, the wind is building, tormenting the trees in the garden. A flurry of leaves drifts down from the heaving boughs.

'Well?' Ida prompts. 'What was it like? What happened?'

'The dead made themselves heard.'

Ida gasps, her hand flying to her chest. 'Really? You honestly believe that?'

'The things that were conveyed through the medium . . . secrets . . . intimacies . . .' Sarah drops her eyes as she shakes her head. 'I know people say it's all a confidence trick, that those mediums find things out about you beforehand or wheedle information out of you without you realising, but that's not what I witnessed.'

'And? Did your brother come through?'

Sarah stands up. She crosses to the table, pausing to set down her teacup and saucer, before moving to the window. She stares out upon the stormy scene hatched by lead, gathering her thoughts.

'No,' she says at last, her voice faint, 'but something strange did happen. The medium was up on stage, conveying these messages to people in the audience, and then . . . then, she looked directly at me and . . .' she turns around. Ida is watching her agog '. . . she said they were drawn to me, the spirits. That they sensed something in me.' Her fingers lace and unlace restlessly. 'That's why I asked, you see . . . whether anything like last night has happened here before because I'm afraid . . . I'm afraid . . .'

'You're afraid of what?' Ida whispers breathlessly.

'Oh Ida!' In a rush, Sarah reaches for Ida's hand, but her confidence fails her, and she lets it fall. Aware of Ida's mounting tension, she finally summons the courage to make the confession that has been hanging over her since her arrival. 'I'm afraid it's me,' Sarah admits, her voice barely carrying the short distance between them. 'I'm afraid I'm the cause of it all . . .'

From far off in the house, the doorbell begins to jangle. Ida looks at Sarah.

'Be an angel and answer that, would you?'

*

It is Victor who looks up first when Sarah offers an apologetic knock on the library door. She hesitates on the threshold.

'What is it?'

He is short with her, still annoyed over the shenanigans of the previous evening, her insistence about the tobacco smoke and the suggestion that something was amiss. He had even caught Maurice and Leonard in conflab after, discussing the likelihood of Ida's absurd suggestion that Hugo might be making his spectral presence known, a notion that had set Maurice's eye twitching beyond control. Victor had duly mocked them for entertaining the idea, ridiculing them as they deserved. After all, hadn't they roared with laughter on reading Sir Oliver Lodge's article asserting that, thanks to the medium Gladys Leonard, he now knew his dead son Raymond, a casualty of Aras, was happily ensconced beyond the veil, enjoying country walks in a place called Summerland, while toasting the afterlife with brandy and cigars?

Such a concept was ludicrous – they had each of them concurred on that point. God knows they had all seen enough death to appreciate, beyond doubt, its finality. This girl, with her insistence of phantom smoke (with hindsight, he felt certain it was the power of suggestion that led him to think it was there) had set an unwelcome cat amongst the pigeons, disturbing their sedate existence. Maurice's affliction was more noticeable this morning. He had even stuttered twice over breakfast, something he hadn't done for months. The girl had sown her insidious seed with no care for its consequences, and now she was staring at him mutely, wide-eyed and gormless.

'Sarah?' he barks, ignoring Leonard's stinging look of rebuke.

'There is a police officer here.'

'Oh, for God's sake.' He closes his newspaper. 'Not that bloody Inspector again?'

'Not an inspector. A detective sergeant by the name of Verity.' Sarah turns to Maurice. 'He wishes to speak to you.'

Maurice blinks. He opens his mouth to object, but when no words form, he shoots Victor a desperate look instead.

Vic's eyes roll heavenwards as he gets to his feet. 'Come on, Maurice,' he coaxes, 'let's go and see what the fellow wants.'

Despite their approach, Sarah continues to block the doorway.

'Is there something else, Sarah?' Victor asks, icily.

'He . . . I don't like to say but, in case . . .' she darts a look towards Maurice.

'For God's sake, woman, spit it out!'

Victor thinks he detects a flicker of contempt in her steely expression.

'The Detective Sergeant,' she says. 'He has no face.'

Victor leads the way from the library, Maurice following behind with abject reluctance. As the reception hall comes into view, Victor begins mentally preparing himself for what he is about to see, determined not to react. He only witnessed one serious facial injury during his time at the front. A man under his command had part of his jaw ripped from his face by shrapnel. Victor had reached him first and was horrified by the sight that greeted him, raw flesh and features so destroyed as to be unrecognisable – a tooth hanging from the remnants of sharded bone, a nasal passage, its cartilage exposed. The young man, no more than twenty, had been sobbing and choking on his own blood and tears, his tongue flapping inside what was left of his mouth. Victor had turned and vomited, before screaming for a stretcher bearer, and then he had scrabbled away as fast as he could, leaving the man to his fate, silently praying for it never to be his own. Sometimes, in nightmares, he still saw that face, flailed of flesh, barely even human. He would shoot upright in bed, gagging on the scream lodged in his throat. Once he had not succeeded in stifling it, but his room was next to Maurice's, and it was easy to convince the others it had been Maurice – poor, weak, damaged Maurice – who had succumbed to his night terrors again. Not him. Never him.

The police officer, a plain-clothes detective, is admiring the carving on the stone chimney breast, his back to the door, apparently oblivious to their arrival. From behind, their visitor appears complete. Victor steels himself for the reality as he crosses into the room, Maurice following as his meek shadow.

'Detective Sergeant Verity, I presume.'

The man turns, startled, and despite his best efforts, Vic's breath catches in his throat. Behind him, he hears Maurice's muttered expletive.

The left side of the man's face is a sculpted copper mask, the features skilfully painted to give the impression of an eyebrow, a staring blue eye, a cheekbone, a nose, a nostril. The top left lip is also painted on, though here the mask curves away. The right-hand side of the top lip and the full bottom lip remain intact, and though there is a little deformity to the bottom left it is passable and strangely rendered less noticeable due to the impact of the mask.

'Good morning, gentlemen.' The Sergeant sweeps his trilby

from his head. His hair is thick and, though neatly parted, it is a little long – Vic presumes this is deliberate, to conceal the mask's fastenings. As the man dips his head in greeting, it becomes apparent that much of his left ear is also missing. His voice is soft, the words slightly slurred, a result, Vic suspects, of the damage wrought upon his mouth, the use of his tongue no doubt encumbered by what he guesses to be a missing palate, or part thereof. He subdues a shudder. It is impossible not to impose the image of the wounded soldier upon the masked man standing before him – he can all too well imagine the devastation the painted copper must hide. His thoughts stray to Leonard. He can't decide which man's deformity is the worst to bear.

Collecting himself, he clears his throat. 'Good morning, Sergeant. To what do we owe the pleasure?'

'My Inspector asked me to call round . . . Mr Monroe, is it? And you must be Mr Stilwell? I recognise you both from his descriptions. Very good at accurately capturing people in a few words, my Inspector.' The man's incomplete lips curve up in a smile. His right eye sparkles with wry humour, whilst the painted left looks blankly on. Victor finds the effect disconcerting.

Perhaps detecting his discomfort, the Sergeant gets down to business. 'He omitted to ask a few questions the other day, and has sent me to discover their answers, if you wouldn't mind indulging me? Oh! But first, before I forget, I am to be postman today as well, it seems.' He bends to retrieve a parcel from the low table between the sofas. 'I found this on the doorstep when I arrived. I meant to hand it to the young woman who answered the door, but she had gone to fetch you before I had the chance.'

He carries it over. It is a curiously shaped bundle, wrapped in brown paper and tied with string.

Victor accepts it, glancing down at the typed label stuck to the front. 'It's for Ida.'

'I see it hasn't been postmarked,' the Sergeant says, angling his head and lifting his finger to indicate the empty space where the franking stamp should have been. 'I presume therefore it was hand delivered. Did no one knock?'

'If they did, we didn't hear them.'

'Is that for me?'

Ida, who has clearly been listening in from her vantage point in the drawing room, now emerges to claim her prize. She pays little attention to the stranger in their midst as she crosses the hall, but as she reaches out to take her package, she casts him a cursory glance and gasps, stepping back, as if his injury might be contagious. Spots of colour immediately blight her complexion. She hastily looks away, stumbling over her thanks as Victor surrenders the mysterious parcel to her possession.

The Sergeant appears unfazed by her reaction. He simply dips his head in greeting. 'Mrs Stilwell, a pleasure.'

Ida offers him a stiff smile. 'Likewise, I'm sure,' she murmurs, before retreating to the sofa on the far side of the fireplace. She sits down, nursing the paper-wrapped bundle. Her fingers begin to work on the knotted string.

The Sergeant turns back to Victor.

'Where was I? Oh yes, my Inspector. As I say, gentlemen, he was hoping you might be able to assist him further.'

'I don't see how, we covered everything we knew last time he was here,' Vic points out. Maurice presses the flickering flesh beside his eye.

'He certainly found you most helpful, indeed. But he just wanted some information on . . .' Reaching inside his jacket, the Detective Sergeant pulls out his notebook. He flicks through pages of scrawled notes. 'Here we are . . . your farm manager . . .'

Victor finds himself distracted by Ida's persistent fiddling. He wishes she had returned to the drawing room to open the parcel, but he suspects she is curious as to why the police have returned and is determined not to miss out. The package's wrapping crackles as she finally succeeds in removing the string, but the paper fold appears to have been firmly glued, and she wears her frustration poorly as her fingers work at its stuck edges, trying to find a way in.

'I understand there's a possibility that your farm manager at the time of the Higgins boy's disappearance might know precisely where on the estate was searched, but I don't seem to be able to find any trace of him since he moved away. I was just wondering whether you knew where . . .' he refers to his notebook, 'Mr Durham went?'

'Did your lot really keep no notes on this at the time? Surely your own records should provide the details of where was searched?' Victor protests.

'I'm afraid the notes are a little . . . *vague* . . . in nature. Mr Stilwell, sir? Might you know? About Mr Durham's whereabouts?'

'I'm afraid I've absolutely no idea.' Maurice draws forward with evident reluctance. 'The family moved away during the war. Home Farm has since been much reduced – death duties, deadly things – so I suspect our current manager, like ourselves, would have no cause to keep in touch with his predecessor.' He issues an awkward chuckle.

'Shropshire.'

They all turn towards the door where Leonard has appeared, Sarah at the handles of his wheelchair. She leans down to whisper something into his ear and he nods. Keeping her eyes low, she discreetly withdraws.

'I know they had family in Shropshire,' Leonard continues, as Sarah's steps fade from the lobby. 'It's highly possible they returned there.'

For a moment the two casualties of war weigh each other up. The Sergeant acknowledges the information, but he makes no effort to jot it down.

'They had a son who went to war with you, I think?' he says instead.

Leonard turns his face to the window. Its leaded panes are dashed with rain, while the wind whistles through its casings. Maurice shifts his weight from foot to foot. He thrusts his hands into his trouser pockets, then immediately removes one to push back his tumbled fringe.

'Yes, their son Joseph – Joe – joined our battalion not long after we'd all gone over,' Vic says.

The Sergeant nods again and appears on the brink of voicing another question when Ida's shriek rips through the room. She scrambles to her feet, whimpering, a gory mess of blood and white feathers dripping from the front of her dress as she thrusts the torn remnants of the parcel onto the table. Her breaths come short and frantic as her face bleaches of colour. Her splayed fingers are stained red.

'My God! Ida!' Victor pushes past the Sergeant to reach her, but he stops short of touching her, repulsed.

She emits a low moan. As her shock fades, she begins to

swipe hysterically at her bloodied front, dashing away the sticky feathers, wailing as tears spill unchecked down her ashen cheeks.

'Ida, darling, please.' Shaken, Maurice hurries forward to pull her away from the pooling blood and clumped feathers, but she yanks herself free and continues to wipe at the mess on her clothing with mounting frenzy, plastering her hands with bloody down. 'Darling, it's all right, you're all right,' Maurice cries, but Ida gleans no comfort from his desperate reassurances. She breaks down in despair, clutching her head. When Maurice finally succeeds in easing her hands away, her blonde hair is streaked with scarlet.

'Dear God, who would do such a thing?' Victor says, looking on with blatant horror.

Leonard begins to giggle. Then he throws back his head and roars with laughter. He laughs until his eyes swim with tears.

'For Christ's sake, Len, shut up!' Victor yells, rounding on him.

But despite this furious display, Leonard struggles to contain himself. 'Oh, come on, Vic, even you have to admit, there's some divine justice here,' he laughs, drying his eyes.

Pushing free of Maurice's embrace, Ida takes an unsteady step towards him, her tears rapidly giving way to anger. 'Was this your doing, Len? Is this your idea of a sick joke?'

'How on earth can it have been me?' Leonard protests, still laughing. 'I'm a one-handed cripple, remember? I'm incapable of anything – as you are so quick to point out at every opportunity.'

'I hate you!' Ida screeches, tears streaking her blood-smeared cheeks. 'I wish you were dead!'

'Well, that makes two of us,' Leonard shouts back, all levity lost.

Releasing a cry, Ida whirls away from him, almost colliding with the Sergeant who takes a rapid step back, his hands aloft to steady her.

'Don't touch me!' she cries, recoiling. 'If you want a bloody crime to investigate, why don't you do something about this one, rather than wasting your time on ancient history?' She spins away from him and dashes for the staircase. Maurice calls out her name, then takes off after her. Their heavy steps resound off the stair treads as they disappear behind the panelling.

'Jesus . . .' Vic drags his hand through his hair, then advances with caution on the unwrapped package, now spread across the table, its bloody contents dripping onto the flags below. He gingerly touches the edge of the brown paper, open now like a blooming flower revealing its grisly heart. He is conscious of the Sergeant's presence, just beyond his shoulder. Close up, he sees why the parcel was so hard for Ida to open. The paper has been delicately stitched to what he takes to be an animal bladder, a pig's most likely, given the size. In ripping the paper open, Ida had inadvertently torn apart the membrane, spilling the contents someone had taken great pains to fill it with.

Tucking his notebook back into his jacket pocket, the Sergeant reaches past Victor to extract a fold of paper from amidst the congealing blood and down. He frowns, his fingertips exploring its strange texture.

'It appears to have been coated in something . . . wax? Perhaps to protect it from the blood?' He unfolds it to reveal a single line of type.

'"Blood on your hands".'

'Well, that's a fair comment,' Leonard says, throwing Victor a belligerent look.

'Might I ask you to enlighten me, Mr Stilwell?' The Sergeant lisps with easy charm as he turns to face him.

Leonard snorts. 'Ida was a most ardent supporter of the war, Detective Sergeant. She believed herself capable of enlisting more men than Kitchener, though her methods were a little more questionable.'

'Len . . .'

Leonard chooses to ignore Victor's growled warning. 'She took it upon herself to hand out white feathers. She wasn't too fussy about who she gave them to. She certainly didn't trouble herself over mitigating circumstances – health, profession . . . age. She'd just thrust one at any poor blighter she deemed big enough and strong enough to be doing their bit.' Victor attempts to stop him, but Leonard merely raises his voice against the interruption and carries on. 'She sent children over to fight, Sergeant. She humiliated fifteen-, sixteen-, seventeen-year-old boys into joining up on the sly, without their parents' knowledge and certainly without their permission.' He shakes his head. 'Boys, Sergeant, little more than boys. It's hardly surprising she's detested around here. People have long memories and little forgiveness in their hearts – mothers bereaved who shouldn't have been, mothers whose sons could have, *should have*, avoided that dreadful slaughter.'

Swallowing hard, he seems to deliberate for a minute. He takes in Victor's pensive expression, then addresses the policeman for a final time. 'She gave one to Joe Durham, you know, the farmer's boy. He was underage, and even if he wasn't, his profession as a farm labourer would have protected him.

But Ida gave him a white feather anyway. No man, let alone a foolish boy, could ignore a slight like that in those days.'

'I think, Sergeant, this is perhaps not the best time for you to be asking your questions,' Victor says, deliberately placing himself between the Detective and his friend. 'Perhaps you could come back on another occasion. I can try and see if we have any records that might confirm where the Durhams went.'

'Yes . . . yes, of course, Mr Monroe, I will do indeed,' the officer mumbles thoughtfully. As he starts to follow Victor from the hall, he turns to catch Leonard's eye. He dips his head in silent communication, then sets down the waxed note upon the side table, pulling out his handkerchief to wipe his fingers clean, before ducking beneath the lintel into the lobby.

Victor already has the front door open, allowing rain to speckle the quarry tiles, but he is eager for the policeman to be gone. The Sergeant, though, is in no hurry. He stands on the threshold, tutting at the inclement weather as he lowers his trilby into place.

'There's much more of this to come,' he warns, his painted mask dulled by the dreary light. Victor cannot think of a suitable reply. He is unsure whether the man is referring to the investigation or the weather.

The Sergeant's deformed mouth issues a hint of a smile, before he makes a dash to his waiting car, having failed to offer any further insight into his meaning.

Chapter Eleven

Sarah emerges from the kitchen a little while later to find Leonard sitting alone in the library. His chair, as always, is positioned before the window, and though a book lies open on his lap, his focus is on the garden spanning out beyond the diamond panes.

'They flew in last night,' he says as she approaches, referring to the Canada geese that are spread across the lawn, pecking at the grass.

The rain has finally stopped, and though the sky remains bruised, with building clouds threatening a fresh assault, the sun's low rays have, for the meantime, bathed the garden in vibrant gold. The trees in the distance appear to stand proud of their violet backdrop, like a layer in an illuminated image.

'Do you want to go out and feed them? There's stale bread in the kitchen.'

He grins up at her. 'I'm not five, Sarah.'

She laughs and folds her arms across her chest. 'Well, I think some fresh air would do you good. You spend too long cooped up in here.'

His smile fades, and he watches the geese again as they waddle to graze fresh patches. 'Yes, perhaps I do.'

'Come along, let's get you outside.'

'Take me to the hall first, would you? I want to speak to Vic.'

Sarah pushes the chair down the passageway. Its thin wheels jiggle over every join in the ornate stone floor, then glide over the lobby's quarry tiles into the reception hall. She fails to stifle her surprise at the sight of Vic on his hands and knees, attempting to clean up what looks like a butchered bird. Hearing the squeaking wheels, he glances up.

'If you've come to gloat, Len, be off with you. You've done enough damage as it is.'

'I haven't come to gloat.' Leonard gestures for Sarah to take him further forward. 'I am curious though.'

'What on earth happened?' Sarah moves out from behind the wheelchair to better survey the scene of devastation: the gloopy pool of congealed blood on the floor; the coagulated drops poised to fall from the edge of the table; the crimson-smeared wrapping; the translucent membrane – the insides of some animal from what she can see; and the white feathers dressing the entire sticky mess. She covers her mouth with her hand.

'Someone sent dear Ida-down a present.'

'Shut up, Leonard. And for God's sake have enough sensitivity not to call her that to her face,' Vic snaps.

'She's hardly sensitive towards me,' Len says, but he doesn't press the point. Instead, he leans forward in his chair, straining to see the wrapping in Vic's hand. 'So, who do you think it was from?'

Victor shakes his head, scrunching the paper in his fist. 'No clue. There's no postmark and the address label was typed: *Mrs M Stilwell.*'

'This was the parcel on the doorstep?' Sarah gasps, looking between them.

'You saw it then?' Vic glowers at her, his eyes narrowing.

'Well, yes . . . that is, I vaguely noticed it when I opened the door, but then I saw the policeman and . . . well, I'm afraid I became rather flustered and immediately came to find you. I didn't even think about the parcel.' She inches closer, appalled by what she sees. 'Why blood and feathers?'

'Ida felt it was her patriotic duty to dish out white feathers during the war. It caused a lot of ill-will in the village – especially when boys and men protected from enlisting ended up dying.'

'It's why they don't want her at the memorial service,' Victor adds quietly.

'What of the note?' Leonard asks.

'Note?' Sarah looks at him. 'There was a note inside?'

'Yes . . .' Victor levers himself up and carefully steps over the mess to retrieve the fold of waxed paper, now spotted with dried gore, from the side table. '"Blood on your hands".' He passes it to Leonard. 'What do you make of that?'

'Succinct and to the point,' Leonard observes drily. He reads the note for himself, turning the paper over as if hoping to find a clue, but it gives nothing else away. 'Impossible to tell, really. Could be a man, a woman, a literate, illiterate. They certainly got the message across. I presume they wanted to make sure she was sufficiently discouraged from attending the unveiling.'

'Well, she won't go now,' Vic says, taking it back. 'Not even Ida's that stubborn.'

'I must say, you have to admire the genius of it. Filling the bladder with all that gunk, then stitching it to a layer of paper so it would explode on opening. Brilliantly horrible.' Leonard peers at the detritus on the table. 'And terribly effective.'

'I'm so glad you approve.'

'I should clear it away,' Sarah says.

'No!' Leonard's fired instruction is accompanied by a furious glare at Vic, intended to suppress any impulse to countermand him. 'You were just taking me outside for that fresh air you prescribed, remember?'

'Yes, I was.' Her lips flicker with gratitude.

'I'll clear it up. I don't want Ida to have to do it,' Victor mutters, discarding the note upon the mess. 'It is curious we didn't hear or see anyone coming.'

'Not really. We were at the back of the house – anyone could have come to the front door and we wouldn't have seen or heard a thing.'

'I suppose so. All the same . . .'

'What?'

'It's so bold, so hate-filled.'

'Mothers lost their sons, wives their husbands. Lives were destroyed by Ida's actions, Vic,' Leonard says, his expression solemn. 'The only thing I find extraordinary is that something like this hasn't happened before now.'

And with that, he squirms round in his seat, gesturing to Sarah that is time for them to go.

*

Though the wind has died down, there is still an edge to it, while the air itself is redolent of damp earth. Sunshine bursts between scudding clouds, illuminating the saffron-hued leaves so they sparkle like gold coins as they drift down to litter the lawns.

They take the path that trails beyond the tended borders towards a large pond fed by a spur channelled from the river.

It is a pleasant spot. Clusters of glossy green lily-pads form archipelagos across the pond's murky surface and willow trees weep into the water, their ancient trunks growing precariously from the pond's banks. There is a sense of tranquillity here that Leonard relishes.

Sarah struggles with the wheelchair which is difficult to manoeuvre over the gritted path, but at last Leonard gestures for her to stop at one of the benches situated near the pond's edge. When she has secured him in place, she takes a seat beside him.

'Sunshine feels like such a gift at this time of year, whereas in the summer we just come to expect it.' Sarah sighs, her chin tilted upwards, her face open to the sun sitting low in the sky. 'It's beautiful here. You're so lucky.'

'Yes, I've always loved the pond – even though it nearly killed me once.'

'The pond nearly killed you?'

'Well . . .' Leonard laughs as she twists round, expectant of an explanation. 'I was home from school, Christmas holidays. How old would I have been? Thirteen? Fourteen? Anyway, I woke up one morning, and the ground was white with frost – it was so cold there was rime on the inside of my bedroom window – and the sun was glinting off the pond, frozen over, like a dusty sheet of glass.

'No one else was awake, other than the servants, of course. I ran downstairs, dug around in the boot room until I found a pair of skates that looked like they'd just about fit, then I ran down here.' He laughs again, shaking his head. 'I jammed my feet into those damn boots – God, they were so small my toes were bent double – then I tottered out onto the edge of the pond. I took a couple of tumbles before I got going, it'd been so long since I'd been skating, but I got the hang of it again, and soon I was having a high old time, flying across the surface. And then I heard a crack.'

'The ice!' Sarah gasps, clearly picturing the scene.

'Yes. It was thick enough at the outside edge, but in the middle it was still thin, and I was too stupid to realise until this great crevasse opened up before my very eyes and I plummeted into freezing-cold water.'

'My God, you could have drowned.'

'I would have – or perished from cold, whichever came first – if it hadn't been for our farm manager's lad, Joe Durham. He'd been walking across the field there and saw me go in. He raced over, knew to spread his weight by lying on his stomach, and he inched his way across to where I was thrashing about. Managed to haul me out and got me back to the house. The look on Cook's face when I appeared dripping in her kitchen, blue with cold, teeth chattering. Good old Joe.' He looks wistful for a moment. 'We were of a similar age, I was a little older, and we became firm friends after that. We'd knock about together whenever I was home from school, exploring the woods, shooting pigeons. Boys' stuff. Our parents didn't approve, of course. Mine didn't think he was the right sort for me to be associating with and I think his were rather wary of having the master's son about, but we solved that problem by keeping out of everyone's way. We didn't care about such things, and when mucking around in the great outdoors, the differences in who we were didn't matter.' His expression grows serious. 'He was a good friend,' he says, his voice suddenly thick.

'What happened to him?'

Leonard doesn't answer immediately. He clears his throat and looks out over the breeze-rippled pond. 'Died in the war.'

'Like so many,' Sarah says, sadly. 'Another lost soul to be remembered. We must remember them all.' Her fingers play with a fold of her skirt. 'I presume Victor is right, that Ida definitely won't be going to the memorial service now. Has it always been like this since the war – the villagers' hostility towards her?'

'Oh yes. I'm not sure many of them liked her even before the war, but since, she's positively hated. She rarely goes out into the village these days. There have been too many incidents now.'

'Incidents?'

'She was spat at once. She had handed a young man a white feather, giving him her usual nonsense about how he should be ashamed of himself, et cetera, et cetera. He had been gassed at Ypres, invalided out because of the damage to his lungs. He could barely speak let alone defend himself against her tirade. So, his mother arrived and did it for him. Tore strips off Ida and then spat right in her face. Disgusting . . .' he grins '. . . but rather satisfying at the same time.'

'You hate her.'

'Hate's a strong word. But perhaps it is the most accurate. It seems I am stuck with her regardless.'

The wind changes direction. Sarah picks a strand of hair from her lips. 'Do you know much about the monument? What they're planning?'

'Not really,' Leonard says, rubbing his nose and hunching his shoulders against the stiffening breeze. 'I suppose it's only right the village should have one. Twenty-three of our parish fell.'

'But there are twenty-two names on the memorial,' Sarah says, confused. 'I heard Maurice say.'

'Twenty-two?' His jaw sidles on its hinges and his eyes dull. He watches a pair of coots descend into the water. 'Twenty-two.' A deep furrow appears between his brows. 'They all deserve to be remembered. They all served, they all laid down their lives, in one way or another.'

'Yes . . . they did.'

'I mean, that's the point of these monuments, isn't it? To list the dead. Record their names.'

He notices her turn her face from him and when she brings up her hand to wipe at her cheek he swears under his breath.

'I'm sorry. Have I made you think of your brother?'

Her surprise is evident as he reaches out to take her hand. She braves a smile. 'Not my brother, my cousin. He made me promise before he went that if anything happened to him, I would plant a pear tree in the garden to remember him. You plant pears for your heirs, isn't that the saying? He said, "If I can't meet your heirs, Sarah, the least I can do is help feed them."' She laughs at the recollection, a fond smile broadening her cheeks. 'That's all any of them ever wanted. They weren't afraid to die, they were just terrified of being forgotten. We must remember them. Every single one.'

'All this talk of war and the dead. The wounds are still too fresh for many of us to even think about things like memorials. The pain is still too raw.'

'I wonder if it will ever cease. It doesn't feel like it. Moving on seems an impossibility.' Sarah eases her hand free of his. 'You're cold. Let me run in and get your coat.'

'No, really, I'm fine.'

But she is already on her feet. 'No, you'll catch cold. I won't be a minute.' She sets off, half-walking, half-running down the path. He watches her cross the lawn, until she has disappeared through the back door.

He awaits her return. Time passes. The coots glide across the pond, leaving chevrons of rippled water in their wake. He shifts in his chair. He is feeling the cold now. He squeezes a fist in an effort to warm his fingers as he twists round to see if he can spot Sarah.

He is surprised to see her loitering, his coat folded over her arm as she aimlessly surveys the small patch of herb garden. She looks up, and realising he is watching her, she holds up her hand and begins to hurry towards him.

'Here you are, pop this on,' she says, opening his coat. 'I didn't want to interrupt you.' She smiles as she guides his arm into the sleeve. 'So, I waited.'

'Waited?'

'Until he'd gone.'

He regards her with confusion as she bends down to do up his buttons. 'Who?'

She laughs and meets his quizzing eyes. 'Whoever it was that was with you.'

'But no one has been with me. I have been alone with my thoughts.'

'Then you must have truly been miles away,' she exclaims, straightening up, 'because when I came back outside, some fellow was stood right beside you.'

The sun is suddenly lost behind a bank of clouds. A gust of wind roughens the surface of the pond and causes the long grass at its edge to shiver.

'What fellow? What did he look like? Describe him to me.'

Sarah lifts her hands in bewilderment. 'He was too far away for me to see in detail, but he was tall, I'd say, broad-shouldered – though there was something about the way he carried himself that struck me as young. He was wearing a pullover, trousers, holding a flat cap by his side.' She shrugs helplessly. 'I presumed him to be a gardener or one of the estate workers. Oh! And he had red hair.' She appears proud of her powers of recollection.

'Red . . .'

'Ginger – a dark ginger from what I could see,' she clarifies.

'What happened to him? Where did he go?'

'I don't know. I went to inspect the herb garden and when I looked up he had gone and you were looking my way, so I came over.' Sensing his disquiet, she crouches down before him, her hand resting on the arm of his wheelchair. 'What on earth is wrong, Leonard?'

Somewhere above them, a crow caws.

'Leonard?'

Despite the extra warmth offered by the coat, he is trembling. When he finally meets her gaze, he bears the look of a man who has made a harrowing discovery.

'I have been alone, Sarah, for the whole time you were away. There has been no one with me. No one at all.'

His voice is barely audible as he draws his conclusion.

'No one living at least.'

Chapter Twelve

Victor is relieved to find Sarah vacating the library, just as he is returning to it. They dance around each other in the doorway, as she accidentally sidesteps into his path. He makes a brazen display of his exasperation as she darts past him, uttering an apology.

He is annoyed to discover the fire has been neglected, though Maurice sits slumped before it. Neither he nor Leonard pay any heed as Vic tuts with disapproval before dropping to his haunches to bayonet the motley collection of charred logs with the poker. Bayonetting the enemy. He had been good at that, Vic reflects. War had suited him. What's more, he had enjoyed it – soldiering, fighting. He stands up, hooking the poker back onto its stand before fishing two fresh logs from the basket and placing them within the grate. He glances at Maurice, now righting himself in the chair and wincing with apology. Vic watches the reinvigorated fire take hold. The war had not suited Maurice at all, but then, he wonders callously, what had ever suited Maurice? He had turned out to be inept at most things in life, though he had proven himself a generous and loyal friend. Victor is willing to concede that, albeit begrudgingly.

'Sorry, I . . . I should have sorted that,' Maurice says, as Vic throws himself into his armchair. 'Time rather got away from me.'

'I've just been with Ida,' Vic says, his disappointment in Maurice so great he can't even bring himself to meet his eye. He stretches over to collect his cigarettes from the table, so he doesn't have to. 'She's dashed upset. Poor girl.' He strikes a match and shields its flame until it has embraced the tobacco tip. 'If I ever catch the bastard who sent that damn parcel—' he flicks the match into the fire and hunches over, staring into the building flames '—I'll rip him apart with my bare hands.'

'Perhaps it was inevitable that the past would catch up with her,' Leonard says, staring out through the window. 'Perhaps the past catches up with us all in the end.' He jabs urgently at his chair wheel until he is facing them. 'You know, I've just had the strangest thing happen.'

Vic looks across at him, still smouldering over Maurice's inherent ineptness, an anger fanned by the memory of Ida's shuddering sobs, as he sat beside her in the drawing room, his arm firm around her shoulders, Maurice having typically absented himself. 'What?'

Bucking up, Maurice at last shows some interest. 'What is it, Len?'

'Well . . . I don't know how to explain it really.'

'Just get on with it.' Vic is in no humour for games.

'All right. I was outside, by the pond, and it was a bit chilly and Sarah—' Leonard is thrown by Victor's derisive splutter. He restarts with stubborn defiance. 'I was outside with Sarah by the pond, and she was concerned I was getting cold, so she

112

went off to fetch my coat. She didn't come back straight away. She dallied by the herb garden. Apparently, she wanted to give me some privacy to talk.

'Talk?' Maurice asks, confused. 'Talk to who, old chap?'

'That's just it.' Leonard pitches forward in his seat, animated now. 'Sarah said when she came back out with my coat, she saw a young man standing beside me. She presumed we were in conversation and so didn't want to interrupt. But I wasn't talking to anyone. There was no young man there. I was alone, the entire time she was gone.'

'That girl's crackers.' Vic blows a stream of smoke towards the plasterwork ceiling.

'You think so?' The warning note in Leonard's voice catches his attention.

'You don't?'

'I asked her what this young man looked like. She described him to me, height, build, his clothing.' He pauses, ensuring he has their undivided attention. 'And then she added he had ginger hair . . .'

Maurice's complexion takes on a waxy sheen. 'Ginger hair,' he echoes.

'Ginger hair,' Leonard repeats slowly, meeting his anxious eye. 'She described Joe Durham perfectly.'

'Oh, for God's sake.' Vic jumps up from his chair. 'What exactly are you trying to say, Leonard?' He screws his cigarette butt into the ashtray beside him. 'That you think the ghost of a dead man was hovering at your side and the girl saw him? Is that honestly, *honestly*, what you want us to believe?' Sniggering, he helps himself to an early glass of whiskey. 'I wonder what the hell is happening to you two sometimes.'

'She described him perfectly. A man she's never met, and there was no one there, Vic, no one beside me.'

'You really do!' Vic realises with amused astonishment. 'You really think this girl saw a ghost.'

'Well . . .' Maurice hugs his crossed knee, as he risks a glance up at Vic, now leaning against the mantel. 'She did smell Hugo's tobacco . . .'

'Hugo's tobacco.' Vic scoffs. 'You two are so gullible.'

'You smelt it too, Vic.'

'I possibly detected a faint hint of pipe smoke in the air. I might remind you both that Hugo smoked like a bloody chimney in this room when he was alive – the furnishings have clearly retained some of that smell, and that's all it was. She comes into the room when for once we're not already in it, smoking away, and she detects the pipe stuffing that tainted the fabrics years ago. Hardly takes a genius to see the logic there.'

'But it was strong! Noticeable – fresh even,' Leonard cries in challenge. 'I hear your argument, Vic, but it doesn't explain why the room suddenly smelt so distinctly of it. It usually just reeks of our stale cigarettes.'

'We're just too accustomed to it.' Victor gathers his arguments, suppressing his urge to ridicule them for their foolishness. 'Look, it's like when we came home after the war; the entire house had an unfamiliar smell. We didn't recognise it anymore, whereas in fact, it smelt exactly as it always had, we were just inured to it when we lived here. I think it's the same in this instance. The room had been vacant that night for longer than it had been in ages. So, coming back in, when the air was still and cold, and . . . well, we were just more aware of it, that's all.'

'I'm not convinced,' Leonard says. 'Sarah . . . she senses something in this house, I'm sure she does. I've seen her jump out of her skin, as if something's caught her eye, and when I ask her what's wrong, she looks embarrassed – she falls over herself trying to change the subject, and yet I'll see her eyes straying back to the exact same spot minutes later, as if something's still there, bothering her. And how could she possibly know what Joe Durham looked like?'

'You're at it again!' Victor drains his glass. 'It's all the power of suggestion. She says she can smell pipe smoke and you decide it's Hugo's. She claims to have seen someone – and quite frankly I think the girl is deluded – and you take her vague description to be that of Joe Durham.'

'Ginger hair? Hardly vague.' Leonard's voice rises in anger. 'How common is ginger hair exactly?'

'I'd have said Joe Durham's hair was auburn, not ginger. You see? Detail! Broad sweeps can be interpreted in any way you want.'

'It's a damned strange thing, that's all I'm saying. And why would she make that up? Why would she say such a thing if she hadn't seen someone with me?'

'Maybe she's a card short of a full deck, I don't know.' Vic returns to the decanters. 'She's a queer fish at the best of times, if you ask me.' He turns back, wafting his glass. 'Maybe it was light and shadow, playing off the water, and she thought she saw something – being of a fanciful nature, she decides it must be a person. People convince themselves they see things that aren't there all the time.' His eyes narrow, a streak of cruelty flaring in their depths. 'You of all people should know that, Maurice.'

Leonard speaks up as Maurice flounders for a response. 'You can say what you like, but I think Sarah is a nice girl, a decent sort.' He pauses, his lips parted. His words seem reluctant to leave, but in the end, he pushes them out. 'And there are people . . .'

'What?' There is something threatening about Victor's fixed expression.

'There are people who are sensitive to things the rest of us can't understand or see.'

Victor roars with laughter. 'What, like mediums, calling up the dead? Letting dear Aunt Muriel know that young Jimmy is having a splendid time on the other side, enjoying a right lark with all the other fellows who got blown to bits in the trenches?' Victor's mockery poisons the atmosphere. Maurice bites his lip and stares at his lap. Victor's resentment hardens. 'Grow up, Leonard. Grow up the two of you. You're both doo-lally if you believe the nonsense peddled by those spiritualists and the like. Crackpots and fraudsters, the whole bloody lot of them. Perhaps that's this girl's game. She's busy laying the groundwork, hoping to fleece us all later with some damn trick or other. I bet she's already been snooping through our things trying to find material to use against us. I said from the start there was something bloody queer about her and, quite frankly, I don't trust her further than I can throw her.'

He pauses, realising he has lost his audience. Leonard and Maurice have been distracted by something behind him. Turning, he sees Sarah standing rigid in the doorway.

'Lunch is ready.'

They listen in silence to the click of her departing steps, quick upon the stone floor outside.

Sarah's cheeks are smarting as she hurries back down the corridor. Her ears, she reflects, should no doubt be burning too. Her steps falter just short of the kitchen door. Ida is sitting at the table, sniffling into a handkerchief, her eyes red and her delicate features bloated from crying. She has changed her outfit. The bloodied clothes from earlier now lie in a heap on the floor beneath the sink. Seeing Sarah, she makes a weak gesture towards them.

'I hope you don't mind. I couldn't bear to have them anywhere near me.'

'No, of course not.' Gathering herself, Sarah continues into the room, snatching up a tea towel to protect her hand as she opens the oven door. 'I'll do my best to get the blood out.'

'I don't think I could face wearing them again. You can have them if you like.'

Sarah focuses on the pie in the oven. 'That's kind,' she says at last.

Ida sniffs. Satisfied it is done, Sarah pulls the pie out and plants the enamel dish upon a trivet on the table.

'I'm so glad you're doing the cooking now. I'm sure the boys are relieved.'

Unsure what to say, Sarah begins to drain the vegetables, clouds of steam rising above the Belfast sink.

'You were saying something.' Ida shuffles round in her chair. 'Before that wretched policeman came, you were telling me about the séance you went to. What was it the medium said to you again?'

Sarah sets down the saucepan on the drainer. She stares out

of the window, entranced by the shimmer of the wind-buffeted leaves. The sky is growing leaden once again.

'She said . . .' Her fingers grip the wooden drainer. 'I know it sounds silly, but she said the spirits were drawn to me. She said she could see them . . . clustered around me.'

'She could see them?' Her tears forgotten, Ida leans forward, fascinated. 'She could, what? See dead people all around you?'

'And I believed her.' When Sarah turns back to face Ida, there are tears in her eyes. 'Because I could *feel* them.'

Ida's swollen lips part in wonder. 'You could *feel* them?'

Sarah nods. She blinks rapidly to clear her vision. 'And I can feel something . . . someone . . . some spirits . . . here, in this house. I have from the moment I arrived.'

'I say, ladies, Victor's sent me along to see if I can lend a hand because us chaps are all starving in the dining room.'

Both women jump at Maurice's unexpected intrusion. Sarah swiftly turns back to the sink, dabbing the tears from her cheeks.

'We're coming now, Maurice, you'll just have to wait,' Ida snaps.

'Sorry, I didn't mean to interrupt,' Maurice says, adopting the air of a chastened schoolboy.

Sarah says nothing. Keeping her head down, she retrieves the vegetable dishes from the warming oven and sets about filling them from the saucepans.

'Smells delicious,' Maurice pipes up with renewed cheer.

'Maurice, you're cluttering up the kitchen.' Ida gets to her feet, leaving her damp handkerchief scrunched on the tabletop. Her tears have vanished. 'Go on back to the others.

We'll be along directly.' Murmuring apologies, Maurice makes himself scarce.

Sarah arranges the filled dishes upon on a wooden tray. As she lifts it from the table, she pauses. 'You won't say anything, will you? To the others. Please don't.'

'Of course not,' Ida assures her. 'Don't you worry, Sarah. Your secret is safe with me.'

But as Sarah follows her from the room, she nurses a nagging suspicion that her secret is not safe. Her secret is not safe at all.

Chapter Thirteen

That night, Maurice's screams wake them all.

Sarah shoots up in bed, her breath catching in her throat as the raw cry carries into her room, penetrating the dark. She hears the faint *clack, clack,* of lifting latches and the creak of opening doors, followed by soft thuds of footfall on the threadbare runner. Muffled voices. Leonard's bell begins to jangle.

Her heart thudding, she reaches for the lamp. Throwing back the covers, she scrambles from the bed, her skin protesting at the sudden assault of frigid air. She snatches up her dressing gown, slipping her feet into her slippers as she knots its cord about her waist. Depressing the door latch, she rushes to Leonard.

She finds him sitting up in bed, his bedside lamp already ameliorating the effects of the darkness as he rings his bell with the vigour of a headmaster announcing the end of break. The clanger rattles to silence.

'Maurice!' he cries before she is even fully in the room. 'What's wrong with Maurice?'

'I don't know.'

'Well, don't just stand there. Go and find out then come

back and tell me!' Stunned by his aggression, she fails to move. 'Go!' he barks, and she flees the room, stumbling in the half-light up the short flight of stairs to the upper landing. Maurice is shouting now. She hears Victor trying to calm him; she finds his soothing cadence surprising.

Ida is standing on the landing, just shy of Maurice's open door, as if she is too afraid to enter. Her hair is sleep tousled, and she is shivering in the satin nightdress that clings so revealingly to the curve of her body that Sarah feels embarrassed to look at her.

'What is it? What's wrong with Maurice?' From where she stands, Sarah cannot see into the room. The sound of Maurice's suffering is so unsettling she is not sure she wants to.

Ida lowers the fingernails she has been biting and shakes her head, her usually smooth forehead corrugated with concern. Unable to speak, she chews her lips, fighting back tears. Sarah moves past her, her heart beating quicker, a strange tightness in her belly. She looks through the doorway.

The room is blazing bright thanks to the ceiling light – no muted lamps soften the darkness, darkness has instead been banished completely. Discarded bedcovers trail across the floor. A wooden chair lies on its side. Though she can hear Victor's calm voice and Maurice's returning whimpers, she is unable to see either man. Stepping further into the room, she finally spots them. Maurice is wedged into the far corner of the chimney breast recess, partly hidden by a velvet-covered armchair. His knees, narrow in his striped pyjamas, are drawn up against his chest so that his chin bangs against them as he sobs. For some peculiar reason, she is struck by how pallid his bare feet are, the jointed tops of his toes darkened by wiry hairs. Victor crouches before him, his unfastened dressing gown hanging loose so that it pools onto the carpet around him. Every time he attempts to reach out a comforting hand, Maurice yelps and presses himself further into the corner so that the walls force his shoulders to curve together.

'It was just a dream, Maurice . . . a nightmare . . .'

'I heard them! I heard them clear as day.' Maurice's ashen, tear-stained face lifts as he addresses his friend, his eyes manically roaming the room, searching. 'They were in my room. I heard them. In my room!'

'Maurice . . . look about you, there's no one in your room but me . . .' Victor catches sight of Sarah from the corner of his eye. 'And Sarah,' he adds, his voice hardening. 'There's no one else here, you're safe, you're at home. You're at Darkacre.'

'No, no . . . no . . .' Maurice's face twists with despair and his fringe flies as his head snaps side to side with every exclaimed contradiction. 'I heard them. Clear as day. Germans, whispering. They were in my room, Germans. I heard their words . . . German words . . . German!'

Victor's expression flickers with impatience. 'There's no bloody Germans in your room, Maurice. For God's sake man, it was just a nightmare. Nothing more.'

'I heard them!' Spittle flies from Maurice's mouth forcing Victor to recoil. Maurice pitches forward. 'I heard them whispering to each other. I heard them, Vic. I damn well heard them. "*Attacke!*"; "*Schießen!*"; "*Töte ihn!*" I heard it all.'

'It was all in your head.' His sympathy spent, Victor rises from his haunches. 'Pull yourself together, Maurice. You're supposed to be past all this damned nonsense.'

The involuntary moan that escapes Maurice is so without

hope and so burdened by shame that it almost breaks Sarah's heart to hear it. Victor mutters something under his breath as he turns his back on his friend's now rocking form. Sarah interprets the look upon his face as revulsion. He barely acknowledges her as he brushes past, though his demeanour softens as he reaches Ida, still poised on the landing, unable to bring herself any closer. His hand lingers on her bare arm as their eyes lock. Leonard's impatient call sounds faintly from down the corridor. Sarah is grateful to answer it.

He has moved to the edge of the bed by the time she arrives, harried and apologetic.

'What the hell took you so long? What's happening? How's Maurice?'

'He's had a nightmare. He thought he heard Germans talking in his room.'

'I must go to him. Damn these legs!' he cries, anger and frustration rough on the words as he brings down an ill-tempered fist upon the stumps that imprison him.

'Here!' Sarah retrieves the wheelchair from the side of the room. She brings it close then helps him lower himself into it.

For once, he doesn't grab the blanket. 'Get me to Maurice. I need to be with Maurice.'

Sarah pushes the chair from the room, but her heart sinks at the seven rising steps that impede their progress.

'I can't . . .'

'Damn it! Damn it all!' Leonard's voice cracks. Tears glisten in his eyes as he slams his hand against the arc of the wheel. He bellows for Victor.

'Hasn't there been enough drama for one night without you adding to it?' Victor doesn't rush to answer Leonard's summons, but instead saunters towards them with an air of resentment, his dressing gown still flapping loose over his crumpled pyjamas. 'He's fine now, Len. It was just a nightmare – you know how he gets. He's fine. Ida's tucking him back into bed; she's given him one of his sleeping pills. There's no point you going to him, he'll be out like a light before you reach his room.'

'I want—'

'There's no point, Len.' His tone brooks no argument. 'Go back to bed. Everyone should just go back to bed. It'll be morning soon enough as it is.'

As he starts to retrace his steps, Leonard calls after him.

'He hasn't had a nightmare for months. Months! Why now?'

Sarah flushes as Victor's narrowed inspection lands on her, before falling upon Leonard.

'Why do you think? There's been far too much foolish talk of ghosts and ghouls lately. Too much raking up of the past. Is it any wonder that Maurice is cracking up again? And you two aren't helping. You might want to think about that, both of you. Now goodnight. I, for one, would appreciate a little more sleep.'

With no other option available to them, Sarah returns Leonard to his bedroom. They maintain a burdened silence as she helps him back into bed. Once he is resettled, she extinguishes the lamp. It is not until she has reached the door that he finally speaks.

'I tell you now, there's something very strange happening in this house, Sarah. And no one is going to convince me otherwise.'

Sarah sets an early alarm to ensure she is the first up – a feat easily achieved, given the household's disturbed night. She forces herself from the cosy comfort of her bed, and washes quickly, dressing in her usual muted attire. Drawing back the curtains, she is unmoved to see another drab day with threatening clouds already clustering, violet in the burgeoning light. She shivers and moves away.

With her usual stealth, she eases up the latch and opens her door, not wanting to wake Leonard or anyone else – she enjoys the solitude of her morning routine. She tiptoes down the landing, choosing to use the back staircase that lies beyond the attic door, as she has done since her arrival.

She descends into the service passage below and carries on into the kitchen, where she lights the lamps and stokes the range, before carving two thick slices of bread, spreading them with butter and jam retrieved from the larder. She fills the kettle from the tap, wincing at the initial squeal of trapped air in the pipes, grateful when it abates. She sets it to boil, pulling it from the hotplate just before it whistles. She makes tea, stirring the leaves vigorously in the pot until the water takes on a pleasing hue. Using the strainer, she pours out a mugful. She fetches the milk from the stone shelf in the larder and sniffs the mouth of the bottle to check it isn't on the turn. Satisfied, she slops a dash into the tea.

Smoothing down her skirt, she makes a mental check of the scene around her, then glances at the clock. She releases a soft sigh, her front teeth tugging at her bottom lip. She clears her thoughts and, leaving the kitchen, she strides out down the corridor, opening curtains as she goes, past the study and the library, through the lobby and into the reception hall, from where she takes the main staircase up.

It will soon be time to rouse Leonard.

Maurice is the last down for breakfast. Leonard's welcome is overly bright and so ebullient it strains at its seams. It is delivered in the same tone used to encourage a shy child to join in with his peers, and perhaps as a result, Maurice sidles to his chair in the manner of just such a child. The twitch in his eye is particularly prevalent, and his hand trembles uncontrollably as he helps himself to a cold slice of toast from the rack. Ida observes him with a sharp, distrusting look, her mouth pinched. She suddenly realises that she herself is being watched. Sarah hastily pours Leonard more tea though he hasn't requested any. He looks surprised but doesn't complain.

Later, Ida comes to find Sarah as she is washing up in the kitchen. The drying rack is stacked with dripping crockery, but Ida makes no attempt to take a tea towel to them. Instead, she drifts aimlessly around the room until at last she comes to rest against the edge of the table.

'Maurice must have frightened you a bit last night.'

Sarah vigorously applies the dishmop to an egg-smeared plate. 'The screams woke me, but . . .' she snatches a glance at Ida '. . . I'd seen men like that during the war.'

'Shell shock.'

Sarah scrubs harder. 'That's what I thought. As soon as I saw him.'

Ida releases a ragged sigh. 'It started after a trench raid. Victor and Maurice volunteered to lead a small group over, to gain intelligence primarily. Victor would never tell me the full details but . . . well, needless to say, it didn't go according to plan. They were lucky to get out. Vic saved Maurice's life that night, but he didn't save his sanity . . . he went to pieces after. His mind started fragmenting. Vic covered for him for as long as he could, then, one morning, on the brink of battle, he just lost it completely. He was hospitalised shortly after, first in France, then he was sent to a place in Scotland. I visited him there once, but . . .' she dabs a fingertip into the corner of her eye. 'I barely recognised him. He wasn't discharged until well after the Armistice. He's not been the Maurice I knew, the Maurice I married, since.'

'It was a cruel war.'

'But not everyone ended up a jabbering wreck, did they? Victor didn't. Even Leonard, after all he went through. He might be a physical wreck, but he's not . . . *mentally* . . . affected. Not like Maurice.'

'War impacts on people in different ways.'

Ida snorts. 'Well, I'm stuck with him now. I could just about tolerate him the way he was, but if he regresses, like he did last night . . .' She shudders, and Sarah suddenly realises her tears were not for Maurice, but for herself, her own tragic predicament. 'If only I knew then what I know now. I would have been so much better off with . . .' She stops abruptly.

'With?'

The smile Ida summons hints at secrets and deception and the alluring possibility of a confidence shared, but the sudden tolling of the doorbell prevents further discussion.

'Now, who on earth can that be?' Ida asks.

But the wariness in her expression suggests she already knows.

Chapter Fourteen

Maurice begins to shake when Sarah enters the library to announce the faceless Detective Sergeant has returned and is awaiting them in the reception hall.

'I c-c-can't face him . . .' he stutters, his voice breaking. 'Not today . . . not after last night.'

'It's all right, Maurice, don't get worked up now.' Leonard leans over the side of his chair, attempting to still the quaking with a reassuring hand, but it proves ineffective.

Rolling his eyes, Victor abandons the ritual study of his stocks and shares and folds his *Financial Times*. The newspaper lands on the floor as he rises from his chair.

'I'll go and deal with him. You two stay here.'

He reaches the reception hall to find the Detective Sergeant is once again indulging his curiosity: this time he is admiring the display of silver-framed photographs, neatly arranged upon a sideboard, which, thanks to Sarah's recent ministrations, is no longer discoloured by a coating of dust.

As Sergeant Verity turns to greet him, the mask of painted copper stuns Victor anew. He finds himself wondering if those more familiar with the man become accustomed to it with time. He can't imagine it. He is morbidly fascinated by a raindrop that glistens upon the tinted cheek and it suddenly strikes him that the Sergeant will be oblivious to its existence. He will not feel the dampness on his skin, he will not realise to brush it away, as Vic would do, without thought, in the same situation, with his perfect complexion and undamaged face. The damp drop catches the light and seems to wink at him, taking him into its confidence, sharing the secret of its presence. He pulls his gaze away and trains his focus on the Sergeant's eyes, only to be discomfited again by the lifeless painted image that in part greets him.

'Sergeant.'

'Mr Monroe! Another filthy morning – I fear we shall all soon be drowned if this wretched rain doesn't let up. I'm sorry to darken your door again so soon, but my enquiries were obviously waylaid last time due to the unfortunate incident with the package. I trust Mrs Stilwell is fully recovered from her nasty shock?'

'As recovered as she might be. It was an unpleasant prank for someone to play upon an innocent woman.'

'Sadly, some seem to believe she is not quite so innocent.'

Victor's heckles rise. He does not appreciate the Sergeant's tone, nor the inference there might be a valid case against Ida, but it is impossible to determine the Sergeant's true opinion due to the confounded mask. What is visible of his mouth for the briefest instance seems to twist into a malicious smile, but it vanishes so quickly Victor wonders whether his own prejudices have led him to misinterpret the fleeting movement. As the Sergeant ambles away from the photographs to join him, his manner relaxed and affable, he continues to doubt himself, imagining slight where in fact there is none. He is not accustomed to being so unsure of himself.

'My Inspector was very keen that I revisit as soon as possible to finish what I had started, so to speak.'

'Of course.' Still rattled, Victor forces himself to concentrate, determined to beat the Sergeant at his own game. He consciously arranges his features into an engaging smile. 'My apologies, Sergeant, I had promised to investigate the Durhams' onward movements, but I'm afraid—'

'Oh, no matter, Mr Monroe, no matter, my own enquiries have provided me with the answer to that particular question. My visit today is on another matter entirely.'

'Really? And what might that be?'

The Sergeant shivers dramatically and stamps his feet. 'Mr Monroe, forgive me for appearing rude, but I don't suppose there might be fire roaring somewhere in this magnificent house? Mackintoshes are marvellous things against the rain, but I'm afraid they do little to keep one warm on these cold autumn mornings and I'm chilled to the bone. May I be so bold as to ask whether we might retire somewhere to continue this conversation in more comfort?'

Victor bites back a refusal. Mastering his ill-temper, he counsels himself to be wise. He has the unnerving suspicion he is being tested in some way and that some form of deep-seated calculation is being craftily concealed behind the Sergeant's off-putting sheet of copper. He wants it exposed.

'Yes, of course. I believe Mrs Stilwell's in the drawing room; why don't we go and join her there?'

'Ahh, perfect. Are the Mr Stilwells . . .'

'I'm afraid that Maurice is unwell. Leonard is with him.'

'I'm sorry to hear that – nothing too concerning I hope?'

'No, nothing a few days' rest can't cure, I'm sure.'

'Well, perhaps I can speak to them another time.'

'If you must.' Despite his good intentions, Victor's smile is glacial.

They cross the expanse of the reception hall, past the faded tapestry that covers the far wall, to the drawing room beyond.

Ida issues a mew of alarm as Victor ushers their visitor into the room with measured good manners. Quickly recovering, she does not bother to get to her feet, and barely manages a civil greeting, but the Sergeant appears unoffended by her lack of welcome, and gratefully takes a seat before the fire, unbuttoning his mackintosh and pinching up his trousers as he sits. Once comfortably in place, he takes the liberty of stretching out his legs until the scuffed toes of his black lace-up shoes rest on the edge of the hearth. He leans forward, rubbing his hands together before facing his palms to the flickering flames. He sighs with contentment. Ida casts Victor a look of utter disdain.

'So Sergeant, what was it you wanted this time?' Victor enquires, as he perches himself on the arm of the sofa. He hopes the temporary nature of this position might convey to the policeman that his presence is likewise expected to be transitory. The Sergeant, however, appears to be making himself at home.

'Ah, yes, now . . .' He retrieves his notebook and pushes back the pages until he finds the relevant place. 'That's it, Mr Joe Durham. Now, Mr Stilwell was indeed correct, the family did remove to Shropshire – beautiful part of the world, have you ever been? I was surprised to discover the apparent reason for the move . . .'

The fire crackles and hisses. Victor looks blandly on, his

arms folded across his chest; he ignores Ida's wide-eyed stare. When it becomes apparent he has no intention of being lured by the Sergeant's tantalising hook, Verity's mask reveals the hint of a smile. He continues undaunted, his voice soft and lisping.

'There was, I understand, during Mr Durham's – Private Durham's – service, a court martial.' He pauses, but still Victor resists his bait. 'I have discovered indeed that Private Joe Durham was subsequently found guilty at that court martial . . . and executed.'

'He was indeed. For murder and cowardice, amongst other things.' Victor brushes some lint from his trouser leg with a practised air of disinterest.

'I understand the boy was underage at the time.'

'He had volunteered. He was serving as a soldier. I don't know his exact age at the time of his execution.'

'Seventeen, Mr Monroe, Joe Durham was seventeen.'

'There were many boys who volunteered to do their bit for their country, as I'm sure you're aware. Numbers were needed and recruitment sergeants weren't too bothered as long as the boys weren't being coerced.'

'Although, in a way, Joe Durham had been coerced.' The Sergeant includes Ida in the encompassing smile that now stretches wide from his mask. She averts her chilly gaze to the fire, her lips a thinly drawn line. 'He can have been little more than sixteen when he signed up. He'd done twelve months of service before his trial, one might even argue he was battle hardened, by that time.' He sighs. 'Murder, threatening an officer, casting away his weapon and deserting the battlefield,' he recalls. 'It's quite a list of charges.'

'You've read his court martial file?'

'No, but . . . I have had access to a first-hand account.'

'Whose?' Victor demands, straightening his shoulders. 'And how on earth can this be pertinent to your investigation into the Higgins boy?'

'I like to be in charge of all the facts surrounding a case, Mr Monroe, even ones that might appear to be unconnected.'

'I fail to see how anything that happened out there can be of any relevance to the disappearance of Bobby Higgins.' Victor gets to his feet with a pointed glance at the doorway.

'Well, a fresh pair of eyes often sees different things and there are allegations made within—'

'The letter,' Victor concludes acidly.

Verity's mask glints as he turns to him. 'That troublesome letter.'

'Which is probably little more than vindictive hearsay.'

'Quite possibly.'

'If you were to let me take a look at it . . .'

'Oh, I'm afraid I couldn't allow that, Mr Monroe.' The Sergeant taps the side of his nose. The copper produces a dull ring. 'Confidential police information and all that.'

'Well, I for one think it's shocking when the police spend precious time on poison pen letters rather than investigating things of proper importance.' Ida declares with a huff, rearranging her skirt over her knees.

'A boy is missing, Mrs Stilwell, probably dead . . . and another shot . . .'

'Joe Durham was executed in accordance with military justice, Sergeant; the two are hardly comparable,' Victor protests. 'I must confess, I'm struggling to see the relevance.'

'The letter alleges that Private Durham was in a shell hole

133

with yourself and the then Lieutenant Maurice Stilwell at the time of the incident.'

'That is a matter of record.'

'Ah, now unfortunately the court martial accounts of these executed men are to remain sealed, but from what I've been told by the very helpful chap at army records, there appears to be some discrepancy between the events as recorded in the letter we have received, and the testimony delivered during the court martial.'

'I am soon going to have to insist you tell me who the author of this mysterious letter is, Sergeant. You seem to be placing a great deal of credence on its authority.' The Sergeant remains tight-lipped. Victor summons a sardonic smile. 'But you're still not going to tell me.'

'Afraid not, sir.'

'Private Durham lied at his court martial, probably in an attempt to paint himself in a better light, knowing what the penalty for his true actions would inevitably be.'

'Death by firing squad.'

'Indeed.'

'Would you mind, then, Mr Monroe, giving me your account? For comparison?'

'Very well. It was during the Battle of Loos. We had been gassed by our own bloody chlorine, thanks to a change in the wind, but we still managed to go over the top when the call came. We made our way across No Man's Land, facing extremely fierce fire – our artillery bombardment had proven as woefully ineffective as our attempt at gassing the buggers. There were a great number of casualties. I won't dress it up, Sergeant. You've clearly seen battle, you know what it was like over there, so let me just say it was a bloody disaster – men dropping like flies, a bloodbath if you will. Maurice and I were advancing with our men when a shell exploded just in front of us. When the dust settled, I saw that Maurice had been knocked unconscious, and I was wounded in the leg. So, I dragged him and myself into the shell crater for cover. Private Jenkins followed us in and Private Durham joined us a short while later, bringing with him another soldier, Private Syms, who was badly wounded.'

'Were Jenkins and Durham wounded?'

'We were all wounded, to one extent or another.'

The Sergeant scratches further notes into his pad, before looking up expectantly, waiting for Victor to continue.

'We were trapped for some time. The enemy shelling and machine-gun fire were relentless. Private Jenkins, after we had been pinned down for an hour or so, scrambled up to the top of the crater to get an eye on the battle but was immediately shot and killed. By this time, Private Syms was in a very bad way. He was in a great deal of pain.'

The pencil continues to rasp its way across the paper – the noise seems intolerably loud to Victor. Ida, pale and withdrawn, stares into the fire, her usually restless body motionless.

'What happened next?'

'We were completely pinned down until nightfall.'

'But matters got out of hand before then?'

Ida inhales sharply as she darts a look at Vic. For a moment, his guard down, Vic looks uncomfortable. Verity waits.

'Private Durham lost his nerve,' he says at last. 'By the evening Syms was making a dreadful noise, and he wouldn't . . . couldn't . . . be quiet. Perhaps for fun, perhaps to force our hand, the Germans began to strafe the crater with machinegun fire. This, combined with Syms' suffering, proved too much for Durham. He scrambled to the top of the crater, intending to make a break for it, but German snipers spotted him and started firing. I dragged him back down and told him to stop being such a bloody fool, but he was ranting like a madman, saying he couldn't take it anymore. Syms was screaming with pain and Durham just . . . He shot Syms in the head before we could stop him.'

Victor relates the account in a trancelike state, bewitched by the leaping flames in the grate, his voice distant, lost to the smoke and fire of another time. He blinks himself free of the past and looks to the Sergeant with momentary confusion. His expression quickly clears.

'Durham had lost his senses. He said he refused to fight anymore. He was going to flee. I told him again not to be so bloody stupid, he'd incur a charge of desertion if he tried, but he said he didn't care, and in truth we both knew there was no way back from the murder he had just committed. He threw down his rifle and made a run for it, over the top of the crater and back to our lines. Miraculously, he made it. Maurice and I got out after nightfall. I reported Durham as soon as we reached the front trench.'

'Durham had a slightly different account, from what I understand. He said—'

'I know damn well what Private Durham said and it was a blatant pack of lies – beyond all credibility. It was merely a desperate man launching a desperate attack in an attempt to save his own skin. Indeed, his own skin was all he ever thought about. He was arrested in the casualty clearing station, getting his wound seen to.'

'But he had reported your position and situation to an officer.'

'Leonard. He told Leonard.'

'And didn't he order Durham to attend the clearing station, to get himself patched up?'

'Well, yes, but only because he was unaware of the full facts, Sergeant; otherwise he would have had Durham arrested on the spot.'

Verity appears to consider this point, before referring to his notes once again. 'The court martial was convened two weeks later, I understand?'

'Army justice is quickly served in an active arena of battle, Sergeant, through necessity.'

'Did yourself or Lieutenant Stilwell sit on the panel?'

'Maurice had brought the charge and as such was unable to sit. I, however, was on the panel, yes. Along with two of our commanding officers.'

'I understand Private Durham appealed to Second Lieutenant Leonard Stilwell to be his Prisoner's Friend. I found that curious, considering it was Maurice who brought the charge.'

Victor blanches. 'How did you know that?'

'I understand that the request was refused.'

'Leonard decided against it.'

'I see.'

'Private Durham was tried by due justice and in accordance with military law, Sergeant,' Victor says, rallying. 'There was nothing irregular about the proceedings brought against him. The verdict was given by two other senior officers in addition to me and was then ratified by Sir John French himself. You

137

might consider military executions unsavoury. They are. But they are at times necessary and, in this case, justified.'

Sergeant Verity says nothing. He merely jots down some further notes. 'I'm sorry, Mrs Stilwell, that you have had to listen to such unpalatable proceedings. Your husband perhaps has discussed them with you already, but then perhaps he chose not to. I understand he was hospitalised sometime after this?'

Ida resembles a rabbit caught in headlights. She defers to Victor who responds with an almost imperceptible shake of his head. The tip of her tongue darts out to wet her lips before she speaks, her voice tight.

'That's right. Maurice spent the rest of the war in hospital.'

'Where was that, Mrs Stilwell? If you don't mind me asking?'

Ida glances at Victor again before clearing her throat. 'Craiglockhart, initially.'

'I believe a great many suffering from shell shock were treated there.'

'That's right.' A cold defiance radiates from her. 'Maurice had endured terrible things in the war by then. He has never been particularly strong; clearly, they took their toll.'

'Indeed. A most unfortunate and complex malady. There is so much we have yet to understand. I saw many men in my own time miserably afflicted. He has my every sympathy.'

'Thank you.' Ida rises abruptly. 'Now if you don't mind, I see no gain in dwelling on the past. If I'm not needed, I've things to be getting on with.'

'Of course. My apologies for causing any delay.' The Sergeant gets to his feet.

She does not offer him a smile and the curt nod he receives seems more of an afterthought. The heels of her shoes rap against the floorboards as she leaves the room. Sergeant Verity watches her departure, his eyes lingering on the doorway long after she has disappeared through it.

Victor clears his throat, capturing Verity's attention. 'I can hardly think there's anything else, Sergeant. Surely you've raked up enough unpleasantness for one morning?'

'She is a very beautiful woman, if you don't mind me saying.'

'I beg your pardon?'

Verity finally turns to face him. 'It is rare to find such beauty and poise in a woman. She is truly a Helen of Troy – that face alone would launch a thousand ships. I'm sure a man would do just about anything to win the favour of a lady like that.'

There is something about the lisped, ill-formed words of flattery that, in Victor's opinion, renders them grotesque. An unwanted image of the destroyed face behind the mask fills his mind's eye again, and even when he banishes it, the erased space behind his forehead seems to throb with its memory. 'I'm sure Mrs Stilwell will be suitably flattered by your praise. Now if there is nothing else?'

The Sergeant appears amused as he tucks his notebook into his inner pocket. To Victor's intense irritation he begins to laboriously button up his mackintosh.

'Forgive my natural curiosity, Mr Monroe, but how did you come to be such an intimate of the family?'

Victor fights an urge to swear at the man. Instead, he takes a deep breath and tries to maintain his civility, now paper thin. 'Maurice and I were in school together. With my own parents abroad, he would invite me to stay for the holidays. His parents were very kind to me, I was always considered one of the family.'

'And you've never left?'

'I suppose not.'

'And who can blame you . . .' the Sergeant's expression remains disconcertingly hidden '. . . when there is clearly so much to keep you here.'

A log slips in the grate, sending a cascade of sparks onto the hearth. Vic recovers quickly from his startlement, but his chest remains unsettlingly tight. 'Allow me to escort you to the front door, Sergeant. I'm sure you know the way by now, but I wouldn't want you getting lost.'

On the doorstep, the Sergeant pauses, mumbling his dissatisfaction with the continued rain. He makes a drama of unfurling his umbrella, retrieved from the polished brass shell case now repurposed as an ornate stand. Victor wishes he would simply make a dash for his waiting car, parked just yards away.

With the umbrella finally elevated, Verity huddles beneath it. 'Well, thank you, Mr Monroe, most helpful.'

'I expect we've exhausted our usefulness now.'

'Oh, I wouldn't say that, Mr Monroe. I'm sure there's much more assistance you can provide, and we are so grateful for it. I have no doubt you will be seeing me again very soon.'

Victor fights to hide his irritation, as he watches Verity avoid the puddles now pocking the sparse gravel. The Sergeant fiddles around at the front of the car, pulling the choke and turning the crank handle until the engine splutters into life. With some faff, he closes his umbrella and thrusts it into the footwell of the passenger's seat before finally getting inside. Closing the door, he issues a cheery wave. As the car trundles off down the drive, Victor's sense of relief is overwhelming.

'Don't hurry back,' he mutters.

He is guarded over the details he shares with the others when he returns to the library. Maurice is circling the room as he enters, the twitching around his eye near constant now, and clearly aggravating. He starts to slap the fidgeting muscles and flickering skin, his aggression building with each landed blow until Victor is forced to grab his hand to stop him.

'It's all st-st-starting . . . again, I know it is,' Maurice stutters.

'Why don't you try some of your therapies, old man,' Leonard suggests, concern etched on his features. 'A bit of woodwork, perhaps. You showed a real flair for whittling things, and it helped, didn't it? You haven't tried it for a while now. Can't hurt to pick it up again, can it?'

After further careful encouragement, Maurice slopes off to retrieve his whittling knife and some wood from the work shed. Once he has gone, Victor divulges the full details of his meeting with Verity. Leonard listens, stony-faced.

'Why would he want to know about the court martial?'

'I've no idea.'

'He can't know the significance, surely.'

'I don't know.' Victor seeks to rub away the weariness that has been threatening to overwhelm him since his dance with Verity, a weariness compounded by Maurice's increasing return to madness. He drags his hand across his face, but it does little to revitalise him, so instead, he resorts to pouring himself a generous measure of whiskey. He is aware that he has started drinking earlier and earlier these days. Perhaps they are all slipping back into old habits, skidding downwards on Flanders mud just as they had before, to the deadly depths waiting to drown them. 'I just don't know. That damn letter.

What the hell's in it, and more importantly, who the hell wrote it?'

'The past catching up with us again.' Leonard stares at the rain-spotted windowpanes and the rivulets blown horizontal across the glass. 'Perhaps the time has come.'

'Perhaps the time has come for what?' Vic asks.

Leonard turns to face him. 'For us all to finally pay our dues.'

Outside, the wind howls like a wolf on the hunt, and the rain falls heavier than ever.

Chapter Fifteen

That night, Sarah returns from emptying the urinal in the bathroom to find Leonard hanging precariously from the bed, attempting to access the cupboard in his bedside table.

'Leonard!' Depositing the bottle, she dashes forward to catch him, forcing him back against his pillows. 'What on earth are you doing? You could have hurt yourself.'

'Bit late to be worrying about that.' There is a hint of wry humour in his voice, and his smile is charmingly sheepish. 'Would you do me a favour? If you look in my bedside table there's a journal, brown leather. Pass it to me, would you?'

'You could have just waited to ask me in the first place,' Sarah scolds, crouching down.

Opening the cupboard door, she begins to rifle through its crammed contents. She lifts dog-eared novels and pushes aside loose change and pens. A balled-up pair of socks gives her pause; she shoves them further to the back. She continues to rummage until at last she finds a leather-bound notebook, its stippled binding pitted with what looks to be dried mud. As she draws her fingertips across it, her heart beats a little quicker. Collecting herself, she passes it to Leonard, then slams the cupboard door to prevent an avalanche.

As she gets back to her feet, she catches him watching her, a strange expression on his face. She issues a nervous laugh, her hand fluttering to her hair.

'What? What is it? Why are you looking at me like that?'

'Is what you told Ida true, Sarah?'

The softly delivered words render her motionless. Indeed, they are both still, like models pinned in a diorama. Sarah's breath catches in her chest. She cannot bear the intensity of Leonard's scrutiny, and yet she is powerless to look away. There is a peculiar hush in the air. The rain pattering on the windowpanes becomes the dominant sound, despite the muffling curtains, now drawn against the dark.

Sarah stoops to pick up an item of discarded clothing, breaking the spell cast by his words. 'And what would that be?'

'That you . . . you think you might be some sort of magnet . . . for the dead.' She hopes he cannot see the quiver in her hands as she returns his shirt and trousers to their hangers in the wardrobe. She knows she must answer him, she *must*, but she cannot bring herself to say the words. She wishes him to be silent, but she knows that wish is futile. This is not what she wants, she realises, and the thought frightens her. She hears him reposition himself on the bed. She squeezes her eyes shut as he speaks again. 'That you can sense the dead. That you sense something in this house.'

She closes the wardrobe door, but she is not yet ready to turn around. She must focus her thoughts. It is the only way. 'I asked her not to say anything.'

'I would have thought you'd have known enough of Ida by now to realise that was a rather optimistic request.'

She smiles despite herself, and finally summons the courage to face him. 'Yes.'

'So, it is true?'

'I don't know what it is. I just know since stepping foot in this house, that I've felt something.'

He leans forward, the side of his face glowing from the lamplight. 'What?'

She considers her answer with great care. 'Discontent. And not just amongst the living.'

'So you do sense a presence? More than one? Several?' He probes with the doggedness of a schoolboy determined to test his master's knowledge.

'Oh, Leonard! I hardly know myself what I sense. I can't explain it. But I feel them here. I feel them around me.'

'Then, it's not just Hugo? You feel others?'

'I suppose . . . possibly.'

'You have a gift.'

'No!' she responds instinctively. When she brings herself to repeat her denial, she imbues it with measured uncertainty. 'I don't know what it is, I can't explain it and I certainly don't understand it. I'm not sure I want to.' She crosses to the medicine cabinet. 'I think it's better not to meddle in such things.' She twists the small key in its lock and opens the door, taking down the brown glass bottle containing his evening medication.

'Sarah, the person you saw me with by the pond—'

'Oh I wish I'd never said anything now!' She sets the bottle down on the bedside table with more force than necessary, rattling the pills against the glass. She wants him to be silent, and yet she wants him to continue, needs him to do so. She presses a hand to her forehead, confused by the distress welling inside her. It is unexpected and threatening. She forces herself to think straight. To focus. Steadier, she pours him a glass of water from the carafe. 'I should have known better than to—'

'Please, I'm curious, that's all. Please.' In a rush, as if fearing an opportunity is about to be lost, he opens the journal in his lap. 'All I want to know,' he persists, as she sets the glass down on the bedside table beside him, 'is whether the man you think you saw me with is in this photograph.'

He hands her a black and white print of a row of soldiers relaxing before a hedgerow. Puttees bind their legs, and their sleeves are rolled to their elbows, the top buttons of their shirts open at their throats, leading her to deduce the photograph was taken in summer, or in one of the warmer months at least. First in the line of eight men, is Leonard. She recognises him immediately, and is struck by how young he looks, little more than a schoolboy, standing with his hands on his hips, his chin dipped against the glare of the sun, his eyes looking up from under long lashes, an impish grin dimpling his cheek. She experiences a pang in her chest, seeing him as he once was, full of youth, confidence, and vigour, and she thinks of the medals and the school sports cups lined up on the mantelpiece behind her. To her surprise, her vision swims.

'Is he there?'

Remembering her task, Sarah scans along the line and then she sees him. She cannot find her voice. She forces herself to remain calm, forces herself to concentrate. A nod is all she can manage.

'Which one?' Leonard shuffles towards her with keen anticipation. 'Show me, Sarah. Which one is he?'

Her fingertip brushes against a soldier sitting cross-legged at the front.

Leonard draws in a short breath. 'You're sure? You're absolutely certain? This is the man you saw?'

'Boy,' she murmurs. 'He looks little more than a boy.'

'Dear God.' He collapses onto the pillows propped against the headboard behind him. 'Dear God.'

She is oddly reluctant to surrender the photograph when he asks for it, but she knows she must. Her legs feel unsteady and the floor uneven, as if the world tipped on its axis while she stood looking at the monochrome image, and she is now listing to match its revised angle.

'Who was he?' She looks at Leonard. 'Who was he to you?'

'He was my friend.' He tips back his head and stares at the ceiling, his Adam's apple bobbing. His voice, when it comes, sounds like a miss-struck chord. 'He was my good friend. My best friend. Tell me . . . did you sense . . . was he angry, do you think? When you saw him?'

'No.' The question takes her aback, but her instinctive answer more so. Is she correct? The unexpected query derails her.

'He wasn't angry . . .' Leonard marvels on a broken whisper.

'What happened to him?' she asks, struggling to right her thoughts.

'He died.' Leonard begins to cry. He splays his hand across his eyes – whether to hide from her or to hide his tears, she cannot tell. 'I failed him . . . and he died . . .' His pained sobs crash like stormy waves upon a shore, angry and destructive. The desperate honesty of his sorrow brings an ache to Sarah's heart. 'I should never . . . I should have . . . I let him . . . And yet he's still here . . . with me . . . showing me more loyalty in death than I managed to show him in life . . .'

Sarah twists away, her throat raw. A fissure opens deep inside her and something pushes its way through, until it settles within her, occupying her completely. Her pulse slows. She lifts her chin, adopting the detached air of a nursing professional, once second nature to her but lost since the war, since the end of her service. But it all comes back to her now.

'Come along, that's enough. It's time for your medication.'

Her hands are no longer shaking as she picks up the pill bottle. She deftly unscrews the top and puts it on the crowded bedside table while she tips the required dosage into her cupped palm. She sets down the bottle.

'Put your hand out,' she instructs, her voice firm.

Sniffling, Leonard wipes away the mucus trickling from his nostrils, his sobs subsiding. He places the pill on his tongue, then takes the glass of water Sarah proffers, drinking deeply to wash the medicine down.

'There we are,' Sarah says, her voice softening. 'You'll feel better in the morning.' She hesitates. 'What's done is done.' She refills the drained glass from the carafe and places it within easy reach. 'He must have been a dear friend.'

'He was,' Leonard says, the tide of his emotion ebbing now. 'He's the one I was telling you about. The boy from here.'

Sarah busies herself tucking in the loose covers. 'The one who saved your life?'

'And I cost him his,' Leonard says miserably, sinking back against his banked pillows as she draws the covers over his chest. 'He was my best friend, against all odds. And I let him down. If I could make amends . . .' he swallows hard. 'Too late now.'

'I'm sure you're not really to blame for his death. It was war. It was chaos.'

'No . . . I *am* to blame. Perhaps not just me, but of all people, I was the one who could have, *should have*, saved him.'

She perches on the edge of the bed beside him. 'Do you want to talk about it? Tell me what happened?'

His head flops listlessly from side to side. 'No. I can't face it. I can't face telling you.'

She purses her lips and looks away. 'You know, guilt is a great burden to carry around.'

Laughter crawls out of him, dripping with gall. 'Oh, you don't need to tell me that. I battle with it every day, and it's killing me slowly. I wish it bloody well would.'

'In my experience, guilt can be assuaged by an act of repentance. Whatever it is you feel you're guilty of, maybe you can seek penance in some way. That's how you escape it, that crushing sense of guilt. You must do the right thing, whatever that might be, to make amends for the wrong you've done.'

'Then what should I do? How can I make amends for something that has happened to a person now lost to me, lost to us all?'

'Oh Leonard—' she places her hand on his '—only you can decide that. It wouldn't be for me to say.' She offers him a half smile as she rises from the bed. 'Shall I turn off the lamp for you?'

'No . . . no, leave it on, would you.'

'Of course.' She hesitates. 'You're a decent sort, Leonard. I truly believe that.'

'I was once.'

'I'm sure you can be again.' When she reaches the door, she turns back. 'Goodnight.'

'Goodnight, Sarah.' As she pulls the door to behind her, he speaks again, his voice hushed to a whisper. 'Thank you.'

She latches the door behind her. The heaviness in her heart is troubling.

Chapter Sixteen

For the second time in as many nights, they are woken by Maurice's cries, but this time there is a difference. This time they emanate from Leonard's room.

Sarah sits up in bed, her heart hammering. At first, she thinks it is a nightmare imposing itself on reality, but when Maurice's frantic calls come again, she swings her legs from the bed and pulls on her dressing gown. Her courage wanes as she reaches her door. She takes a breath, steeling herself for what awaits, then plunges out onto the landing.

Victor is running down the bedroom corridor towards her, with Ida, still pulling on her satin wrapper, close behind. He leaps the steps and dashes past Sarah to reach Leonard's room first.

Maurice is sitting on the bed, Leonard's lifeless body caught in his arms. His face is torn apart with distress, tears streaming down his cheeks. Victor curses out loud as he races forward, while Sarah, fearful now, hovers in the doorway, taking in the glass lying on the floor, and the brown pill bottle stark against the white bed sheet.

Maurice repeats his brother's name over, and over again, keening. Victor digs his fingertips into Leonard's neck, then lowers his ear to his mouth.

'Jesus, Maurice! He's not dead, he's still breathing.'

He roughly wrenches Leonard's inert body from Maurice's arms. Puling, Maurice, stumbles from the bed. He wraps his arms around himself, looking broken and utterly terrified in equal measure.

'For God's sake, Sarah, you're a nurse, help me!' Victor shouts.

Jarred from her paralysis, Sarah hastens to the bedside. Leonard is deathly pale, but when she checks, she too feels a faint pulse, and his chest rises and falls with coy breaths that brush her cheek as she leans over him. She gently eases back his eyelids. The lamp is still burning, just as she had left it, and she pulls it towards her now, shining the light as best she can into Leonard's eyes. His pupils contract. Releasing his eyelids, she sets down the lamp, a bewildering myriad of thoughts and unexpected emotions muddling her mind.

'Is he going to die?' Ida enquires with ghoulish fascination from the doorway. Sarah realises with some distaste that she is relishing the drama of it all.

'I need an emetic.' The words tack onto the dry roof of Sarah's mouth. She gulps. 'Three tablespoons of mustard in a cup of warm water, Ida – now!'

'Me?'

'Now Ida!'

Pulling a face, Ida disappears.

'Is he conscious enough to take anything?' Victor sounds dubious.

'We need to rouse him if we can. Hold him.'

Securing Leonard on the bed, Sarah snatches up a flannel from the washstand, and soaks it in water from the half-empty carafe. Barely wringing it, she applies it to Leonard's face while urging him to wake.

Leonard weakly snatches his head to the side. He mumbles incoherently. Sarah's heart stutters, while behind her Maurice mewls with relief. Ida makes a breathless return, her nose wrinkled in disgust at the cup of liquid she holds before her.

'Are you really going to make him sick? That's rather revolting,' she complains as she sets it down on the bedside table.

'We need to purge his stomach, we need to make sure there's nothing left in there for him to absorb,' Sarah says. 'Victor, help me prop him up.'

Victor raises Leonard from the bed enabling her to layer the pillows behind him. His protests are increasing, though his eyes remain shut and his utterances nonsensical.

'Leonard, you need to drink this,' Sarah implores, as she brings the cup to his mouth. Barely conscious, his head lolls one way then the next, forcing her to chase his clamped lips with it. Her tone becomes stricter, and in the end, with Victor's help, she holds Leonard's nose and prises open his mouth, trickling the emetic inside, before pushing up his chin, forcing him to swallow. Leonard splutters, chokes and gasps, but eventually most of the foul concoction goes in, the escaped excess dribbling down his chin to drip yellow stains onto his striped pyjama top.

With the cup emptied, Sarah grabs the porcelain bowl from the washstand. She stands by the bed, bowl in her hands, waiting. Praying.

'We need a doctor!' Maurice cries.

'They'll cart him off to some asylum, Maurice,' Victor warns, over Ida's declared fears of ignominy. 'What I want to know is how the hell did he come to have access to the pills in the first place? They are supposed to be shut away, *every, single time.*'

Sarah keeps her focus on Leonard, but there is no escaping the guilty blaze upon her cheeks. 'I must . . . I must have forgotten . . .'

'I told you, Sarah, I told you that very first day,' Ida preaches, her arms folding across her slack chest.

'I didn't know . . . you never said . . .' Sarah whips round to look at her. 'Has he done this before?'

Ida thrusts up her narrow chin. 'Yes.'

Wiping the tears from his blotched cheeks, Maurice fights back a fresh deluge. His right eye spasms as he speaks. 'He's tried it a couple of times since . . . since . . .' He waves his hand over his brother's decimated frame.

'What a bloody mess.' Victor drags his hand down his jaw.

'Is he going to be all right? I really think we should get a doctor. To hell with what anyone says if it gets out. If he dies what's—'

'Tell me about the other times,' Sarah says, cutting dead Maurice's hysteria.

'Pills and whiskey . . . twice.'

Her grip tightens on the porcelain. 'Well, there's no whiskey this time, that'll help. I remember wondering whether there were enough pills . . .' she murmurs. 'To last . . .' she adds hurriedly, seeing Ida's appalled expression. 'I thought he was running out and I made a mental note to ask about requesting more.'

'So how many do you think he might have taken?' Victor asks.

Harried, Sarah shakes her head. Tears prick her eyes. 'I don't know . . . but he's still alive, so I'd be surprised—'

Leonard starts to wrestle against the bed in apparent discomfort, his stomach gurgling. He attempts to sit, his belly convulsing as he begins to retch. Sarah springs forward, one hand supporting him, the other holding the bowl, as he purges the contents of his stomach in three horrendous gushes. Ida cries out, twisting away in disgust, her hand across her mouth as if fearing she may follow suit. She is only too eager to volunteer her services when Sarah calls for someone to fetch more water.

Wrung out, Leonard slumps back against the pillows, his forehead beaded with sweat. His skin is the colour of bleached bone and his breathing is laboured, but at last his eyes flicker open, and though woozy, he scans the room.

'You silly bugger,' Victor mutters.

Maurice crumples down onto the bed beside his brother. He flings his arms around him, sobbing into his shoulder.

'Promise me you'll never try that again. Promise me. Promise me!'

Leonard stares dead-eyed over his shoulder, bearing the look of a soldier who has fought with all his might, only to discover the battle had been declared lost hours before.

'I cocked it up again?' he croaks at last, his voice raw and rasping. The first sob rips him apart, rips the room apart, and all within it. They stand rigid, watching him, unmoving, each of them absorbing some of his agony as he succumbs to heartbroken despair. 'I was praying for it to be third time lucky,' he gasps, swearing brutally through the spittle, tears, and snot. 'Why? Why didn't you just let me go, for God's sake?

What right do you have to make me go on suffering this way? You've no right, no right at all . . .'

None of them attempt to answer.

Sarah volunteers to spend the remainder of the night in Leonard's room, to ensure there is no relapse, though the emetic had proven effective. For once, Maurice is grateful for the German voices that infiltrated his sleep, rousing him from his bed to seek his brother's comfort. Sarah can't help thinking if he had, instead, sought comfort from his wife, the night might have had a very different outcome.

She does not mean to doze off, but she must do, for she wakes with a start and a shooting pain in her neck. Her head is angled awkwardly against the back of the armchair she dragged to Leonard's bedside after the others had left, so she could sit and watch him sleep. His rest has not been peaceful. Even in unconsciousness, he tossed fitfully, his face screwing with pain or distress – she could not tell which. Perhaps both. Small, unhappy noises had escaped his twisting lips, and she had sat forward, watching him with a pang of disquiet, on more than one occasion.

But eventually, as the grey light of dawn began to trim the curtains, he had fallen into a more peaceful slumber. Only then had she allowed her head to tip back against the chair, but even so, she had intended to resist her heavy eyelids. Now, righting herself in the seat, she massages the pain from her neck and wonders how long she has been out.

'You're awake.'

Leonard's voice is rough, his throat no doubt sore from the repeated vomiting. He bounces his head against his pillow and stares unblinkingly at the ceiling. 'Another day.'

'You're very lucky.'

He snorts. 'Am I really?'

'If Maurice hadn't found you—'

'Damn Maurice and his damned nightmares.' He turns his head towards her. His cheek is almost as white as the pillow it rests upon. 'If he hadn't come in, I'd have succeeded, wouldn't I? This time? You wouldn't have found me until morning, and it would have been too late. Your foul emetic wouldn't have worked then, would it?'

'It might have been too late,' she concedes quietly. 'It depends on how many pills you took, I suppose.'

'Every last one in the bottle. I didn't count them. I didn't wait. I couldn't believe my luck when I saw you'd left it there like that, lid off and everything. Like a gift.'

Flushing, Sarah rises from the chair and crosses to the window. Reaching up, she throws the curtains apart. The lawn is so waterlogged puddles have begun to spot its surface.

'My mistake,' she says, looking out into a whitewashed sky.

'Was it? I wondered whether it was an act of kindness.'

The Canada geese are back, grazing between the puddles. The river looks swollen, even to her untrained eye. The air shimmers. She realises it is drizzle.

'I wonder will it ever stop raining.' She turns away from the window to face him. 'It was a terrible oversight on my part, leaving those pills there like that. And it hadn't been made clear to me . . .' She looks down at the dust-silvered floorboards poking out from under the rug. They should have been cleaned by now.

'That I'd done it before?'

'No.'

'Third time lucky I was hoping, but there we are.'

'Do you mean that?'

'Yes, I bloody do.' He raises himself up on his elbow. 'Look at me. Look at me!' He yanks back the covers, exposing what is left of his body. She wants to look away, but she can't. 'Why would I want to live on like this?'

'Men do. You could too. You could try prosthetics.'

He covers himself back up, as if he can't bear to see what he has become. 'I've told you. I tried and couldn't take to them.'

'There are better ones—'

'I don't want a body made whole with bits of bloody metal and wood!' His anguish vibrates off the beamed walls. 'If I was a dog, or a horse, or even a fucking cat, I would have been put down by now. It would be considered the kindest thing to do, putting me out of my misery. And they'd be right. Can't you see the irony, Sarah? We look at an injured animal and we can decide what's in their best interests. We see their three legs, or their broken pelvis and we say, poor blighter, it's not right to let him suffer. That animal can't argue against the decision. They can't say, "Actually I can get about fine on three legs, I'll manage, and it doesn't hurt, so, let me live, would you?" No, it's decided by us that their quality of life is sufficiently impaired that putting an end to their handicap is the kindest thing to do.

'And yet here am I, a fairly intelligent, sane, rational man, able to communicate that the life I have been left with – my body destroyed as it is beyond repair – is not a life I wish to live. I can convey that I am in misery every day, and yet I am not afforded the same consideration of kindness as that dumb animal. The quality of life I have been left with is not taken into account. I can say, competently, I no longer wish to live. I can beg to be released from my suffering. And yet it seems I am not worthy of the same level of compassion given to an animal we deem to be in distress. I am expected to bear my suffering until the end of my days, ideally with good grace. And why? Because my wanting to die makes other people feel uncomfortable. It is an uneasy subject to discuss. So, they choose not to. They leave me to suffer instead. To save themselves any sense of discomfort or loss.'

'Other men—'

He slams his hand down on the mattress beside him. 'Other men can do what they damn well like, Sarah. I don't care! I don't care what other men – better men than me clearly – are content to endure. The fact is this is *my* life, and *I* don't want to live it like this. Doesn't that matter to anyone? I don't want to be like this any longer. I don't want to depend on someone to carry me up and downstairs like a child, cutting up my food, feeding me like an imbecile, dressing me, helping me piss and cleaning up my shit – I don't want that humiliation. It's not that people are unkind in any way, everyone is so willing to help me . . . the fact is, *I* don't want to live like this a minute more. And if anyone had an ounce of Christian kindness in their souls, they would bloody well help me escape this torturous existence, rather than doing everything in their power to prolong it.'

'You don't mean that. You have people that love you.'

'And I love them, but that doesn't give them the right to force me to live when I don't want to. *I don't want to,*' he reiterates slowly. 'My choice, my right. They're not living like this, they've no idea, *no idea* what it's like for me, so they have no right to dictate to me, no right to decide that the proper thing to do is to force me to continue in this pitiful existence as half a man. Perhaps other veterans can find purpose and contentment with their destroyed bodies, Sarah, and I applaud their courage and dogged determination, but I can't. I don't want to. Not now, not ever. And don't try and tell me it will get better with time, that I will come to accept and perhaps even enjoy my fate because I won't. And I will hate you for suggesting that I might.'

'You never promised Maurice . . .' she realises, thinking back on his brother's plaintive pleas.

Leonard sinks back against his pillows. 'I don't believe in making promises I have no intention of keeping.'

Silence fills the room. Leonard's focus returns to the plasterwork ceiling. His forehead ripples with private thoughts he is clearly not prepared to share.

'I'll go and fetch some water for your ablutions,' Sarah says at last. He turns his face to the window.

As she reaches the door, he speaks again, but the words are so softly delivered she is unsure whether they are even meant for her.

'Maybe I don't deserve to succeed. Maybe I don't deserve to die. After the sins I've committed, perhaps being trapped alive in a living hell is exactly the punishment I'm due.'

Chapter Seventeen

'All I'm saying is it's a damn good thing you got spooked last night, Maurice. If you hadn't found Leonard when you did, well, I doubt we'd be sitting here now tucking into our tea and toast.'

Victor reaches for his cup of coffee, casting a glance at Maurice who has not eaten or drunk a thing since taking his place. Instead, he sits huddled in his chair at the far end of the table, his narrow legs tightly crossed, his arms binding his concave middle, as if he is keen to take up as little space as possible. The strained knit of his limbs has at least concealed the shaking in his arm, which had been particularly pronounced when he joined Victor and Ida for breakfast. As Victor takes in his friend's gaunt face, the feverish rambling of his gaze and the sweat glistening on his forehead, he feels a tug of concern the like of which he hasn't experienced since that night in the shell hole, trapped with Maurice in the chaos of No Man's Land. He takes another glug of coffee, but it fails to alleviate his unease.

He transfers his observations to Sarah, who is unobtrusively collating a range of breakfast items upon a tray to take up to Leonard. He watches her as she scrapes butter across a cold triangle of toast, sees her deliberation over strawberry jam or marmalade, though in the end, she plumps for the jam. She too bears the mark of the night, the shadows beneath her eyes more prevalent than before, and he suspects her quiet confidence has taken a blow.

'What I still find appalling is how Leonard came to be left with the pills,' Victor says, sitting back, raising his voice a little.

Ida's head shoots up from the pages of the society magazine she has been absorbed in since taking her seat. 'I said, didn't I? I said that very first day, Sarah, that Leonard's medication must be returned to the cabinet every night.' She leans forward, the edge of the table pressing against her as she addresses Victor. 'Every night! I couldn't have been any clearer, Vic.'

'It was an accident.' Sarah does not lift her eyes from the tray. Her fingers tighten on the handles. 'We had been talk-ing . . . he became upset . . .' Finally, she braves their peevish scrutiny. 'I must have been distracted, comforting him. By the time he settled, I just wanted him to have some peace and quiet, to sleep. In my rush to leave him be, I must have . . .' She bites her lip.

'I told you.' Ida is like a terrier shaking life from the rat caught in its jaws. 'I told you they must not be left around!'

'I didn't realise . . . I didn't fully appreciate the dangers.'

'You must have left the top off and everything.' Victor eyes her coldly. 'If you had just bothered to replace it, he would never have managed to unscrew it.'

'I know . . .'

'I c-can't lose him,' Maurice squeezes his eyes shut as he battles to eject his words. 'I can't lose him.' He begins to rock in his chair.

Victor sets his coffee cup back down upon its saucer. He skewers Sarah with his steely glare. 'It can't happen again. Do you understand?'

Whispering her assent, she lifts the tray and leaves. Victor takes a surprising amount of pleasure from the fact she has been put in her place.

'Oh, do stop that, Maurice!' Ida spits, her face creasing in distaste at the sight of her husband's rocking form. She pushes back her chair. 'He's alive, isn't he? Good God, I get more sense out of Mr Tibbs.' Clutching the magazine to her chest, she leaves the room.

'You heard voices again, then?' Victor asks, pushing away his plate, and turning in his chair to give himself room to cross his legs. He taps a cigarette free of the box sitting on the table.

'Voices.' The word escapes Maurice as a dreamlike whisper. He blinks and starts. His arms close around his middle. 'I heard them again.'

The hushed admission is delivered with the shame of a tawdry secret shared in a confessional.

Vic bats out his burning match. He draws deeply on his cigarette.

Maurice pitches forward, suddenly fervid. 'I heard them, Vic. I know you think I didn't, but I did, and it's not in my head, Vic, it's not in here.' He hammers his knuckles to his temple, his skin reddening under the assault. 'The Germans were in my room, whispering. I heard them. Heard their damned voices. I'm telling you. They were right there. Plotting to kill me!'

'Jesus, Maurice.' Vic uncrosses his legs and sits up in his chair. 'There's no bloody Germans in your room. Even you must be able to appreciate the absurdity of that idea.'

'I can't explain it, I don't know how they're managing it, but I'm telling you they are in this house. I heard them.'

'In your imagination!' In an explosion of movement, Vic springs up from his chair and crosses to the fireplace, his muscles singing with the frustration he is trying hard to contain. 'Those voices are in your head.' He taps at his temple. 'Nowhere else. There's no ghastly Germans hiding underneath the floorboards at Darkacre, old man.' He tries to make light of it, to chuckle, but his contempt is too thick, and the words come out mean and mocking. He wants to do better. He wants to be kinder. 'This nonsense has got to stop, Maurice.'

'It's not nonsense!' Maurice erupts from his seat with such violence his chair topples backwards, clattering against the floorboards. The drama of it proves too much for Victor's resolve.

'Oh, go and whittle some wood or whatever the hell it is you need to do to calm your nerves.' Like a placid dog who has been too much tormented, he snaps and snarls and mauls Maurice now, his instinctive restraint tested beyond its bounds, his patience broken. 'It's all in your head, Maurice. It's all in that weak little head of yours and it's about time you stop inflicting this foolishness upon the rest of us.'

'I hear them, Vic . . .' Maurice pleads, with the confusion and distress of a bitten child.

'No, Maurice. You only think you do.'

Maurice's face crumples. He snatches his plate from the table and with a furious cry he flings it into the beamed wall behind Vic's head. Victor barely flinches as the plate explodes on impact, its shattered fragments clattering onto the hearth below. Maurice flees the room with the guttural cry of the wounded.

Victor retakes his seat, china fragments crunching under his shoes. He pours himself a fresh cup of coffee and butters another slice of toast. After some deliberation, he chooses marmalade.

*

Ida ekes out a listless existence in the drawing room. Her magazine lies discarded and, having grown tired of Mr Tibbs' demoralising failure to affirm she is indeed a *pretty lady*, she now stares out of the window at the waning rain, wondering whether Maurice is heading for another breakdown, and feeling quite miserable over her sense of imprisonment. She has always had a tendency towards self-pity and her maudlin indulgence elicits threatening tears. This is not the life she had anticipated when she accepted his proposal all those years ago.

Though initially piqued to learn that Maurice, as second son, was in fact only entitled to a share of the estate used to lure her, Ida had quickly realised he was still a profitable catch, and Walter Stilwell had assured her father Maurice would be well set up for married life.

The wedding was a glorious affair. Edwina Stilwell insisted on hosting – and as her own parents could offer nothing as grand as Darkacre Hall, Ida agreed without hesitation.

The cooks worked flat out in the kitchen for days; the gardens were preened to perfection and extra staff hired to assist with the waiting. Thirty tables, all dressed with starched linen, the best silver and gleaming crystal, were set up in the Great Hall at the far end of the house, with the estate carpenters building a dais at one end for the use of the top table and, later, the orchestra. Every table was decorated with beautiful arrangements of cream roses, white peonies and delicate lily of the valley. Pedestals bearing stunning floral displays filled every corner of every room on the ground floor – save the study, which Walter Stilwell insisted be out of bounds for the day.

The ceremony itself passed in a blur – Ida knew only a tiny fraction of the two hundred guests invited. A horse-drawn carriage bedecked with ribbons and flowers returned them to the Hall, and Edwina was quick to usher them inside, pausing only to remove petals of confetti from Ida's headdress.

'Hurry now, my dears, the photographer from *Country Life* is waiting in the reception hall and he assures me the light is simply perfect.'

She and Maurice stood side by side, as Edwina herself arranged Ida's ivory train and flowing lace veil into a luxurious pool at their feet. The exploding flashbulb left stars dancing before Ida's eyes and her heart swelled at the thought of *her* photograph gracing the pages of such an esteemed society publication. The very thrill of it took her breath away.

Later, she danced to the orchestra, her cheeks flushed from excitement and copious coupes of champagne. She soon found herself in Hugo's arms, spinning a waltz.

'You're quite beautiful, you know,' he said, just loud enough for her to hear above the violins and cellos. 'I'm amazed Maurice managed to hook you. If Mother wasn't so intent on me marrying into landed gentry, I would have been tempted myself.' He pulled her closer, his breath hot on her ear as he whispered, 'Perhaps we can explore our options another time . . .' He released her the moment the music stopped, offering a bow that hid his suggestive smile from the crowd, before leading her back to her husband who was patiently awaiting his turn. Initially stunned, she was unsure whether to be flattered or insulted, but there was something in Hugo's backward glance that made her feel she was being toyed with. In that instant, the new Mrs Stilwell resolved to never be anybody's fool.

Naturally, she did not mention the incident to Maurice. Hugo returned to his regiment the day after the wedding, having already joined the army *for the dashed fun of it*, given it would be a while before he would be assuming the reins of the estate. No one saw the war coming back then, of course.

He ended up coming home for a few days' leave just prior to leaving with the British Expeditionary Force. Edwina was anxious and Walter proud, while Leonard sulked terribly for being too young to join up, though his eighteenth birthday was only a matter of weeks away.

They lined up on the gravel to see Hugo off, perspiring in the baking heat. Only Hugo himself looked cool, every inch the dashing hero in his uniform.

'Make sure you come back. I need to know there will be a safe pair of hands at the helm when I've gone,' Walter Stilwell told his son.

Hugo accepted his father's gruff embrace and then moved on to gently tease Edwina for her tears, before jesting with Leonard that he would save him a spot. Victor kept his handshake brief, and his smile seemed a little perfunctory, but then Ida had noted a change in his demeanour towards Hugo since the wedding. When Hugo ignored her proffered hand to kiss her cheek instead, she sensed Victor stiffen by her side.

Maurice stepped forward when his turn came.

'I'll help hold the fort here while you're away, Hugo, don't you worry. I'll make you proud.'

'Well, you can but try.' Hugo's smile appeared sardonic as he clapped Maurice on the shoulders. 'Do your best, eh? Don't let me down, Floppy.'

'I won't, Hugo. I promise.'

Ida found Maurice's rather desperate display insightful. For the first time, she saw her husband for what he was: a weak boy, yearning for approval. The realisation proved sobering and the rose-coloured lens through which she had been viewing her future suddenly turned crystal clear. The fear that she had merely settled, when perhaps she ought to have held out for more, had plagued her from that moment on.

'I'm sorry, I didn't realise you'd still be in here, I can come back . . .'

Gasping, Ida whirls round from the window to see Sarah standing in the doorway.

'I'm so sorry, I didn't mean to startle you.'

Extracting herself from her reverie, Ida beckons her in. 'No, no, come in. I'm not doing anything really. I'd welcome the company.'

Head down, Sarah scurries across to the grate with a bucket in one hand and a trug of cleaning equipment in the other. Ida collapses upon on the sofa, her desolation forgotten as she reflects on the events of the night before and the niggling suspicion that kept her awake long after they had all returned to their rooms.

'I hope I didn't come across too strong earlier,' she says.

There is no alteration in the rhythmic *shush, shush, shush* of the hand brush as Sarah sweeps the grate clear of ash.

Soot tickles at Ida's nostrils as she leans forward, the points of her elbows digging into the tops of her knees as she cradles her face in her palms. 'At breakfast. I had to be cross, you see, the others would have expected it.'

Sarah sweeps the ash into a dustpan. Ida sighs and throws herself back against the sofa cushions. She smooths her hands over the empty seats either side of her.

'I do have to wonder whether it was an accident, of course.'

'It was.'

The ghost of a smile haunts Ida's lips, and she feels a sliver of satisfaction for having provoked a reaction at last. Sarah has inadvertently cracked open the door – Ida will wedge in her foot to prevent it closing. She leans forward again. 'You know, I wouldn't blame you one bit if it wasn't. In fact, I'd think all the better of you.' Sarah does look round now. Ida meets her shock with a bewitching smile. 'I would think it a great kindness.'

Sarah's confusion is evident. 'It was an oversight on my part,' she says, as she tips the contents of the dustpan into the bucket.

'If you say so.'

'It won't happen again, I swear.'

'Well, that's a shame.' Ida rests back, playing with the beads looped over her chest. 'Release . . . that's all poor Leonard has ever wanted. Who wants to live like that? Helpless and humiliated.'

Sarah scrambles to her feet. She snatches up her bucket of ash. 'I need to put this on the garden.'

'You would have been doing us all a favour, you know,' Ida calls after her, swivelling on the sofa to face her as she stops in the doorway. 'Dear Leonard most of all.'

Sarah savours the sting of cold air on her cheeks as she shakes ash onto the withered borders, unkempt now and past their best. The rain has abated just in time, but even so, she is forced to avoid puddles on the gravelled path, and the first dusting of ash dissolves into the sodden earth. Looking towards the pond, she sees Maurice huddled on a bench at the far end, where the surface is smothered with waxen-leafed waterlilies.

Setting down the bucket, she wanders over. He doesn't acknowledge her approach but instead remains intently focused upon the bit of wood that he is whittling into shape with his knife. Even when she stands over him, he does not react to her presence. She watches the blade slice through the grain, curled shavings tumbling to the ground. It is a striking tool to be sure, its polished hilt inlaid with pearl from what she can see, and as another sliver of wood falls, she notices the blade is ornately engraved with Maurice's initials.

Now that she is here, she cannot think what to say, so instead she watches reflected clouds scud across the surface of the pond. Maurice radiates an intensity she finds unsettling. The blade moves in frenzied sweeps. She considers how sharp it must be to pass through wood with such little effort.

'Whittling again?' she says, watching the coots peck at the pondweed wavering below the surface.

'It calms me.' He speaks through gritted teeth, his words belying his taut physique. The air vibrates with his pent-up frustration. One miss-word, and she is sure he will erupt. Perhaps this is what makes her take a step back. Fear for her safety.

But he says no more. The knife carves and slices. The shavings drift downwards. In the end, she decides being with him is a pointless exercise; there is nothing to be achieved while he is in such a disturbed state. Even so, as she makes to leave, she says, 'Well, be sure not to leave that knife lying around. I wouldn't want Leonard to get hold of it.'

'Do you think I would?' His head snaps up and his bloodshot eyes bore into her. She is taken aback by the naked aggression in his voice, but more than that, she is taken aback by how ill he looks, how haunted. His tormented nights are taking their toll.

'Of course not.'

His eye flickers like a lightbulb about to blow. The hand clutching the knife begins to shake. She can see it takes a different kind of concentration now for him to guide it safely through the wood.

'Go away,' he whispers.

She does not make him ask twice.

Chapter Eighteen

Sarah remains in the kitchen long after she has cleared away the dinner things. She finds extra chores to prevent her accepting Ida's nightly invitation to join the others in the drawing room, and even when she has run out of reasons to stay away, she sits in the gloom, grateful for the knowledge that no one will think to come and find her.

Leonard might have insisted, had he been there, but Leonard has not been down all day. He has taken his meals in his room, though in truth he has eaten little, his appetite quashed by disappointment. He has shown no remorse for attempting to take his own life, only regret that he wasted the opportunity. There has been no epiphany; he is not grateful for his second chance at living. He is instead angry. Some of that anger he has taken out on Maurice, who had visited his room earlier, only to leave it a short time later in a fresh flood of hysterical tears, Leonard's screamed accusation that Maurice only wanted him to live for his own selfish reasons chasing him down the corridor.

'I find emotional displays in men vaguely repellent,' Ida confided to Sarah later, when she came into the kitchen to request more tea. 'You wouldn't catch Victor behaving like that,' she muttered, as she sneaked a cigarette at the back door, her exhaled smoke hanging fog-like in the dank air.

Sarah finally rouses herself just after ten o'clock. Filling a carafe with water, she heads up the back staircase to Leonard's room to help him with his nightly ablutions and dispense his medication. It is nearly eleven by the time she returns to the kitchen to begin shutting up for the night, locking the back door, and turning down the gas lamps after she has stoked the range for a final time. She is strangely nervous as she makes her way down the service passage to the reception hall and the drawing room beyond, her steps resounding off the stone floor.

'If there's nothing else you need, I'll be off to bed now,' she says, framing herself in the doorway.

Ida looks up from her game of patience, then glances at the mantel clock. 'Gosh, I didn't realise it was so late.'

'I might turn in myself.' Vic's words are distorted by a stifled yawn. He folds the pages of *Sporting Life*, before pushing himself up from his armchair. Without consulting Maurice, who is staring sightlessly into the fading fire, Victor crosses to the gramophone and lifts the stylus from the spinning disc. Such an abrupt silencing of Puccini's gently swelling strings seems somehow brutal to Sarah. Beauty extinguished without care or consideration.

'I'm done in too.' Ida sets down her cards.

'Has Leonard turned in?' Victor asks.

'Yes. I saw to him half an hour ago,' Sarah says.

Victor abandons the gramophone. 'Maurice, we're all going up. Are you coming, old man?'

Apparently hypnotised by the dying flames, Maurice does not respond until Victor snaps out his name a second time.

'No. I'm not going to bed. I'm not going to sleep.'

'Of course you're going to sleep,' Ida protests, sitting back in her chair. 'Everyone has to sleep sometime.'

'Not me. I can't. I can't, I tell you. I can't take the risk.'

'What risk?' she demands. 'For goodness sake, Maurice. What drivel are you spouting now?'

'I can't go to sleep!' Maurice's voice rips through the room, causing Ida to jump. 'They come when I'm asleep.'

'Who come when you're asleep?'

'They do. You know who . . .' he pushes the words out through gritted teeth. 'The Hun bastards . . .'

'Oh dear God, Maurice,' Vic chuckles. 'What is it going to take to convince you? There are no German soldiers lurking under your bed. Now come on up with the rest of us. You need sleep more than anyone else in this room.'

'No, I'm not going!' Maurice leaps to his feet. 'I'm not going up there.'

'Don't be ridiculous, Maurice—'

'I'm not going, I tell you!' As if fearing he is about to be bodily removed from the room, Maurice scrambles to put the armchair between him and Victor. 'I can't. They'll know I'm there. They'll come for me.'

'No one is going to come for you, Maurice.'

'I'll hear them if I go up there. I can't do it, I tell you, I can't. I don't want them to come for me, I don't want to hear them whispering . . . plotting . . .'

'Oh leave him.' Ida rises contemptuously. 'Leave him down here to cry like a baby. Maybe I'll get some sleep tonight if he isn't in his room, waking us all up with his screams.'

Sarah bumps against the door frame as she makes way for

Ida to sweep past. Maurice remains, chuntering to himself, his breaths catching like sobs as he cowers from terrors unseen. When Vic makes a move towards him, he retreats with a whimper.

'Enough, Maurice. It's over, all of it, it's in the past. Whatever you think is happening now is just your imagination, nothing else. You must take hold of yourself, man.'

'N-no . . . no. I can't Vic, I can't go up there. I can't . . .' Maurice's face is ashen. 'I can't.'

Cursing under his breath, Victor strides across to him, undaunted as Maurice shrinks away. 'You'll lose her, if you keep up this nonsense . . . you'll lose her.'

'I j-j-just can't . . .'

Breathing hard on his fury, Victor storms towards the doorway. Sarah steps aside. 'Leave him here, he's impossible,' he snarls as he passes her. 'Just bloody leave him be.'

The shouting wakes them all, but tonight it has a different tone again. Leonard's bell jangles, demanding and persistent. Frantic. It matches Maurice's voice.

Sarah emerges from her bedroom just as Victor and Ida are descending onto the landing. Maurice is already in its midst, twisting left to right, dashing towards the service stairs before racing back, pushing past Victor to mount the steps to the bedroom corridor, all the while hollering with increasing desperation for his lost brother. For Hugo.

Leonard's impatient shouts soon join in, and Sarah throws open his door. He is sitting up in bed, bathed in a pool of lamplight.

'What's going on?' he cries, the bell hanging heavy in his

hand, but all Sarah can do is shrug in dumb confusion. She moves aside so he can observe his brother's bizarre behaviour for himself.

'What the hell is it now?' Victor demands.

Maurice spins towards him, euphoric. 'I saw him! He was here. Here, I tell you. I followed him upstairs.'

'What the hell are you talking about?'

'Can't you smell it?'

Suddenly everything is still. Even Maurice overcomes his fizzing energy and freezes in a hush of anticipation. They collectively hold their breaths, for, sure enough, faintly lingering in the air, is a familiar scent.

'It's Hugo's pipe tobacco,' Ida murmurs with wonder, drawing closer to Victor.

'Of course it is!' Maurice whirls round to face her, alive with fervour. 'He was here!'

'What the hell . . .'

'He was here, Vic! You can smell it, can't you? His pipe – don't tell me you can't. Len! Len!' Maurice makes a dash for Leonard's door. 'Can you smell it? In there, is it drifting in? It's unmistakable. Just as in the library.'

He challenges them all to deny it, but no one can, because it is true. The air is threaded with the unmistakable smell of tobacco. Maurice glows with triumph.

'He was here. I saw him!'

'What do you mean, you saw him?' Vic asks, looking harrowed in the wan light of the wall sconces.

Maurice makes a visible attempt to calm himself. He starts slowly, his voice steady and determined. 'I'd fallen asleep in the drawing room. I don't know what woke me, but I woke

176

with a start. The door was open, it was cold, the fire had gone out. The lamp was still burning on the table beside me, but that was the only light. Something . . . something caused me to look towards the open doorway, and there, just beyond, in the hall, in the darkness as if waiting to come into the light . . . was Hugo.'

'Hugo?' Victor qualifies, doubtful.

'I smelt his pipe. I saw him.'

'You saw Hugo?'

'Not his face, it was too dark, but I saw his cap, his officer's cap, and his greatcoat over his uniform. I called his name . . . *Hugo* . . . and he turned to leave, but waited, as if he wanted me to follow him. And then he started to walk away. I thought perhaps I was imagining it, that I am mad, just as you keep telling me, so I leapt to my feet and ran to the door, and there he was! Retreating through the hall, up the stairs. I couldn't believe my eyes. Hugo!' He gulps down a sudden swell of emotion, determined to relate his story. 'I hurried after him . . . the smell of his tobacco was like a trailing cord guiding me to him . . . but by the time I reached the landing here, he had gone. But I saw him! I swear to you, Vic, I saw him. Len, are you hearing this? It was Hugo! I'd know him anywhere.'

'It's impossible, Maurice.' Victor rakes his fingers through his hair. Though the aroma of tobacco smoke has left a visible dent in his certainty, he forges against it. 'You were asleep . . . you were probably dreaming of him and woke up. You're just confused.'

'I'm not, I tell you!' Maurice's joy is swiftly replaced by anguish. 'I saw him, I followed him up the stairs, he was here, he was right here.'

'And then he conveniently vanished?' Whatever shifting sands Victor had unexpectedly found himself upon have now solidified. He treats Maurice to a mocking hitch of his eyebrow, an amused smile playing at the corner of his mouth. It does nothing to soften the hard glint of contempt that flashes deep in his eyes.

'Damn it, Vic! Why won't you believe me? You can smell the tobacco smoke. I know you can.'

'What I can smell is lavender,' Vic said, his nose creasing.

'That's me . . . from my room,' Sarah admits. She had been careful to shut her door. 'I use lavender oil. It helps me sleep.'

'Well, that's what I can smell.'

'I can smell it,' Leonard calls from his room. 'I can smell Hugo's tobacco, it's drifting into here now. I can. And I smelt it in the library before.'

'I can smell it too,' Sarah says softly. 'I can smell it despite the lavender.'

'I have to say, Vic . . . I can as well,' Ida says, apology in her voice.

'Good God! All of you?' Vic rubs his forehead in a display of exasperation. 'I tell you, it is nothing more than the power of suggestion. Look, Maurice here wakes up, probably from a dream of Hugo though he doesn't know it, gets spooked by the dream and the dark, then convinces himself a shadow is in fact Hugo's ghost. He comes upstairs, shouting Hugo's name loud enough to wake the dead but merely wakes us up instead. Having roused us from our beds, he swears blind he can smell Hugo's bloody pipe smoke. Is it any surprise then, that suddenly, in our sleep-fuddled, barely conscious states, we all think we can smell it too?'

'So you admit it then, you can smell it,' Maurice cuts in.

'What? No—'

'You said *we*.' Maurice preens in triumph. '*We* can all smell it. You do smell it, but you want to pretend you can't because you *want* everyone to think I'm going mad, don't you? You *want* everyone to think that I'm becoming unhinged again, but I'm not I tell you, I'm not!'

'Why on earth would I want that, Maurice? And quite frankly, if you carry on like this, I won't have to persuade anyone. They'll be reaching that conclusion all by themselves.'

'What if Maurice did see someone?' Ida interrupts, with renewed fear. 'There is another possible explanation none of you have considered. What if we have an intruder?'

'An intruder with a penchant for smoking Hugo's blend of tobacco. Wasn't that the suggestion last time too? Oh really Ida, do you think it's likely?'

'Well, maybe this time it is! The tobacco may well be suggestion as you say, but perhaps the figure is real.'

Struggling to maintain his equilibrium, Victor closes his eyes, as if hoping to find the occupants of Darkacre pleasingly rational again when he reopens them, but instead their taut expressions greet him unaltered. He might be embattled, but it is obvious he has no intention of being beaten. 'An intruder? Very well. Maurice, you say you were right behind this figure on the stairs?'

'I was, he was just in front of me.'

'And he definitely came this way?'

'Yes.'

'So, he would have had to come past you if he had turned back on himself?' When Maurice concedes this point, Victor moves into the middle of the landing, as if he is an actor taking centre stage, ready to perform to his rapt audience. He considers his next line. 'And he'd vanished by the time you got to the landing here?'

'That's right.'

'Well, let's see . . .' Vic passes Leonard's room, and Sarah's closed door. The bathroom door is open, and the room is evidently empty. Moving on towards the service stairs leading down to the kitchen, he pauses long enough to rattle the attic door. 'Locked. Note the key is here on the outside.' Maurice starts after him as he descends the service stairs. The rest of them listen to the creak of the treads, and Victor's faint call that the kitchen door is also locked. Ida and Sarah are both shivering with cold by the time the two men return via the main staircase.

'No one in the house . . . *again*,' Victor announces as they approach. 'And no ghostly smell of tobacco smoke either, surprise, surprise.'

'Well, it would have dissipated by now,' Maurice counters, but his conviction has been undermined, and its foundations weakened.

Victor thumps down the steps to join the women clustered together on the lower landing. 'Look, I think it's best everyone goes back to bed. Especially you, Maurice. You need to get some sleep, man, some proper sleep, to stop your mind playing tricks on you. That's all that's happening here.'

'I saw him . . . I did, Vic, I promise you I did.'

'I'm going to bed.' Victor sighs, starting back up the steps. 'And if the rest of you have an iota of sense, you'll do the same.'

'Wait!' Ida hurries to catch him. 'I don't want to walk back in the dark on my own, ghost or no ghost.'

Len calls out to his brother, uncertainty in his voice now. 'Are you going to be all right, Maurice? Perhaps Vic is right: perhaps you just woke up all muddled from a dream.'

Maurice claws at his forehead, his frustration and confusion as evident as the fight draining from his limbs. 'I don't know . . . I don't know anything anymore . . .'

'Try and get some rest,' Sarah suggests gently.

He surrenders to his defeat, looking lost now, and heartbreakingly deflated. 'Len, can I come in with you? I don't want to go to my room. I don't want to be alone.'

'Of course, old man.'

Broken and slumped, Maurice retreats into his brother's room. The door closes behind him, leaving Sarah alone on the landing. She releases a shuddering breath and waits until her unsteady pulse has become reassuringly regimented. Only then does she return to her own room, grateful for the strong scent of lavender that disguises the unmistakable odour of tobacco.

Chapter Nineteen

Maurice vacates the room the next morning when Sarah arrives to get Leonard ready for the day, but he is swift to return. She is pleased to see he has washed and shaved, but his eyes remain ringed with shadow, and the haunted look that was so striking in the night has become an inescapable part of him. The twitching beside his eye plagues him still, and as he helps Leonard into his chair, she can't help noticing that an involuntary tremor now affects both hands. Not wanting to stare, she instead opens the wardrobe and fingers her way through the wooden hangers until she finds what she is looking for.

'What are you doing with that?' Leonard demands, when he sees his dress uniform folded over her arm.

'I need to get your uniforms ready for the memorial ceremony.'

'I told you I'm not going. I thought you understood that.'

'I . . . I don't think I can g-g-go,' Maurice stammers. He looks everywhere but her face. 'I don't think I'm up to it.'

'What's this?' Victor fills the doorway. 'What's going on?'

'I was intending to get the uniforms ready for the memorial ceremony, but . . .' Sarah's voice fades to silence.

'I'm not going, I've made that clear.' The stubborn line of Leonard's mouth coupled with his jutting chin seems to accentuate his youth. Sarah is struck by the fact that despite all he has gone through, he is still so young. A boy cursed with the heart of a jaded man.

'And I'm not sure I can do it either,' Maurice confesses in a broken whisper.

A muscle ticks in Vic's freshly shaven jaw. 'Don't be ridiculous, Maurice, you've got to. For God's sake, your own brother's name is on that memorial. Len I can just about understand, though for what it's worth I don't think it's right and I don't think Hugo would be impressed. He was never one to flinch away from his responsibilities, and he would expect you both to live up to yours. You have a duty to show up, Maurice, and by God you will. You deserted the poor buggers for long enough during the war. The least you can do is honour their memory by showing up now.'

Maurice keeps his face directed at the ground. For the first time that morning, his cheeks flush with colour.

'Vic—'

'He's going, Len!' Victor snaps, ignoring the warning note in Leonard's voice. 'My God, he left us to face death alone while he cowered away in the safety of a hospital – easier to give in to weakness than to fight. If you have any sense of decency, Maurice, you will attend this ceremony and be the commanding officer you bloody well failed to be during the war.'

'Vic, that's enough!' Leonard shouts.

Maurice is shaking uncontrollably. A solitary tear trickles down his cheek.

'Maurice, Maurice, it's all right.' Leonard nearly slips from his chair as he strains to reach for his brother's hand. 'You were ill then. You didn't desert anyone. You weren't well. You weren't yourself.'

'I'm a coward, Len. Victor's right, Hugo would be ashamed of me.'

'You're not, you're not a coward, Maurice, you were ill, that's all, ill, and Hugo would have understood that. But you're better now,' Len insists. 'Do you hear me? You're better now.'

'Am I?'

Sarah catches her breath at the vulnerability betrayed in the question. Leonard pulls his brother into a firm hug, though Maurice's arms remain limp. Victor regards them both, grim-faced.

'Get his uniform looking shipshape, Sarah,' he instructs. He crosses to the embracing brothers. His hand hovers before coming to rest on Maurice's shoulder. Maurice does not respond to the contact. Vic clears his throat. When he speaks, his tone is conciliatory. 'You'll regret it, old man, if you don't show willing and do your bit. We have a responsibility. We can't shirk it.' He pats Maurice's shoulder and seems relieved to move away. 'Now come on, let's get downstairs. I don't know about you two, but I'm bloody famished. I want my breakfast.'

Following them onto the landing, Sarah watches in silence as the three men engage in the familiar exercise of transporting Leonard downwards, reburying as they do so the dormant resentments that had sprouted so unexpectedly. But this display of unity does nothing to thwart her suspicion that those ancient grudges persist, just below the surface. Waiting to rise again.

After lunch, having installed Leonard with Maurice in the library, Victor pulls on his shooting jacket and shoves his feet into his gumboots, before snatching his tweed cap from the peg. He stalks down the corridor towards the kitchen, irritation coursing through his veins. His need to get out of the house, to get away, if only for a brief period, is overwhelming.

As he slinks past the kitchen door, he hears Ida wittering on to Sarah about Mr Tibbs' failure to learn a new phrase. He rolls his eyes as he finds himself summoned by her shrill voice.

'Where are you off to?'

'I'm going to Home Farm to fetch a gundog from the kennels and then I'm going shooting.'

'Shooting?'

'It's the season, isn't it? I'm sure Sarah would appreciate a brace of pheasants.'

Sarah looks round from the sink. 'I could do them for dinner tomorrow, perhaps.'

'See?' He looks to Ida. 'I do like to make myself useful.'

He carries on to the gun room, taking a shotgun from the rack and filling his pockets with cartridges, before heading out via the back door.

Striding down the drive, his sense of liberation is as refreshing as it is complete, and he realises just how sick he is of Leonard's moping and Maurice's twitching and foolishness. The nonsense over the war memorial is the last straw. Backbone. That's what makes a man, he reflects. God knows Maurice has always been sadly lacking in that department, but Victor has covered for him long enough. He is growing intolerant of his best friend's weakness.

Glancing up at the livid clouds gathering above, he wonders how long he has before the rain starts and hopes it will be time enough to bag a few birds. He can almost feel the satisfying buck of the shotgun against his shoulder. It will do him good to vent his frustration.

As he nears the woods he hears the drone of an approaching car. His steps slow as a Model T Ford Coupelet emerges from the gloom. It is horribly familiar.

'Oh God.'

The car draws closer. He considers keeping his head down in the hope he won't be recognised, but given the state of both Maurice and Leonard, he isn't sure it's safe to let the vehicle reach its intended destination, so when it begins to slow, he prepares himself, fixing a smile.

'Mr Monroe, I thought that was you!' Verity calls from the lowered window as he draws abreast, the engine running. 'Off for a spot of shooting?'

'If I can, depending on the weather,' he says with a pointed upward glance.

'Oh well, I won't detain you. I was just off to the Hall, hoping to speak to Mr Stilwell.'

'I'm afraid Maurice is still unwell, Sergeant Verity. I'm not sure he's up to visitors. Leonard's with him.'

'Still? Oh dear, nothing serious, I hope?'

'A recurrence of an old malady. It should soon pass. Perhaps you could come back another day, though I struggle to believe there can be anything else we can help you with.'

The car falls silent as Verity kills the engine. The Sergeant's masked features give nothing away, but even so Victor's heart sinks a little as the Detective opens the car door and stands out.

'Well, you see, Mr Monroe, our investigation into the Higgins boy is proceeding apace,' he says, straightening his mackintosh as he eases the door shut. 'I'm afraid it's going to be necessary for us to have a poke about in Darkacre's woods.'

'I'm sorry, you've lost me.'

Verity smiles. 'Further scrutiny of the original investigation has revealed the woods here were, in fact, never included in the search area for the boy. The new information we have received suggests, well, perhaps we ought to.'

'Search our woods?'

'Search the Stilwells' woods, indeed.'

Victor notices the slight but does not react to it. He nods, rapidly collecting his thoughts. The wind is picking up, and the clouds above are melding into a threatening mass. 'Don't you need a warrant or some such?'

'Well, we were rather hoping, given Mr Stilwell's willingness to assist us with our enquiries, that – as I'm sure you've nothing to hide – there would be no objection to us having a team come and take a look.'

'Of course we have nothing to hide,' Victor says. The Detective Sergeant's expression remains elusive behind the painted copper. 'When are you proposing to start?'

'We would like to make a start in the morning. I can certainly confirm the details with you once the arrangements have been made. I wouldn't want us to just turn up and invade, so to speak.'

'Well, thank you, that would be appreciated.'

'The last thing we want is to cause you any inconvenience, especially when you have been so accommodating.'

'Indeed.'

Verity glances up at the sky as the light takes on a sickly yellow hue. 'Thank you so much for your time, Mr Monroe,' he says, making his way to the front of the car. 'Once our curiosity regarding the woods has been satisfied, I hope that we shall be able to leave you all in peace, but it would be remiss of us if we ignored this new information. We must think of his poor mother, and ensure no stone is left unturned this time.' He bends down to pull out the choke.

A raindrop strikes Victor's cheek. 'The woods here are pretty extensive. Forgive me for saying this, but I fear it'll be like searching for a needle in a haystack.'

Verity chuckles. 'Well, I'm relieved to say our informant has provided some details which we're hoping will narrow things down a little.'

Somehow Victor manages to remain impassive as he absorbs this titbit of information. 'Still, it's six years ago now. Things change.'

Verity tips his head in acknowledgement. 'Of course. There is no guarantee our search will prove successful, but if the boy did meet with an unfortunate end . . . he will be there, waiting to be found.' He gives the crank handle a firm turn. The engine putters into life.

'Quite.' Victor steps back as Verity opens the car door. Rain begins to patter. 'Well, I would say I wish you every success but I'm not sure that's quite the right way to put it.'

'Never fear, Mr Monroe. I understand you perfectly.' Verity lowers himself into the driver's seat. 'I fear you may have to abandon your shooting, Mr Monroe. It's going to be raining pitchforks and hammer handles out here in a minute.' He chuckles at Victor's expression. 'Not heard that one before?'

'No, I have . . .' Vic frowns, something gnawing at his memory. 'I just can't quite place where.'

The Sergeant pulls the car door shut. He leans towards the open window. 'I will be in touch before the end of the day to confirm our arrival time. Until tomorrow, Mr Monroe. Let's hope this wretched weather has passed by then, otherwise it'll be like reliving the mud and muck of the trenches and I'm sure none of us wish to do that.'

To Vic's surprise, the very thought provokes an involuntary shudder. 'Certainly not. I don't envy your men their task.'

'You know—' Verity looks through the rain-spotted windshield at the waterlogged grounds '—I often think of the brave souls who have remained in France to retrieve the dead, to secure them a decent burial. The sights they must be seeing.' The Sergeant shakes his head. He turns back to Vic, huddled against the rain. 'If Bobby Higgins has met such a fate, I think it only right we try and do the same. Everyone deserves to have a decent memorial to their life, to be properly remembered. Don't you agree?'

'I do indeed. And if you're right, if the boy is out there somewhere, I hope he can be found and laid to rest in a respectful manner.'

'Oh, I hope so, Mr Monroe. I certainly hope so. Now, I suggest you get inside, this rain is setting in. I say, that river is looking very swollen. Does it ever flood?'

'On occasion, but it's never reached the house yet, thank goodness.'

'I'm glad to hear it. Well, I won't detain you any longer. I'll be in touch.' Verity raises the window, then puts the car in gear.

Victor steps onto the grass to give him room to turn around, the narrow tyres sinking into the wet ground before returning to the stone driveway. The Sergeant departs with a cheery wave.

Victor watches the car disappear into the woods, his mind churning, a sick feeling in the pit of his stomach. He turns on his heel and heads back to the house.

It is not the rain that has scuppered his shooting. He now has far more pressing plans for the day.

Chapter Twenty

Sarah brings the afternoon tea tray to the library to discover Leonard is its only occupant.

'I've been deserted it seems,' he says with a wry smile.

She sets down the tray. 'Have they left you to freeze? You want a good blaze going to keep out the damp chill on days like this.' She adds two extra logs to the neglected fire and positions his chair closer so he can enjoy its benefits. When he asks, she locates a volume of poetry upon the shelves she has yet to dust, and hands it to him. As he begins to flick through the pages, the book spread in his lap, she moves to the window, sighing over the inclement weather. From her vantage point, she can see the angry swell of the river, the surging brown waters pushing eagerly against the tops of the banks. Already in places it has burst free, creating lakes where previously there had been shingle scoops and fallow land.

As she takes in the scene, her attention is caught by the sight of Maurice and Victor, tugging at sou'westers flapping on the wind as they stride out across the lawn, shovels in hand. Sarah frowns as they make their way towards the wooden footbridge that links the gardens to the meadow and woods on the far side of the river.

But just as he is on the brink of crossing, Maurice throws down his shovel and begins to back away. Victor is already part way across by the time he realises he is alone. She watches as he turns back, shouting words at Maurice that she has no hope of hearing, words that are greeted by tossed-up hands and backward steps. Victor makes a frantic dash, catching Maurice in a few long strides. He grabs his arm and when Maurice snatches himself free, Victor grabs it again. They stand face to face in the rain, and though Sarah cannot make out their features from this distance, the hostility in Victor's stance is easy to discern. Maintaining his hold on Maurice, he marches him back to the discarded shovel. He stoops to pick it up, never releasing his grip, then thrusts it against Maurice's body. With the briefest of hesitations, Maurice's hands close around its wooden handle. Victor nods in clear approval. His flattened palm rests between Maurice's shoulder blades as they walk side by side back to the bridge.

'Sarah? What are you looking at?'

'Victor and Maurice. They're walking towards the woods – with shovels. What on earth are they doing out in this?' She turns back to Leonard, perplexed. 'They'll catch their deaths – it's foul out there.'

Before he can answer, Ida bustles through the doorway, a dress slung between her arms.

'Oh Sarah, there you are. I was wondering whether you might be able to sew a button for me. One's come off the neck of this—'

'Ida, what are Maurice and Victor doing?'

Piqued by Leonard's blunt interruption, Ida is mealy-mouthed. 'How should I know?'

'They've gone outside. In this weather.'

As Ida follows his gesture to the rain-lashed windows, her look of petulance is fleetingly exchanged for one of fear, like a stylus displaced by dust before returning to the record's groove. She, too, rediscovers her tune.

'Oh, for goodness sake, Leonard! Maurice was concerned about the river getting too high. They've probably gone out to see if there's anything they can do to prevent it flooding. Maybe they're intending to dig some overflow channels or something, I really couldn't say.'

'Can you still see them, Sarah?' Leonard asks, his eyes locked on Ida's shifty expression.

Sarah looks again through the rain-distorted glass to the squally scene beyond. She scours the length of riverbank.

'I can't see them now.'

In the grate, the flames cower from the wind baying down the chimney.

'Ida—'

'Just leave them to it, Leonard. They're doing what needs to be done.' Ida scrunches the dress in clenched hands. 'Sarah, if you could see to this button. I'll leave it in the kitchen for you.'

'Yes, of course.'

'Ida—'

Ida parts her lips, but whatever rebuff she has for the dogged Leonard sits on the tip of her tongue unfulfilled. A moment later, only perfumed air remains of her presence.

'Oh God . . .'

'Leonard?' Alarmed by his sudden pallor, Sarah abandons her watch at the window and hurries to his side. She crouches down by his chair, her hand on the wheel for balance. 'Leonard, what is it?'

Keeping his own counsel, he fails to answer.

The storm erupts in earnest just after four o'clock. By Sarah's reckoning, the men have been gone for an hour. The rain, a steady, shimmering gauze when they left, turned to curtain rods soon after, fierce and unrelenting, and by four o'clock, the light has drained from the sky, and the wind, which has been teasing the trees all day, suddenly takes a vicious turn, growing angry and petulant, vindictive and aggressive, pulling and pushing, heaving and thrashing, stripping the trees of their rich autumnal dressing as if jealous of their finery. The darkening skies drain the tumbled leaves of their jewelled sheen, and the continuous downpour drowns their last vestiges of vibrancy. They smother the ground, sodden and bland, their shining beauty but a memory.

'Surely Victor and Maurice shouldn't be out in this?' Sarah protests to Ida when she comes to the kitchen to enquire about the evening meal.

'They are grown men, Sarah, and perfectly capable of looking after themselves. I suggest you concentrate on preparing dinner – they'll be grateful for a hot meal when they come in.'

But as Ida flounces out, Sarah detects flaws in her carefully constructed complacency.

Another hour passes, and there is still no sign of them. Sarah takes a fresh pot of tea to Leonard in the library.

'Are they back?' he asks, as soon as she enters. His concern matches her own. 'Take me to Ida, would you?'

Sarah gladly abandons the tea tray. The wheels of Leonard's

chair jiggle over the stone floor as she pushes him down the corridor. Rambling rose branches scrape at the windows, their thorns screeching against the glass as the wind buffets them loose from the outside walls. Leonard observes the increasing violence of the storm with a grave face.

They are crossing the reception hall when a white flash dazzles through the leaded windows followed by a deafening crack of thunder that stops Sarah in her tracks, her breath seizing from the sheer, unanticipated shock of it. Even Leonard leaps in his seat. There had been no warning, no distant rumble, just the eruption of electricity. Leonard's fingers grip the side of his chair.

'Come on, Sarah.'

Gathering herself, she guides him past the sofas, to the doorway of the drawing room.

Ida does not greet their arrival. She is standing at the window next to Mr Tibbs' cage, one thin arm covering her narrow waist, the other crossing her chest so that her fingertips rest heavily on her heart.

'Ida!'

Leonard blasts her name, matching the violence of the thunder. Unable to ignore him, and perhaps afraid to, she turns from the window just as lightning flashes through the room. Her face is deathly pale, and to Sarah's surprise, she has been crying. She jumps as thunder booms again.

'What are they doing, Ida?' Leonard's fingers form a vicelike grip on the arm of his chair, and Sarah suspects he would be shaking his sister-in-law now if he only had the legs to reach her.

'What do you think, Leonard?' Ida hisses. She turns back to

the window. 'I'm sure they won't be much longer,' she asserts, but this time there is no trace of her earlier glibness. 'They can't be.' Her words ring with desperation. And fear.

She flinches as white light illuminates them all. Without pause another crack splits the air.

'Maurice won't cope with this,' Leonard murmurs.

For once, Ida does not contradict him.

Chapter Twenty-One

Maurice does not want to be in the woods. The building wind thrashes through the autumnal canopies and the trees creak in protest, the sound as discordant as a poorly played fiddle. He shoots them an anxious look, fearful one of the swaying giants might crash down at any minute.

'We should leave . . . come back after the storm,' he calls above the soughing wind, but Victor doesn't even glance around.

The days of relentless rain have turned the narrow paths that weave their way through the woods into ribbons of slippery mire and the resulting black slime sucks at their boots. In places, chaotic patterns of cloven-hoofed tracks pit their way, and all well-worn ruts are now filled with brackish water. Above the wind, the angry rush of the river demands to be heard, warning of nature's unstoppable force.

Trudging on through the treacherous mud, Maurice's attention is reeled in by a broken tree whose bleached spine stands jagged above the woodland floor. His sluggish steps slow to a standstill as it tugs at a memory, projecting him into the past, to a summer's day six years before. Sounds of trilling birdsong, splashing water and laughter fill his ears. He closes his eyes, recalling the warmth of the sun on his face and the rosy glow behind his eyelids.

'Maurice!'

His eyes snap open. Victor stands before him. 'This is no time for bloody daydreaming!'

'No . . . I . . .' Maurice is confounded by vague recollections of days gone by. Something remains tantalisingly beyond his grasp, but he doesn't know what. The nagging sense that it is something significant, something he should remember, *needs* to remember, troubles him. But trying to capture it is like closing his fingers over a plume of smoke – when he opens his hand, there is nothing there, though the acrid scent on his skin hints at its existence.

'What?' Vic demands.

'I feel like there's something . . . something trapped in here—' Maurice presses his hand to his forehead '—something I can't get out, but I need to, I need to get it out. Something troubling me, but I just can't remember—'

'Then it can't be important,' Victor says, raising his voice against the storm. He glances up through the threadbare branches at the dulling sky. 'We haven't got time for this nonsense, Maurice, we must press on.' He turns back to the path.

'But—'

Vic spins around, cursing now. 'Let it go, Maurice! Whatever it is you think you need to remember, just let it go. If it really mattered, you would remember, wouldn't you? So just forget it and move on!'

Abandoning the path, they crunch over the brittle bones of bronzed bracken and are pricked by spurting holly. Unruly tangles of bramble block their way like nature's barbed wire – this truly is No Man's Land. They find gaps in the growth and push their way through, yanking themselves free when they become snagged on thorns. Soon, blood seeps from the scratches on their ice-cold hands.

'Vic, this is pointless,' Maurice calls over the howling wind and the hammering rain. He brushes his drenched fringe from his forehead then tries to waylay Victor's determined advance. 'Let's go back.'

Vic curses and throws him off. 'We can't do that Maurice. We have to move the body.'

'But what are the chances of us even finding it? And if we can't find it, the police won't either.'

Cursing again, Victor closes the gap between them. 'I've told you already. They know where to look. And what do you think will happen when they find it?'

'They'll just find a body. It doesn't mean it has anything to do with us.'

'For God's sake, Maurice, can you be more stupid?' Victor draws so close Maurice's icy skin is warmed by his breath. 'If that letter can lead them to the body, what else do you think might be in it? If someone knows enough to say where the body is buried, perhaps they know enough to say how the body came to be there in the first place.' He takes a step back, wiping the rain from his face, though his irritation is harder to dispel. 'If the police find that body where the letter tells them to look, then they're more likely to believe whatever else it says, and I don't know about you, but I'm not willing to take that risk. We move the body. If for no other purpose than to throw doubt on the rest of the letter's contents. Whatever they might be.'

'But if it implicated us in any way, wouldn't we know by now? Wouldn't that Inspector or Sergeant Verity have said something? You might be leaping to conclusions, Vic.'

'Those policemen are wily devils, and I can't shift the feeling Verity is playing with us in some way. We could already be suspects for all we know, but if we are, I have no intention of making it easy for them.'

Maurice catches Vic's arm as he starts to turn away. 'But Vic, even if we do dig the body up, won't they know? Surely they'll see the signs?'

'We'll be careful how we go about it. The ground's sodden, we can tamp it back down, replant some weeds, cover it up with leaves and brambles. I don't know, Maurice, but we'll find a way. I don't see that we have any other choice.' For the first time, Victor looks uncertain. The slip in his characteristic confidence shakes Maurice to his core. Victor draws his hand over his mouth. 'Look, maybe the letter isn't as precise as Verity's hoping, in which case, they might miss the site completely, but the important thing is, we can't let them find that body. And we'll stay here all night if needs be, to make sure they don't.' He grips Maurice's arms. 'Think of Leonard, Maurice.' He gives the thought time to sink in before releasing him. 'Now come on, I think it's around here somewhere.' He moves away, struggling through a tangle of briars to reach a new track carved across the woodland floor. 'Hurry up, Maurice!'

Maurice shudders, but the trembling continues. His body does not feel to be his own. He knows it is not a reaction to the cold, or the wind, or the rain. It is his demons rattling their cage, reminding him they are stirring. Reminding him he is powerless to contain them.

Battling against the force of his growing desperation, Maurice surveys the overgrown morass around him. His gaze passes over a vibrant laurel bush, planted as partridge cover, before stopping abruptly upon a fallen tree, rotten and decayed, furred by moss that gleams with rain. An image of his cream blazer draped over that very same trunk flashes into his mind's eye.

Here's as good a place as any.

His fingernails throb with the pressure of trapped dirt. The sensation is so overpowering that he looks down at his hands. Though they bear trickles of blood and streaks of mud, he is bewildered to see the fingernails themselves are clean. He looks back at the tree trunk and bellows Vic's name.

When Victor finally hears him above the storm, he tramps back. Maurice gestures towards the fallen tree, and then watches as Vic travels back through his own memory. He reaches the same destination.

'Yes.' Breaking into a relieved smile, he claps Maurice on the arm, but Maurice feels no sense of satisfaction. Only dread.

They scrabble from the path through the undergrowth to the fallen tree. Victor paces around it.

'Here. This is the spot,' he calls with absolute certainty. 'Come on, Maurice, let's get this over with.'

He raises his shovel and rams it into the ground.

An hour later, they are only three feet deep. The excised soil forms a muddy scrag heap to their side. The saturated excavation fills so quickly with rainwater that mud soon plasters their trousers and starches the bottoms of their sou'westers.

Maurice's freezing fingers grow stiff around the slick handle of his shovel. He has already lost all feeling in his feet, numbed by the pooling water soaking through his boots. His teeth chatter incessantly, though whether solely from the cold, he cannot tell.

'Come on, Maurice,' Victor grins, 'this is just like the good old days in France.' He thrusts his shovel in again, levelling off a blade full of dirt which he scoops over his shoulder. As he swings back, he stops. He darts Maurice a look. Maurice follows his eyes down.

Setting his shovel against the side of the trench, Victor drops into a squat. Plunging his fingers into the slime, he scrapes away the top level. Maurice peers over his shoulder. His stomach turns.

A scrap of cloth.

An ivory bone.

Without warning, lightning dazzles and thunder booms like an exploding shell. Out of sheer instinct, Maurice throws himself face down into the bottom of the trench, knocking Victor off his haunches. Mud plugs his nostrils and brackish water fills his mouth as Victor shouts his name. Gagging and retching, Maurice pushes himself back up. Lightning flashes again, brightening the sky like a phosphorous flare, illuminating spike-helmeted figures advancing through the trees. A scream rips from his throat.

'Jesus, Maurice!'

Maurice stares transfixed at the rifle-bearing soldiers, his chest so tight he cannot breathe. Words of warning lodge in his throat as thunder shudders through the air. He lifts a quivering hand.

'H-H-Hun.' The stammered word flies free like a glob of

phlegm. He sees the confusion on Victor's face as he twists round to study the gloaming.

'There's nothing there, Maurice.'

Brilliant lightning fleetingly eradicates the gloom. Maurice blinks. He wipes the rain from his eyes. The figures have vanished from the shadows. Only grey tree trunks stand before him. 'I thought I saw . . .' he starts, his heartbeat as chaotic as his thoughts.

'You saw nothing,' Victor says. 'We have to get this body out, Maurice.'

An eruption of thunder deafens them both. Maurice cries out as his legs buckle. He collapses into the sodden trench. Exposed roots scrape at his shoulders like skeletal fingers clawing free of their graves. Lightning bursts like a Very light overhead, its eerie illumination revealing a Tommy huddled at the far end of the trench. Rain drips from the lowered rim of his helmet, while the butt of his rifle sinks into the mud as his filthy fingers tighten around the barrel rising between his bent knees. Maurice chokes on his scream as thunder crashes.

You murdering bastard

Lightning forks through the blackened sky, the bolt striking a nearby tree with an ear-splitting crack. Bark explodes like shrapnel. Flames leap skywards, pillars of smoke rising against the gunmetal clouds. The bitter smell of burning clogs the dank air and as the fire takes hold, crackling and roaring, something deep inside Maurice's brain begins to shift, like a nut twisting loose from the threads of a bolt. The Tommy raises his head.

I'm done keeping your secrets

The nut tumbles free.

'Maurice, what are you playing at? Damn well get up and help me!'

Maurice looks at Victor like a blind man suddenly able to see, only to discover the world is an ugly place.

'Maurice! Get up!'

Victor reaches for him, but Maurice scrambles backwards, using the wall of the trench to work himself onto his feet.

'Don't touch me!'

'Fine!' Victor flings up his hands. 'I won't fucking touch you, but we need to get on.'

'No.' Thunder rumbles as Maurice clambers free of the trench. Victor follows suit. They stand over the half-dug grave that is on the verge of surrendering its secrets.

'What the devil is wrong with you?' Victor demands.

'I remember, Vic!' Maurice yells, leaning into the words, spittle flying.

'What the hell are you talking about now?'

'I remember the shell hole. I remember that night in No Man's Land.'

'Look at us, Maurice!' Rain drips from Victor's outstretched arms as he presents himself, his boots sinking into the mire, rivulets streaming the length of his sou'wester. 'It's hardly a wonder you remember; it's like we're bloody there. Back in fucking No Man's Land. So let's just dig this bloody body up so we can get *the fuck* out of here.'

'No!'

'For fuck's sake . . .' Victor launches himself at Maurice. Grabbing his sou'wester he yanks him forward so they stand nose to nose in the darkness. Sheet lightning silvers their filthy faces. Thunder booms.

'I remember, Vic,' Maurice hisses, quaking. 'I remember what Joe Durham said in the shell hole, about what really happened that day with Bobby. I know, Vic. I know the truth. God help me . . . *I remember*!'

Chapter Twenty-Two

The years of effort, of hiding secrets and telling lies, of suppressing passions and nursing disappointments, come tumbling down on Victor all at once. He is weary beyond belief.

'Jesus, Maurice.' His shoulders sag and his head sinks from the exhaustion of it all. 'Maurice, whatever you think you remember, whatever you think you know—'

But his words are lost to a thunderclap. It proves too much for Maurice's fragmenting mind. He screams again, cowering, and as the rumble disperses, he sets off running, slipping chaotically through the mud. Victor's bellowed appeals are drowned out by the wind-beaten trees crashing above him like storm-tossed waves upon a ruthless shore.

Vic battles his way through the brambles, their piercing spines tearing his sodden clothing and ripping his skin. They almost bring him down as his foot catches on a stubborn spurt, forcing him to hop to keep his balance until he can wrench himself free. Finally, he breaks through, and smashes his way beyond the dripping bracken to the path. He skids on the rain-slickened earth like a hapless skater on ice. His heart pounding, he pushes on, the mud slurping greedily at his boots.

It isn't long before he catches up with Maurice's fleeing

figure. Dazzling sheet lightning sends Maurice careering into a tree trunk, his arms flying up in self-protection as his knees give way beneath him.

'Christ, Maurice!' Victor gasps, doubling up, hands on his knees, trying to catch his breath.

Maurice looks up at him. Rivulets of rain run through the dark hair plastered to his scalp onto his cheeks, mingling with the tears Victor suspects he is crying, his eyes red and swollen as they are. The trees whine and moan in a cacophonous symphony. A branch crashes to the ground just beyond them. Maurice shrinks against the tree trunk.

'Maurice . . . Maurice! Come on!'

Maurice pushes himself to his feet. Breathing hard, he wipes his nose with the back of his hand. With a flare of defiance, he staggers back to the path.

'Jesus, Maurice, wait!' Victor's patience has shredded. Maurice is making his ungainly escape, his progress impeded by the treacherous conditions – the mud, the rain, and the wind that seems determined to beat him back even as he pushes against it. Victor bellows with fury, then takes off after him.

The edge of the wood comes into sight, the final row of trees forming inky striations against the darkened sky. Victor closes the gap between himself and Maurice. As soon as he is within reach, he lunges for him.

Maurice yelps with surprise, whirling round, his fist flying so aimlessly it is easy for Victor to recoil beyond its range. He is bigger, stronger than Maurice, and always has been. He grips Maurice's upper arms, his teeth gritted as icy rain streams down his furious face – but deep within him, his desperation is rising.

'God damn it, Maurice! This isn't you. You must calm yourself.'

'I know now, Vic,' Maurice's assertion seems to lend him strength as he yanks free of Victor's manacles. 'I know the truth . . . I *know* . . .'

'You're confused.'

'No!' Maurice shoves him hard. Victor staggers back, unprepared for the force of it. 'You betrayed me, Vic . . . you . . . you *lied* to me . . .'

'Maurice . . . this isn't you . . . this is like before . . .'

Vic sees his insidious words provoke a flash of doubt, but even so Maurice seems determined to deny them leverage. A flash of lightning fleetingly turns night into day as another clap of thunder sends him charging towards the tree line. Though exhausted, Vic sets off in pursuit, the wind chasing behind like a pack of hounds baying for blood.

Bursting from the woods, Maurice runs across the meadow towards Darkacre Hall, silhouetted against the steel horizon. He stumbles on hassocks of glistening grass and when his foot catches the edge of a rabbit hole, he is sent flying. He hits the ground hard, but before Victor can reach him, he is on his feet and making a determined sprint for home.

'L-L-Leave me alone!' he cries, spinning back, before racing on again.

As they approach the river, their feet splash into lying water. Victor draws up in surprise. Lightning flashes off the fluid surface spread wide around him. His steps become tentative. He is fearful of the hidden bank, aware he could plunge into the river's torrid depths without warning. Maurice is showing no such caution. He careers through the ankle-deep water without care. Ignoring his better judgement, Victor jogs after him, sloshing through the freezing flood that now covers the meadow. Ahead of him, Maurice has reached the footbridge. Gaining in confidence, adhering to Maurice's route, Victor pushes on.

By the time he reaches the same spot, Maurice is already running across the lawn on the other side. Victor hears splashing and realises with sobering shock that the water has spread both sides of the river. He tries to hurry, keen to intercept Maurice before he reaches the house and blurts out God only knows what, but his boots slip on the bridge's rain-greased planks and his feet fly out from underneath him. He lands hard on his side, pain exploding in his hip. Through the gaps between the planks he sees the surging torrent gushing beneath him, usurping the river's natural channel. Cursing, he hauls himself up, his thigh smarting. Gingerly placing his feet, he forges ahead.

Once off the bridge, he tries to hail Maurice a final time, but his efforts prove futile. Leaving the lawn, Maurice races across the forecourt, scattering chippings in his haste to reach the front door, where a pinprick of light flickers behind the diamond-leaded panes of the small window beside it, a warming beacon in the darkness, guiding weary travellers to safety. And safety seems to be paramount in Maurice's mind, as he grasps the twisted metal of the bell pull and yanks it down.

*

'The storm must have knocked out the power,' Sarah calls out, placing a candlestick on the stone ledge of the lobby window, before continuing into the reception hall with the oil lamp she has brought from the kitchen. Its golden glow guides her through the dimness to where Ida and Leonard are waiting by the fireplace. She sets the lamp down on the table. 'I'll light the fire,' she offers. The anxiety etched on Leonard's face knots her stomach.

'They should never have gone out there,' he says, his voice rough.

Ida says nothing; she doesn't need to. Her growing concern is evident to all. She moves aside to give Sarah access to the grate. The wind gusts down the chimney, and Sarah wonders if she will manage to get a fire going at all. She strikes a match and nestles it amongst the screwed-up newspaper and kindling laid earlier. The paper catches, its edges charring as flames lick and crackle. She waits until the fire has taken to the kindling in earnest before adding a pair of logs. She gets to her feet just as the doorbell jangles with frantic alarm.

'It must be them!' Ida cries, but rather than run to answer it, she shrinks back against the wall of the fireplace, as if fearful of what she will discover. Wiping her hands clean, Sarah hurries across the stone flags, her heartbeat as frenzied as the tolling bell.

'Damn it, Ida, don't just stand there. Wheel me through,' Leonard demands.

Sarah is relieved she has not been left to answer the door alone. The bell tips side to side, deafening, as her butterfingers struggle with the bolts. It takes a firm hand to turn the key, but, at last, the door is released from its constraints.

A sudden gust of wind snatches the ancient timber from her hands, and she yelps with fright as it flies back into the wall. Gasping and sobbing, Maurice stumbles into the gloomy lobby on legs barely able to hold him. Victor runs in behind, panting heavily. Sarah wrestles the door shut and a strange hush descends, the wail of the wind muted by the dense oak that now holds it at bay. Wet leaves gusted onto the quarry tiles stick to the soles of her shoes.

'Dear God, Maurice.' Ida gasps, drawing back.

'Stay away from me!' In his haste to distance himself, Maurice trips over his feet and collides with the coat stand. The brass shell case clatters onto its side.

'Maurice . . .' Victor pushes dripping hair from his forehead. He takes a cautious step forward, approaching Maurice as he might approach a skittish horse, his hands open-palmed and held wide.

'Stay back! All of you! Stay away from me!'

Lightning pierces the window, irradiating the vestibule, making a mockery of the candle's mean glow. Maurice cringes as thunder shudders through the building. The candle's flame crackles and dips, as wind rattles the casement against its frame.

Bang. Bang. Bang.

Ida screeches, jumping out of her skin in time with the violent hammering on the front door.

'What the hell . . .' Victor mutters, spinning back to face the roughly hewn wood.

The brass bell set high above the door tips manically from side to side.

'Don't open it!' Ida begs.

Bang. Bang. Bang.

'We can't just ignore it.' But Sarah's protestations fail to provoke a response. They stare at the door. No one moves.

The bell clangs again. Darting past Victor, Sarah forces round the key and lifts the latch. The wind steals the breath from her lungs as she struggles to hold the door. Rain slants into the hallway, speckling the russet tiles.

On the doorstep, stands a figure wreathed in shadows. His trilby hat is low on his forehead, while his buttoned mackintosh hangs heavy, drenched below the knees, and his trouser legs are so wet, they cling to him like a second skin.

'I'm so sorry to trouble you yet again . . .' the words lisp from him, discernible though monstrously distorted. 'But I've run into a spot of bother. Do you mind?'

A mercury flare illuminates the visitor's features, flashing off his mask of painted copper. Thunder crashes.

The faceless man steps inside.

Chapter Twenty-Three

Having forced the door shut, Sarah fights to steady her thudding heart as she turns to face their new arrival.

'You're soaked through.'

Small puddles form on the quarry-tiled floor as rain drips from Sergeant Verity's saturated clothing.

'Well, it could have been a lot worse,' he chuckles ruefully, removing his sodden trilby. 'I was coming, as I promised Mr Monroe, to tell you our intended arrival time for tomorrow. The river has quite thoroughly burst its banks, you know, and I saw as I came up your drive towards the bridge that it was raging high, but . . .' He taps his hat against his hand, provoking a flurry of raindrops. 'I should have turned back at that point, but I'm afraid, rather foolishly, I decided to risk it.'

'What happened?' Ida asks.

The Detective Sergeant sighs, his painted mask ghoulish in the flickering candlelight. 'I was halfway across when the bridge collapsed.'

'Collapsed?' Victor exclaims.

'Yes.' Verity twists round to address him. 'It gave way beneath my car. I thought I was a goner, I can tell you. One minute I was driving over, the next thing I know the car is being swept downriver. If it hadn't jammed into the bank, I fear I wouldn't be here now. As it is, I was able to scramble out to safety.' He opens his arms to present himself. 'Though I got a little wet in the process.'

'The bridge has collapsed?'

'I'm afraid so, it's quite gone, and the flooding is widespread, as you can imagine. I hate to say it, but I think you might find yourselves rather stranded – unless there's another route out of the valley? Ah . . . I feared not. I feel awful about this, but it may be necessary for me to impose on your hospitality for a little while.'

He tries to smile, but his body is now quivering within the freezing layers of wet clothing. His teeth chatter over ragged breaths.

'You'll perish in those wet clothes,' Sarah says quickly. 'Come through to the kitchen, it's warm in there by the range. We'll find you something dry to put on.'

Instinctively, she appeals to Leonard.

'Oh please, help yourself to anything of mine,' he says. 'I shan't be needing them anymore.'

'Right, this way.' Sarah raises a hesitant hand to the Sergeant's elbow, while the others look on with mounting horror.

'You are most kind. I'm so sorry to be such a nuisance.'

As Verity casts wide his look of apology, he spots Maurice on the floor, tucked in tight against the edge of the settle, his knees drawn up to his chin, his arms banding his legs.

'Good evening, Mr Stilwell.'

Ida opens her mouth, but promptly shuts it again. Even Victor appears at a loss, while Maurice simply fails to respond at all. The side of the Sergeant's mouth curves out from the harsh edge of the copper plate as he turns to Sarah.

'Please, lead the way.'

She nods dumbly, then starts off down the corridor, her steps confident despite the low light. The Detective Sergeant follows close behind, his shoes squelching. They are soon swallowed by shadows, vanishing from sight.

'Dear God! What are we—' Ida begins, but Victor's hand darts up to silence her. He indicates for them to withdraw somewhere private. Fretful, she nods her agreement, but before she can leave, Leonard grabs her wrist. With some reluctance, she takes the handles of his wheelchair and pushes him towards the reception hall.

Victor shrugs off his dripping sou'wester and hangs it on the coat stand, Maurice scuttling further into the corner as he does so. He regards the tight knot of Maurice's figure with conflicting emotions.

'You can stay here if you like, but if you've got a grain of sense left, you'll come with us. We need to talk.'

He starts for the doorway, but before he reaches it, he whips around and drops to his haunches. 'Whatever you think you remember, Maurice, I can tell you now, it's not true. You must trust me. You've always trusted me, and I've always seen you right. I've always looked after you, Maurice. You've got to let me do that now, do you understand?' When Maurice refuses to respond, he leans towards him. His voice comes low and venomous. 'If you fuck this up, we'll all be swinging from Pierrepoint's rope.' He rises. Maurice does not move. Vic bites back his temper as best he can. 'Now, be a good fellow, get a grip, and come and join us.'

Maurice tightens his overlapping tangle of his limbs, pressing his forehead into the hard wall of his knees. Realising he is fighting a lost cause, Victor joins the others in the reception hall.

Firelight spills over the hearth to catch the ends of the sofas, while the oil lamp on the low table provides an extra pool of light for Leonard's wheelchair. Ida has positioned herself before the fire, her palms open to the flames, and yet she is shivering uncontrollably. She welcomes Victor's arrival with relief and takes a faltering step in his direction, but then catches sight of Leonard watching her. She remains where she is.

'What on earth are we going to d—' She stops abruptly, distracted by the shifting darkness in the doorway. Fearful the Sergeant has returned already, Vic is relieved when, instead, Maurice shuffles into the room. He does not come to join them but hovers, uncertain, in the shadows.

'Come in, Maurice,' Leonard implores him. 'Come on.' He holds out his hand, and the solace he promises seems to encourage Maurice. He slumps onto the sofa beside Leonard's chair, his head hanging low. No one speaks. The fire crackles between them.

'What are we going to do now?' Ida asks in a hushed voice.

Victor takes a place on the empty sofa opposite Maurice, who immediately inches further away. Victor notices the shun as he contemplates what is now at risk. His heart aches more than he had anticipated. Already exhausted and now beleaguered, he buries his face in his hands, trying to think, trying to determine a route to lead them to safety once more. Whether any of them have ever appreciated it or not, it is what he has always done – or tried to do – though at times his motives have been laced with more self-interest than perhaps they ought. As he raises his head, he realises for the first time his hands are filthy, mud-covered, and scraped, the cuts beaded with dried blood. He wonders if the Detective Sergeant noticed. And if he did, what he must have thought.

'What were you doing out there?' Leonard asks, looking to Victor when Maurice fails to lift his head.

'What do you think?' Closing his eyes, Victor rubs his forehead. 'I shouldn't have taken Maurice out.' He glances at the figure opposite. 'Conditions as they were . . . it was too raw. Too reminiscent.'

Ida turns back to the fire. Her fingers retract into little fists, the fabric of her skirt caught in their midst.

Leonard's breath shudders from him. 'You shouldn't have gone.'

'What choice did I have?' Victor springs to his feet and begins to prowl away from the sofas, crisscrossing the flagstone floor. 'As it is, we didn't even get the job finished. And the damned police are coming tomorrow morning,' he whispers harshly.

'They won't be now.' Leonard's observation brings Victor's restless movement to a halt. 'If the bridge is out, they won't be able to reach us.'

'Can they find another way into the woods?' Ida asks, turning back to them.

Leonard shakes his head. 'That area of the woods is cut off by the boundary wall. The only other entry point would be from Home Farm, but if the river's burst its banks all along, the likelihood is the access lane there will be impassable too.

My guess is, they won't attempt any investigations now until the floodwater has receded.'

'And what about us, here?' Ida drops down to perch on the edge of the sofa. 'If the bridge is out, we're cut off too, aren't we? That awful man is going to be staying with us until we have a way of getting him out of here.'

'I'll find a way around that.' Victor leaves the shadows to return to the light. 'I'll bloody row him back across the river myself if I have to.'

'I can't help feeling judgement day is coming,' Leonard says, staring into the flames.

'Look.' Victor sits down abruptly. He scans them all – Maurice dejected, Ida terrified, Leonard resigned – and he feels a surge of desperation. 'The past is done and dusted. We are still here—'

'Perhaps we shouldn't be.'

Victor chooses to ignore Leonard's interjection; instead he transfers his attention to Maurice, broken yet belligerent. He is by far the greatest threat.

'Let's not forget, we did what we did to protect Ida.'

Ida looks down at her hands, trembling upon her knees. Vic shuffles forwards, the sofa wheezing beneath him. 'That boy . . .' he fights to keep his voice steady. 'We had to protect Ida. Especially you, Maurice . . . as her husband . . .'

Maurice rises slowly from the sofa. The firelight plays upon his harrowed features.

'Her husband,' he echoes. He swallows hard. 'I told you. I remember now what Durham said about that day when we were in the shell hole.'

'Joe Durham was a liar, Maurice.' Victor leaps to his feet,

matching Maurice in height and surpassing him in stature. He glances towards the door, remembering to be on his guard. He drops his voice. 'Do you remember what he accused you of? Do you? And that wasn't true, was it? You wouldn't have done such a thing, would you? You couldn't have.' Seeing his seeds of doubt are falling on fertile ground, he presses his advantage. 'So everything else Joe Durham said must have been a lie too. Whatever you think you remember—'

'What did Joe say?'

Vic bats away Leonard's untimely interruption. 'It doesn't matter.'

'It does.'

'You know what he said. And for God's sake keep your voice down,' Vic hisses.

'Not about that day, I don't. I had no idea he'd said anything about it.' Leonard's persistence doesn't drop with his pitch. He looks up at his brother. 'Maurice? What did Joe say? What did Joe tell you in the shell hole?'

'He said . . . he said . . .' Maurice's voice falters. 'He said, Bobby Higgins wasn't attacking Ida that day . . . he was trying to save her . . . he thought he was saving her . . .'

'Saving her from who?' Leonard asks, bewildered.

Maurice looks to his brother. Then his gaze shifts.

'Victor.'

Chapter Twenty-Four

'What nonsense.' Ida's head jerks up. Her voice quavers. 'Why on earth would I need saving from Victor?'

'How could he possibly know that?' Leonard asks. 'How could Joe know what Bobby was thinking?'

'Because he was there.' Agitated, Maurice stalks towards the towering window overlooking the front. The curtains have not yet been drawn against the deepening night. The wind batters the rain-dappled panes, forcing its way through the lead mouldings and the gaps in the frame. The infiltrating draught insinuates itself through the fabric of Maurice's damp clothing and circles his neck like an icy chain. Away from the warmth of the fire, he begins to shiver anew. 'He said he was there in the woods, with Bobby.' He seeks out his brother. 'That's what he told us in the shell hole. I remember! I remember it all now. It's like . . . it's like a dam has burst in my brain. I can remember everything he said that night.'

'What *he said*,' Victor growls. 'Weren't *we* there in the woods that day too? Didn't *we* see it all with our own eyes? Why would you believe him, even for a moment? He was a liar, don't forget that, Maurice. Joe Durham was a liar. Or have you conveniently forgotten the lie he told about you? He'd say anything to save his own skin. He was nothing more than a damn coward and a liar.'

Maurice's conviction falters again. 'What he said about me . . .'

'That's right. The allegation he made against you . . . it wasn't true.'

'It wasn't, was it, Vic?' Maurice whispers, lost in the past again, struggling to make sense of competing memories and distorted recollections. 'What he said . . . I didn't . . . did I?' His breathing grows rapid as tears fill his eyes. 'Did I, Vic?'

'Of course not, old man.' Vic crosses to him swiftly. Taking hold of his arms, he speaks with reassuring authority. 'You would never do such a thing.'

Leonard looks away with the aversion of a surgical student queasy at the sight of blood.

The sound of approaching footfall hushes them all. Ida rises unsteadily. Gathering herself, she hurries to Maurice, slipping her arm through his. Victor rakes his fingers through his drying hair and faces the blank doorway in anticipation of the imminent arrivals.

'You're looking somewhat drier, Sergeant,' he says when they appear, his voice a little too loud.

'Yes, indeed, Sarah here has been most kind.'

Verity ambles into the room, neatly dressed in flannels, shirt, and jumper. Sarah follows a few respectful paces behind, a candlestick in her hand, its light licking her cheek. Ida takes advantage of the interruption to guide Maurice back to the sofa, and as she sits, she tugs him down with her. She presses herself against his side.

The Detective Sergeant watches them closely from his position just beyond the lamplight. He steps from the shielding darkness to better address Leonard. 'And I'm very grateful for the loan of the clothes, thank you, Mr Stilwell.'

'Leonard please. And you're welcome. They look much better on you than they would on me.'

A log slips in the fire. Conversation eludes them all. Victor draws the curtains. The harsh scrape of the rings on the pole sets his nerves on edge, like fingernails down a chalkboard.

'I'll just set an extra place at the table,' Sarah says, filling the uneasy silence. Her steps patter off the flagstones. She disappears through the dining room door.

'I must apologise most profusely again for imposing on you like this.' Verity rocks on his heels, his hands clasped behind him.

With apparent effort, Leonard adopts the role of host, though he looks ill-at-ease with the responsibility. 'Not at all. It couldn't be helped.'

'No, no indeed, this storm . . .' As if to reinforce Verity's words, rain clatters against the window and wind moans in the chimney breast. 'Well, the weather of late . . . quite horrendous.'

'I would imagine it'll put a kibosh on your plans for digging up the wood tomorrow?'

Verity sighs. 'Yes, I fear so. In this weather it would be a near impossible task.'

'I dare say there are people you'll need to notify?' Victor interjects.

'Well, ideally, yes, but regrettably it's not possible, in the circumstances.'

'In the circumstances?'

'Sergeant Verity has tried to telephone already,' Sarah's disembodied voice drifts from the shadows. A flicker of light appears in the dining room doorway and Sarah looms into sight behind it. 'The lines must be down.'

'Yes indeed,' Verity confirms regretfully. 'I drove here because I'd had no joy trying to get through on the telephone.'

'Dinner shouldn't be much longer.' Sarah draws nearer, her face a picture of concern as she looks between Maurice and Victor. 'If anyone wants to change, now would be the time.'

'Forgive me,' Verity says, 'but I couldn't help noticing Mr Monroe, Mr Stilwell, that it looks as if you too have been caught out in the storm?'

'Yes—' Victor summons a bold smile '—Maurice and I decided to survey some of the fields, to evaluate the damage being done by all this rain. Our timing couldn't have been worse. We were drowned rats in no time. In fact, we'd only just got back when you arrived.'

'Then I am mortified my turning up has delayed you from getting dried off.'

'Sergeant Verity is right,' Ida pipes up, a tell-tale waver in her voice. 'You must change.'

'Indeed we must. Maurice?'

'Yes.' Maurice's voice is faint, but chivvied by Ida, he rises from the sofa.

'Please excuse us,' Victor says, his confidence restored. 'We'll rejoin you shortly. In the meantime, Sergeant Verity, do make yourself at home.'

The atmosphere in the dining room is tense. After polite opening pleasantries, they eat in a depth of silence better suited to the refectory of a Holy Order. Only the occasional teeth-tingling screech of cutlery on porcelain punctures it. Periodically, Ida glances across at Maurice, who sits subdued, pushing his meagre portion around his plate with little enthusiasm and a great deal of distraction. His raised fork betrays the tremor in his hand, and he appears to forget his purpose, until, with a little jolt of surprise, he remembers to insert the skewered mouthful, chewing with preoccupation as his eye twitches and flickers.

It does not escape Ida's notice that she is not the only one watching her husband. The Detective Sergeant's surreptitious inspection renders her uneasy, but it is impossible to know what he is thinking behind the painted visage with its fixed look of indifference. Realising he has been clocked, Verity returns his attention to his dinner. She finds herself watching on with morbid fascination as his loaded fork advances towards his mouth, but she looks away at the last minute, repulsed by the thought of what she might inadvertently glimpse, the distortion that lurks behind the mask – the missing teeth, the gummy jaw, the malformed palate. Her stomach turns.

'Damn nuisance about the telephone lines,' Victor says at last.

'Do you have anyone at home who will be worried about you, Sergeant?' Ida asks, unable to contain her curiosity.

Verity doesn't answer immediately. He finishes his mouthful, rests his cutlery on his plate, then reaches for his wine glass to take a sip of the Chateau Margaux Leonard insisted be brought up from the cellar. He savours it with clear appreciation, then sets the glass back down.

'Would it surprise you, Mrs Stilwell, to learn that I am indeed married?'

Ida experiences a sudden rush of heat to her cheeks, perturbed that the Sergeant has somehow managed to perceive exactly what she was thinking. It is incomprehensible to her that someone so horribly disfigured could garner anyone's love and devotion. She stumbles over her rejoinder and reaches for her own wine glass to cover her embarrassment. She gets the distinct impression that he is enjoying her discomfort, an impression reinforced by his soft chuckle.

'I suspect it would,' he says, when he clearly feels she has been humiliated enough. 'After all, what sane woman could possibly love this?' He presents his face with a sweep of his hand. 'And yet, one such woman does exist. In sickness and in health. I am blessed that she will, right now, be awaiting my return.'

'Won't she be worried?' Leonard asks. 'If you don't come home?'

'I dare say she will deduce the weather has detained me. She is not one to panic, or to create doom-laden scenarios in her mind. She is a woman who has great faith in me, and in truth . . . well, she would not deem it fair that I had survived the war against all odds . . .' his fingers stray to the metal mask '. . . only to perish in a foolish flood. And because of that conviction, she will no doubt, quite sensibly, believe I am safe and well, but temporarily out of touch.'

'You are lucky to have the love of such a woman.' Victor takes a gulp of wine. He does not look Verity's way.

'I am indeed. And I am grateful for it every day.'

'And how did you meet this . . . paragon?' Ida asks icily, aware that Maurice's pain-filled eyes now seem to be evaluating her. When she meets them, they fall back to his plate.

The soft chuckle comes again, warmed by fond reminiscence this time. 'She was the sister of one of the men serving in my platoon. I was a platoon sergeant by the time the war started, you see, a career soldier, and given the nature of the job, I had never expected to marry. We had a few days' leave and one of the lads was insistent I join him at a teashop where he'd arranged to meet his sister. I must admit I was rather reluctant to do so, but the alternative of too much drink in a dubious public house with the rest of the boys didn't hold much appeal either. So I went along, thinking I would say hello, take a cup of tea, then make my excuses and leave.

'She was already seated when we arrived, at a small round table draped with a white cloth and decorated with a tiny cut-glass vase of wildflowers, and the moment she looked up and smiled, I knew I wouldn't be going anywhere. I wouldn't be able to. She had ensnared me, you see, with that one, simple, heartfelt gesture, a smile that lit her eyes, and wrapped me in warmth the like of which I had never thought existed.' He huffs, mocking his own sentimentality. 'And so, it started from there. After that first meeting, we entered into correspondence, and if I hadn't already fallen in love with her in that little teashop, I certainly did so through those letters.'

'Were you married before . . .' Ida stops herself just in time.

'No . . . no . . .' Understanding her immediately, the Sergeant smiles at her blatant curiosity. 'We had become engaged, but when I was wounded . . . when I came to appreciate the extent of my injuries . . . I dictated a letter to her from hospital, releasing her. I told her she would be happier without me now, that it would be best if she found someone else.'

He pauses, the pain of the memory evident in his halting

voice and the flicker in his natural forehead. 'I received a reply by return. A single sheet of notepaper, with a solitary word written in its midst: *No*. She had underlined it three times.'

He smiles. 'There was no changing her mind. She took it upon herself to nurse me back to health and gave me a reason to carry on when I thought my life was over . . . when my life should have been over. I am indebted to her, and I do not say that glibly. There is not a day goes by when I am not in awe of the love she shows me – and it never fails to amaze me that it is possible to be so consumed by my feelings for her. We are in perfect harmony, and, believe me, I know how fortunate I am to be able to say that.' He plays with the stem of his glass, the ruby-coloured wine glowing intermittently under the auspices of candlelight. 'There is nothing I wouldn't do for her. I would walk through fire if I thought it would make her happy. Whatever she might ask of me, it will never be too much – her love has made me a rich man.'

Leonard sets down his fork. Ida brings her glass to her lips, in part to conceal the misery now written in the pull of her mouth. Maurice's gaze remains trained upon his plate, while Victor drains his glass and pours himself another.

The Detective Sergeant surveys their responses, his thoughts concealed in copper. He picks up his cutlery and compliments Sarah on her excellent stew.

Afterwards, they retire to the drawing room. The wind continues to gust down the chimney, buckling the flames in the grate, while rain crackles against the windowpanes, though the sound is muffled by the thick velvet drapes closed against the darkness.

Victor plays host, distributing glasses of whiskey to the men, and sherry to the women, while Maurice occupies the armchair closest to the fire, lost to silent contemplation, his left knee bouncing. He has yet to speak half a dozen words to the Detective, and Victor burns with resentment that, once again, it is being left to him to carry the evening and safeguard them all from their unwanted guest.

After a hushed conversation with Ida at Mr Tibbs' cage, Sarah leaves the room. Sergeant Verity notes her departure.

'She's just gone to make you up a bed,' Ida explains. 'I'm afraid it won't be aired, but then we weren't expecting guests.'

'I'm sure it will be quite comfortable. I really am extremely grateful to you, Mrs Stilwell, for your generous hospitality.'

Ida receives his gratitude with cool accord, then returns to the company of her parrot, which is moving up its cage, its claws locked around the vertical bars, its beak clicking against the metal as it hauls itself towards the domed roof, while issuing a dazzling array of clicks and chirrups.

'What a magnificent creature,' Verity observes.

'He's an African Grey Parrot,' Ida says brightly, relieved to find comfortable territory with the man. 'A present from Maurice. He's the cleverest thing. I'm teaching him to speak, you know. Show the Detective Sergeant how clever you are, Mr Tibbs. *Hello*.'

'*Hello*.'

'There!' She beams at the Sergeant. 'Isn't that marvellous?'

'Quite surprising, indeed,' Verity says, raising his glass to toast the silver bird.

With the conclusion of Mr Tibbs' performance, they fall silent once again. A log splutters and bangs in the grate, causing

Maurice to gasp and flinch as sparks arc outwards onto the hearth rug. They are quickly stamped out by Victor. Maurice's fingers blanch around his whiskey glass.

'Shall we have some music?' There is a hint of desperation in Leonard's suggestion.

'Yes . . . yes, why not?' Victor says, crossing to the gramophone. He selects a shellac disc of ragtime and cranks the gramophone handle. Its energetic rhythm assaults the silence. Maurice screws his eyes shut and begins massaging his temples. Abandoning the bird cage, Ida moves across to the sofa, careful to give Verity's chair a wide berth. The toe of her shoe taps the rug in time to the jaunty music and she shares a smile with Victor as he hands her a fresh glass of sherry.

Sarah returns, offering to make coffee, but the consensus is for more alcohol, so Victor does the honours while she takes a seat towards the edge of the room, her chair a little removed from the comfortable circle formed by the others.

Fragments of soot loosened by the rain tumble down the chimney into the fire.

'What a night,' Sarah observes.

'*Floppy. Floppy. Floppy.*'

Maurice's head jerks up, his face suddenly waxen. 'What did you say?'

'I was just commenting on the weather . . . what a night.' Sarah's shoulders lift with bemusement.

'*Floppy. Floppy. Floppy.*'

Ida's hand flies to her mouth. Victor's raised whiskey glass fails to reach his lips.

Maurice rises on unsteady legs, staring at the parrot now bobbing its head.

'Floppy,' he whispers.

'Jesus.' Leonard manoeuvres himself to face the domed cage. Sarah absorbs their collective horror. 'I don't understand.'

Maurice whirls towards Ida. 'Did you teach him that?'

'Of course not! Why would I?'

'I must confess I too feel as if I am missing something.' Sergeant Verity regards them both quizzically. He finds himself ignored.

'He's never said that before. I promise you, Maurice, it wasn't me.' Ida's desire to impress her innocence upon her husband brings her to her feet.

'Floppy was the nickname our brother Hugo gave to Maurice, because of his heavy fringe,' Leonard says, taking pity on the Detective's evident confusion. He half-laughs at the memory, but his humour proves transient. Something else replaces it, something far more serious. 'Hugo died in the war.'

'No one has ever called me that . . . only him.' Struggling to master his emotions Maurice rounds on Victor. 'I told you. I told you – he's here. He's with us. He's here in this house with us. Still!'

'Maurice . . .' Victor's low voice is filled with warning. 'Forgive Maurice, Sergeant Verity. Hugo was more than just a brother, you see. He was Maurice's hero in many regards. It is hard to accept the loss of such a larger-than-life character.'

'I know he's dead, Victor,' Maurice counters. 'I'm not stupid. But I also know that of late, I have sensed him in this house, sensed his presence. We smelt his pipe tobacco—' he appeals directly to Verity '—we all did, in the library. And then I awoke the other night to find him watching me, from the doorway—' Agitated, he dashes across the room to stand on the wooden threshold. 'He was right here. I had been asleep on the sofa there and woke up to the smell of his pipe and the sight of him, watching over me. He turned and led me upstairs. I followed him and then he disappeared on the landing. But he was there, I tell you, right there!'

'Maurice, you're working yourself up, old man.' Victor sets his glass down on the piano. 'We don't want the Sergeant to get the impression you're crackers.' His attempt at genial laughter fails to impress.

'I'm not mad!'

The roar is sudden and jarring. Ida gasps. In her chair, Sarah flinches, but she keeps her face down, the embodiment of an unwilling witness to a family dispute. The bird trills and clicks as it clambers about its cage, oblivious to the furore it has caused.

Maurice makes a renewed approach to Verity, perching on the chair across from him. 'What would you make it? You're a detective. Taking the evidence before you, what would you deduce?'

'I'm sure Sergeant Verity works on facts and reality not fanciful nonsense or spirits and spectres, Maurice,' Victor says.

'Actually, Mr Monroe, you might be surprised.' Verity displays his typical unruffled calm. He sets his barely touched whiskey down on the table beside his chair. 'You were at the front. You must have been aware of the extraordinary tales men told.'

Victor laughs. 'Phantom cavalrymen and angelic saviours? Works of fantasy, Sergeant Verity. Simply hallucinations born of terror and tiredness.'

'Indeed. You are right, no doubt. And yet . . .' Verity rests back in his chair, crossing his legs '. . . there were some stories which defied explanation. Appearances that couldn't have been possible, and yet were impossible to refute. I heard a fellow tell a story one night, of how he'd been sleeping in a dugout near Vimy, when he was woken by his brother. His dead brother.'

With the skill of a practised raconteur, he pauses, garnering the hushed attention of the room. 'He recalled that the hand his brother laid across his mouth to stifle his joyous cries was "warm". Imagine that. This chap claimed his brother then led him from the dugout into some ruins nearby where he promptly disappeared. Now this fellow, as you say, Mr Monroe, believed it to be nothing more than a waking dream, or a hallucination induced by exhaustion, and certainly he was too tired to return to where he'd come from, so he lay down where he was and went back to sleep. And yet, in the morning, when he woke, he learnt that the dugout he had been sleeping in had taken a direct hit after his departure, killing everyone inside. But there he was, alive . . . and all thanks to the watchful care of his dead brother.'

'That can't be true.'

The Sergeant tips his head to the side and offers his palms. 'The soldier concerned was most convincing. And I heard other such stories. I'm sure you must have too.'

'I did,' Leonard pipes up. 'A fellow I was in hospital with swore blind he was carried from the field by his dead pal. They'd been hit in the same blast. They lay together, dying. He watched the life leave his friend's eyes and yet moments later, he was being thrown over his shoulder, and carried back to the trenches. Some of our lads found him, propped up at the bottom of a scaling ladder, half out of his mind with pain, while his dead pal's body was left to rot in No Man's Land. He was convincing too, I must say.'

'What do you say about it all, Sarah?' Ida asks suddenly.

Sarah looks up, startled.

'Well?' Ida challenges. 'Of all of us, you should know whether the dead truly walk amongst the living.'

Victor cuts across Sarah's stuttered protest. 'For God's sake, Ida . . .'

'You have the gift, don't you, Sarah?' Ida persists. 'You've felt the spirits before.'

'You've seen spirits here,' Leonard adds, albeit with an air of apology.

'I . . . I . . .' Sarah bites her lip, her eyes stealing towards Verity, who cocks his head with interest. 'I have felt something . . . someone . . . here, yes, that's true. But I don't have a gift . . . I wouldn't say that.'

'You're too modest,' Ida chides. 'The spirits clearly like you. And, as you say, you have felt things since you arrived.'

Sarah does not respond. She stares at a fixed point ahead, avoiding them all.

'Can you feel Hugo, now?'

Sarah's lips move, but no sound comes out. There is no need for her to say anything. Her pained expression gives her away.

Fervour shining in her eyes, Ida turns to her husband. 'Maurice, imagine, just imagine, you could speak to Hugo one last time!'

'Ida, don't talk such bloody rot.' But Victor's attempts to rein Ida in are in vain. She doggedly pursues her unfurling idea.

'You'd gain so much comfort from that, wouldn't you, Maurice? A chance to say goodbye. The chance you never got.'

'He's trying to tell me something. I know he is . . .'

Ida traps Maurice's hand in her own. 'He's trying to give

you peace, I'm sure of it. Why else would he still be here, if not to give you comfort?'

'Ida, I'm not sure—' Leonard starts, but she doesn't let him finish.

'Imagine if we could summon Hugo. Hear him, for a final time.'

'Ida . . .'

Spots of colour brighten her cheeks. 'We could, you know! With Sarah, we could do that. Through a séance!'

'I don't think I . . .' Sarah stands up in protest. 'I couldn't do anything like that . . .'

'But of course you could, you've just never tried!' Still gripping Maurice's hand, Ida sets her sights on Sarah. 'Look what happened when you attended a meeting. The medium there said the spirits were drawn to you. You! And the things you've seen here, the things that have been happening since you arrived. You've given power to something with your very presence, Sarah. You can bring Hugo back to Maurice.'

'Ida, that's enough. You're letting your imagination run away with you,' Victor says, attempting to douse her growing enthusiasm.

'No . . . no . . . she's right.' Emerging from his glum pre-occupation, Maurice now leaps to his feet with the joy of a convert who has seen the light. 'If there's a way of making contact with Hugo, even if only for a short time, I want to try it. I want to try.'

'Is it wise to meddle in such things, Maurice?' Leonard asks.

'Len!' Maurice crouches before his brother, resting his hands on his blanket-covered stumps. 'He's here, with us, I know he is. How can we ignore him? How can we not at least try?'

'I'm not a medium,' Sarah protests. 'I've never done anything like that. I wouldn't know how.'

'Nonsense, all we need to do is sit in a circle holding hands,' Ida says, as if it is as obvious as forming a queue at a bus stop. 'And I have every faith in your appeal, Sarah. I don't think you need to do anything – I think they'll come to you.'

'No, please . . .'

'Of all your crazed ideas, Ida, this one really takes the biscuit.' With little choice remaining, Victor appeals again to Verity. 'Detective Sergeant, please, help me out here, add some rational sense to this conversation.'

'Well now, Mr Monroe, if Mrs Stilwell is quite set on the idea, far be it for me to interfere – I am merely an unexpected houseguest here, after all,' Verity says, smiling. 'I'm in no position to lay down the law.' He chuckles at his own joke.

'Then it's settled!' Ida claps her hands with ill-concealed delight. 'Once and for all, we'll try and get to the bottom of the extraordinary events of late. We'll try and make contact with Hugo. Sarah?' But she is not seeking Sarah's agreement. The decision has already been made. 'It will be quite a night!'

Behind them, Mr Tibbs flutters onto the swing in his cage.

'Floppy, Floppy, Floppy.'

The bird begins to preen.

Chapter Twenty-Five

Under Ida's enthused direction, they push back the sofa and armchairs to make space in the centre of the room for the games table, which Maurice – growing in resolve by the minute – carries from its place against the side wall and duly unfolds. Chairs are brought through from the dining room and placed around it. Voices rise with eager suggestions, and suddenly the leaden atmosphere grows effervescent with excitement more characteristic of a weekend house party. It proves so infectious that even Leonard, initially unconvinced, joins in the spirit of the preparations. Sergeant Verity also gamely partakes, carrying through dining chairs when requested. Victor continues to be vocal in his dissent, but he soon finds himself shouted down by the others and when teasingly declared a party-pooper by Ida, he succumbs at last, giving in with good grace. Only Sarah remains averse to the enterprise, chewing her fingernail as she watches on. As Verity sets down the final chair their eyes meet.

'I'm not sure about all this,' she murmurs.

'Oh, come now, Sarah, it'll all be fine, you'll see,' Ida insists as she tweaks the chair's position.

Sergeant Verity leans towards Sarah. 'Courage, Miss Hove.'

She glares at him and moves away.

'Does anyone know how one of these things actually works?' Leonard asks, as Maurice tucks his chair into the space created for him.

'I think it will all be down to our resident medium,' Ida declares, earning a horrified look from Sarah. She attempts a further desperate protest which Ida impatiently halts with a raised hand. 'Now Sarah, don't fuss. If you do have the gift, as we suspect, I think the spirits will quite naturally use you as a conduit. You might find you don't have to do a thing. You'll see things, hear things, I imagine. That's what's happened before, isn't it? You've felt their presence?'

'I've never tried to communicate with them.'

'Then this will be an experiment for you too.' Ida takes Sarah's hands. 'Let's just see what happens. Perhaps nothing will. Or perhaps we will finally find out what's been going on of late. Maybe Hugo *will* come through. It must be worth a try. Nothing ventured, nothing gained.'

'We shouldn't meddle.'

'Nonsense, they can't hurt us—' Ida grins, dropping her voice to a stage whisper ' —they're *dead!*'

'I still think this is a load of old rot,' Victor mutters, recharging his glass.

'Victor, I don't want you spoiling it,' Ida insists. 'If nothing else, it'll just help pass the evening. We're stuck in, the weather's frightful, this will be a bit of fun – and you never know, it might produce results.'

She sidles over to him. Ensuring the others are all preoccupied, she lowers her voice for him alone to hear.

'You can see Maurice is coming apart and we can't afford to let that to happen, as you well know. Look how the mere prospect of a word from Hugo has lifted him. He's been obsessed of late – maybe this will prove beneficially diverting. And you never know . . . perhaps there is something in it.'

Her fingers fleetingly brush his arm as she moves away. She claps her hands to garner the attention of the room.

'What else do we need? Candlelight, obviously! We'll turn down the lamps in here. Sarah, can you fetch a candle? Will the fire make it too bright, do you think?'

'I hardly think the dead are going to be put off by a bit of firelight.' Reluctantly, Victor joins the others as they take their seats at the table. 'Come on then, what do we need to do?'

'Let's all sit,' Ida instructs. 'Sarah, you there, Maurice, you next, then I'll sit this side of you Sarah, Vic, do you want to sit next to me too, then Len and, oh . . . Sergeant Verity, are you all right there, by Leonard?'

They take their allotted positions. Sarah turns down the last of the lamps before joining them at the table. The solitary candle placed in its midst flickers under the influence of the seeping draught that adds a chilly edge to the air. Outside, the wind pushes against the house, while the fire hisses as rain drips down the chimney.

Sergeant Verity smiles. 'I must say, it's very atmospheric.'

'We should form a bonded circle,' Ida says officiously, the candle flame highlighting her intense excitement. 'Isn't that what they say? Join hands, everyone.'

'That might be difficult,' Leonard observes.

'What if I rest my hand on your shoulder?' Verity suggests.

'I don't see what else you can do.'

With the circle formed, they wait in breathless anticipation.

'Aren't you supposed to say something?' Ida whispers to

Sarah, betraying the nervous giggle she is trying to contain. 'To see if anyone is there?'

'I told you, I have never done—'

'Yes, yes,' Ida cuts in, tiring of Sarah's objections. 'But you are now. Just . . . throw yourself into it.'

'Don't do anything you're not comfortable with, Sarah.'

'Oh, hush-up, Leonard! Do you want to hear from your brother or not?'

'Can we just stop arguing and try,' Maurice pleads. He looks to Sarah. 'Please.'

Perhaps taking pity on his desperation, Sarah releases a long breath. 'Hugo . . . are you there?'

The candle flame gutters then flares. Ida squeaks at the drama of it, eagerly exchanging glances with those around her.

'It was just the draught, Ida,' Victor says, dour as ever.

'Try again, Sarah.'

Sarah shifts in her seat.

'Should we close our eyes perhaps?' Ida whispers.

'Oh, for God's sake.'

'Just give her a chance, will you?'

'Go on, Sarah.'

Sarah fidgets again but appears resigned to her fate. 'Is there anyone with us?' She focuses on the candle. 'Is there anybody there?'

She has barely finished talking when the table jerks. Ida screeches as it stills abruptly. With shallow breaths, they all exchange stunned glances.

'Hugo . . .' Sarah says tentatively. 'Is that you?'

They wait. The fire crackles and wheezes. Mr Tibbs issues a shrill whistle, causing Ida to jump. The clock ticks. Outside, the wind-beaten roses scrape against the windowpanes. A gust of draught chills them all. The candle flame bends and straightens.

'Hugo?' Sarah attempts again. She turns to Maurice. 'Perhaps if you tried.'

His hesitant nod sends his heavy fringe into his eyes, but he makes no move to brush it back, not wanting to break the circle. Instead, he peers up through the curtain of hair.

'Hugo? Hugo it's me, Maurice . . . are you there? Because . . . well . . . I think you might be, old man.'

Again, they wait. Ida squirms in her seat, but for once holds her tongue.

'All right then . . . is there someone other than Hugo with us?' All of them detect the uncertainty in Sarah's voice.

Ida screams as the table shudders towards her, forcing her and Victor to scramble backwards in their chairs.

'Jesus,' Victor gasps, his swagger evaporating under the candle's insipid light.

'Can you feel anything, Sarah? Like you felt before?' Ida's voice wavers with fear.

Sarah is staring into the flame. She nods slowly. 'Yes.' Her whisper lacks substance. 'I do feel a presence. There is someone, something . . . I feel it.'

'Can you see anything?' Leonard leans towards her.

Sarah's chin tips up. She stares into the deepening darkness behind Victor. Her features widen with terror.

'Sarah?'

'I see a soldier . . .' she gasps, her shock as great as theirs. Vic jerks round to look over his shoulder.

'I see a soldier . . .' Sarah's chest lifts and falls on short, sharp breaths.

'Hugo? Is it Hugo?' Maurice cries.

She shakes her head slowly. 'No . . . a soldier not . . . just a soldier . . .' She frowns, her eyes narrowing as if trying to discern something. 'A private . . .'

'Joe?' Leonard cannot contain himself. 'Good God, is it Joe?'

Sarah's face scrunches with pain. She cries out, pulling away, forcing Ida and Maurice to tighten their grip on her hands to keep the circle intact. Her breathing grows jagged as she presses herself against the back of the dining chair.

'Sarah? Sarah, are you all right?'

'What's wrong with her?' Ida cries.

With a guttural cry, Sarah sits upright, her eyes fixed before her. The pain vanishes from her face, her features suddenly lax and still. Her lips part.

'I know . . .'

'Sarah?' Leonard manages little more than a whisper.

'Not Sarah . . .'

The voice she speaks in is uncharacteristically low. Leonard frowns, then gawps.

'Joe?'

'I know . . .'

'What the hell is this?' Victor interrupts. 'What game are you playing, Sarah?'

Sarah's blank eyes move to bore into his, unblinking. The effect is so disturbing, so unnatural, Victor pulls back, as if straining to place himself beyond their reach.

'Died . . . for you.'

'What's happening?' Ida whines. All traces of her previous excitement have vanished. Horror moulds her features.

'Woods . . . Bobby . . . shell hole . . . lies . . .' Sarah pauses. 'Fire!'

The barked order takes them all by surprise. Maurice begins to whimper.

'Murder.' Sarah's face contorts with rage, her teeth bared. 'Murder. Murder.'

'Stop it! Stop it!' Maurice jumps up with such force his chair tips backwards and thuds onto the rug, evoking a shriek from Ida. 'Make it stop!' he yells, clutching his head.

Sarah cries out, the pitch of her voice her own once more. She slumps in her seat, her head lolling forward. Leonard shouts her name. Verity leaps to his feet and Victor is close behind. The circle has been well and truly broken.

'Enough of this malicious nonsense!' Victor's demand sounds above the melee of voices.

'Is she even conscious?' Leonard cries, his palm pressed to the table. 'For God's sake, help her someone.'

It is Verity who goes to Sarah's aid, the candlelight catching on the painted white of his eye and the black spot of his fake pupil.

'Miss Hove?' He gently places a hand on her arm. When she fails to react, he lisps her name again. She issues a faint moan, her head lifting, albeit woozily. She looks around, glazed and befuddled.

'What . . . What happened?'

'My God, Sarah! Are you all right?' Leonard reaches across the table to take her hand.

'I don't . . . what happened?'

'Let's get you onto the sofa, my dear,' Verity suggests, helping her to her feet. His arm remains around her back as he guides her across the room. Once she is seated, Verity adjusts the dial on the oil lamp beside them, banishing the immediate gloom.

'I don't feel well.'

'A drink perhaps? Mr Monroe, would you mind?'

Verity looks to Victor, but Victor does not move. 'What the hell was all that about?' His voice vibrates with anger.

'It was hardly Sarah's fault,' Leonard protests, pushing himself away from the table. 'Maurice? Maurice . . . Stop it, please!'

But Maurice doesn't stop. He is pacing in tight, repetitive circles, switching one way, then the next, moaning to himself, visibly trembling, the flesh beside his eye flickering like a frantically hammered SOS.

'Maurice!' Ida takes a step towards him but holds back. She is shivering.

'For God's sake, Maurice.' Grabbing Maurice's shoulders, Victor forces him to stand still, though he continues to sway and mutter and sob. 'Come on, Maurice. It was nothing, nothing at all, just a foolish parlour trick.'

'How can you say that?' Ida cries. 'How can you say that? You saw Sarah. It wasn't her. It wasn't her saying those dreadful things.'

Releasing Maurice, Victor turns on her. 'If you expect me to believe it's some bloody ghost—'

'How else do you explain it?' Leonard works the wheel of his chair, so he too is facing Victor. Verity continues to attend to Sarah, taking it upon himself to furnish her with a restorative tot of brandy, which she sips gingerly.

Victor remains unmoved. 'Bobby Higgins, Joe Durham

'– both of those men have been discussed in this house of late,' he says, his voice rising in anger. 'And then, with all this—' his hand sweeps out towards the abandoned games table, the candle still burning in its midst, molten wax spilling down its side '—this ridiculous exercise instigated by Ida, it's hardly surprising the girl blurts out such things, pressured as she is into fulfilling this crazed expectation that she has some supernatural gift.'

'An interesting theory, Mr Monroe.' With Sarah's assurances, Verity abandons her care and rises from the sofa.

'A far more logical one than the alternative,' Victor argues.

'"Murder",' Verity mulls.

Victor huffs. He aims for the drinks table, snatching up the whiskey decanter. 'After all this time I think it's pretty bloody obvious no good has come to Bobby Higgins.'

'And yet . . .' Verity taps his chin; the tinny echo on his mask is disconcerting. '. . . the commonly held belief is that the boy met with some unfortunate accident.'

'Well, this letter you have clearly suggests otherwise, doesn't it?' Victor points out, tipping back his whiskey. 'Otherwise, you'd hardly be wanting to dig up our woodlands after all these years.'

'Perhaps.' The mask renders it impossible to deduce what the Sergeant is thinking, but at last he says, 'The reference to the shell hole was curious, was it not?'

'She must have overheard us discussing the court martial when you came the other day.' Victor shrugs off Verity's comment with careful disinterest.

'I didn't hear you.' Sarah's mouth forms a defiant line. 'I know nothing about Joe Durham . . . other than he was a friend of Leonard's. That's all I know.'

'Finish him off! Finish him off!'

Victor's glass thuds onto the rug. 'What the . . .'

The bell attached to the mirror hanging inside Mr Tibbs' cage tinkles as the bird catches it with its outstretched wings.

'Jesus,' Leonard murmurs.

Maurice crumples upon folded knees and begins to rock back and forth. Ida stifles a sob.

'I warned you,' Sarah says quietly. 'I warned you all. No good ever comes from meddling with the dead.'

Chapter Twenty-Six

The next morning, Sarah once more ensures she is the first to rise. Waking at dawn is an increasing struggle – her much reduced sleep is beginning to take its toll, but as she descends the back staircase to the kitchen, achingly tired and tearful, she tells herself things will soon improve; she must simply manage until they do. After all, she endured much worse during the war.

The power, she discovers, is still out, so she lights an oil lamp to alleviate the early morning dullness as she stokes the range and sets the water boiling. After the disastrous séance, the evening had drawn to a fraught close with Ida beseeching Victor not to wring Mr Tibbs' neck – she had only managed to prevent his murderous advance, by clinging to his arm and dragging him to the drinks table, where she was quick to ply him with another whiskey. Sarah wonders, though, whether she will enter the drawing room this morning to discover the bird has met an unfortunate end. She hopes not.

Victor had been forced to engage the assistance of Sergeant Verity when it came to getting Leonard upstairs to bed, as Maurice had been in no fit state to perform his usual duties. In fact, the two of them had first escorted him, jabbering and whimpering, to his room. Verity had passed no comment on Ida's absence from her husband's bedside. Indeed, the Detective Sergeant had not so much as batted his remaining eyelid at any of the night's events. With Maurice safely ensconced, and Leonard delivered to the lower landing, he had dipped his head and wished them all goodnight, before cheerfully following Sarah to the room she had prepared for him.

'I wonder what on earth that man must think of us,' Leonard had said, when Sarah returned to get him ready for bed. 'To give him his due, he seems completely unfazed by tonight's events.'

He had tried to gently prod her then, about her experiences in the drawing room, but she had no recollection of the words that had fallen from her lips, only an overpowering sense of someone standing before her.

'What do you think it all meant?' she had asked, unable to let the matter lie.

But for whatever reason, he had failed to share his thoughts. He had simply wished her goodnight, drawing a line under it all. Though dissatisfied, she had issued her parting pleasantries, turned off the lamp, and headed for the door.

'Good people sometimes do bad things, Sarah, often for what seem to be the right reasons at the time. But on reflection, they realise they should have done better. Whatever happens, please don't think ill of me.'

She had stood in the darkness, the metal latch cold in her hand. 'What did you do?'

'I chose family over friendship. And though there are times I have regretted that – indeed, felt weak for doing so – faced with the same dilemma again, I'm not sure my choice would be any different. Life isn't black and white, Sarah, and the decisions we find ourselves having to make are often mired in the vast stretch of grey in between.'

'Then all we can do is own those decisions come judgement day.'

'Do you believe that? That we must all face our maker? A vengeful god seeking justice?'

'I believe in justice, certainly.'

'Do you believe in empathy? Compassion?'

She had hesitated a moment. 'Yes.'

'Then I hope the god I must face will manage to extend some compassion and empathy to me when we meet. Goodnight, Sarah. I hope, despite the events of this evening, you manage to rest well.'

With the kettle boiled, she gathers up the ash pail, dustpan and brush, and makes her way through the house, intending to start the fires in the dining room and drawing room, perhaps the reception hall since they are entertaining, to at least take the frigid edge off those rooms before the others appear.

On reaching the reception hall she comes to an abrupt halt. The Detective Sergeant is standing at the vast window overlooking the front of the property, leaning into the hands he has planted on the windowsill. The soft rattle of her bucket as she sets it down on the hearth gives her away, and he glances round, before turning his attention back to the view beyond the panes.

'Look.'

Wiping her hands on her apron, she joins him. Her eyes widen. The lawn has vanished. Overnight, the river has spilled across it, transforming the verdant expanse into a vast sea of brown water. A duck swims where only yesterday there was a flowerbed. The water laps at the edge of the gravelled forecourt, as if testing its reception should it decide to impose further.

'It's quite perfect,' Verity murmurs. He turns to look at her, the dashes of colour on his copper mask muted by the grey light. 'Almost biblical.'

Sarah's heart beats faster. She steps back from the window. 'I must ready myself for the day.'

'Of course,' he lisps softly. 'Don't let me detain you.'

Breakfast proves to be a subdued affair. Maurice fails to surface so it is left to a sullen Victor to carry Leonard downstairs while Sarah struggles behind with the wheelchair, bouncing it clumsily over each descending tread.

Ida is already loitering in the reception hall.

'I can't go into the dining room!' she hisses as Victor lowers Leonard into the chair and Sarah absents herself to the kitchen. '*He's* in there already.'

'We have to find a way to get him out of here.' Victor drapes the blanket for Leonard, then leaves him to tuck it into place. 'Given the state Maurice is in—'

'I'm worried about Maurice,' Leonard says.

'We're all bloody worried about Maurice, Leonard. If he carries on the way he is, we'll each of us be swinging from a rope before long.'

'Perhaps that's no more than what we deserve.'

Ida rolls her eyes. 'Oh, do be quiet, Leonard, no one wants to be subjected to your reflective angst.'

'You might wish yourself dead, Len, but I'm afraid I rather like living.' Victor rubs his chin, deep in thought. 'I'm going to see about getting rid of him today, this Detective.'

Ida clutches at his arm. 'Victor, you can't!'

Amusement plays across his face. 'As in getting him out of the house, Ida, not bumping him off, for Christ's sake.'

Chuckling, he takes the handles of Leonard's chair and the three of them make their way to the dining room.

Sergeant Verity rises from the table as the wheels squeak over the worn wooden threshold.

'Good morning.' He greets them with a courteous dip of his head.

'Morning, Sergeant.' Victor positions Leonard at the table. 'I trust you slept well.'

'As well as can be expected, given the circumstances.' Verity sits back down, returning his napkin to his lap. 'It was quite an eventful evening.'

'Yes, well, I think everyone got a little carried away last night,' Victor observes drily. 'What with the flood and the power cut and the events of late. Well, you can see how the human mind can work against itself sometimes.' It irritates Victor that the impassiveness of Verity's mask leaves him so uncomfortable, but it does. He dislikes finding himself at a disadvantage. 'I think we have to take it for what it was – heightened emotions and fanciful foolishness. Maurice has not been well of late.'

'Shell shock?' Verity's presumed diagnosis forms unpleasantly in his damaged mouth.

'Yes.' Leonard abandons his attempt to butter the piece of toast of his plate. 'We might bear the scars of the war differently, but it damaged each and every one of us.'

'Yes, yes, it did.'

'We really must see about getting you home today, Sergeant,' Victor announces, reaching for the teapot. 'We have a rowing boat, you know. I'm sure we could get you across to the main road.'

Verity rests his cutlery on the edge of his plate and dabs his mouth with the napkin. He leans back in his chair. 'I'm not sure I would advise that, Mr Monroe. The velocity of the water was quite terrifying last night. The force of it was something to behold, I can tell you. It was a raging torrent – the currents will be treacherous. I'm not sure I would be comfortable with either of us risking our lives in a little rowing boat.'

'All the same—'

'No, no, I could not allow you to take such a chance, Mr Monroe. My conscience would not bear it. If any harm were to befall you, I would hold myself solely responsible. I'm afraid you may just have to suffer my continued presence a little longer – but I do promise you this, I have no wish to impose on your hospitality. I will be seeking to leave as soon as it is safe to do so.'

'Well . . . tomorrow maybe,' Ida says, with forced optimism.

Verity concurs with a hint of a smile. 'I do hope so, Mrs Stilwell.'

*

Sarah is on her way back to the kitchen, but as she passes the open door of the library, she stops and retraces her steps.

'You came down.'

Maurice is perilously perched on the edge of the chair by

251

the fireplace, like a fledgling preparing for flight – it strikes Sarah that he might slip from the seat at any minute. But he shows no signs of discomfort. He is completely preoccupied with the task in hand: whittling. Sarah cannot tell whether it is the same piece of wood he was working on previously, but he is just as intent as he skims it with his knife. When he finally notices her he glowers, and jabs the knife in deeper, gritting his teeth at the extra force needed to guide it free.

'I'm doing breakfast. Won't you join the others in the dining room?'

'Is he in there?'

'Sergeant Verity?'

'I don't like him.'

The hollows around Maurice's eyes seem to have deepened overnight and grown even murkier, while something plays behind the eyes themselves that renders Sarah uneasy. 'You should eat,' she says at last.

Maurice throws the piece of wood into the fireplace. It strikes the stone back and falls into the grate. Getting to his feet, he begins to pace across the hearth rug, opening and closing his knife. His eye flickers uncontrollably and for the first time she detects the musk of his unwashed body.

'Were you pretending last night, Sarah?'

'No, I wasn't.'

'Why did you say those things?'

'I told you, I don't know what I said.'

'Tell me!'

The unexpected violence of his demand takes her aback. Seeing her fear, Maurice drops the knife. It thuds onto the hearth rug as he clasps his head.

'I'm sorry . . . I'm sorry . . .' he says, slapping his skull with both hands.

'Stop! Please stop that!' Recovering her shock, Sarah starts forward, but then changes her mind. She is still close enough to have a head start for the door should she need it.

'I just want to try to understand what's happening.' His thumbnail finds the groove between his front teeth. He begins to pick at it repeatedly.

'I don't know what's happening.' The soles of her shoes whisper against the rug as she takes a step towards him. 'But it seems to me the dead are revisiting this house, for whatever purpose, and if you have any reason to fear them . . . then you should.' His forehead ripples like water where a plunging stone has disturbed the calm. She straightens her apron. 'Now I think you should go into breakfast. Everyone is expecting you.'

She sees his instinctive objection rise, but something – perhaps her matron-like authority – leads him to suppress the retort and instead he follows her meekly to the door. She waits, her arms folded, blocking the corridor so the only choice he has is to head for the dining room.

'I'm scared.'

'Good men never have anything to fear.'

The flesh by his eye stutters.

'Perhaps that is why I am so afraid,' he says.

*

Victor stalks across to the reception hall window to evaluate the state of the weather. He had intended to go out and assess

253

the extent of the flood for himself, but the heavens have opened once again, and the wind has reached gale force – it has already brought down one of the cherry trees and he is concerned for the poplars. With no possibility of escape, he starts to make his retreat towards the library, but before he can reach the doorway, Ida comes scurrying out from the dining room and latches onto his arm.

'Don't you dare think of abandoning me.'

Before she can further her appeal, Verity appears on the threshold, looking somewhat at a loss. Ida's fingers dig deeper into Victor's arm, and with some reluctance he invites the Sergeant to join them in the drawing room.

'That would be most pleasant.' Victor is beginning to find Verity's inexhaustible blitheness tiring. 'I wonder if the psychic Mr Tibbs will perform for us again today, or does he save his intuition for the drama of the night?'

Victor responds with a wilting smile, as he ushers Verity before them. He and Ida hang back slightly, and once the Sergeant has entered the room, Ida tips her chin towards Victor's ear.

'I hate him,' she whispers.

'I think we all do.' But they dutifully follow him through all the same.

That sense of duty, however, is not so deeply instilled in Leonard. When Maurice angles his chair towards the drawing room, Leonard twists around in his seat and pointedly mouths *library*. Maurice, catching sight of a photograph on the sideboard of Hugo flanked by his parents, is conscious of letting the side down yet again, but he feels no compunction to spend time with either the Detective or Victor. He redirects the chair without comment, and they are soon sneaking away to their inner sanctum.

On arrival, Maurice wheels Leonard towards his usual place in the window but Leonard stops him.

'Actually, I think I fancy being closer to the fire today. Can you put me there, between the chairs? Here! Yes, that's perfect.' He slaps his hand against his lap. 'Oh, damn it all, I left the book I was reading in my bedroom. Could you bear to fetch it for me? It's on my bedside table.'

'I'll light the fire first though, shall I?'

'No, don't . . . do that when you get back. I won't be able to fix it if it needs any attention.'

Maurice slopes off to Leonard's room, but despite a thorough search, he returns a short time later empty-handed.

'There was no book that I could see.'

'Wasn't there?' Leonard says, breathlessly. He looks, to Maurice, a little red in the face and the rise and fall of his chest seems more pronounced than usual. 'I wonder where on earth I've left it?' he muses, before issuing a sudden smile that is so warming it serves as a salve upon Maurice's own ill-humour, and he feels his heart lift for the first time that day. Len shrugs. 'Not to worry, pass me down that collection of Thomas S. Jones poems I like, would you? *From Quiet Valleys*, that's it. I like the way he puts things.'

Maurice runs his finger along the spines on the poetry shelf until he comes across the well-thumbed volume that Leonard is after. He flips it over in his hands as he walks back to him, asking with contrived insouciance, 'What do you think it meant last night, Len? All those things that Sarah said. Do you think that was Joe?' But despite his best efforts at conceit, he is betrayed by the trembling hand that holds out the book to his brother.

'I don't want to think about any of it, Maurice, and I don't think you should either. Both of us have dwelt too much on the past of late. We should leave unhappy memories behind us. I know we've made mistakes down the years but we don't have to let them define us, do we? Haven't we always tried to do better since? And you have your whole life ahead of you, Maurice. You can lead a good life and you should, you must. Do you hear me?' Maurice flinches as his brother grabs his hand, but he appreciates the comfort of Leonard's reassuring squeeze. 'You must overcome your demons, Maurice.'

To his surprise, Maurice finds himself pulled down into Len's firm embrace. He welcomes the touch, sincere and loving, missed for so long. Leonard has been largely undemonstrative since his injury, believing others to be as repulsed by his body as he is, but Maurice has never felt that. He clings to him now, relishing the physical contact. Pure and uncomplicated, it soothes his troubled soul. Leonard's tender smile as he releases him elicits a pang so profound it almost reduces Maurice to tears.

'We're moving forward to better things, from this moment on, Maurice,' Leonard says, giving his hand a final squeeze. The flesh tingles pleasantly even after he has let go and Maurice feels better all at once. 'Now, shall I read to you? Would you like that?'

'Yes please, Len. I would like that. I would like that very much.'

Maurice slumps into the armchair next to him and nestles his head against the wing. He feels very young again, like a boy, and he longs for those carefree days before the war. He closes his eyes to conjure them, warm memories, unsullied by what was to come.

Pages flutter. There is a long pause before Len starts reading, his voice gentle.

Across the fields of yesterday
He sometimes comes to me,
A little lad just back from play –
The lad I used to be.
And yet he smiles so wistfully
Once he has crept within,
I wonder if he hopes to see
The man I might have been.

Maurice hears the book close. The fire's sputter fills the sombre silence.

When at last he opens his eyes, he sees his brother's cheeks are awash with tears.

Chapter Twenty-Seven

In the drawing room, playing host to the enigmatic Detective Sergeant Verity, Ida has exhausted all safe topics of polite conversation – the weather is indeed frightful, he joined the force at the end of the war, his family come from Lewes, yes that part of the south coast is certainly worth a visit, and his first child is on the way.

'How delightful,' Ida says, with a thin smile and an upsetting ache in her heart.

Suppressing the unexpected surge of personal disappointment, Ida looks across to Victor, who is prowling around Mr Tibbs' cage in a most disturbing manner, irritated that he is doing nothing to relieve the strain of the Sergeant's unwelcome presence. Verity himself is also being frustratingly taciturn. He is polite enough in answering her questions, and she is becoming accustomed to his fixed expression, but whether through ignorance, ill-manners, or just plain disinterest, the conversation has remained one-sided, with him not asking *her* any questions, making it a struggle to prolong. She is quite at a loss what to do about it. She offers him more tea – or coffee perhaps – out of growing desperation, but is thwarted when he assures her he is quite sated. As a result of all this, her practised smile is now fraying at its edges.

She is therefore more than a little relieved when Victor, having clearly been pondering the mysteries of her talking parrot, decides to quiz her on her training practices, though she remains piqued that he has, up to this point, abandoned her to the laconic policeman.

'It's all very well asking about it now,' she says, sulking, 'when you've always ridiculed me for it before.'

'Never mind that.' Victor swats away her comment as if it is an irritating fly. 'It's repetition, is it? You say the same phrases over, and over again?'

'Yes, of course, you *know* that.'

'But how do you make him say something when you want him to? Do you have a trigger word?'

'Well, I'm sure I don't know. I just try to get him to say back to me the phrase I'm teaching him.'

'But what if you wanted him to say a specific phrase at a specific moment? Could that be done? Perhaps if you trained him differently?'

'How would I know, Victor?' Ida throws up her hands in ill temper. 'I've never tried anything like that. I simply train him as I train him. I've never tried any other method. Why on earth are you asking me all these questions?' Unhappy that rather than alleviating her stress he has exasperated it, Ida prevents further interrogation by cutting him off with a question of her own. 'Will you make up a four for whist? You'll play, won't you, Sergeant Verity? And Sarah will, I'm sure, if asked. She's squirrelled away in the kitchen; no doubt she'd welcome a break.'

While Ida enjoys some blessed relief, scurrying off to fetch Sarah, Victor abandons his study of Mr Tibbs and makes himself useful by unfolding the games table. The sight of dried candlewax on the felt gives him pause.

'What did you make of it all, Sergeant? You've been rather quiet about last night's events.'

Verity reaches for the pack of cards Victor has produced. 'It's difficult to say. Pure chance? A freak coincidence perhaps, the bird picking up a few stray words and linking them together?' The deck slides from the tapped box into his hand. 'If you don't mind me saying, Mr Monroe, you seemed very shaken by his phrasing. Is there a reason why?'

'Not really.' Victor bristles before he can govern his response. He recovers quickly. 'Just took me by surprise.'

'"*Finish him off*".' Verity takes his time, lingering over the words. The effect is unsettling. 'Does that have a particular resonance with you?'

'Not at all.' Victor twists sideways in his chair to cross his legs. He can't quite bring himself to look at the Sergeant. He shrugs. 'It's a brutal phrase. Incongruous in a domestic setting such as this.'

'Brutal,' Verity echoes thoughtfully. 'Yes, indeed. Most off-putting.'

Victor is suddenly eager to change tack. 'You didn't fall for Sarah's little performance last night, did you?'

With what he interprets as a smirk, Verity begins to shuffle the deck. Victor is entranced by the waterfall of cards, and how, with a subtle tilt of his hand, Verity can change its flow, making the cards vanish within the pack.

'You think it was a performance?' the Sergeant asks at last.

Victor breaks free from the hypnotic stream of colour. 'Of course. I'm not saying the girl was trying to be malicious.

She found herself bamboozled into doing something she didn't want to do, and probably felt compelled to try and live up to expectation. I suspect she was stressed and afraid, and . . . well, you saw in the trenches how some men were affected by such things; the consequent tricks their own minds could play on them.' Victor pulls a face as he delves into his pocket for his cigarettes. 'I think it was just the same with her. As I said last night, she's no doubt picked up things since her arrival – she knows about your investigation into the missing boy, she knows Joe Durham was a friend of Leonard's, he's told her as much, and perhaps she wasn't listening at doors, but there's many ways she could have picked up titbits about the events that led to his execution.' He turns a cigarette over and over between his fingertips. 'I daresay, consciously or not, in her panic she connected all those ideas together and yes, spouted nonsense in the hope it would bring the séance to an end.' He takes the cigarette between his lips.

The cards continue to whisper in Verity's hands. 'An interesting theory indeed.'

'The most sensible one, I would have thought,' Victor says, the cigarette jiggling on his words. He strikes a match to light it.

'Curious that she connected Joe Durham to knowledge of some sort.'

'Ah, Detective, here I'm going to do your job for you.' Victor's eyes narrow as he blows out his smoke. 'Sarah simply said she saw a soldier, not an officer, just a private. It was Leonard who decided it must be Joe and, well, let's just say Leonard has been talking to Sarah about Joe quite a bit lately.' He sits back in his chair, a superior lift to his chin as he takes another drag. He gesticulates with the cigarette caught between his fingers. 'There's a danger in jumping to conclusions.'

'Indeed there is, you have me there, Mr Monroe.' The cards tumble for a final time. 'It's still curious though, isn't it, that consciously or not, she linked the Higgins boy's death with events in the war.'

'Well, that's exactly my point.' Victor swivels round on his chair, leaning his elbow onto the table, eager now to convince Verity to look the other way – in any way, but theirs. 'It's all fantasy. How can she possibly know that? She's only been here a few days, she's not from the area. She'd never heard of Joe Durham a week ago, or Bobby Higgins for that matter.' He reaches for the ashtray on a nearby table. 'So, unless she really is a conduit for the dead – which I think we can safely assume she isn't – last night was just a panicked display of imagination.'

'You are now in danger of making assumptions, Mr Monroe.' Verity sets the shuffled deck down on the table before him. 'You are assuming that spirits don't exist, and that mediumship is a con trick, a fallacy. But if it isn't . . .' The implication is clear in the Sergeant's silky voice. Victor laughs.

'The dead are dead, Sergeant. And if you're going to try and convince me that somehow they linger or rise again . . . well, I'm afraid you're preaching to the unconvertable.'

'You're very definite, Mr Monroe.' Verity's fingers smooth the top card in the deck. 'You bear your convictions well.'

'And you? What's your position, Sergeant Verity?'

Verity smiles. He taps the top card, then pushes the stack away, as if he is too tempted to deal them. 'I have always been a tremendous admirer of Sherlock Holmes, Mr Monroe.

How does he put it? "When you have eliminated all which is impossible, then whatever remains, however improbable, must be the truth".'

Victor takes another drag on his cigarette. He taps the crumbling ash into the tray. 'That may be so, Sergeant—' his words carry on threads of pungent smoke '—but you'll forgive me if I continue to keep an open mind for the time being. You see, I, for one, am not entirely convinced the impossible has yet been fully eliminated.' He treats the Detective to a wolfish grin. 'I'm inclined to carry on with my investigations.'

*

As soon as there is a break in the rain, Leonard asks Sarah to take him to the pond. Given the conditions outside, she feels the trip is unwise, but he persists and cajoles until, in the end, she agrees. They do not manage to reach their favoured spot. The pond has also swelled beyond its usual parameters, though not as dramatically as the river to the front. The tributary that feeds it has escaped the constraints of its narrow channel, and the pond itself has engulfed the gravel paths leading to the benches.

'Never mind, this is close enough,' he says, as they stop short of the lying water, now ruffled by the wind. He relaxes into his chair. 'I love everything about this place.'

The sun breaks through the clouds as if presenting itself for his pleasure, and he tips back his head and closes his eyes, savouring its warmth on his skin. He finds himself thinking of an early September day, a last adventure before the start of term, when he and Joe had fashioned a raft from spare wood and knotted rope. They had carried it between them to the pond's edge, stripping down to their shorts before guiding it through the shallows, silt oozing between their toes as water chilled their calves. They had scrambled aboard with mixed success, hooting with laughter, but it had, to their pride, stayed afloat. Joe had brought a broom handle, purloined for a punt. Taking to his feet he had eased them into the depths, while Len had basked in the late summer sun, his fingers trailing in the water.

But as clouds smother the sun once more and a cool breeze skirts across his face, his warm memories succumb to colder recollections, discomforting reminders he finds himself unable to suppress.

He slipped on the icy cobbles as he followed the provost sergeant across the courtyard to the stone building awaiting them. He only just managed to keep his footing.

'*All right, sir?*'

'*Yes, thank you, sergeant. Damn slippery out here.*'

The sergeant came to a standstill before a wooden door. Snowflakes speckled the khaki serge of his uniform as he selected a key from the crammed ring brought from the guard-house. He grunted as it turned stiffly in the lock. The door groaned as he pushed it wide.

'*Visitor for you,*' *he called, stepping clear of the doorway so Len could enter.*

The straw thinly carpeting the small room rustled as Len moved inside. Through the gloom, he saw a table and chair against the back wall, and a narrow army cot pushed to the side. Sitting upon it, a standard-issue blanket wrapped around his shoulders, was Joe.

Seeing Len, he rose to his feet while maintaining his grip on the blanket, his only source of warmth in the frigid room. It dropped onto the bed as he took a step forward into the pale light cast through the room's sole window, a tiny affair, its square panes filthy and skimmed with ice. Len caught his breath at the sight of him. Stubble blemished his unwashed face, its sparse and intermittent growth betraying his youth. His eyes were red-ringed and bloodshot. Len's first thought was that he had been crying.

'You can wait outside, sergeant.' Len's voice caught on the order, but the sergeant appeared not to register his unguarded emotion, and silently withdrew, closing the door behind him.

'I wasn't sure you'd come.' Joe took a further step away from the bed.

A hundred thoughts and responses rushed through Leonard's mind, but in the end all he said was, 'Oh Joe.'

'I didn't do it. I didn't do any of it, any of the things they say I did. You have to believe me, Len.'

Len sank his face into his palms. He did believe him. That was the problem.

'Christ, it's cold in here,' he muttered, dragging his hands clear.

'It's no worse than being in the trenches.'

They stood in silence, the raw air encircling them.

'Len . . .' His name was made visible by Joe's breath. 'Can you talk to Maurice? Can you persuade him to withdraw the charges?'

'Oh, Joe!' Len looked away, surprised by a rush of tears. 'It's too late for all that.'

The truth of his statement weighed heavy between them.

Joe muttered something Len failed to catch, then turned to face the tiny window. Delicate white flakes drifted past the dirty glass. The room's chill permeated every layer of Leonard's clothing.

'Then I have a favour to ask you,' Joe said, his voice low. He waited for Len to meet his gaze. 'I want you to be my Prisoner's Friend.'

Len felt his blood drain. 'I can't—'

'You're the only one who can help me, Len. I need you to defend me against the lies they're telling.'

'I can't, Joe . . . you can't ask me—'

'I'm not asking you, Len, I'm begging you!' Joe's desperation rang off the dank walls of his makeshift cell. 'As your friend. Please.'

'Joe, for Christ's sake!' Len's throat constricted. 'Do you realise what you're asking?'

'You know what they'll do to me.'

'You're asking me to choose between you. And I can't, you must see that . . .' Leonard stifled a sob. He whirled away, burying his face in his hands once more.

'Len . . .'

'No.' His voice firm, Leonard destroyed all evidence of his tears before turning back to face his friend. 'I can't do it, Joe. I'm sorry. I can't stand for you against Maurice.' His brow rippled with distress. 'Please understand that. Please.'

Joe turned again to the window. Snow was gathering on the sill outside. A trim of glistening crystals pressed against the grimed panes. His voice, when it finally came, was flat.

'I forgave you. I gave you the benefit of the doubt because I thought . . .' His brows drew tight. He squeezed his eyes *shut, and when he opened them again, he swallowed hard, but his efforts failed to banish the tremor from his words. '. . . I truly believed that you weren't like them, not really, not deep down.'*

'What are you talking about?'

Joe snorted and shook his head. His expression hardened. 'I thought I knew you, Len. Turns out, I didn't really know you at all.'

Returning to his cot, he stooped to retrieve the blanket. It billowed as he flung it around his shoulders. The cot slats protested as he laid his weight upon them. Pulling the blanket tight, he bellowed for the guard.

Leonard opens his eyes and takes in the cavalcade of storm clouds moving above him.

'Are we alone, Sarah?'

She fails to understand him at first, but when the penny finally drops, she averts her gaze to the far side of the pond.

'Yes.'

He is surprised by the depth of his disappointment. 'Well, I can hardly blame him,' he whispers, the pain in his heart so great all he wants is for something, anything, to take it away.

And then he remembers the promise of the day, and the ache begins to alleviate, as his spirits dare to lift once more.

As the day wears on, Leonard's lost happiness returns, and his good humour prevails anew. Even the tense silences over lunch and dinner do not thwart him. When they retreat en masse to the drawing room after dinner, it is Leonard that calls for the gramophone, dictating the music choice, calling for Vic to play this record, then that. As soon as a disc circles to its hissing end, he suggests the next. Victor fulfils his requests with wry amusement, grateful, Sarah suspects, that someone is maintaining the sociable atmosphere that Verity's presence seems to threaten.

It is Ida who brings Leonard's party to an end. Frazzled from a stressful day of awkward entertaining, she is first to retire, and Maurice is quick to his feet when she announces her decision. In an unusual display of unity, they leave the room together, watched by Victor.

'I should turn in too,' Verity says, getting to his feet. 'I very much hope the floodwaters have receded sufficiently by tomorrow that I might be able to take my leave. I'm sure you're all sick of the sight of me by now.'

'Your wife must be very worried,' Leonard says. 'I say, did you check the telephone today?'

'I've tried it a few times during the day,' Sarah says. 'No joy, I'm afraid.'

Verity makes a resigned gesture. 'I suppose it all depends on what damage has been done and where. Not to worry, I'm sure Mrs Verity will take the position of no news being good news. This flood must have impacted the entire region. I'm sure there is chaos all about.'

'Well, let's try and make a concerted effort to get you home tomorrow,' Victor says.

Bidding them all goodnight, Verity takes himself away.

'Come on, Leonard, we'd best get you up,' Victor says, putting down his empty glass. 'Sarah, do you think you can manage the chair again? If not, I'll carry Leonard up first and come back for it.'

'I'll manage.'

'One more song?' Leonard pleads.

'I'm done in, old man. It's time we were all heading up the wooden hills. We'll play them tomorrow.'

Casting a wistful look towards the gramophone, Leonard relents without battle. Victor takes the wheelchair, while Sarah follows behind, extinguishing the lamps as she goes. When they reach the staircase, Victor cradles Leonard in his arms and carries him up, while Sarah drags the chair backwards over the treads in a rather cumbersome fashion, but they get to the top eventually, and Leonard is soon settled on his bed.

'Thank you, Victor. I do appreciate all you do for me, you know.' Leonard grasps Victor's hand. 'The way you lug me about without complaint. It's good of you.'

'Well, someone's got to do it.' Vic pats Leonard's shoulder, the sentimental expression of gratitude having seemingly evoked a mix of fondness and embarrassment. ''Night, Leonard.' He wishes Sarah goodnight as an afterthought, and then he is gone, the door closing behind him, the room strangely still without his presence.

'That was nice of you,' Sarah says, as she unbuttons Leonard's shirt.

'I was hoping to chat to Maurice, but he went up so quickly. He's not at all himself these days.'

'No, he needs a good deal of rest, I would say. He has the look of a hau . . .' she stops herself.

'The look of what?'

'He looks like he needs a good night's rest,' she qualifies, easing off his shirt.

'Yes. I think you're right.' He waits as she helps him with

his pyjama top. 'I know you don't know what happened to you last night—'

Sarah groans. 'I don't want to talk about this again. Can we not?'

'No, I don't want to, not like that,' he assures her. 'All I was going to say was, I took solace from it. I don't know what happened, how it happened, or why, but it gave me hope.'

'Hope?' She secures the last button. 'What do you mean by that?'

'That there's more to our existence than just this life. That death isn't the end.' He seems suddenly embarrassed, dropping his chin as his fingers fiddle with the hemmed edge of his top. He appears a little abashed when he looks back up, and it restores the youthfulness so often lost to his simmering gall. 'During the war I wasn't sure. You saw so many things. It was hard to know. Hard to have faith, I suppose. All those people who claimed to have contacted their dead loved ones and so on . . . well, it smacked of desperation – self-deception, if you like – rather than truth. But if something has been in this house, Hugo . . . Joe . . . it gives me hope that there is life, existence of some sort, afterwards, and that maybe we will all meet again, in a better place. And if that is the case . . .'

'What?'

'Then maybe we have a chance to apologise to the people we've let down, a chance to express our remorse for decisions made that we wished we hadn't.'

'You're talking about Joe?'

Leonard smiles. It is boyish, sunny, carefree. She imagines it is the smile that graced his face always, before the war, before the shell blast that destroyed his body and changed his life, changed him, beyond measure.

'It'd be good to see Joe again. I would welcome the opportunity to make amends.' His sunny smile clouds over. 'Do you think he would forgive me?'

'I think that would depend on what you had done and whether you are truly sorry for it.'

'I am sorry. I'm sorry for everything.' The light in Leonard's eyes drains like a dimming bulb. 'I let him down, and I regret that. I would welcome the opportunity to apologise to him for my weakness.'

Sarah gives him privacy as he shuffles out of his trousers and underpants and into his pyjama bottoms. When he is done, she hands him his medication, which he dutifully takes with a slug of water from the glass she holds out for him.

'Do you think, if there is an afterlife, I will be fully restored in it?' He settles himself back against his pillows. 'I wouldn't want to go there if I had to remain like this.'

'Isn't that what the bible teaches us?' Sarah says, putting the medication away in the cabinet before returning to tuck in his covers. 'That in heaven our earthly afflictions are corrected?'

'Well then, that's something to look forward to, isn't it?'

His grin is vibrant and infectious. 'It is indeed.' She snuffs out the candle on his bedside table. 'Goodnight, Leonard.'

'Goodnight, Sarah.'

She finds her way across the darkened room. As the door-latch clacks from its rest, his voice comes again.

'I'm glad you came here, Sarah.'

The sincerity in his words gives her pause. 'So am I,' she says, matching it, before closing the door behind her.

Chapter Twenty-Eight

Sarah does not scream. The smell, that unmistakable tang of iron, hits as soon as she opens the bedroom door the next morning, projecting her straight back to France, to the make-shift operating theatres and triage tents. Images of torn-apart men on canvas stretchers flash in her mind's eye with such bewildering rapidity that she falls back against the door she has closed behind her. It is all she can do to prevent herself from sliding to the floor. Though she shuts her eyes, the horror remains, the images burnt on her irises. She talks calmly to herself, regaining control of her rapid breathing, until at last she feels ready to face what awaits her.

She is hesitant as she approaches the bed. Once there, she surveys it all, gritting her teeth to hold herself together. The profundity of the sadness that washes over her is a surprise, as are the unexpected tears that sting her eyes. She dashes them away with a stiff reprimand.

Leonard lies on his back. Blood has soaked the pillow and the sheet beneath, and there is blood spatter on the wall. She absorbs all of this, without shock, without surprise, and without fear – her years as a nurse have inured her to such things. She takes a step closer to the bed, careful not to let her clothes touch the blood. She sees the knife and recognises its ornately etched blade. She stares at the wall on the far side of the bed, her mind ticking.

She drops her gaze to his face, her expression softening, her heart aching. A deep-seated instinct leads her to close her eyes and her lips move in silent prayer, each word heartfelt. When she has finished, she cannot stop herself from gently touching his hair. There is a smile on Leonard's face, and that brings a fragile smile to hers.

She is filled with a mystifying combination of darkness and light as she walks to the door. Her hand on the latch, she considers the scene behind her for a final time, then she opens the door. Lengthening her stride, she crosses the landing, before dashing up the steps.

Only then does she begin to shout.

The doors open rapidly one after another. Victor responds to her urgent cries first, a single path cleared through the shaving cream that frosts his face; then Ida, still in her nightdress. Sarah is aware of Sergeant Verity's door opening, but she does not turn to him. Instead, she hammers upon Maurice's door with the side of her closed fist.

'It's Leonard!'

Impatient, and ignoring the harried enquiries flying towards her, she throws open the door. Maurice sits up, disorientated by the sudden clamour.

'You must come.' She spins about to address the cluster of bewildered faces behind her. 'You must all come.'

They follow her down the landing, growing in frustration as she fails to answer their desperate questions. In her haste, she stumbles on the short flight of stairs, and her hand darts to the wall to save herself, setting her heart pounding as it has not pounded before.

She pauses as she reaches Leonard's room. 'I'm so sorry.'

She pushes the door open and moves aside, allowing them entry. Ida's hand flies to her mouth. She sways, and it is Victor's arms that shoot out to catch her, as Maurice releases a howl of agony. There is no chance of a mistake this time and certainly no chance of reprieve. His brother is dead. He wraps his arms over his head and keens.

Verity cuts a quiet swathe through the drama. The detachment with which he approaches the bed reminds Sarah of her own. His face, what can be seen of it, matches the blankness of his mask.

'I'm sorry for your loss,' he says at last in a soothing lisp.

'How can this have happened?' Maurice sobs. 'Leonard!'

Sergeant Verity leans over the bed. He takes a handkerchief from the pocket of his trousers, for he alone is dressed. He shakes it free from its crisp folds then reaches over, using it to retrieve the knife lying just below the stump of Leonard's left arm. He turns back to face them, studying the blade.

'It appears to be your knife, Mr Stilwell.'

'What?' The revelation jars Maurice from his grief, his eyes red-rimmed, tears fresh on his cheeks. 'It can't be.'

'I damn well told you to keep that blade safe at all times.' Snatching the towel from Leonard's washstand, Victor furiously wipes the shaving cream from his face.

'I did. I swear I did.'

'I saw you,' Sarah says quietly.

'What?'

'I saw you in the night.' She unburdens herself, unflinching under the pressure of their aghast stares. 'I was thirsty. I got up to get a glass of water from the kitchen. As I left my room, I saw you, down the end of the corridor, leaving yours. I noticed in particular because you looked strange, vacant, but I didn't think any more of it. I went down by the rear staircase and when I came back up, you were at the top of the steps there, walking back to your room. I just thought maybe you'd used the bathroom . . . or had gone in to see Leonard.'

'I d-didn't,' Maurice stutters, confused. 'I didn't leave my room last night.'

'I saw you.'

'I . . . d-didn't I tell you . . . I didn't!' He begins to pace, his breaths growing more frantic with each passing second, the flesh below his eye spasming chaotically. 'I . . . I . . . d-d-didn't . . .'

'Did anyone else hear or see anything last night?' Verity asks.

Ida's fingers stray to her chin. 'I'm not sure, I don't know . . . I think I might have heard a door open at some point. It could have been . . .' her eyes slide towards her husband.

'Maurice . . .' Victor's voice comes out low and halting. 'Is it possible . . . you weren't aware . . .'

'No! No, I tell you!'

'Did you hear any voices last night, Maurice?' Victor persists unsteadily. 'Any German voices?'

'No . . . no, I didn't . . . I tell you now, I . . . d-didn't have any nightmares last night and I didn't leave my room, not once. I'd remember.'

'But sometimes you don't remember,' Ida says, staring at her husband. 'Do you, Maurice? You've sleepwalked before, you know you have. You don't know what you're doing when you're in one of your episodes.'

'I'm b-better now.'

'No, Maurice,' Victor says, grave-faced. 'I think we've all seen that of late. You're not better.'

'Can you explain, Mr Stilwell,' Verity asks, 'how else your brother might have come by your knife?'

'I d-don't know . . . I would never have let him have it, not willingly.' Maurice slaps his forehead. 'I can't remember.'

'Try, Maurice! For once, try and remember.' Ida chokes on her tears. 'Leonard's dead, for God's sake. Sarah saw you coming here last night. Did you do it? Did you kill him?'

'No!' Maurice's cry echoes through the room. 'He's my brother. My brother, for God's sake, I love him.'

'And he was suffering,' Sarah says, her voice breaking. 'You saw his suffering every day, and yes, you loved him . . . perhaps . . . perhaps you thought you could release him from that torture. Is that why you did it?'

'No! I tell you, I didn't. I . . . d-didn't d-do it!'

'When did you last have this knife, Mr Stilwell?'

'He's never parted from it.' Ida's words are cut with bitterness. 'He keeps it with him always of late, to whittle. To whittle away his madness.'

'Ida.' Her name proves an effective reprimand on Victor's tongue, but though she falls silent, her eyes continue to burn with defiance. Victor takes up Verity's line of questioning. 'Maurice, might you have left it somewhere by accident? Somewhere Leonard could have found it?'

'No . . . I don't know, I can't remember. I don't know. Stop saying these things, I didn't do it. I didn't kill him. I loved him.'

'And we are often prepared to do the most heinous things for those we dearly love,' Sergeant Verity says, his words gently formed.

'No! I tell you no!' Maurice is trembling now, his limbs quaking as Sarah has never seen them quake before, while sweat beads his forehead. 'I didn't do it. I would never hurt Leonard. Never, I tell you.'

'Never knowingly.' Victor's head sinks and all at once he is like a full sail stripped of wind, limp and impotent.

'Never!' Maurice whimpers. 'Never!' With growing desperation, he searches their faces for some hint of support, but when it dawns on him that he has already been tried and convicted, he lets out a cry of such despair that even Ida seems moved. He pushes through them to reach the door. 'If I can't be trusted . . . if you can't trust me . . . if I can't know myself . . . Then I'm not safe to be amongst you.'

They pursue him on to the lower landing, calling after him with half-hearted appeal, but he does not respond. He races to his room, slamming the door behind him. The key clunks in the lock. A deathly hush follows.

Swearing under his breath, Victor mounts the steps and goes to Maurice's door. His knock is light at first, but his fist grows heavier with his growing agitation, his voice hardening as Maurice refuses to open up – indeed, he loudly declares that he will never open the door again.

'He won't do anything silly, will he?' Sarah asks.

They can hear Maurice crying, his sobs muffled by the ancient oak.

'Short of breaking down the door, there's not a lot we can do,' Victor says, returning to the lower landing. 'I wish I could say his hurting Leonard was an impossibility, but given the state he's been in of late . . .'

'Let's just leave him for a little while. Perhaps he'll be more rational when he's calmed down,' Ida suggests.

'Poor Leonard,' Sarah whispers, blinking back a sudden glaze of tears.

'What do we do about it?' Ida asks.

'Unfortunately,' Verity says, 'with the telephone out and cut off as we are, there isn't much that can be done for the time being. I suggest the room remains closed and undisturbed, until we are able to notify the authorities – my colleagues on the force—'

'The police?'

'A suspicious death, Mrs Stilwell, demands investigation.'

'If it was Maurice, what will happen to him?'

'If there is sufficient evidence to implicate him, he will be charged with his brother's murder, Mrs Stilwell.'

'Good God.' Ida covers her mouth with a trembling hand. 'That we are come to this.'

'I don't care what you say, Sergeant, we have to find a way across the river now,' Victor says.

'Mr Monroe, please, I can't allow you to risk yourself. Mr Stilwell is unfortunately dead, nothing will change that. What I can't have is recklessness adding to tragedy.'

'So what are we supposed to do? Just sit here with Leonard's . . . *corpse* . . . in the house?'

'That in itself is not such an unusual event really, Mrs Stilwell.'

'It is when he's had his throat slit,' Ida snaps.

Verity remains serene despite the mounting tension. 'I appreciate it's unpleasant, but I'm afraid we must do our best to proceed as we are, for the time being.'

'I can't bear it.' Tears spill down Ida's cheeks.

'Might I suggest we repair to our rooms for now – none of us are quite ready to face the day,' Verity adds in light of Victor's part-shaven jaw. 'Miss Hove, is there a key to this room? Good, then please lock the door.'

As Sarah obeys his instruction, he moves to the landing window. The curtains still conceal the day that awaits them. He pushes aside one edge to take a peek.

'Unfortunately, it is still raining—' he lets the curtain fall '—but let's hope it relents at some point today, and that the floodwaters have a chance to recede.'

'One more day, Sergeant.' Victor is resolute as he addresses Verity. 'That's all I'm giving you, and then, come what may, I'm finding a way out of here.'

Verity regards him steadily. 'Very well, Mr Monroe. One more day. After that, I won't try to stop you.'

Chapter Twenty-Nine

Victor sinks onto the end of his dishevelled bed. Through the walls, he can hear stark evidence of Maurice's heartbreak and it accentuates his own searing pain. He rubs his face, trying to dispel the horror of the scene that lingers ghostlike before him, translucent, yet strangely tangible. Leonard. He tilts back his head, as misery, his old friend, greets him again with a heavy arm around his shoulder, clutching him in a suffocating embrace, crushing the breath from his lungs.

He stands up, pacing the room, dragging his hands through his sleep-mussed hair, unable to suppress the terrifying feeling that everything is falling apart. He flattens his palms against the beamed wall separating his room from Maurice's. He leans into them, his rage surging like lava. Of all the Stilwells, Leonard had been the best. Hugo had been arrogant and assuming, and Maurice, while great fun when the going was good, had proven to be a gutless coward as soon as the going got tough. Only Leonard had possessed a good heart and enviable character.

Victor remembers the boy he was – ebullient, active, always laughing and messing about – but he remembers him at the front too, a boy-man who was able to lead men twice his age over the top without question. He had garnered their respect, their trust. He had the courage of a lion, and everyone saw it. But he had cared too. He had refused to be careless with their lives and displayed a characteristic decency that never floundered. Until it was tested. Until he was made to choose. Family or friendship. Truth or lies. He and Maurice had placed Leonard in an impossible position, and Leonard had never truly recovered from the damage it had done to him. His physical wounds from the shell blast may have mended, but the wounds the two of them had inadvertently inflicted on his character, his sense of decency and self, had never healed. He realises that now.

Victor pushes himself away from the wall, no longer able to bear the sound of Maurice's grief – grief further fuelled, he suspects, by Maurice's guilt over his heinous act. As Victor considers what his friend has done, he turns over the events of the past few days. Maurice had seemed so much better of late, calmer, the quivering in his limbs finally banished, the stutter a mere memory. Only the intermittent flickering of his eye remained to remind them of what he had once been reduced to, how he had suffered, how he had been. His recent deterioration has been sudden and unexpected. Victor thinks back on what Verity said. *The improbable.* Why does he feel he is missing something?

He finishes dressing and completes his shave with a rushed hand. On leaving his room, he is drawn to Ida's door, but hearing her muted sobs, he moves on. He doesn't care what Verity says, he needs to see the extent of the flood for himself. He needs to know if they truly are marooned.

Hurrying down the main staircase, he tries the light switch

at the bottom, but the electricity is still out, so he makes his way across the darkened reception hall from memory so ingrained his steps remain fluid and sure. From the lobby he can just detect the faint sounds of Sarah preparing breakfast, but he ignores the twist in his stomach. He shrugs on his sou'wester and pushes his feet into gumboots still encrusted with mud. For some reason, he chooses not to throw back the door bolts, but instead he eases them gently from their beds. Instinct renders him unwilling to announce his departure. The door creaks as it opens. He darts a cautious look about him and, though he feels foolish for his cloak and dagger tactics, he maintains his stealth as he closes the door behind him.

It is teeming with rain. The floodwaters have now encroached onto areas of the gravelled forecourt. The lawns are but a memory, and the resulting lake holds siege to the house, stretching as far as the eye can see. Victor's gaze comes to rest on the woodland before him. The unexpected overflow may have bought them a day or two, but at some point – and some point soon – he will have to address the issue of the partly dug grave and, more importantly, its contents. Though the thought chills him, it reaffirms the pressing need to rid themselves of Verity.

His mind freshly focused, Victor sets off with the pace of an escapee, splashing through the lying water that has also swallowed the drive, so that the row of poplars now stand guard over a murky mirror that reflects their stripped branches.

The wind blows gusty and cold, chopping the floodwater and pricking his face with rain. He shoves his hands deep into his pockets and whirls around, walking backwards as his narrowed eyes rake the windows of the Hall to see if anyone is spying on his departure. He thinks he detects a shadow of movement at an upstairs window, but he can't be sure. Facing forward, he picks up his pace, the water closing over his boots with every step.

The sheep stand huddled under a cluster of oaks deep in the park, the far side of the drive, away from the floodwaters. They pay him scant attention as he sloshes past, though their bleated complaints carry on the breeze. Soon the woods that stand guard between the parkland and the estate walls rear up to greet him.

The grey light drains as he enters, but for the time being at least he has escaped the floodwaters. The canopies above interfere with the present downpour, but the wind continues to wear them ragged and they rustle and groan, though below, protected by an army of tree trunks, Victor finds he is largely shielded from its belligerence.

He hears the river long before he reaches the bridge. Its roar drowns out the wind and smothers the thrashing of the branches above. Trepidation stirs inside him as he makes his advance. He is unsure how much damage to expect, although he is prepared for the worst. Even now, hearing the river's deafening fury, his imagination conjures images of what he is about to discover – collapsed arches, crumbled parapets, a fractured roadway with a jagged-edged drop into the torrent below. He now suspects Verity's veto on the rowing boat was wise indeed.

At last, he spots the bridge rising above the brown water covering its approach. Within the channel of the river itself, the water gushes ferociously, frothing like a rabid dog. Its force is in fact terrifying, humbling in the extreme, and a primal fear of its power almost holds him back. But he needs to go forward. He needs to assess the damage to the bridge.

Wincing at the noise, he progresses with caution, keeping in line with the bridge's gently elevating approach, his boots splashing into the lying water that covers the drive once more.

He stops, his brows knitting as he stares at the sight before him, momentarily confused. The humped bridge rises over the river and descends into the lying floodwater on the other side. It appears completely intact.

Bewildered, he walks downstream to visually inspect the bridge front on, conscious that the damage could well be beneath, to part of its supporting structure, but as he looks back, he sees at once that this is not the case. The water surges below the stone arches, and whilst the crest of the frothing torrent brushes against the domed underbelly of the bridge, he can see no loose stonework, no eroded mortar, no crumbling gaps, or fractured piers. The bridge looks as sound as ever.

His mind racing, he wades back to the approach and begins to cross. He is deliberate in the way he places each step, testing its safety, half-expecting the bridge to give way beneath him. He finds himself imagining the terrifying plunge and the shock of the freezing rapids as they engulf him. When he reaches the other side without mishap, he is staggered beyond belief.

He splashes through the waiting floodwater and within a few yards finds himself returned to the stony drive.

'What the devil?' He turns full circle, trying to make sense of it all.

And then he spots it. He staggers a few uncertain steps, unsure at first what he is seeing, as some attempt has been made to hide it. Leaving the drive, he moves between the widely spaced trees, following a set of tyre ruts that lead to where two laurels have grown so large the tips of their glossy-leaved branches touch.

He shakes his head in disbelief.

'Well, well, well. What have we here?'

A car stands parked between the two trees – their overlapping branches almost completely conceal it. It doesn't take him long to place the vehicle. It is the same Model T Coupelet he has seen parked on the forecourt of Darkacre Hall. The car supposedly lost to the raging river. The very car from which Detective Sergeant Verity had apparently made his miraculous escape.

He pushes back the low-hanging laurel boughs, eliciting a shower of rainfall from their slickened leaves as he works his way alongside. He cups his hand to the rain-speckled glass of the passenger window and peers in. He is rather disappointed to see only a leather-bound road atlas lying on the seat, along with a flask, nothing of import. He tries the door handle but finds it locked and though he considers breaking the window, in the end he decides against it.

Clambering out from underneath the laurel, he critically reassesses the events of the past few days. They have always assumed the Detective Sergeant is exactly who he says he is – why would they not? But he wonders now whether Sarah had the wit to ask for a warrant card before permitting him entry, or whether she had just taken him at his word when he introduced himself at the door. For that matter, could Ida have made the same mistake with Inspector Hume? Was either of them who they claimed to be?

He curses himself for not having been more thorough, for not having telephoned the police station himself to check the legitimacy of their visits. He had just taken for granted they were who they said. Remembering it was Verity who had delivered the bloody package to Ida, his anger rises. Has the improbable indeed come to pass?

With a new sense of urgency, he hastens back to the drive, swashing through the water. Confident now of its sturdiness, he jogs over the bridge.

He needs to get back to the house. He will confront the wretched Sergeant and demand to see his warrant card, demand to know exactly why he lied about the bridge, and what he hoped to gain by doing so. And if the man has, as he increasingly suspects, no warrant card to show him, and no affiliation with the police to boast of, he will demand to know exactly who he is, how he knows what he does, and what his motives are for deceiving them as he has.

But more than anything now, he must get to Ida. He must ensure she is safe.

A new fear takes him. He begins to run.

Chapter Thirty

He bursts through the front door, his heart hammering in protest at the exertion so rudely thrust upon it. He sets about wrenching off his dripping sou'wester and prising off his boots before the door has even closed behind him. He is just about to head into the reception hall when he sees Sarah coming along the corridor, carrying a tray laden with crockery.

His unexpected presence startles her. She pauses to take in the discarded gumboots lying on the floor and the cast-off raincoat now leaving puddles on the quarry tiles.

'Have you been out, already?' she asks with surprise.

'Where is everyone?'

'I don't know. I've been seeing to breakfast. No one else has come down yet, as far as I know. Not that that's surprising, given the circumstances.'

The tray is clearly heavy, and she carries on around him, but he calls after her. She sighs and turns back, her eyebrows peaked in query.

'Detective Sergeant Verity – that very first time he came, did he show you any sort of identification? A warrant card?'

She appears taken aback by the question and ponders upon it, visibly searching her memory. 'No . . . now you mention it, he just introduced himself, and because I knew the Inspector had been the day before, I . . . well, to be honest I didn't think to question it. After all, who's going to lie about being a police officer?'

'Who indeed.' The blood pumping through Victor's veins runs cold.

Sarah carries on, the crockery rattling upon her tray.

'Ida is still upstairs then?' he calls again.

'They all are, as far as I'm aware,' Sarah replies over her shoulder.

Victor takes the front staircase, aware of Hugo watching over him as he reaches the first half-landing, but he does not dally to consider what the eldest Stilwell boy would think of the developing events. Reaching the bedroom corridor, he hesitates, intending to go straight to Ida, but something sends him in the other direction, towards Leonard's room. Shocked by the morning's tragedy, he had failed earlier to examine the scene. Such an unpleasant task had seemed unnecessary, and Ida had needed his succour, but now he has reason to regret his oversight and he intends to rectify it.

Maurice's grief remains audible as he passes his room. When he reaches Verity's door he pauses, angling his ear to the wood, but unable to hear anything within, he carries on, taking the descending steps lightly, careful to avoid the creaking boards. Darting a look back the way he has come, he heads for Leonard's door. He puts his hand to the latch and pushes, but the door refuses to give. He tries applying more force, but still the ancient timbers hold fast. And then he remembers the Sergeant's insistence the room be locked, to preserve the scene, and he silently curses his earlier lack of curiosity. His failure to question.

Abandoning his lost cause, he is just about to head back to Ida's room, when he catches sight of the attic door. He frowns. It is hanging slightly ajar – and yet it is always kept locked. He tries to fathom who might have needed access and why, but he can think of no reason for anyone to go up there on this of all mornings.

He eases the door wider. Unvarnished wooden steps curve round, rising to the floor above. He takes them warily, his senses heightened in a way they haven't been since the war. The pitched eaves slope sharply into the boarded space that stretches before him. The small windows set low in the walls are smirched with dirt and draught gusts through their ill-fitting frames, while rain patters onto the roof tiles above him. The supporting joists are linked by garlands of cobwebs, and he sees evidence of rodent infestation – a pile of yellowed newspapers shredded to confetti and a scattering of black droppings.

The attic is crammed with boxes and crates, old school trunks marked with the various Stilwells' initials, discarded furniture and long-forgotten toys. The space is divided by a chimney breast that rises through the floorboards to form a wall across the breadth of the attic, leaving just enough space to pass on either side before the sloping eaves guide it through the roof. Victor's attention is drawn to this brick monolith by the old curtains, mildewed and moth-eaten, that have been laid like drugget across the floorboards from the top step of the stairs to its far side – by whom, he cannot think. His suspicions as to their purpose though are confirmed as soon as he begins his cautious advance – each step is deadened by the fabric, disguising his footfall from the bedrooms below.

He proceeds along the drugget pathway to the chimney breast. Its hand-hewn bricks are rough against his palm as he moves past it, his heart thudding in anticipation of whatever it is he is about to discover on the other side. His stomach drops as he takes in the scene.

'Jesus.'

Dropping to his haunches, he plucks up the blanket strewn across a makeshift mattress, exposing a pillow that still bears the indent of the head that slept upon it. As he looks about him, he sees a modest pile of empty ration tins, but it is what he finds beside them that takes his breath away. He swears with disbelief. An officer's forage cap sits upon a neatly folded trench coat. Bewildered, he picks it up and his heart stutters. Hidden beneath is a pipe and a tin of tobacco. Hugo's favourite blend.

His blood pounds through his veins as he bounces back up to standing, his thoughts tangling chaotically as he tries to make sense of his discovery. He searches for a rational explanation, but he knows there is not one, though the alternative – and increasingly the most likely explanation – seems too fantastical to be true. His gaze snags on the chimney breast before him, where a small area of bricks lie awkwardly upon each other. He sees the issue at once – there is no mortar holding them in place, brick rests upon brick. His curiosity piqued, he draws closer, noticing as he does so a heap of thick grey dust and mortar fragments on the floorboards below.

Puzzled, Victor eases out one of the bricks, turning it in his hand. Each edge bears scrape marks, as if caught by a blade. Setting it down, he removes another, then another. Every brick bears the same chisel marks to its surface. He releases a ragged breath. There is only one way to interpret the evidence before him: the mortar securing the bricks in place has been deliberately worked away to facilitate the bricks' removal, but he cannot understand why. And then he sees the rubber hose.

It lies coiled like a resting snake just beyond the ration tins. He looks between the hole in the chimney breast and the hose, trying to piece the two together, knowing instinctively they are somehow connected. He steps back perplexed and confounded. On a whim, he puts his ear to the gap. Swirling air bites at his face, but there is something else. He draws away, then forces himself to listen again. Faint on the draught, he hears Maurice sobbing.

He rights himself, thoughts racing. He conjures a mental image of the house, then feeds the chimney breast through his imaginary plan, trying to ascertain what rooms it serves. As the images meld in his mind's eye, he realises with a bolt of cold certainty that he is indeed directly above Maurice's room. Maurice, who so recently has been tortured by the resurgence of his night-time terrors, with the voices of German soldiers penetrating his sleep, filling his room at night, tormenting him from his slumber.

Victor begins to rapidly feed the pipe through the gap in the brickwork, lowering it – all six or seven feet of it, he estimates – inside the chimney. When he has run out of length, he brings its end to his mouth. He is about to speak Maurice's name, but something dark and perverse shifts deep within him. His thoughts turn from Maurice, to Leonard, then to Ida. His humour sours and his resolve hardens. The hollow end of rubber tube encircles his mouth. He takes a deep breath.

'*Achtung*! *Achtung*!'

Maurice's harrowing cry carries up through the attic

floorboards and echoes within the chimney. Victor's lips twist with grim satisfaction. He retracts the hose, leaving it to slither into a heap upon the floor. He has discovered all he needs to know. His calculations are correct. Questions begin to fill his mind. But answers also.

'The improbable indeed,' he murmurs.

Chapter Thirty-One

Victor makes a stealthy descent. Darkacre Hall is no longer the safe haven it has always been, and whilst he doesn't possess the answers to all of the questions swirling through his mind, he has deduced enough to be on his guard. His primary concern now is to find Ida.

The lower landing is empty as he inches open the attic door. He crosses swiftly, making as little noise as possible. In the bedroom corridor, he pauses again outside the room of the man claiming to be Detective Sergeant Verity, but no noise greets him as he cocks his ear to the wood, and he cannot ascertain whether the room is occupied or not. Discovering the true identity of this faceless man who has insinuated his way into their midst has become Victor's obsession, as he speculates as to what might have driven him into this charade and, more crucially, what he hopes to achieve by it. Is he simply a crank? Does the copper mask hide not only a damaged face but also a deranged mind? He cannot dismiss the disturbing fear that something sinister is afoot.

He passes Maurice's room and heads directly to Ida's. Wishing to avoid all chance of detection, he does not risk announcing his presence, but merely lifts the latch and lets himself in. His disappointment at finding the room empty is profound – only a cloud of Coty Chypre remains of her. The tantalising scent elicits a wave of desire. He leaves at once, his need to see her, speak to her, urgent now.

The fire is crackling when he reaches the reception hall, though it does little to alleviate the chill in the air. No sounds emanate from the dining room. Suspecting Ida will be unwilling to face breakfast alone for fear of having to entertain the enigmatic Detective, he heads for the drawing room. He ensures his tread is light upon the flags as he keeps his wits about him.

'Oh, there you are! Where have you been?' Ida asks, pushing a slice of apple through the bars of Mr Tibbs' cage. The parrot takes it from her with infinite care, whistling its gratitude.

'Ida . . .' Victor softly closes the door behind him. He crosses the room in a few strides, then takes the plate of apple from her hand and sets it down on the piano top.

She looks at him as if he has lost his mind.

'What on earth—' But there is something in his expression that kills her laughter, and the sparkle dies from her eyes.

'Have you seen our friend Verity since this morning?'

'No. No, that's why I'm in here, waiting for you. Maurice is clearly in no fit state to come down and I didn't want to have to breakfast with that frightful man on my own.' Her tone changes in the face of his sobriety. 'Victor, what's going on?'

'I don't know. But something is.' Pacing away from her, he drags his hand through his hair. 'I've been out, down to the bridge.'

'Oh.' She takes a half step towards him. 'Is it bad? Is there any chance of getting across the river do you think?'

'Ida, the bridge is intact.'

It takes a minute for his words to sink in. 'What?'

'The bridge is as undamaged as it's ever been.'

'But . . . but Sergeant Verity said . . . why would he say it was gone?'

'To keep us here.'

'What? What on earth are you talking about?'

Victor steals a look at the door then lowers his voice another notch. 'I found his car parked up, partially concealed in the woods the far side of the river. I don't know what his game is, but I believe he told us the bridge was out because he didn't want us to think we had any chance of leaving the house. Ida . . . that man . . . he's been lying to us all along.'

'Lying to us? But why would a policeman lie to us?'

'Is he a policeman? I checked with Sarah this morning – he never showed her any form of identification and she never thought to ask for it. She took him at his word. We all have.'

Ida struggles to absorb his revelations. Her features crease with confusion. 'But why would he lie? Who is he? What could he possibly want with us?'

'I don't know, but I think he's been in this house for longer than we think. I found the attic unlocked this morning, which I thought was curious since no one has reason to be up there, so I went up to investigate.' He hurries over to her. 'Ida, someone's been sleeping up there, living up there by the looks of things, and there's more. There was officers' garb, just like Maurice said he'd seen Hugo wearing. And I found a tin of Hugo's tobacco.'

Ida's cheeks lose their colour like sun-bleached fabric. 'Dear God.'

'There was also a length of rubber tubing, and someone has taken the trouble to remove bricks from the chimney breast that serves Maurice's bedroom. Ida . . .' his fingers close around the soft swell of her arms 'those German voices that he's suddenly been hearing? I don't think they were in Maurice's imagination after all. I think someone has been up there deliberately torturing him, playing with his mind. I tried it out myself. I suspended the tubing down the chimney, and I spoke into it. Maurice heard me. I was in the attic, but Maurice heard me in his room. Ida, somebody has been up there driving him to madness.'

'That's impossible.' Ida pulls away from him. 'How could someone be in the house and us not know? And you've had cause to check, *twice* now!'

'I know. Somehow he has been moving around this house, avoiding detection.'

'And you really think it's this Detective Sergeant Verity? That it's been him all along?'

'I am struggling to think who else it could be. A stranger turns up, he delivers that God-awful package to you, then he comes day after day asking question after question, and finally he tells a blatant lie in order to be offered shelter in this house.' Victor falls silent. 'And then of course there's Leonard . . .'

Ida begins to tremble. 'Dear God! You don't think it was him who killed Leonard, not Maurice?'

The full implications of their predicament strike Victor anew. His energy drains as an image of Leonard's body flashes before him. 'I don't know, Ida. But I think we have to consider it a real possibility.' He grabs her arms again, forcing her to focus. 'Ida, listen to me, we have to get out of here. We don't know who this devil is. We don't know what he wants with us or what he's capable of, but we do know he's intent on keeping us trapped here and I, for one, don't want to wait around to find out why.'

'What can we do?'

He can see she is afraid. The strength of his instinct to protect her shocks him. He knows in that instant that he will do whatever it takes to keep her safe, and the realisation steadies him, giving him a greater sense of purpose than ever before. 'We leave, now. We can take the car and get into town. We'll go straight to the police.'

'What about Maurice and Sarah? We can't just abandon them with a mad man.'

'Sarah can come with us if she can get away, but I'm not waiting for her.'

'I must try to speak to Maurice.' Ida attempts to pull free, but he tightens his grip, keeping her in place.

'Ida . . . Ida, for whatever reason, this man has attacked Maurice in the cruellest possible way. He's unleashed Maurice's demons, demons that were only ever barely contained in the first place.' He searches her face, desperately seeking for a glimmer of something, *anything*, that will give him hope that what he has always wanted may at last have a chance of coming to pass. He grapples for the right words to help make it happen. 'Ida, I don't know that Maurice will ever recover from this. You've seen him, you've seen how he is. And what if Sarah's right? What if it was Maurice?'

'What are you trying to say, Victor?'

'Ida—' he tugs her closer, and when she doesn't resist, his heart soars '—you know how I feel about you, how I've always felt about you. I know you said we were never to speak of it again, and I've respected that, all these years, but the fact remains if that bloody simpleton hadn't interrupted us, we would have given ourselves fully to that desire.'

When Ida finally finds her voice, it is a featherlight whisper. 'Victor . . . we should never have let it go as far as it did . . . if we hadn't . . . oh God! If we hadn't the awful events of that day would never have happened.'

'But we did, we couldn't help ourselves . . . and then we did what we had to do to protect our secret.'

She jerks free of his hold, and panic grips him, panic the like of which he has never experienced before, not even under fire.

'And look what happened! Dear God, Victor, we lied to protect ourselves and look what happened!'

'Ida, please.' She twists away when he tries to touch her, and he realises she is slipping away from him. The distance between them in this very moment is greater than it has ever been in the six years since that sultry summer's afternoon. 'Ida, I never meant for him to . . . when Maurice and Leonard came running, I just said the first thing that came into my head. I couldn't let that boy blurt out the truth, I had to protect us, I had to protect *you*, Ida. I said what I did to protect you more than myself. I never thought my accusation would lead to . . .'

'Mob violence.' There are tears on Ida's cheeks. 'That's what it led to. You all fed off each other. A simple punch, then a kick, then another kick, then all of you kicking and punching.' Ida hides her face in her hands.

'It got out of hand, I know, but what's done is done. We can't bring him back, but at least . . .'

'At least what?'

He is careful not to reach for her, though it requires him to deny his every impulse. He meets her challenge with gentle appeal. 'If you and I were finally together, it would all mean something, surely? No, don't turn away – listen to me. I know you don't love Maurice. He's not even the man you married anymore, and we both know the estate is in hock. I know money is what persuaded you to choose him over me in the first place. I could never compete with the Stilwell fortune, but Ida, the Stilwell fortune has gone. Whereas my investments have served me well. I can look after you, give you the life you've always wanted, the life you deserve.'

'And what of Maurice?'

'What of Maurice?' He bites his tongue too late. He sees his barbed lash land and regrets the slip immediately. Time is pressing upon him. He is acutely aware that Verity is somewhere in the house, prowling, circling, preparing – though for what he does not know, and this fact alone concerns him above all others. He needs to get her out. He needs her to see sense. 'Maurice has cracked. You can get a divorce; nobody could blame you for doing so now. Or we can just go abroad, to the continent, somewhere no one knows us. I have the funds for us to escape, Ida. The South of France maybe. You'd like that, wouldn't you? An elegant life on the Côte d'Azur? Live it with me, Ida. You're all I've ever wanted.'

Her hesitation stings, but as he watches her, he sees her shock morph into shrewd calculation, and it gives him hope. He can see her picturing swathes of golden beaches, the crystal-clear seas, the villa smothered in ruby bougainvillea, the coupes of champagne they will sip, sitting on the terrace in the scorching sun. He sees it all play through her mind and he knows, at last, he has won. He has her. The light that used to shine so brightly within her before the war, the light that for so long has been extinguished, glows again.

'All right.'

He kisses her then, pulls her to him, rougher than he intended, but he is overcome with euphoria that at last he has conquered the mountain he has been struggling to climb from the very first second he saw her. The path may have been rocky, and he has endured setbacks along the way, but he never doubted he would succeed in reaching the pinnacle, somehow, someday.

He crushes her against him, his desire rising, and though she is stiff with resistance at first, the memory of that late summer day in the dell, when they were still wet from swimming in the river, their white cotton clothes clinging, translucent, to their sun-warmed skin, comes back to them both, and the passion they felt then, forbidden but irrepressible, surges to the surface once more.

He recalls how he pushed her against the tree, their teeth clashing with a furious, aggressive lust; how he pulled up her damp skirt as her demanding hands tugged his belt from its buckle; how his fingers became tangled in her satin knickers as she wriggled to free herself of them and how his pulse careered as she pushed his trousers away. He can remember vividly the pleasurable torment of plunging inside her and her accompanying cry of yearning that had driven out all reason, as her moans of need met his own.

And then the damn boy, blundering from the undergrowth, demanding he release her. Victor barely had time to pull up his trousers and fix his belt before Maurice and Leonard came running, half-dressed and still dripping from the river. Victor had no choice but to throw that first punch, fuelled by the frustration of thwarted passion, rage, and fear. The boy went straight down. The accusation that Bobby had attempted to attack Ida flew unconsciously from Victor's mouth, and Ida stepped into the role of damsel in distress without hesitation, plucking at her dishevelled clothing, weeping prettily, until Maurice, his features creased with fury, unleashed a kick worthy of a fly-half converting a try. Leonard followed suit, like an eager puppy copying its littermates, a little unsure at first but determined to join in the fun. And then they were all at him, kicking and stamping, while the dolt of a boy rolled on the ground, his arms pulled up in pathetic protection, as he pleaded with them to stop.

But it was he, bloodied and broken, who stopped first. He fell still and silent, and finally they did too, their chests heaving, the red mist before them gradually clearing. They stood above him, nudging him with the toes of their shoes, ordering him to get up. Strangely, it was Leonard who took the lead, Leonard who crouched down and with a trembling hand reached out to feel for the boy's pulse. Leonard who fell back onto the seat of his pants, his jaw slack, his eyes wide. It was Leonard who first realised what they had done.

Victor and Maurice buried Bobby Higgins – Leonard was too upset to help. Victor watched him escort Ida back to the house, where they would have to pretend nothing was amiss. Ida glanced back at Victor as they left, her chin to her shoulder, and as her eyes found his, he knew they would never speak again about the events that had led to this calamity, that they would never again give voice to the passion between them. As he rolled Bobby's body into the hastily dug grave that day, Victor felt he was consigning a part of himself to the ground with him. But now both have been disinterred.

Ida gently prises herself away. She dabs her fingers to her swollen lips, her dry eyes wide with startlement.

'So what now?' she whispers.

It is a struggle to ground himself, but one thought of Verity and Victor's passion is quelled, and his sense of urgency is restored. 'We must leave at once.'

'I need to get some things from my room.'

'All right, but just grab what you must. Your jewellery,' he says quickly. 'Bring all of it, just in case we don't come back.'

She clings to him. 'Will you come with me? I'm afraid.'

'I need to get Maurice's revolver, it's in the study. You'll be all right. Just go straight up to your room—'

'But what if I see him?'

He captures her flushed cheeks in his palms. 'Remember, he doesn't think anything is amiss. Act as if nothing has changed, then lock yourself in your room – don't open the door to anyone but me. I'll deal with Verity if needs be. Whoever he is.'

They start for the door, Ida's fingers loosely threaded through his. As he reaches for the handle, she stops him. 'Victor, why is he doing this? What can he possibly want with us?'

He squeezes her hand. 'I don't know, but he seems to know an awful lot about Bobby Higgins, and he knows what happened that night in the shell hole.'

'But how? How could he know about all of that?'

'I don't know,' Victor admits, grim-faced. 'But I'm sure as hell going to find out.'

Chapter Thirty-Two

Despite Victor imploring her to act as if nothing has happened, Ida dashes across the reception hall and takes the staircase like a tag-playing child racing to make the safety of home.

She feels physically sick by the time she reaches the bedroom corridor. She snatches a look over her shoulder, convinced the faceless man is in pursuit, but the staircase is empty, and, as she surveys the full length of the landing, she is relieved to find he is nowhere in sight.

Even so, she still runs to her room, not even allowing the sound of Maurice's tortured grief to waylay her. She fumbles with the latch, then falls inside, slamming the door shut behind her. She rests heavily against it while she catches her breath, her eyes closed with relief. When she opens them, she issues a startled cry.

'Oh Sarah! You frightened me.'

Sarah is in the middle of making the bed. Recovering from her surprise at Ida's dramatic entrance, she proceeds to fold down the top sheet, tucking it neatly beneath the mattress.

Ida's heart is still hammering. 'Sarah, have you seen Detective Sergeant Verity?'

'Not since breakfast, I'm afraid,' Sarah says, plumping the pillows.

Ida absorbs this information with a distracted nod. Her fingers knot together as she takes a step further into the room. 'Sarah . . . Victor and I are leaving.'

Sarah looks up. 'Leaving? I'm sorry, I don't follow.'

'Oh Sarah!' Desperate to share Victor's terrible revelations, Ida hurries forward. 'Sarah, he's lied to us all.'

'Who has?'

'Verity,' Ida spits. 'He's lied about everything. The bridge? The bridge isn't out at all. There's nothing stopping us going for help over Leonard.'

Reassured by the security of the room and Sarah's stalwart company, Ida bustles over to her dressing table beneath the window. She begins pulling out the drawers, gathering her jewellery boxes into a pile.

'He's not who he says he is, you know. Victor suspects he's not a policeman at all.' She pauses to look back over her shoulder. 'He was the one that brought that ghastly package into the house for me – it was all his doing.' Taking huge satisfaction from Sarah's evident astonishment, she busies herself once again with her valuables. 'We don't think he found it on the doorstep at all. And Victor thinks he may have had a hand in Leonard's death – Leonard's *murder*! Pass me the vanity case in my wardrobe, would you? And the worst part of it all? Victor thinks he's been hiding in the house, Sarah. All this time, hiding in the attic! And all that nonsense Maurice has been spouting about Hugo and the Germans, Victor thinks it's been him, all of it, all along. So, we've got to get away from here as quickly as possible and get the police involved. You must come with us, Sarah.'

With her jewellery boxes clustered on the dressing table,

ready to be swept into the vanity case, Ida finally turns around. She is surprised to see Sarah standing by the bedroom door, a pillow in her hand.

'Sarah, did you hear a word of that? We have to get away.'

Sarah locks the door.

'Oh yes! Good idea,' Ida flattens her hand against her chest. 'Victor said to lock myself in and I plain forgot. I was so scared that man was going to catch me before I got here. Now come on, help me pack a few things, not much of course, just enough for the next few days. Goodness knows what's going to happen.'

Sarah turns away from the door, both hands on the pillow now.

'Sarah?'

'He was sixteen when you handed him that white feather,' she says softly. 'He had his birthday just a fortnight before. Sixteen. Too young to fight, but old enough to know right from wrong. Old enough to know that he'd witnessed a murder.'

Ida is motionless. 'What are you talking about?'

'Joe struggled with his guilt. It had been his idea, you see, to go to the woods that day. He'd wanted to try his hand at snaring some rabbits. Bobby had pestered him into letting him go along too, and Joey was a good sort, he didn't mind Bobby's company. He knew the boy was harmless. Simple, but harmless, with a heart of gold.'

Sarah begins a slow advance into the room. Ida takes a step back, jarring the dressing table. Her perfume bottles dance, tinkling against each other. A ring box lands on the floor with a soft thud.

'They hid, of course, as soon as they heard you coming.

They didn't know if you would be cross with them because they were closer to the river than perhaps they ought to have been, especially with you lot drunkenly cavorting in it as you were. So, Joey pulled Bobby down, and they hid in the bracken, intending to run for it after you'd passed by. But of course, you didn't pass by. Victor Monroe caught up with you. Maurice must have been blind not to see it. I've noticed the attraction between the two of you since the day I arrived.'

'Sarah—'

'And Bobby didn't understand, the innocent that he was. He thought, with all your moaning and groaning, that Victor Monroe was hurting you, and Bobby didn't like that. Joey tried to hold him back. He told me how Bobby's shirttail slipped through his fingers, and then he was there, berating Victor, and poor Joey, he was paralysed. Didn't know what to do. Had no idea the length you people would go to, to protect your sordid secrets.'

'Sarah . . . now listen to me . . .' Ida edges along the dressing table, her eyes darting to the door.

'Do you know what it was like for Joe to witness what they did to Bobby?' Sarah's fingers tighten on the pillow. 'He filled his mouth with dirt to stop his own screams. And the guilt – the guilt of having done nothing to stop it – ate him up. Until at last he found the courage to confront you, a few weeks later, at the Harvest Fair. There you were, all prim and proper, full of self-righteousness, handing out white feathers to any man or boy you could see, not stopping for a minute to consider there might be a good reason why they weren't in uniform.'

'I didn't know he was sixteen,' Ida murmurs.

But in her heart, she knows it would have made no difference, even if she had.

She paused in the shade of a beech tree to take stock of her afternoon's success, a little distance away from the Harvest Fair with its skittles and stalls and milling crowd. She had felt as valiant at Boudicca as she handed out white feathers to men so unsuspecting they had accepted them with confusion rather than comment. Only one had managed to gather his wits in time to hurl an insult in her wake, but it had not tempered her triumphant smile as she walked away.

A glance now in her handbag revealed her supply of feathers to be sadly depleted, meaning her campaign would have to rest until another day – another day soon, for the sense of power gleaned from her endeavours was addictive and she was already yearning for more.

It was then, as she was closing her bag, that she noticed him, skulking. It took her a moment to place his face, but she finally realised it was the Durham boy, Leonard's rather inappropriate friend. As their eyes locked his apparent agitation provoked a stir of unease.

'I've been watching you,' he said, his voice unsteady. 'Handing out your white feathers, looking mighty pleased with yourself, like somehow you're better than the rest of us.' He appeared to gather his courage before taking a step closer. 'Quite the queen of virtue—' he shaped the title with sarcasm '—but some of us know the truth about you.'

'I have no idea what you're talking about.'

'I was there,' he hissed, drawing nearer. 'I saw you.'

'I have no interest in what you saw, just as I have no

interest in wasting my time listening to your ramblings.' She turned to leave.

'I know the truth about you and Victor Monroe. I saw the two of you that day by the river. You couldn't keep your hands off each other.'

His words stopped her in her tracks. She was thankful her back was to him, so he couldn't see the shock on her face. She willed herself to walk on, but her treacherous feet refused to move.

'And I heard your lies. And I saw what you did to Bobby Higgins.'

She whirled around, her heart skittering. She stared at him, her breaths short and sharp. He nodded slowly, his mouth hard with contempt. 'Oh yes, I saw it all and I'm done keeping quiet about it.' His face crumpled. 'His poor mother . . . beside herself wondering where he is.' He paused long enough to regain his self-control. 'The whole village went out looking for him and I went too, playing along because I didn't know what else to do, because I was too bloody scared to do the right thing, but no more! I can't do this no more.'

'You hold your tongue, Joe Durham.' It was Ida who now advanced, driven forward by furious self-preservation. 'You'll hold your tongue, and you will tell no one.'

'I can't—'

'You will!' There was only a hair's breadth between them. She glared into his glistening eyes. 'Because if you don't, I'll have your family evicted from Home Farm without notice and I'll take steps to ensure no one employs any of you again. Your family will be out on the street, without a roof over their heads or food in their mouths, with no prospects. And

all of it will be your doing, Joe Durham. You will bring that misery on your parents. How old is your father now? And your mother doesn't have the best of health from what I hear. Are you sure you want to do that to them, Joe, at their time of life? Because I'll make damn sure it happens if you breathe a word to anyone.'

Satisfied her message had been received, she took a step back. 'You know, any decent young man would be taking up arms to defend his country right now, not trying to threaten a married woman. Only a coward would behave in such a way—' delving into her bag, she plucked out the last remaining feather and thrust it into his chest '—so this is what you deserve. You should be ashamed of yourself, Joe Durham.'

The delicate white curl drifted downwards, its descent watched by the ashen-faced boy before her. As Ida walked away, she had the satisfaction of seeing him crouch down to claim it.

'Even if you didn't know his exact age, you must have had a damn good idea he was too young for the army,' Sarah says now, displaying chilling dispassion. 'You gave him that feather to get rid of him.'

'Who are you?' Ida whispers.

'I'm Sarah Durham. Hove is my mother's maiden name, I thought I'd use it just in case, but I didn't think you'd know me. I was away working by the time Dad took on Home Farm. Joe was my baby brother. And I loved him dearly.'

'I don't know what you think happened, but it's not true, Sarah. None of it.'

'Oh don't. Don't do that. Don't insult me.' As Sarah circles towards her, Ida tries to back away, but she is cornered. The bed now lies between her and the door. 'Joe wrote to me. His final act before they shot him for cowardice. And that's another story, isn't it? More Stilwell guilt, more covering up of lies. But our Joe, he wanted the truth to come out. So, he wrote it all down. If only he'd told me sooner, I might have been able to do something.' Sarah swallows hard. Tears glaze her eyes. 'He made sure that account reached me directly. He knew he couldn't risk it getting into the hands of his commanding officers . . . your husband, Monroe . . . it was clear he couldn't even trust Leonard anymore, Leonard who he'd turned to for support, his best friend.' Sarah snorts. 'Even Leonard betrayed him in the end. Though at least he had the decency to come to regret it. No, Joe couldn't risk anyone getting hold of that letter. So, he entrusted it to the one person he knew would get it to me uncensored. Who would deliver it by hand. His platoon sergeant. My fiancé.'

Goosebumps wash across Ida's shoulder blades. 'That man . . .'

For the first time, Sarah smiles, her eyes shining. 'That man is the most loyal, most generous, kindest man I have ever met. It is my privilege to love him, and to be loved by him. I am cherished, and I pity you that, Mrs Stilwell, because I don't think any man has ever cherished you. I wonder whether they have even ever loved you, though they have, without doubt, wanted you. Desired you. Lusted after you.'

'Sarah, please . . .'

'The war memorial will be revealed at the service on Sunday. Twenty-two names. I cannot claim to know them, I didn't grow up here, I was never amongst these people. But I do know one name is missing. Our Joe's name won't be inscribed.

We had all wanted it there and Mum tried, bless her.' She swallows again, her voice straining with emotion. 'She dug into her savings and wanted to make her contribution, but they wouldn't accept it. They wouldn't have our Joe's name on it, and the thought of his service not being recognised, the thought of his name being forgotten, has broken my mum's heart. That memorial is for the "courageous dead", not the so-called cowards, the men shot at dawn, like our Joe, even though he fought with bravery when he was too young to be fighting anyway. Even though the only thing he was guilty of was daring to cross the mighty Stilwells, daring to challenge their lies. My mum cries herself to sleep every night, while all of you get to walk away with your heads held high.'

'Is that what this is all about?' Ida asks, nearly crying with relief. 'Sarah, I can use my influence.' Seeing a glimmer of light at the end of a perilously dark tunnel, Ida ceases to cower. She almost laughs at the fuss being made and smiles at how easy it will be to resolve. 'I can insist Joe's name is added. He will be remembered. I can make that happen.'

Sarah tries to stifle a chuckle, but it slips out as a gleeful giggle. Her entire face lights up with amusement, and Ida finds herself beaming in delighted response.

'You?' Sarah says at last. 'The person they hate so much they've asked you not to attend? You think *you* can make them add our Joe's name?' Her laughter dies. 'This village hates you, Mrs Stilwell. Your name is barely uttered, and when it is, it is with loathing.'

'Then what do you want?' Ida cries, slapping her hands against her thighs in frustration. Fear pricks her anew. 'What do you want from me?'

'I want you to be punished, Mrs Stilwell, to be punished for your crimes, for the damage, for the *death*, they have caused.'

'And so what?' Ida demands, growing belligerent. 'You're going to tell the police, are you?'

'Oh, we have told the police.' In contrast to Ida's defiance, Sarah's tone is conversational. 'That is to say, we fulfilled Joe's dying wish, that his letter, his witness account of all that happened, should be handed over to the authorities, for them to take whatever action they see fit.' Sarah tuts with dissatisfaction. 'But you see, so much time has passed, evidence will have been lost, and at the end of the day, it's just a dead man's word against the living. So we knew, despite our best efforts, justice could never, would never, really be done. For that to happen, for there to be proper justice, we would have to mete it out ourselves.' Sarah regards her steadily, her face impassive. 'Rough justice. Just like the rough justice handed out to Bobby Higgins, even though he was innocent of any wrongdoing. But you, Mrs Stilwell, you're not innocent. You're as guilty as sin.'

Sarah lunges. Ida tries to scramble across the bed, her eyes trained on the door, but Sarah grabs her, yanking her down onto the mattress, rolling her over. Before Ida can recover, Sarah is upon her, straddling her, pinning her in place. She sits so heavily on Ida's stomach that Ida can barely gather breath.

She lashes out with clenched fists, but Sarah, stony-faced, absorbs each impact without so much as flinching. Panic-stricken Ida wriggles and bucks, hitting and scratching, her desperation growing as she calls out for Victor.

But her cries are soon muffled by the pillow covering her face.

Chapter Thirty-Three

Having left Ida, Victor stalks down the corridor towards the study. Volleys of rain clatter against the windowpanes as the wind batters the house. His blood is up, and his senses are humming. He feels as if he is on a trench raid. He feels like a hunter. He feels alive.

There are three things in the study he needs: the keys to the Lagonda; Maurice's service revolver which is kept in the desk drawer; and the petty cash box – the last time he caught a glimpse inside, it was packed with bank notes and bonds. He will take it all. And then he will take Ida.

He lets himself into the study and crosses immediately to the desk. Seeing the candlestick telephone, he lifts the receiver to check whether the lines have been restored.

The connecting cord has been sliced through.

He swears under his breath at the audacity of it and curses his stupidity for not having checked such things earlier. He vows never to be so gullible again.

Yanking open the bottom drawer, he extracts the cashbox. As ever, Maurice has left the key in the lock. He twists it round and lifts the lid, a satisfied smile tugging at his lips. He has often told Maurice he was a fool for keeping such large quantities of cash around, but Victor is now glad his warnings fell on deaf ears. Relocking the box, he opens the desk's top drawer, fully expecting to find the Webley inside, but all he can see is a carton of bullets. Frowning, he ferrets through the drawer's contents, suspecting the weapon has been shoved to the back.

'Looking for this?'

Verity rises from one of the winged chairs facing the fireplace, their backs to the desk behind them. In his leather-gloved hand, pointed at Victor, is the pistol.

'It's strange, having one of these back in my hands,' he says. The distortion to the words is almost unnoticeable to Victor, he has become so accustomed to it. 'Can you remember the last time I held one?'

'How can I?' Victor straightens up, the muscle in his jaw twitching. He refuses to give the masked man the satisfaction of seeing his discomposure.

Verity chuckles. What remains of his lips forms a wry smile. 'You should remember it. What was it Mr Tibbs said? *Finish him off.* You looked so terrified when he said that I almost laughed . . . but that would have given the game away.'

'Who the hell are you?'

'Don't you recognise me, sir? Well,' Verity gestures to his mask, 'I suppose I have changed a bit since the war.'

And then, to Victor's rising horror, he removes the copper moulding from what is left of his face and drops it upon the chair.

'Is that better?'

It is as if the side of his face has been caved in. Where there should be the line of a jaw and the ridge of a cheekbone, there is a deep dent covered with skin. Where there should be an eye, there is a scooped hollow. He has no nose to speak of, just flattened skin that stretches down to where once there were lips. And yet, despite the evident destruction, something nags at Victor's memory. Surveyed in full, without the distraction of the painted mask, he sees a hint of someone vaguely familiar. He squints at Verity, attempting to mentally rebuild his face in his quest for its true identity.

'Coming back to you now, is it?' Verity lisps.

'I never knew a Verity.'

'A pseudonym, of course. I thought it rather apt, verity meaning . . .'

'Truth.'

'Indeed.' The deformed mouth moves into the semblance of a smile. 'There we are, you're getting it at last. It's a wonder it took you so long. A smart officer like you, I was worried you'd have me rumbled from the off. I wasn't too concerned about poor old Maurice, knowing the state he'd been in, and Leonard . . . well, I didn't have so much to do with him, so that seemed to be a risk worth taking.' The faceless man studies him intently. 'No, it was you, you were the one that I was worried about. That keen mind of yours was a possible fly in the ointment. But it seems you're still so distracted by a certain person, that you didn't stop to question anything.' He chuckles. 'It was a risky plan, certainly. A fifty-fifty chance of working at best and yet . . . here we are.'

'Sergeant Dakers.'

'There you have it.' Something akin to pleasure shines in his eye. 'I'd salute but—' he tips the gun to one side '—you understand, I'm sure.'

'What's this all about, Sergeant?'

'Goodness me, sir, I must say this is all very disappointing. I thought you'd have it all worked out by now.' Dakers' tone remains disconcertingly genial. Other than the weapon trained on Victor, there is nothing in his manner to suggest they are anything but two former comrades, catching up after a chance meeting – except Victor is keenly aware nothing has been left to chance over this reunion.

'Well, forgive me, Dakers, but I seem to be a bit slow on the uptake,' Victor says, trying to match his former sergeant's cool demeanour, though his mouth is dry and his heart is racing.

'It's not complicated, sir.' Dakers perches on the arm of the chair. 'It's just a little story of revenge. And justice being served, that too of course.'

'Justice? For what?'

'For forcing me to put a gun to an innocent boy's head and then ordering me to pull the trigger . . . *sir*.' For the first time, there is a betraying quiver in Dakers' voice, but he quickly suppresses it. 'That's my part, at least. But there's so much more. My Sarah—'

Victor's stomach drops. '*Your* Sarah?'

Dakers chuckles again. 'My wife, Sarah. You've been enjoying her cooking these last few days, I believe. Grand cook she is, and the best wife a man could have. Loyal, loving, devoted. I told you I would do anything for her, and now you can see for yourself, I meant every word.'

'Sarah . . .' Victor flexes his fingers by his sides. His palms are sticky. 'Where's Sarah now?'

'Seeing to Mrs Stilwell, I should imagine.'

Victor makes a dash for the door, but Dakers easily cuts

in front of him. 'Now, now, now . . .' he keeps the Webley pointed at Vic's middle. 'Bit rude to dash off when we haven't finished our chat.'

'I have nothing to say to you.'

'That's as may be, but I have a thing or two to say to you, Captain Monroe. I think if a man's going to die, he should know what for.'

Victor's throat constricts. His pulse is rapid now, his thoughts distracted. He tries not to imagine Ida alone with Sarah, but instead he focuses on how he can get to her. On how he might disarm Dakers.

'All right. Talk.'

Dakers appears pleased he is to be humoured. His body relaxes again, and if he is aware of the intense scrutiny he is under, he does not show it. This lackadaisical attitude towards his own safety gives Victor hope. He concentrates his attention on the man before him. Waiting for his opportunity.

'Do you remember how I said I came to meet my wife?'

Victor blinks, trying to recall. 'One of your men introduced you.'

'Yes, that's right. A young boy, too young to be fighting, I saw that straight away. A young lad by the name of Joe Durham.' It is clear to Vic that Dakers enjoys seeing the shock this bit of intelligence evokes. He tries to steel himself, preparing for more revelations, determined not to give him any further satisfaction. 'Lovely lad, Joe, and despite his age, he was as brave as any of them in my platoon. Too young to have the sense to be afraid maybe. Too young to consider his own mortality. He never told me how he came to enlist. I just presumed he'd pulled the wool over the eyes of some unscrupulous recruitment sergeant and his MO. That's how it was at the start, wasn't it? Let the eager beavers have a chance of adventure before it's all over, no matter if they're a little too young. It was only later that I came to learn the real reason he'd joined up. How a white feather wrongly given had filled him with shame he had no right to feel. But I also think he wanted to escape, escape what he had seen, escape the betrayal he felt he had committed.'

Dakers dabs at the corner of his mouth with his free hand. Victor attempts to take advantage of his momentary distraction to shift his position, but his subtle move does not escape Daker's notice, and the Sergeant's lips curl with amusement, his eye narrowing. He raises his eyebrows in reprimand before gathering himself to continue.

'He insisted I accompany him one time when we had a few days' leave. His sister, older sister, was nursing in the nearby hospital. He'd arranged to see her and harangued me into coming along. To think now I nearly didn't go.' His expression softens, his voice dropping. 'Best thing I ever did, going to tea that day.'

His damaged features harden. 'And then suddenly, little Joe, he's charged with murder, cowardice, abandoning his weapon, threatening an officer. I couldn't understand it, it was all so out of character. You lot ensured he was quickly put under guard, but I got in to see him. As his sergeant and all, I pulled a few strings. And that's when he told what had actually happened.'

'He lied.'

'No,' the soft contradiction comes with a shake of the head. 'No, Joe wasn't like you. He wasn't a liar. He carried a wounded man into that shell hole where you and Maurice were hiding.'

'We weren't hiding,' Vic asserts, surprised by the tremor in his voice. 'We were injured. We were taking cover.'

And before he can stop them, the memories rush in.

The blast blew him off his feet. One minute he was leading the charge, Maurice a yard or so to his left, and the next he was flying. He landed heavily, the wind knocked from his lungs as a cascade of soil and stone tumbled upon him. Prostrate in the dirt, he tried to breathe, his ears ringing, his senses numbed. His eyes raked the ground before him, watching boots charging past. Groaning, he rolled onto his side, staring up into the gauze of smoke, the smell of cordite burning his nostrils. His tongue was foul with the metallic taste of blood.

And then he saw Maurice, face down beside him, a thin covering of earth over his inert body.

'Jesus, Maurice!'

He scrabbled sideways, ignoring the cacophony around him, the thuds and screams, the zip of bullets, the shouts and booms, and the drilling ack-ack-ack of machine-gun fire that was spitting up the nearby ground. He shook Maurice's shoulder, and when that failed to elicit any response, he pushed him over onto his back. 'Maurice! Christ, Maurice, come on!' he cried, oblivious now to the men still charging past them, many crumpling as German bullets found their mark. 'Maurice!'

Maurice jerked. His eyes flared wide as he drew in a ghastly wheezing breath that seemed never-ending. His limbs began to flail as he battled free of Victor's hands, sightless eyes ranging over the scene around him. And then he began to scream.

'Christ, Maurice. It's all right. It's all right!' Grabbing

319

Maurice's strapping, Victor hauled him to his feet, desperately fighting for control as Maurice continued to struggle and yell. He dragged him towards the cover of the fresh shell hole, but a searing pain in his thigh took his leg from underneath him and he toppled down, bringing Maurice with him.

'Let me go! Let me go!' Maurice screamed, his eyes wild, his face contorting.

'I can't do that, old man,' Victor gasped. Tightening his grip on Maurice's strapping, he threw himself over the edge of the crater.

They tumbled downwards on a landslide of earth. When they finally reached the bottom, Vic lay panting, his eyes screwed against the burn in his leg while Maurice whimpered beside him. Gathering his resolve, Vic looked down at his thigh, prodding at the hole in his trouser where the khaki was turning russet. He pulled the field dressing from the inside pocket of his tunic and applied it the wound, ignoring the searing discomfort as he drew it tight. He collapsed back against the crater wall, trying to steady his racing breaths. Only once he had succeeded did he turn his attention to his friend.

Maurice was huddled beside him, his whole body shaking violently, and when he at last raised his head in response to Victor's insistent summons, the side of his face appeared in constant spasm. Victor sank back against the dirt, filled with dread. He had already noticed the warning signs – the stutter, comic at first but increasingly pronounced, and involuntary twitching he had chosen to dismiss. But now, there was no denying the shell shock that had seized control of Maurice's mind.

A *fresh landslide* of dirt hailed the arrival of Private Jenkins. Panting heavily, the arm of his uniform bloodied, he looked from Victor to Maurice, in a daze.

'Sir. They're cutting us to shreds, sir.'

Before Victor could respond, another soldier scrambled into the crater, dragging a wounded man with him. They slid down to the bottom, the injured soldier crying out with every jarring inch.

'You're all right now, Symsie, you hear me? You're all right now.'

The new arrival glanced around. When his eyes landed on Victor, he froze.

'Private Durham.'

'Sir.'

Victor's gaze shifted from Durham to the man next to him. Syms' uniform was ragged and bloodsoaked at his belly. Durham himself had blood streaming down his forehead, but he merely wiped it away with the back of his hand before setting to work on Syms, exposing his wound.

'Jesus . . .'

'Give me a field bandage, Jenkins,' Durham ordered. Jenkins fumbled for his dressing pack and passed it over. 'Easy, Symsie,' Durham said, 'I'm going to try and stop the bleeding.'

'Fucking hurts,' Syms cried, gasping. 'My stomach . . . Jesus, my insides are on fire . . .' his hand strayed to the bloodied mess. Realising the severity of his injury, he began to swear hysterically.

'Easy now, easy!' Durham cried, grabbing his wrists. 'Look at me, look at me now, John. It's all right, do you *hear me? You'll be all right. I'll get a dressing on it. You'll be all right.'*

Durham worked swiftly to bandage the ripped flesh, using his own field dressing as well as Jenkins' to cover the wound, but blood was already soaking through by the time he had them secured in place. Syms was sobbing with pain. Maurice shrank away, his back to them, rocking chaotically in a hunched ball.

Above them, the battle raged on, bullets kicking up dirt at the crater's rim. Despite Durham's pleas to keep still, Syms was writhing with agony, swearing, and crying in torment.

'I'm going up to see if there's any chance of a stretcher bearer,' Jenkins said, gripping his rifle.

'You'll get picked off as soon as you stick your head up,' Victor warned.

'I can't stay here, sir,' Jenkins said, taking in Maurice and Syms. 'Someone's gotta do summat.'

Jenkins scrambled up the side, loose earth skittering in his wake. The ground shuddered as a shell impacted nearby, and he flattened himself as detritus rained upon them. Straightening his tin hat, clutching his rifle, he pushed himself above the rim.

He immediately flew backwards, landing heavily in an unnatural heap at Maurice's feet. Staring at Jenkins' dead eyes and his obliterated chest Maurice began to scream, scrabbling backwards, though the crater held him fast. Victor grabbed, him, trying to shake some sense into him, but Maurice was too hysterical, and in the end, Durham hauled Jenkins' lifeless body away to the far side of the crater, rolling him face down in the dirt so Maurice could no longer see the gore.

Syms was growing pale. 'Don't let me die, Joe. Don't let me die.' He sobbed, screaming and swearing through each excruciating wave of pain.

'Make him stop. Make him stop!' Maurice pleaded, plastering his palms to his ears.

But Syms couldn't stop. He wailed and shrieked, cursed God, wept for his mother, and roared in agony. Durham tried to calm him, but to no avail.

'Make him stop that noise!' Maurice screamed in chorus.

'He can't help himself, Maurice,' Victor shouted, his own nerves shredding.

'He's got to stop!' Maurice cried, plucking at his holster.

It all happened with shocking speed. Durham was trying to soothe a screaming Syms, as Victor yelled at Maurice to calm down.

The shot exploded between them.

Syms' head lolled to the side.

On the battlefield above, machine guns rattled as shells whistled and boomed. But in the crater, in that moment, all was silent.

'Jesus Christ!' Durham gasped. 'Jesus Christ, you killed him!'

The Webley shook in Maurice's grip. He stared at Syms' motionless body. 'He's quiet now,' he whispered. 'That's better . . .'

Victor stared in disbelief. He drew his hand over his mouth, in part to contain the rush of bile burning the back of his throat.

'You bloody killed him!' Joe cried again.

'Put the gun away, Maurice,' Victor said, his voice steady

though his mind was thrumming. Maurice, quaking but submissive, holstered his pistol.

'You murdering bastard!' Tears choked Joe's words. 'You murdering bastard!'

'That's enough, Durham,' Victor snapped. 'Syms was never going to make it. Lieutenant Stilwell did him a kindness.'

'A kindness?' Joe cried out. 'He might have made it. You can live for days with a stomach wound . . .' But he was too dumbfounded to continue. He stared at Maurice, now eerily calm, though his face was twitching, and his limbs still shook. 'You murdered him in cold blood, just like you murdered Bobby Higgins.'

'What?' The word shot from Victor's mouth before his mind had a chance to catch up. 'What did you say?'

'You heard me.' Joe shifted his position in the dirt. 'I watched you kill Bobby Higgins.'

Maurice frowned, his expression distant. 'Bobby Higgins . . . he hurt Ida . . .'

'He didn't hurt Mrs Stilwell. He thought he was protecting her.'

'Protecting her?'

'Shut your mouth, Durham,' Victor hissed.

'Protecting her?' Maurice said again, confusion competing with his twitching features.

'That's right. Your so-called friend here had her up against a tree like a common whore.'

'I said shut your mouth!' Victor roared.

'Except she didn't need saving – Bobby was just too bloody innocent to realise what's what.'

'Ida?' Befuddled, Maurice turned to Victor. 'You and Ida?'

'And then he blamed Bobby, and the three of you beat him to death like a dog – all because your best friend didn't want you to know he was screwing your wife—'

'I said shut the fuck up!' Victor lunged at Joe, but Joe swung up the butt of his rifle into Victor's stomach. Winded, Victor fell against Maurice who shrieked in alarm. Joe scrabbled to his feet, his rifle raised.

'I'm done keeping your secrets. You're bloody murderers, both of you.'

'If you know what's good for you, you'll stop talking, Durham.' Victor's hand strayed to his holstered weapon.

'Why? You going to kill me too?'

'It may just come to that.' Victor whipped his pistol from its leather holster, but Joe proved quicker. The butt of his rifle connected with the Webley's barrel just as it fired, knocking it from Victor's hand. Maurice screamed at the deafening report. Cowering, he mewled hysterically as Vic yelled in frustration, but Joe was already running. He hurled himself against the side of the crater and began scrambling towards the top as Victor swooped to retrieve his gun. Seeing Victor straighten, Joe abandoned his cumbersome rifle. Unhindered, his hands and feet worked in swift unison as the loose soil shifted beneath him. Gun in hand, Victor took aim but just as he levelled his sights, Joe rolled over the top of the crater into the chaos of No Man's Land. Vic let off a hopeful shot, but Joe pressed himself into the battle-churned earth and the bullet flew by him. Lurching to his feet, he ran, ducking as another shot whistled past.

Thwarted, Victor let the Webley fall to his side. He might

have lost the battle, but he had no intention of losing the war.
Joe Durham was a dead man.

He would see to that.

Victor shakes off the memory and forces himself to focus. Dakers is talking again, the gun still steady in his hand. 'You intended to silence Joe the same way you silenced Bobby, while hoping Maurice's mind was so scrambled he wouldn't remember what had been said. Joe ran for his life that day. You left him no choice. And yet, despite all that, when he got back he tried to get up a rescue party – would have gone back himself if Leonard hadn't ordered him to the regimental aid post. That's the man Joe Durham was. A true man, regardless of his age. And what did you do?' His voice thickens with contempt. 'As soon as you'd made it back, you accused him of shooting Syms. You had him up on charges before you could say how's your father. A firing squad at dawn had all your problems solved.'

'He was court martialled by due process.'

'Due process my arse.' For the first time Dakers' patience frays. 'You lot rallying around, the officers above you too busy to question the detail: "Oh, make an example of him whether he deserves it or not. It's just one more dead soldier, after all".' Daker's voice grows unsteady with ill-suppressed rage. 'You had Joe killed to silence him once and for all. While he lived, he was a threat to you. The only surviving witness to your adultery and the murder you'd committed to cover it up.'

As Dakers pauses to conquer his building emotion, Victor considers making his move, but as if able to read his mind, the faceless man becomes the battle-hardened sergeant once more.

326

'I didn't want to be on the firing squad. I told Joe that when I went to see him. I told him straight I wouldn't do it, but he begged me, *begged me* to take part. He wanted there to be a friendly face, he said. And then he asked me to get him a pen and some paper. He wrote through the night, barely slept by all accounts, writing down his testimony, all of it – Bobby, the white feather, what happened in the shell hole. All of it. He handed it to me when I went in to see him that final time before dawn. He told me to tuck it inside my tunic, where no one would see, and asked me to get it directly to Sarah. Then he shook my hand and thanked me for my help. And he asked me to look after his sister . . .' Dakers fights to get his words out '. . . and told me how he'd never seen her shine before the way she did when she was with me.'

He gulps for air, working to maintain his composure. 'I marched out that morning, wishing I was anywhere else on earth but there. He looked so bloody young when they led him out, but he held himself with such pride, such courage. No crying from him. No wailing. No pleading for mercy. He even refused the blindfold. He looked at me and bloody winked.' Dakers' disbelieving laugh cracks. 'He was seventeen, but he was a man all right, a fine man, a braver man than I would have been in the circumstances. And you, standing there looking idly on, enjoying yourself. That's what struck me, at the time. You looked like the cat that had got the bloody cream.

'I still wake to the echo of those shots ringing out. Wake in a cold sweat, I do, even now. Even after all that's passed. But he was still alive. When the MO shook his head, my stomach sank. And then you, you unclipped your bloody revolver and pressed it into my hand. "Finish him off, Sergeant," cold and callous as you like, yet without the guts to do it yourself, as you should have. I stood above him, I didn't think my legs would hold me, but they did. He looked straight up into my eyes, with such understanding, such forgiveness. God help me,' Dakers begins to weep, his sobs breaking, 'I did it . . . I finished him off.'

Victor lunges forward, knocking the gun upwards. Caught unawares, Dakers stumbles back as the gun flies from his hand. Vic takes him down with a rugby tackle and they crash to the floor, struggling. He splays his hand across Dakers' absent face, digging his fingers into the malformed flesh. Dakers emits an agonised cry before hurling Victor off, slamming him into the desk's solid front. Victor wheezes, winded by the impact, while Dakers scrabbles on his hands and knees towards the cast-off revolver. Seeing his intent, Victor grabs his ankles, hauling him back. Prostrate, Dakers stretches desperately for the gun, his fingertips grazing its hatched grip. Roaring with effort, Victor flings himself forward, his hand outstretched, the gun in his sights.

Grappling, the men wrestle for control of the Webley.

A shot rings out.

The wind falls silent.

The rain has stopped.

Chapter Thirty-Four

Hearing the gun's dull report echo through the house, Sarah begins to run.

She races down the landing, her feet hammering off the threadbare runner. The pain in her chest is unbearable – she feels as if her heart has been ripped out and stuffed down her throat.

In her haste, her foot slips off a step. She catches herself just in time but collides with the wall. She rests heavily against it, her mind spinning.

'Davey . . .' she whispers brokenly. Pushing herself up, she carries on.

By the time she is crossing the reception hall, panic has consumed her. Casting caution aside, she cries out his name, yearning for a response, but none comes. Breathing hard, tears impairing her vision, she tries to judge what room the shot came from. Instinct drives her down the corridor to the kitchen, the mosaic floor blurring beneath her feet. She careers to a stop outside the library, bracing herself in the doorway as she rakes the room, but she finds it empty.

'Oh God, Davey.' She runs on.

Seeing the study door ajar, her steps slow. She stands outside, her sobs catching as she prepares herself for the sight she fears more than anything. It will be her fault. If she has lost him, it will be her fault.

Her thoughts are only on Davey as she pushes the door wide. The arrangement of furniture conceals the truth. All she can see are two sets of legs lying across the floor, shoes sole to sole, toes to the ceiling.

Her knees buckle. A moan rises from deep within her as she sinks to the floor.

One set of feet move.

'Sarah . . . Sarah love . . .'

Her head lifts, hope flaring in her heart. With a groan and a curse, Davey Dakers pushes himself up, the Webley hanging from his gloved hand. He regards it with ill-concealed disgust, before setting it down on the desk.

Sarah scrambles to her feet, and at last they face each other. It takes just two strides for him to reach her. He pulls her into his embrace, holding her firm against him, cupping the back of her head as she sobs into his shoulder. He presses tender kisses into her hair while murmuring words of comfort, his own voice breaking as he does so.

At last, as her hysteria eases, he gently holds her away so he can peer into her eyes.

'Ida?'

Sarah shakes her head. He wraps her in his arms, closing his eyes as he contemplates the justice that they have between them served.

'Is it over?' Sarah whispers into his shoulder.

'Nearly,' he says.

*

They huddle together outside Maurice's room. They can hear him, pacing and weeping. He seems to be talking to himself, though it's hard to make out what he's saying through the door.

'He must have heard the shot,' Sarah whispers. 'You'd think he'd come out to investigate.'

'Maybe it just served to turn the key, locking him into the prison he's already in.' Davey takes her hand. 'Come on, we'd best get on. We'll listen out for him, take action if needs be, but if he remains like this, it might just serve our purpose well.'

On the lower landing, they split up. Sarah goes into her bedroom. She takes down her suitcase from the top of the wardrobe and sets it on the chair. Opening it up, she dons the leather gloves lying inside and proceeds to strip the bed. She neatly folds the quilt and lays it on the floor of the wardrobe, before placing the used linen into her case. She then packs away her things, eradicating as she does so all traces of her presence. Finally, she takes a damp cloth and wipes down every surface. By the time she has finished, the room has the abandoned air of disuse. Closing the door behind her, case in hand, she hurries to Davey's room and repeats the process.

In the attic, Davey collects the officer's cap and greatcoat, the pipe and tobacco, and bags up the discarded ration tins. He returns the bedding used in his internal bivouac to the various packing trunks it was pilfered from, before folding up the improvised drugget, leaving the curtains in a neat pile. He notices that the bricks he so carefully liberated from the chimney breast are now on the floorboards. He pauses to consider them, then gathers up the rubber hosing, and takes a step back. Surveying the scene before him, he decides the bricks might provide someone with an interesting conundrum, one that will undoubtedly elicit much speculation, but alone they are hardly damning evidence. Satisfied, he descends the stairs and locks the attic door behind him.

Setting the collected items down upon the landing, he takes the key to Leonard's bedroom from his trouser pocket and unlocks the door. He winces as he opens it, assaulted by the ferrous smell and appalled anew by the brutal scene. He sighs as he reinserts the key into the inside lock.

Sarah reappears on the landing and sets about packing the attic haul into her case. When she has finished, she picks up her damp cloth and, with some reluctance, comes to the open doorway.

'It wasn't me, you know.' She sags against the doorpost, her voice strained. 'I didn't know he had the knife. After the pills, I didn't think I'd be able to go through with it. I'd left them for him, of course, but I was relieved when they didn't work. Relieved, Davey! Of all of them, I came to like Leonard. I felt so sorry for him. I remembered how fond Joe was of him, how proud he was that the youngest boy from the big house was his friend. I remembered how Mum warned him off messing about with his betters and how Joe argued Len wasn't like that. He trusted him so much. He thought Len had got swept along by the others over Bobby, but he always believed the boy's death troubled his conscience. Still, he never thought Len would turn his back on him the way he did, not when the stakes were so high.'

Sarah draws further into the room, though she avoids looking at the bed. 'But he was sorry for it. I know that. And I'm glad I found that out before he died. He saw what had happened to him as a just punishment, I think, for the bad choices he'd made, the wrongs he'd done. But release was what he wanted more than anything. He must have seen Maurice's knife lying around and taken his chance.'

'You were quick-witted to point the finger at Maurice.'

'It was a wretched thing to do. But he deserved it,' she says, her voice turning cold.

'Yes. They all deserved what was coming to them, truth be known. We came here to make them suffer and pay. I reckon we did that all right. But let's not forget, they all had a chance to repent and only Leonard did. Things might have worked out differently if the others had shown an ounce of remorse.'

He takes the damp cloth from her hand. 'I'll wipe down in here,' he says gently. 'You go see to the rest, and I'll be along to help as soon as I've done.'

*

It is sometime later when they are finally ready. Everything has been meticulously cleaned. Having witnessed the state of the house on her arrival, this cleanliness, Sarah fears, is the weak point in their plan, but Davey, from the beginning, has insisted nothing must connect them to the house or the family. Fingerprints have become his obsession. Fingerprints get people hung.

Satisfied they have eradicated all traces of their existence from the property, they meet by the front door, Sarah's case now bulging.

'Oh wait! One more thing,' Sarah cries, before hurrying down to the kitchen, to retrieve the last of the monkey nuts from the pantry. Though Davey's painted mask is in place once more, she can detect his bemusement. The mask never conceals from her what he is thinking. She knows him too well.

In the drawing room, she takes out a nut and feeds it through the bars of the bird cage. Mr Tibbs snatches it from her fingertips.

'You're a clever boy, Mr Tibbs,' she murmurs, reflecting on the hours she has spent coaching the bird while the rest of the house slept. 'And a fast learner when given enough reward.'

She empties the bag of nuts into the bottom of the cage, then stuffs the paper bag into her coat pocket.

'Bye-bye.'

'Bye-bye.'

She is smiling when she returns to the lobby.

'Ready?' Davey asks.

'Ready.'

He opens the door. 'Blimey.'

Thick white fog shrouds the world beyond the doorstep. It is nearly impossible to distinguish the sky from the ground. Davey lifts the case and lets Sarah go first, drawing the door to behind him. There is not a breath of wind, and he has the strange sense of leaving a nightmare and stepping into a dream.

'It's a real pea souper out here,' Sarah says, buttoning her coat against the damp air.

'It is indeed. I'll be glad to be back in Brighton. I wonder what delights Mrs Gibbons will have cooked up for us.'

'She's a dear woman. I'm glad she accepted our offer. Without her absence, I would never have been employed.'

'For what they were willing to pay, no one else was going to take her place. Hardly wonder they bit your hand off.'

Sarah looks through the mist towards the river, clumps of trees just visible in the blanketing fog. 'Do you think they'll ever find Bobby?'

'Well they know where to look now, thanks to Joe.'

'If they believe the contents of his letter.'

'We must hope they do. Joe put everything in it, too much detail for it to be dismissed as fantasy. The very fact that Inspector followed it up is encouraging.'

'I hope so,' she says with a pensive sigh. 'I hope all of this has been for something. He might not have his name on that war memorial, but our Joe's still a hero in my book.' She brushes a tear from her cheek.

'He was a brave lad and a thoroughly decent man.' Davey turns to her with a smile full of tenderness. 'That's what our little one will know of their Uncle Joe.' He presses his flattened palm to her belly. She starts with surprise, but then smiles broadly, covering it with her own.

'Let's go home, love.'

Hand in hand, they walk across the gravel, the fog closing around them, hiding them from sight.

Epilogue

The Inspector stands before Darkacre Hall, watching a mallard waddle across the soggy lawn to reach the receding floodwaters.

The forecourt behind him is crowded with vehicles. The Inspector's own motor has been joined by two police cars, two ambulances, and a Black Maria, the back doors of which hang open in anticipation. Maurice Stilwell, his wrists handcuffed behind him, is led out through the front door, flanked by two burly police officers. He is gibbering manically, his eye in near constant spasm as he begs and pleads and sobs uncontrollably. As the policemen guide him inside the van, the young Detective Sergeant following behind breaks off, crunching across the gravel to join the Inspector.

'Has he said anything more?' the Inspector asks.

'No sir, same drivel as before. Keeps going on about a faceless man and a maid. Says they must be responsible for it all.'

The Inspector pulls a dubious face. 'There was no sign of a maid when I came, and from what I hear, there haven't been any servants employed since the last one left. No one would work here, apparently. And a faceless man?' He tuts.

'The mind boggles, sir.' The Sergeant rolls his eyes just as their attention is drawn to the clang of slamming doors.

'The mind is a curious thing,' the Inspector muses, 'cruel when it wants to be, yet kind when it wishes to protect itself from the horrors of which it is capable.'

'You think he did it all then, sir?' the Sergeant asks, falling in step beside him as he starts for the house.

'I sadly think so, Sergeant,' the Inspector says, ducking under the lintel into the lobby.

They step aside for the pair of medics carrying a stretcher from the direction of the library. A red blanket covers the unmistakable form of a body. The men pause for the Inspector to lift its corner, revealing the vacant eyes of Victor Monroe. Lowering the blanket, he nods them away. With the Sergeant at his heels like a faithful dog, he crosses into the reception hall and takes the main staircase up to Ida Stilwell's room.

She lies supine on the bed, surrounded by a skittering of white feathers that appear to have exploded from the pillow used to suffocate her. The Inspector feels a stir of regret as he leans over to peer into her frozen face, her eyes wide with shock, devoid of the spark that had been present when he first met her. Her lips are tinged with blue, and taking it all in – the white feathers, the blonde hair and pallid skin – he is put in mind of an ice princess from some ill-fated fairy tale.

He sighs and shakes his head. 'Pity.'

'What do you think set him off, sir?' the Sergeant asks. 'What caused him to do away with them all?'

'We might never know, Sergeant. That man's mind was fractured long ago. He spent months in a mental hospital during the war, and after, you know. Shell shock. Even when

I met him a few days ago, you could see the condition still plagued him. Who knows what might have caused him to finally snap?' He pauses, a sly smirk, a hint of devilment, appearing on his mouth. 'Jealousy perhaps. It was clear to see Ida Stilwell was not enamoured of her husband. It was also clear to see that Victor Monroe was very much enamoured with his best friend's wife.' He looks about him. 'If only these walls could talk. Maybe things just came to a head. These things usually do. And jealousy is a vindictive master, whose lash is harsh and ruthless.'

'But to kill his own brother too?' The Sergeant looks doubtful.

The Inspector's features soften into a different kind of regret. 'Ah, but that potentially was something else altogether. Leonard Stilwell was a physically destroyed man and deeply unhappy – that was plain for all to see. Perhaps we should not consider his death as murder, but rather an act of loving mercy.' He moves away from the bed and the Sergeant follows. 'Of them all, that is the one death I don't feel sad about, for I can't see it as tragic. I suspect an end to his suffering is what that young man wanted. Some badly injured men have found a reason to carry on, a purpose, but we shouldn't judge those who feel differently, Sergeant. We cannot imagine what it must be like to live a life as altered as theirs.' He steps out into the corridor. 'And if they choose not to live it, well, who are we to prolong their misery? What right do we have to insist on their suffering? That's my view on the matter, for what it's worth. Who knows what happened in this house . . . but I can't help feeling Leonard Stilwell secured the outcome he most wanted.'

'He certainly died with a smile upon his face,' the Sergeant says glibly, before reddening at the crassness of his comment. The Inspector lets it pass.

Clearing his throat to cover his embarrassment, the Sergeant hurries after his striding superior. 'And what of the woods, sir? Do you still want us to dig them up? I know that was our initial reason for being here today, but is it still necessary?'

'It is more necessary now than ever, I'd say.' The Inspector pulls a folded document from his mackintosh pocket and rattles it as he descends the stairs. 'Our unexpected discovery has rather negated the need for this warrant, but we must carry on with the dig regardless.'

He walks purposefully across the reception hall, passing the returning medics as they head for the stairs with an empty stretcher in hand. He finally comes to a halt outside, at the edge of the forecourt. He looks through the lingering mist towards the river and the waiting woods beyond, absorbing as he does so the distant bleating of sheep from the park and the closer caws of crows clustered in a nearby oak. He slaps the warrant thoughtfully against his open palm, turning over the morning's unanticipated events in his mind, while his Sergeant huddles against the cold, shifting his frozen feet in the gravel.

'Yes,' the Inspector reaffirms, 'we carry on as intended. If Bobby Higgins is in those woods, I want him found. That letter was quite specific on the location, so we'll soon know whether there's any truth in it or not.' He claps the man beside him on the back. 'Come on, Sergeant, let's get to it. It seems this is a good day for finding bodies.'

Acknowledgements

Thank you for choosing to read *The Good Liars*, and I really hope you enjoyed it, but this book isn't just my work. Well, the words are, but the actual product exists, and has been made available, due to the combined efforts of a dedicated team of people at HQ Stories/HarperCollins and I am grateful to each and every one of them, from the copy editor to the typesetter, the proof-reader to the cover designer, the printers to the distributors, and many more besides. I am especially grateful to the sales, marketing and publicity teams who have worked so hard to get this book before readers.

In particular though, I would like to thank my brilliant editor Kate Mills, for skillfully guiding another one of my stories out into the world, ably assisted as ever by her wonderful assistants Becky Jamieson and Rachael Nazarko.

I am, as always, indebted to the amazing booksellers who stock and recommend my books, and I'm eternally grateful to those bloggers and readers who take the time to post reviews or shout about my work on social media. Never doubt that you are much appreciated!

I would be lost without the fantastic writers that I am now lucky enough to call my friends, who provide priceless support,

encouragement and, most importantly, laughs. I also cherish my non-writing friends, who continue to prop me up in real life. You know who you are, and I am so grateful for each and every one of you.

My family, as ever, are the keystone of my existence and I would not be able to do what I do without their unfailing love and support.

And last but by no means least, I would like to thank my agent David Headley, to whom this book is dedicated. He has far more faith in me than I ever have in myself, and he constantly proves himself to be my indefatigable champion. I'm very lucky to have him. And we're both very lucky to have the ever-fabulous Emily Glenister.

ONE PLACE. MANY STORIES

Bold, innovative and
empowering publishing.

FOLLOW US ON:

@HQStories